Sink the Hood

and

Sink the Bismarck

Duncan Harding is a pseudonym for Charles Whiting, who also writes as Leo Kessler and John Kerrigan. Holder of the Sir George Dowty Prize for Literature, he is one of the most popular borrowed authors in UK lending libraries.

Sink the Hood

and

Sink the Bismarck

Duncan Harding

Pan Books

Sink the Hood first published 2000 by Severn House Publishers
Sink the Bismarck first published 2001 by Severn House Publishers

This omnibus edition published 2001 by Pan Books
an imprint of Pan Macmillan Ltd
Pan Macmillan, 20 New Wharf Road, London N1 9RR
Basingstoke and Oxford
Associated companies throughout the world
www.panmacmillan.com

ISBN 0 330 39880 6

1 3 5 7 9 8 6 4 2

A CIP catalogue record for this book is available from
the British Library.

Printed and bound in Great Britain by
Mackays of Chatham plc, Chatham, Kent

SINK THE HOOD

Prelude to a Mystery

It was nearly dawn now.

Everywhere from the galleys to the gun turrets the sailors tensed. The 'buzz' had gone its rounds. They all knew, even in the depths of the great ship's engine room, where the motors thundered mightily, that the moment of truth was approaching. The enemy would be soon in sight.

On the bridge the admiral, legs firmly astride against the motion of the battle-cruiser going full out, eyed the heaving grey-green waste of the sea through his glasses. Around him his elegant staff officers did the same. The periodic reports from the radar operators and the engineers below came up the many tubes and were relayed to the admiral in whispered tones. It was as if they were all in some ancient cathedral, afraid to disturb its heavy brooding silence with any undue noise.

Now Admiral Holland's Number One started to count off the range, as worked out by the unseen radar operators below. "Thirty thousand . . . twenty-five thousand . . ."

The tension started to mount. Number One could feel it almost tangibly. A cold trickle of sweat started to run down his spine . . . "Twenty thousand . . ."

"All closed up for battle stations?" the admiral queried. His voice seemed unreal to the staff officers. It was as if another man, one they had never met before, was in command.

"All closed up, sir," Number One snapped, breaking off the countdown.

Below them in the morning gloom, the last of the deck ratings were diving for cover, dropping their brooms and pails, knowing that once the great fifteen-inch guns opened fire they'd be dead men, swept over by the mighty blast or blinded and deafened, unprotected as they were. Not far off, the fire control parties, looking like alien creatures from another world in their asbestos masks and gauntlets, crouched in the steel companionways, ready to spring into action immediately if the ship were hit.

"Eighteen thousand—" Number One broke the count-down off.

A sinister, sleek shape, heavy with menace, had slid silently into viewing range of the twin circles of glittering calibrated glass. He could hardly believe the evidence of his own eyes. It was her, all right! How often had he imprinted her outline on his mind from the recognition tables in his copy of *Jane's Fighting Ships*?

"It's the . . . the *Bismarck*, sir," he quavered, hardly recognising his own voice.

"I see her, Number One," Admiral Holland answered, in full control of himself again now. "Thank you for your identification." He adjusted the glasses with a hand that was steady as a rock. It was as if he was used to spotting the most powerful enemy ship in the world at every dawn. He nodded to his Number One.

No words were needed. They had all been waiting for this moment for the last thirty-six hours – indeed, an imaginative person might have said, all their lives. Number One knew what to do. He spoke hurriedly into the tube which connected the bridge with the gun turrets and those deadly fifteen-inch monsters. "Guns?"

"Sir?"

"Closed up and standing by?"

"Closed up and standing by, sir." For a moment Number One had a vision of the senior gunnery officer, dressed in his anti-flash gear and looking like some medieval knight in armour ready for the joust.

Somewhere to port, the great ship's companion warship opened fire. A silent scarlet flame stabbed the grey dawn gloom – once, twice, three times. A moment later the officers on the bridge heard the boom of the *Prince of Wales*' guns.

At once the assembled officers focused their glasses. A great splash of whirling wild white water erupted on the horizon, followed a moment later in rapid succession by a series of others.

"Missed," someone cried almost maliciously. "Not a single bloody hit."

Number One allowed himself a careful smile. The comment was typical of the rivalry existing between the *Prince of Wales*, the Royal Navy's youngest ship, and their own, the fleet's oldest.

"Give 'em a bigger firing arc," Admiral Holland decreed. "Two point turn to starboard."

"Two points to starboard!" Number One called down the tube to the engine room, as the petty officer at the helm swung the 42,000-ton ship almost effortlessly to starboard.

There was no more time to be wasted. They could see the tremendously powerful shape of the German battleship *Bismarck*, a stark black outline on the horizon. She'd open fire herself any minute now and all of the British officers on the bridge knew enough about the enemy's newest ship to fear the striking power of her batteries.

"*Fire*!" Holland commanded.

"Open fire!" Number One echoed, yelling down the tube.

Below him, 'Guns' cried, "FIRE . . . FIRE . . . FIRE!"

They tensed.

For what seemed an eternity nothing happened. Then, suddenly, a hollow boom. Steel striking steel. A strange hissing sound. Gas escaping. A scratching as of a diamond on glass. A louder boom. The bridge trembled slightly. They tensed even more. Another moment. Then it would happen.

Suddenly, even surprisingly, although they knew of old what was coming, the whole of the great ship – some three football pitches in length – shuddered like a live thing. The three great guns of A turret crashed into action. Scarlet flame stabbed the gloom. The three huge missiles screeched overhead.

The men gritted their teeth. Others clapped their hands to their ears, as if afraid they would be deafened by that bansheelike howl. Here and there on the bridge officers gasped, as if they had been abruptly struck in the guts.

Another shudder. It set the plates off squeaking and

creaking in metallic protest. An instant afterwards, the B turret's guns followed with another tremendous, awesome salvo.

Great splashes of whirling white water spouted on the horizon. The *Bismarck* disappeared from sight. On the bridge officers held their breath and prayed. Could it be possible? Others swallowed hard and waited for the spouts to disappear. Then they too would be certain.

Admiral Holland kept his right cheek from trembling with an effort of sheer willpower. Was he going to go down in the history of great conflicts as the hero of the Battle of the Denmark Strait – for that's what they might call the battle if it were a British victory – or as the commander who had lost the Senior Service its three-hundred-year-old command of these northern waters? The next few minutes would tell . . .

Thus the most decisive naval battle of World War Two in the West commenced. It was five thirty-five Central European Time. The position was sixty point five degrees north and thirty-eight degrees west in the Denmark Strait. HMS *Hood*, once known as the 'Pride of the Royal Navy', and her sister ship, HMS *Prince of Wales*, had taken up the enemy challenge.

Some eight miles before them steamed the most modern warships in the world, the German battleship the *Bismarck* and her sister ship the *Prinz Eugen*. Defiantly they had thrown down the gauntlet. Now the battle of the Titans could begin.

The awesome challenge for mastery of the northern seas was under way.

Our Author is Exasperated

God, why am I doing this?

It's not the advance payment from the publisher. That's pitiful anyway. Besides, I've passed my three score and ten. I've got enough to last me out – and I certainly don't need the hassle, as they say today.

Surely there must be other things I could be doing in my declining years. Why should I be delving into a long-forgotten past, which as far as I can see in this 'Glorious Year of the Millennium' has absolutely no bloody relevance to my potential readers? Who cares what happened so long ago in our brave new world?

After all, there were only three survivors and since that May day in 1941 when it all took place, their relatives and those of the hundreds of dead must have long passed on, or have been locked away totally gaga in some cheap nursing home to which a thankful state – and naturally their family – have consigned them. Even if those who do not dribble food from toothless gums as they perch in their Parker Knolls with the pisspots beneath *do* remember those long-lost 'boys in blue' – those dead youths – the memories of their eternally young and cheerful faces must have long been eased into the darkening recesses of their failing minds.

The place in which I write these words does not improve my mood one bit, gentle reader, I can tell you. It's one of those coastal places. You know – plenty of free accommodation in winter and cheap.

Cheap these places might be, but they do tend to be gloomy. Indeed, mostly they're bloody miserable – rooted, too, like the memory of that great ship so long ago, in a kind of faded, bitter past.

The wind off the sea is – as usual – fresh and invigorating. But the sea is inevitably grey-green, choppy and mournful. Even Nature seems to do little for these winter-forgotten seaside 'resorts'. And they're all the same, whether they're located on the North Sea, Atlantic, even the Med. In winter such places invariably smell of damp plaster, rotting underwater timbers, seaweed, and – let's face it – defeat.

Why defeat? you may ask. I really don't know. But they do. Perhaps it's due to the people who live in these coastal dumps in winter. The tourists, the drunken trippers, the screeching kids with their candy floss and rock have departed. With them they have taken the bit of rowdy, beery spunk these places possess. Those who stay on know that they have been left behind to serve a full sentence, as it were. Perhaps they're even 'lifers' bound to die here. God forbid!

I take a drink of whisky. The eternal fuel of hack writers with writer's block. It'll help for a little while. The burn in the throat often burns into the imagination, gives it a kick-start. But after a while the fuel burns up –

it always does – and the imagination stops rolling. You're back where you started.

I get up and walk to the window. It's cold outside. The panes are steamed up. I don't rub them clean. There's no need. I know what I'll see out there: the white combers curling inwards in those graceful icy rolls, time and time again, on and on, as if they'll never cease until they've washed the defiant land away for good.

Of course, I know that it's not just writer's block which is giving me the 'heebie-jeebies', as they used to say in my youth. It was the sheer bloody-mindedness of the Association. It wasn't just that I was a 'scribbler', as I heard one of the old farts say when he thought I was out of earshot – of course I am. It was because they seemed to feel that the great doomed ship belonged solely to them; as if they had an exclusive right to its story and that terrible disaster which overtook the ship in May 1941.

At first when I'd met them in the pub (and paid for several rounds of rum and coke, followed by beer chasers – old farts they may be, but they can still knock back the booze) they were just stand-offish, feeling me out, wondering what I was after. They'd nod sagely and say, when I raised a point, "Old Chalky White, now he'd have been able to tell you that, but he isn't with us any more," or "Funny you mentioned that, Mr Harding," – or 'Dunc', as some of them were calling me after the third round of double rums – "but the committee's decided we're not going to talk about that. You might not understand, not being a matelot like, but we've got to protect our old shipmates."

Afterwards, when the booze really started to talk,

they were snappy, irritable in that grumpy old man's fashion, as if I were trying to trick them, betray their 'glorious past'. One of them actually used the phrase. Christ Almighty, as if the 'glorious past' means anything in the year 2000! Most of the young people I deal with, especially in publishing for instance, don't even remember what happened yesterday in the decidedly unglorious past.

Still, as I grew increasingly hot under the collar, wishing I'd ordered a real drink instead of that paint stripper masquerading as rum the old boys were drinking, I told myself they were trying to fudge the issue – hide something.

Hadn't it been the same with the toffee-nosed civil – very uncivil really – servants of the Ministry of Defence? The archivists at Kew had been little better. Polite and as efficient as they were, they weren't releasing anything more on the subject than they had done over half a century ago. The ship and what really had happened to it seemed to be taboo subjects. All of them were hiding something, I was sure of that.

I gave the old codgers another whirl. In essence they weren't bad blokes. They were just trying to protect their 'glorious past' and cover up what really happened in 1941. So I told them my sad tale of the old woman in the slitted boots. How she came running down the passage in her dirty floral pinny and a man's pair of boots, with the sides cut open on account of her corns; how she brushed by the terrified lad from the GPO who'd brought the fatal telegram; and how she screamed and screamed and screamed yet again, "The

Hood . . . my boy's gone down with t'Hood . . . BOY . . . GONE DOWN . . . HOOD . . ."

Even today, now that I'm old, I can still remember how that cold finger of fear traced its way down the small of my back as I watched, petrified, with the other kids, that woman's overwhelming grief. I'd never seen anyone overcome by such terrible hysteria before and haven't seen much like it since, over the intervening sixty years. That scene on that overcast muggy May afternoon in the middle of World War Two etched its way on to my mind's eye. It is there to this very day.

But my youthful memory cut no ice with the old codgers of the Association. Perhaps they had seen worse in their time. Perhaps it was something beyond their comprehension. But then they hadn't gone down with her. They had only good memories of her. They remembered her when the ship had been the 'Pride of the Royal Navy': the ship they sent to show the flag all over the Empire in those halcyon days of the twenties and thirties – all gleaming brasswork and sparkling white decks. They were intent on preserving the memory of a vessel in her prime, when Britannia ruled the waves and all that sort of thing. Understandably, they didn't want to know her blazing from end to end, all hope gone, virtually destroyed in eight minutes' battle against the German enemy, for which she had been preparing ever since she had been launched back in 1918.

And of course, they certainly didn't want to hear about their former shipmates, the survivors dying in their hundreds in those frozen northern waters until there were just exactly three of them left. No, naturally they didn't wish to be reminded of that tragedy . . . *just three out of a crew of nearly two thousand . . .*

So where do I stand? It was the same question I had asked myself at that reunion of the old codgers in their neatly pressed blazers, immaculate grey flannels with all their 'gongs' polished and sparkling. Standing at the window today, staring out of it at the eternal sea, as, undoubtedly, many thousands of other lonely men and women do throughout the kingdom, I posed it yet again. It remained without answer, as it mostly does.

So why do I ask it, as undoubtedly all those other ordinary men and women do? Perhaps it is because we feel threatened by some sort of nameless doom. Why, we do not know. What that doom is, unless it's death itself, we know neither. All we *do* know, I told myself, as the soaked postman staggered up the path to the cottage, buffeted by the wind and rain, the heavy bag dragging him down at one shoulder so that he looked like a hunchback, is that we – *I* – must do something. Anything. If we don't, surely we must go under.

The postman rings the bell and I realise that events are taking a new course. They have to do so. I force a smile and hurry to the door . . .

One

"*Habt acht!*"

The harsh metallic command echoed and re-echoed the length of the quay. As they had been trained to do, the five thousand sailors, the ribbons of their caps streaming in the wind coming off the sparkling Baltic, straightened their shoulders, youthful confident faces suddenly set and determined.

The officer in charge of the great final parade bent stiffly to the microphone set up on the podium. All around were the flags of the old Imperial Navy and those of the New Germany snapping and cracking in the breeze like live things.

"*Still gestanden!*" he barked.

All five thousand pairs of jackboots stamped to attention. On the quayside the frightened gulls rose in hoarse cawing protest.

Slowly the long black Mercedes, followed by the outriders, gently revving their motors, started to roll towards the platform. Along the route, tall marines came to the present, their gloved hands slapping the wooden stocks of their polished rifles audibly. All was proud pomp and circumstance, while the sun blazed down, the sea sparkled a crisp, hard blue and in the distance, the garrison band blared out 'Preussens Gloria', the big drum thumping out the cadence like the beat of some gigantic heart.

Standing stiffly to attention, young Oberfahnrich Klaus von Kadowitz felt his heart almost burst with pride. What a spectacle they made! These men, young and as tremendously fit as he was, each man dedicated to the service of the Folk, Fatherland, and Führer; every one of them prepared to sacrifice his young life for the cause if necessary. He gripped his ceremonial dirk ever tighter, his lean face under the cropped corn-yellow hair set and determined.

Beyond, the great ships which would be soon setting sail for their first cruise against the English enemy glistened in the grey wartime paint, mighty symbols of the New Germany's power. Who couldn't fail to be proud of his country, his countrymen and the weapons of war wrought by German men and women? No wonder the Führer and his *Wehrmacht* had beaten the decadent effete French the year before. How could he not do so with such power behind him? Now, soon, it was going to be the turn of the perfidious monocapitalist English.

The Mercedes rolled to a halt. An adjutant, all lanyards and gleaming braid, opened the door for the old admiral, who had built this fleet from the shambles of a defeated, humiliated Germany back in 1919. Slowly, fumbling a little with his ceremonial sword, Grand Admiral Raeder, wearing the high, starched wing-collar of the Imperial Navy, rose.

Kapitän Horsthagen, in charge of the parade, raised

his right hand in salute and bellowed at the top of his voice so that, a suddenly amused Klaus von Kadowitz told himself, the poor old admiral must be deafened, if he wasn't deaf already.

"*Mannschaften der Kriegsschiffe* Bismarck *und* Prinz Eugen *angetreten und melden sich zur Stelle, Herr Grossadmiral!*"

Slowly, very slowly, as befitted an old and very important man, Grand Admiral Raeder, head of the German Navy, touched the rim of his brilliant, gleaming cap and replied simply, "*Danke.*"

He paused while they waited, the thousands of them hardly daring to breathe, as in the distance the brass band blared and somewhere a donkey-engine clattered on one of the Polish docks. The admiral's old eyes swept slowly around the rigid ranks, his gaze pausing every now and again, as if Raeder was attempting to etch each and every one of those keen, tremendously fit young faces on his mind's eye; as if it were important to do so; as if he might well be seeing them for the first and last time. Finally he ordered, "You may stand at ease." It was more in the nature of a suggestion than a command.

Once more the sailors' right feet shot out, hands folded behind their backs in the position of 'at ease', the movement one solid uniform crash on the wet jetty, and then utter silence. Both the band and the donkey-engine had suddenly ceased their noise. It was almost as if even the humble donkey-engine operative had realised just how important this moment was: that it was a moment of history.

"Sailors of the *Bismarck* and the *Prinz Eugen*," the

admiral began, voice suddenly very loud and harshly metallic. "*Kameraden*!"

It was the customary form of address, the young Oberfahnrich knew, but at this particular moment he felt that the admiral was overcome by some inner emotion, perhaps the memory of his own fighting youth, and was aware of the significance of what he was to tell them. That 'comrades' was his signal that he felt at one with them when they sailed away on the high seas to do battle with the treacherous enemy English.

"I will not waste words, comrades," Raeder continued. "Back in September 1939, at this very place, units of our High Sea Fleet took part in the action that destroyed the Poles." The old admiral could not quite resist a sneer in his voice at the mention of the inferior Slavic subhumans. "Then one of our battleships, the *Schleswig*, shattered and battered them into surrender just on the other side of that sound, which is today German again." He meant *Westerplatte*, Klaus knew, where the trapped Poles had held out for a week, some of them committing suicide before they would surrender. His handsome young brow creased in a frown. Perhaps one should not talk of one's defeated enemy like that, even if they were only 'Polacks'. They *had* been brave men.

"That ship," Raeder continued, "had been a trusty but old one, laid down before the Great War. It had triumphed against the enemy, although for some of us of the old navy it had been a symbol of our defeat and military emasculation after that war, stabbed in the back by those traitors of the Home Front. Now," his old voice rose with scarcely concealed pride, "those bad days are over. You, comrades, will go into battle not in an old keel, but in two of the most powerful and most modern ships in the world." He paused as if he expected applause, like some politician addressing a party rally.

He got it, too. Captain Horsthagen cried, "*Ein Hoch für den Grossadmiral*!" Thousands of bold bass voices rose in a hearty cheer, which once again sent the gulls rising into the May morning sky in protest. Raeder actually flushed.

Klaus von Kadowitz could have sworn that momentarily there were tears in the old man's eyes. His heart warmed to him. As the Führer had often stated, they were one great community, pulling together not for personal and selfish reasons, but for the good of the whole.

Raeder nodded his appreciation and his face grew hard and serious once more. "Comrades, many of you have never been in battle before. Now you have a chance to prove yourselves in that bloody, awesome field. Make no mistake. There is a kind of beauty in battle, but there is also that sombre reality." He paused so that his words would have full impact when he spoke them. "It is that someone – perhaps even you, yourself – must die."

At that moment, carried away by it all, Klaus was tempted to break ranks and cry with all the fervent patriotism of his young heart, "Herr Grossadmiral, we are prepared to die in battle – and die gladly – for the honour of the fleet and our Fatherland!" But he restrained himself just in time. The von Kadowitzes did not indulge themselves in that kind of showy patriotism.

For nearly three centuries the family had served Germany honourably and faithfully, ever since the days of the great Prussian king, Frederick the Great. They had shared Germany's victories – and her defeats! But they had kept their feelings to themselves. After all, wasn't the family motto, engraved over the portal to their decaying, impoverished estate not far from the new border with Russia, '*Mehr Sein Als Scheinen*' – 'to be more than to appear'? Let others gain the kudos of victory – and the rewards. All the von Kadowitzes aimed to do was to carry out their duty faithfully and to the best of their ability.

"The English are defeated on land," the admiral was saying. "We all know that – thanks to our brave soldiers. But their navy is still a force to be reckoned with. Their chiefs will attempt to lure us out of our harbours and, massing their ships, which clearly outnumber ours, they will do their utmost to blow us off the high seas. But since when – in this war – have the English been calling the tune?" He answered his own question. "Those days are over. Now New Germany makes the decisions and the English dance to our tune. Now *we* decide when and where we do battle with the Tommies."

Obermaat Hansen from the *Prinz Eugen*, his rum-reddened eyes filled with unsurpressed excitement, his brawny chest, heavy with the medals of the Old War, could not contain himself any longer. He lurched out of the ranks, fist upraised in an unconscious salute from those days when he had been a brief member of the Communist Party during the Kiel Mutiny, and cried, "God bless you—"

The rest of his words were drowned by the first lowering boom of flak artillery from the west, as the twin-engined bombers came zooming in at mast height.

"Great crap on the Christmas tree," Klaus yelled, for Hansen was in his division and in a way he was responsible for the tough old petty officer – that is, if anyone could claim to be responsible for him. But he had no time to give the matter of discipline any thought, for already the fleet was taking up the challenge and the quick-firers and multiple machine guns which lined the decks of the two great ships had begun pounding away in frantic fury. In an instant the sky was full of exploding balls of angry fire and officers everywhere on the docks were yelling urgent orders for the divisions to disperse while they could still do so.

Klaus, yelling out orders, snapping to his men to dive for cover, barking directions to the quayside air-raid shelters, caught sight of the first flight of 'Tommies' coming in low. They were twin-engined Wellingtons, spread in a tight camouflaged V, their pilots guiding their planes through the lethal criss-cross of bursting flak shells and puffs of brown smoke like experts. Even at that moment of extreme tension, he told himself the English were veterans. They had come so low now that they were flying below the level of the warships' flak cannons to port and starboard. It was being left to the deck gunners armed with their multiple popguns to bring them down. And Klaus von Kadowitz knew that the Wellingtons, with their wooden latticed frame fuselage, could take one hell of a lot of punishment.

Obermaat Hansen, broad drinker's face glowing excitement, breathing rum fumes all over the younger man, cried above the boom of the flak and the deafening roar of the racing plane engines, "Them buck-teethed

Tommies are gonna get away with it! They're gonna plant one big square-egg of shit right down—"

The rest of his words were drowned by the shrill whistle of bombs hurtling down, headed right for the *Prinz Eugen*, and Klaus flung himself instinctively on to the jetty.

Just in time. The blast wave slammed against his face. He gasped for breath. The air was being sucked out of his lungs. Next moment, the concrete rose and slapped his shocked face.

"*Heil* Churchill!" Hansen cried next to him. "Buy combs, lads . . . there's gonna be lousy times ahead!"

There weren't. For in the very same instant that the *Prinz Eugen*'s gunners gave up the hopeless battle against the low-flying Wellingtons, whose prop wash was lashing the sea below them into a white-frothed frenzy because they were so low, the first of the ME-109s came zooming in at four hundred kilometres an hour, their machine guns and cannon already chattering frantically.

Klaus's heart skipped a beat as he caught a glimpse of the first fighter pilot's face behind the gleaming perspex of his cockpit. The Luftwaffe had timed it exactly right. And they had the decisive advantage. They were coming into the attack right out of the sun. The Tommy gunners were momentarily blinded.

On the wet concrete, the young sailors raised their heads and cheered like spectators at some deadly game of soccer with the home side going in for a sure goal.

The first Wellington was hit. It staggered. Desperately the British pilot tried to maintain control – to no avail. The pilot of the Messerschmitt didn't give him a chance.

He pressed his trigger once more and tracer hissed in a lethal white morse towards the stricken bomber.

Frantically the rear gunner spun his turret round. He didn't make it. The perspex of the turret disappeared behind a crazy spider's web of cracked gleaming fabric. The port engine feathered momentarily. Then it cut out altogether.

The fighter pilot showed no mercy. He fired again – carefully, aiming this time. The starboard engine was hit. The propellor sailed away seawards.

"Hard shit," Hansen cried above the snap and crackle of the merciless duel in the sky. "These Luftwaffe gents ain't got no hearts, have they, Oberfahnrich? Going to get the poor Tommy shite-hawk come what m—"

The words died on his lips. The Wellington fell out of the sky abruptly. Smoke and flame streaming from its shattered fuselage, it plunged nose-first into the boiling, white sea. No one got out.

But the English were not to give up as easily as that. Decadent though their masters might be, coming from a nation which had corrupted the world with their golden sovereigns, they were still desperately brave, Klaus could see that. Perhaps, he told himself, as he watched one of the Wellingtons heading straight for the *Mowe*, one of the escort minesweepers which was to clear the channel for them through the Baltic, this kind of thing was the last desperate fling of a nation that knew it had had its day. These brave young RAF pilots were sacrificing themselves for a cause that was already lost. It was almost as if they wished to die in the heat of battle with their blood roused rather than suffer the ignominy of the defeat that was surely soon to come.

Powerless to do anything, Klaus watched with a hypnotic, limb-freezing fascination. Next to him the hard-bitten Obermaat had pulled out a flatman filled with schnapps and was taking great greedy swallows of the fiery liquid, as if he were a spectator of some entertainment that had absolutely nothing to do with him.

By now the *Mowe* had realised the lone Wellington was heading straight for her. Her gunners opened up. At that range they couldn't miss, however wild and panicked their aim. The Wellington was being shredded in mid-air. Klaus and Hansen, surrounded by their gaping comrades on the jetty floor, gawked open-mouthed like village yokels at this duel to the death.

Still the Wellington flew on. The cockpit was shattered. A dark shape slumped forward over the controls. The pilot, dead or unconscious – it didn't matter. With grim inflexibility the Wellington came ever closer.

On the deck, some of the younger gunners had already panicked. They were abandoning their weapons as the Wellington loomed ever larger. Flame was pouring from her shattered fabric now.

Hansen groaned. "Heaven, arse and cloudburst," he shouted desperately, though no one could hear in that racket, "jump over the side . . . jump, you bunch o' frigging wet-tails!"

But it was already too late. As the starboard wing of the dying plane was ripped off and came floating and twirling down like a great metal leaf, the Wellington smashed into the side of the minesweeper. Her nose crumpled and the

Mowe reeled under the impact. A great searing flame tore the length of the ship like a gigantic blowtorch and, in the next instant, her gun locker went up. Small-arms tracer started to zigzag in crazy profusion into the livid sky. The minesweeper heaved and her bow reared up like a metal cliff as she broke in half. Before they could really grasp what was happening, there was one last tremendous, eye-searing flash.

Something struck the young officer a glancing blow on the side of his head. Vaguely, as if he were far, far away, he heard Hansen call, "Over here . . . over here, you slow sow-arses . . . can't yer see the frigging Oberfahnrich has been hit . . . *Los, beeil' euch, Menschenskinder.*" Then everything went black and Oberfahnrich Klaus von Kadowitz knew no more.

Two

All was back to normal in the former Polish port of Gdansk, now once more the German Danzig. Outside the great ship, there was the sound of a riveteer's hammer, echoing like that of an irate woodpecker. Fire control parties swabbed down the jetty with their hosepipes. Trucks bearing ever-fresh supplies for the fleet weaved their way in and out of the controlled chaos. Now the only sign of the terror which had recently taken place in the naval harbour was the scorched quay and the neat line of blanket-covered dead on stretchers waiting to be transported away.

Grand Admiral Raeder nodded silently, as if in approval of what he saw, then turned to Admiral Lutjens, a shaven-headed man who was tough looking in a professional, controlled manner, as befitted a senior naval officer.

Raeder said quietly, "Herr Admiral, let's go below. I have a few words to say to you still before I leave again for Berlin – and the Führer." He added the last words with a slightly sour smile, as if Lutjens must realise they conveyed more than he could express openly in front of all these officers, officials and flunkeys.

Lutjens, the fleet commander, gave a slight, stiff bow,

but his face expressed nothing – neither approval nor disapproval. Instead he said in his harsh North German accent, which revealed he came from this same Baltic coast, "As you wish, Herr Grossadmiral."

A few moments later, the *Bismarck*'s main ammo lift had taken them to his state cabin, where white-jacketed mess stewards waited with their silver trays at the ready under the eagle eye of a chief steward petty officer. Again Lutjens nodded in that stiff awkward manner of his, as if his whole body was worked by tightly coiled steel springs.

"*Getranke, meine Herren*?" the chief steward queried and without waiting for a reply indicated that the waiters should step forward. Swiftly they went from guest to guest, handing them the chilled glasses of ice-cold Steinhager, the rims of the glasses stiff with sugar as if it were frost.

Raeder raised his glass, held at the level of his third tunic button as naval tradition prescribed. "*Prost, meine Herren . . . Ex*!"

"*Prost*," a dozen self-important voices echoed.

As one they drained their glasses, again in the traditional naval fashion.

Lutjens' hard face above the Knight's Cross revealed nothing. The others had flushed momentarily as the strong alcohol had burned its way down their gullets. Not the Vice-Admiral. He might just as well have swallowed water.

"*Wegräumen*!" he snapped at the chief steward petty officer.

In an instant the waiters, the glasses and bottles had

vanished, as if by magic. They might well never have even been there. Raeder sat down gratefully. Now Lutjens could see just how old the C-in-C was. He seemed to have aged ten years in the ten months since the fleet had last been engaged in the Reich's invasion of Norway. He could guess why. It was the constant fight to keep an active fleet of surface ships. He knew that Hitler thought that Doenitz's U-boats could do the job for him in the battle against the English more effectively than Admiral Raeder's new surface fleet.

"You know the general picture," Raeder commenced. "And you know the Führer's attitude." He looked to left and right, as if he half expected a Gestapo spy might well be listening to his words for any hint of treachery.

Lutjens frowned. Why didn't Raeder have the courage to stand by his convictions and stand up to the Führer? If Vice-Admiral Doenitz had his way, all the Kriegsmarine's great new ships would be damn well mothballed or turned into steel to make more of his shitty U-boats. But he kept his peace and listened.

"You are all aware of our basic problem. It really is twofold," Raeder continued. "We must convince the Führer that our battle fleet can hit the English hard. But our individual raiders, even if they are powerful ships which outgun and outspeed the Tommies, cannot tackle the English convoys without risk – and the Führer will not tolerate the loss of one of our great ships. We all know his reaction to the loss of the *Graf Spee* in '39."

There was a murmur of agreement and understanding. The Führer had gone into one of his frightening rages when he had heard that the Pocket Battleship, as the

English called the German ship, had been trapped in South America by the English fleet and would have to be scuttled if it were not to fall into enemy hands.

"So the plan is to assemble a fleet of our own powerful enough to tackle the English convoys even if they are escorted by capital ships and are within sailing distance of English Home Fleet at Scapa Flow. That is what we have been trying to do for the last few months."

He let his words sink in. Outside the sirens of the ambulances wailed dolefully as they came to collect their cargo of death. Lutjens frowned at the thought of those dead young men, killed before they had the chance to live. But the admiral told himself that it was no use, served no purpose, to dwell on such matters. There would be many other such young men dead before all this was over.

Raeder must have taken the look on Lutjens' face for one of disapproval, for he said, "I know, my dear Lutjens, you wish this operation to be cancelled until we are fully, one hundred per cent, ready to meet the English in battle. But that can never be. There will never be a time when we are completely prepared to tackle them. You see from this raid today that they are aware we are up to something. There was a similar raid on the *Scharnhorst* and *Gneisnau* at Brest last week. They are trying to knock out our ships before they even sail."

Lutjens wasn't about to cross swords with the Grand Admiral. He knew better than that. If he did he'd be dismissed and then some hack would take over and do anything that the Grand Admiral required, regardless of losses. "It is a question of an appropriate target, Herr

Grossadmiral," he commenced, his voice purposefully neutral and without emotion. "We need to plan better where we are to strike the—"

"In the terms of this operation," Raeder interrupted him firmly, "the sands are running out, Lutjens. You know the business with the invasion of Russia. The Führer is impatient to deal with the English problem before he turns his full and complete attention to the east."

Lutjens gave one of his stiff, wooden nods and lapsed into silence. He knew there was no use persisting. Raeder was carrying out orders – *the Führer's orders* – and that was that. End of message.

"Let me sum up then, gentlemen," Raeder said with an air of finality. "Once we march east, we of the navy shall receive no more top priorities. I know that we are not ready. We haven't managed to get the *Scharnhorst* and the *Gneisnau* out of that little trap yet, and it might take some time before we do so. But under present circumstances – which are not in our favour, I must emphasise – an eighty per cent readiness is better than none."

"So the operation is as scheduled, Herr Grossadmiral?" Captain Lindemann, the commander of the *Prinz Eugen*, rasped. As usual he wasted no words.

"Yes," Raeder agreed. "Operation Exercise Rhine will commence exactly as planned. The fleet will sail from here on the evening of May 18th. The Baltic will, as you know, be cleared of all merchant shipping, including that of neutral Sweden, to ensure that your ships are not observed moving westwards. Two days later you should be well into the Skagerrak before you're sighted. By then we can confidently hope that it will be too late for the English to assemble an attack force to engage the fleet. With the smallest bit of luck we'll have found our own target by then . . ."

Lutjens was no longer really listening. Raeder's plan had as many holes in it as a piece of Swiss cheese. Two days in the Baltic, normally filled with Swedish ships supplying the Reich! Even if they did manage to convince the neutral Swedes to run for harbour while the fleet passed up the inland channel, bound for the North Sea, their captains would be suspicious. They'd know there was something going on. The whole complex harbour-and-customs clearance operation that allowed them to enter German ports would tell them that. And although the Swedes were overwhelmingly pro-German, there were enough British agents in Stockholm to pass on the captains' suspicions to the British Admiralty. No, he told himself, suddenly sunk in a gloomy reverie, filled with dark and sinister forebodings, things were not going to work out. He knew that in his bones.

Admiral Lutjens raised his head and suddenly caught a glimpse of himself in the wardroom mirror opposite. He caught his gasp of shock just in time. Staring back at him was a death mask . . .

Up on the deck, saluting Grossadmiral Raeder, as rigidly at attention as if he were still a fresh-faced cadet, Captain Lindemann was still shocked by that look on Admiral Lutjens' face which he had glimpsed reflected in the mirror. What had been going through the fleet commander's mind at that moment? he asked himself as, to the shrill tune of the bosuns' whistles, the elderly C-in-C proceeded down the gangway towards the waiting Mercedes, which would take him back to Berlin and – naturally – the Führer.

Lindemann could only guess. But the result didn't please him one bit. It had been nearly a quarter of a century since the Battle of the Skagerrak where he had had his first taste of action – and he didn't like the idea of it any more than he had done as a young naval cadet back in 1916. Not only did a sailor face shot and shell like a soldier in the line, but he also was confronted by the possibility of a lonely, slow death in the water, with not a soul to hear his last prayer. Lindemann shook his head as if to ward off that fearsome vision and told himself that whatever happened now, he was not going to waste his ship and the lives of her crew. He and they would survive. What did they say: "*Die* for your country? No, *live* for it!"

Three

"*Armer kleiner Mann,*" the Polish whore said softly. She raised her hand from Obermaat Hansen's lap to dab the blood still trickling from his head wound. "Let me soothe you, my little snuggle-puppy."

"Snuggle-puppy yer mitt back on me lap," Hansen barked. "That'll soothe me more, I can tell yer. My senses is coming back. Keep up the good work, and I'll give yer a real diamond-cutter, if yer lucky."

Anna Olga Dora, known in the trade as AOD, laughed wearily in that tired 'seen it all; done it all' whore's manner of hers and did as the tough old sailor requested. She wondered, as she did so, if men kept a stiff 'un even after they'd snuffed it. They always seemed to have one in her long professional experience.

Bei Anna was a typical sailors' waterfront bar. A zinc-covered table, usually awash with suds and schnapps. A dirty picture, curling at the yellow edges, of two women with cropped hair doing something impossible to each other. A fly-blown reproduction on the wall, depicting a curly-haired blond youth in an old-fashioned sailor suit urinating into a pool of water with the legend beneath it warning, "Don't Drink Water! Kids piss in it!" Next to it was a large sign in Polish and German advertising 'Pivo Krakov – Makes Strong Men Stronger'. That and the usual collection of drunks, misfits and morose young sailors crying into their beer with homesickness made up the bar's decor, plus, naturally, AOD, the regular Polish whore.

"What do you think is going to happen?" AOD asked in her harsh Silesian German. She had been born a German, but was of Polish ancestry. Her names came from the old imperial princesses Anna, Olga, and Dora. But she was Catholic, which indicated to Hansen, who was no fool, drunk as he was most of the time, that the family was basically Polish. Those who wished to be taken for pure Germans had usually converted to Lutherism back in the nineteenth century. So, although he didn't quite trust the whore – only a fool would trust a whore whatever her nationality – he liked her. Often when he was stony broke in between pay-days, she'd give him a free 'rub-off,' or if she was particularly generous even let him dance a 'mattress polka' with her in the squeaky old brass bed upstairs, where she took her regular clients to copulate under the cheap reproduction of the saintly Black Virgin of Krakow.

"Happen?" he echoed a little morosely, taking a careful sip of his Pivo Krakov, for he was about broke again, "the usual. The big shots'll decide that it's time us poor sailor lads went and got our frigging turnips blown off again. They ain't won many medals of late."

She gave his penis an encouraging squeeze through the thin serge of his trousers and smiled her gold-toothed smile at him. "Never say die," she said without thinking of her words. She licked her pink tongue around her broad generous lips so that they gleamed an inviting red. "Play your cards right, old house, and I might give you something special when you've finished your beer."

"Yeah," he said gloomily, finding it hard to shake off his mood, "like frigging leprosy, perhaps." He sniffed. "Besides, that kind of piggery costs extra, don't it?"

Her professional smile grew ever larger. "For you, my little cheetah, if you're good to old AOD, it comes free."

Hansen lowered his glass of beer with a bang on to the zinc-covered bar. The barman looked up sharply, hand flying to his mouth with alarm.

"*Free*!" Hansen cried and wished, next moment, that he had not spoken so loud. Something like a sharp wire had bored itself into the back of his right eye with a stab of red hot pain. "Frigging wonders never frigging cease."

Now she laughed and squeezed his penis even harder. "Nothing's too good for our boys in the service." She used the old phrase.

Before he could react with the usual contempt he felt on hearing the propaganda phrase, the tinkling bell of yet another convoy of ambulances heading for the *Marinekrankenhaus* started to race by in a great hurry, scattering the Polish dock workers coming off shift and weaving in and out of the blue-and-white trams dangerously. Hansen frowned as he spotted the scarlet drops of blood coming from the rear of the boxlike contraptions. Next to him, AOD crossed herself in the elaborate Polish Catholic fashion. "Poor boys," she exclaimed.

Obermaat Hansen didn't comment. He was a hard-bitten old salt who had seen some rotten things in his time, during two major wars. Yet the thought of young men dead for a cause that they didn't, perhaps, understand or which meant nothing to them always affected him. "Full of all that piss and vinegar, mates," he would comment to his fellow petty officers when the subject was sometimes raised, "and buggered without ever using it."

He looked at himself sombrely in the fly-blown mirror at the very same instant that the thick felt curtain, which functioned as a blackout after dark, was thrust aside to admit two middle-aged men with their felt hats pulled down far over their faces.

AOD's hand holding his penis gripped so hard that Hansen almost yelped with the sudden pain. He knew why. The two middle-aged civilians were cops. They had Gestapo – Secret State Police – written all over them: the hats, the long green ankle-length leather coats, the supercilious look on their evil mugs. No, there was no mistaking them. They were the frigging Gestapo all right.

"Funny pong in here suddenlike," Hansen said aloud. "Wonder if that frigging roof hare" – he meant a cat – "bin pissing on cops' boots again? I suppose," he added with studied insolence, "that it's only right that they piss on cops."

The bigger of the two, his metal identification disc in his hand, flushed an ugly red and snarled, "You're risking a thick lip, sailor – and worse." The threat was undeniable.

It didn't worry Hansen. He knew he could say what he liked *now*. As torpedo-room senior mate, the *Prinz*

Eugen's skipper wouldn't let the Gestapo do anything to him. The armoured giant needed him now that they were going into action at last.

The thought emboldened Hansen. Besides, he was slightly drunk and he had never been frightened of cops even when he was sober. "Oh dear, oh dear, woe is me," he simpered in what he imagined was a female falsetto. "I do think I'm gonna faint the way that naughty policeman is addressing me."

Some of the older sailors in the bar laughed until a look from the bigger cop wiped the grin from their faces. Next to Hansen, AOD pressed his penis even harder.

"Knock it off," she hissed urgently, and there was no denying the fear in her voice now, "you'll only get us into trouble. Leave it be and I'll be especially nice to you – you know how."

He looked at the still handsome woman. There was genuine fear written all over her broad slavic face. For a moment he wondered why. AOD was not usually afraid of the law. She paid them their monthly bribe and when necessary she granted extra favours. Why should she be afraid?

He had no time to dwell on the answer to that unspoken question, for the cop he had insulted creaked closer in his heavy boots and hissed, "All right, arse-with-ears. Get the dirty water off yer chest with that pavement pounder of yourn and then back to your ship while you still can." He thrust his ugly mug forward threateningly.

A hot retort sprang to Hansen's lips, but he didn't utter it. The whore cut in with, "Come on, lover boy. You've paid your money, let's get it over with." She dragged at his brawny arm almost angrily.

The cop sniggered. "Watch he don't come all over yer belly, Anna. These sailor boys don't know no discipline. Yer wonder why they waste their money in knocking shops. I mean – the five-fingered widow could do it for them for nothing." He made an explicit gesture with his clenched fist and burst out laughing.

Red-faced, Hansen allowed himself to be dragged to the stairs behind the bar while the cops, still laughing at their great sense of humour, as they supposed it to be, started to examine the other occupants' papers.

Hansen waited until he and Anna started to clump up the creaking wooden steps that smelled of stale sweat and ancient lecheries before snorting, "*Du machst doch in die Hose, Mädchen*! Why are yer worried about them two flatfoots? You know they're both blowhards. Besides they need the bribes they got off'n you pavement pounders to pay their old women back home in the Reich."

Before she answered, Anna looked fearfully behind her, as if she were afraid the cops might be listening at the bottom of the dark stairs. "It's not that," she said. "There's something going on."

"What?"

"It's something to do with the bombing of your ships a bit back."

"Shit on the shingle!" Hansen cursed. "You're talking like a five-groschen novel, Anna. Talk some sense, wench."

She looked at him. Abruptly the fear had gone. It was dark on the stairs and he couldn't see her face very clearly. Yet he sensed somehow that there had been a change in her expression: a new quality of proud defiance which he had never encountered in her before – or in any other cheap whore like her, for that matter. "You're asking too many questions," she said quietly, the fear vanished from her voice now. "People who ask too many questions can get themselves into trouble."

"And what's that supposed to mean?" he demanded, surprised.

She didn't answer his question. Instead she said, pulling him round the corner to the untidy bedroom, "Come on, get your pants down and get on with it. There isn't much time left."

Obediently he did as she commanded. There wasn't, and, as he had confessed to his fellow petty officers that very morning, "Comrades, I've got so much ink in my fountain pen, I don't know who to frigging well write to first." But later, when he was on his way back to the *Prinz Eugen*, with uniformed cops and naval sentries everywhere, he considered her phrase once more. What had she meant – 'There isn't much time left'? For *who*? And *what*?

Four

The Führer farted.

His facial expression didn't change. But then he farted all day long and was no longer aware of the fact. It was due to the vegetarian diet he preferred and the laxatives he swallowed constantly to keep down his weight. But if Adolf Hitler wasn't aware of his wind-breaking, those around him were. Their faces went pale. Even Blondi, his Alsatian bitch, whimpered and fled into the corner, tail between her legs.

Next to Canaris – the head of the Abwehr, the German Secret Service – Admiral Raeder flushed and whispered out of the side of his mouth, "The man's impossible. Breaking wind like that – and ladies present." He indicated the two young female secretaries poised next to Bormann of the Reich Chancellory, their notebooks at the ready.

Admiral Canaris, sallow-faced, small and secretive, made no comment. He rarely did. As head of the German Secret Service, he made it his policy to say as little as possible in public. It was better that way. He had too many enemies. It was wise not to give them any possible ammunition they might use to shoot him with.

The Führer beamed as if he had achieved something of importance. The fart had eased the usual turmoil in his guts temporarily, Canaris told himself, but in five minutes or so he'd fart again. After all, he, Canaris, should know. Naturally he had a file on the Führer, which included details of both his unusual sexual habits and the state of his unruly, gas-filled guts.

"*Meine Herren*," Hitler greeted the two admirals, as if they were the oldest of friends, though in fact he had very little time for them and their Navy. After all, he was an Austrian, who had never even seen the sea till he was in his late thirties and who was seasick as soon as he stepped on a boat, even when it was safely at anchor in some protected harbour. "Welcome."

Both of them clicked to attention and gave the master of Western Europe a stiff bow. Behind the Führer, Bormann nodded to the older of the two secretaries and stepped further into the background. As he did so, he gave the cowering Alsatian bitch a malicious little kick in the ribs. He smiled slightly, as if the action had given him some kind of pleasure.

"Gentlemen," Hitler commenced, as the secretary began to take down his every word at Bormann's instruction, "we do not need to waste any more time on Operation Exercise Rhine. It is, I take it" – he shot a sharp look at Raeder – "all taken care of?"

"It is."

"Good, Raeder. Deadline?"

"The fleet under Lutjens will leave Danzig on the tide in the evening of May twentieth under the cover of darkness. With a bit of luck, *Gneisnau* and *Scharnhorst* in Brest will be ready to sail and meet them off the coast of Greenland."

"Excellent. I am pleased, Grand Admiral," Hitler said quickly and raised his right haunch slightly.

The secretary knew the movement of old. It was the signal he always gave when he was about to break wind. Discreetly she moved back a few paces and prepared to hold her breath.

"Now the question of a target . . . something which will hit the English hard before what happens in the East next month makes them believe" – he grunted and broke wind once again, his face giving a fleeting sign of relief, but no other to indicate what he had just done – "that there is still some hope for them. Churchill, that drunken sot, is a rabid anti-Soviet, a man after my own heart in some ways, but he'll make the most of the fact that the Reich will now be engaged in a war on two fronts to East and West and that this will take the pressure off his precious British Empire."

Hurriedly the pale-faced secretary, who had paused to pat her nose and mouth with her handkerchief to prevent herself from gagging at the stench coming from the Führer, attempted to catch up with one of his typical long sentences, sweating visibly.

In a way Hitler answered his own question with, "Naturally we can destroy one of their convoys. Even with just the firepower of the *Bismarck* and *Prinz Eugen*, should the Brest ships fail to make the rendezvous, the fleet would be able to make short work of a collection of merchant ships and destroyer escorts. But is that enough,

I ask you gentlemen?" He searched the two admirals' faces with his piercing hypnotic gaze.

Raeder opened his mouth, presumably to defend his fleet and say that it was. The humble little head of the Secret Service in his shabby uniform and dingy gold insignia beat him to it.

"There is a possibility of a great naval victory, *mein Führer*, if luck is on our side," he said softly. "Luck is the vital element, I repeat."

Hitler's sombre face lit up. He even forgot the noisy rumblings in his stomach, which sounded like a drainage system that had gone seriously wrong and badly needed urgent dismantling. "Go on," he urged. "Tell me more, Canaris." He grinned. "I know your devilish mind. What arcane trickery have you dreamt up now?"

Canaris was not impressed. Indeed, he wished he was not being forced – due to Raeder's predicament with the Brest ships – to disclose his plans. After all, he trusted no one, not even the Führer. He preferred to fight his battles, dirty and underhand as they mostly were, in the shadows where they belonged.

Instead of looking directly at the Führer who stood there, waiting in eager anticipation for whatever surprising rabbit his head of the Secret Service was about to produce as if from some magician's top hat, he stared numbly at his feet and mumbled, "*Mein Führer*, it is a combination of English pride centred on an eighteenth-century British admiral of theirs; English cheapness; and love for short-term results – and a fat lady, who, supposedly, is a medium with an excellent ability to raise the spirits."

The Führer's mouth dropped open. Behind him the secretary broke the point of her stenographer's pencil with surprise, and Admiral Raeder exclaimed, flushing a brick red above his old-fashioned stiff collar, "What in three devils' name are you talking about, Canaris? . . . My God, man," he spluttered, hardly able to find the words to express his exasperated bewilderment, "you're talking in riddles!"

Canaris kept his head bowed, a lock of his snow-white hair – which had earned him the nickname of 'Father Christmas' among his enemies of the Gestapo – falling over his brow, and let the wave of shocked surprise run over him. But his cunning devious mind was racing electrically as he did so.

Suddenly Hitler was intrigued. He clapped his hands. Bormann emerged from the shadows at the back of the great hall immediately. "*Mein Führer*?"

Hitler didn't even look at the servile secretary with the face of a boxer gone to seed. "Tea for myself and coffee for the gentlemen," he ordered. "I believe that Admiral Canaris has an interesting tale to tell. Let us take some time to enjoy it. Ensure that my other appointments are postponed for at least thirty minutes."

"*Jawohl, mein Führer. Zu Befehl.*"

Five minutes later they were all ensconced in the *Sitzecke* – the 'sitting corner', as the Germans call it – drinking tea and coffee, plus *Enzianschnaps*, the Führer's own favourite tipple made from herbs, served by jackbooted, white-clothed SS giants. They looked for all the world like a cosy little group of middle-class folk enjoying the traditional German *Kaffeeklatsch*.

Swallowing yet another *Pfefferkuchen*, Canaris, who enjoyed his food, licked his fingers and prepared to relate his story: one that indirectly would result in the tragic end of a great ship and the death of nearly two thousand British seamen . . .

"So," Canaris said, as the old clock in the corner next to the *Sitzecke* ticked away the minutes of their lives with metallic inexorability, "you can see, *mein Führer*, why the English wanted to give the name of that eighteenth-century admiral to their newest and most powerful ship back in 1918."

"*Natürlich*," Hitler agreed, taking another delicate sip of the peppermint tea that his doctors had recommended to soothe his upset stomach, which was beginning to gurgle yet again in an alarming manner. "He was a typical pirate disguised as a naval admiral. I wish that more of my own admirals were like that – not so cautious." He looked pointedly at Raeder. The latter went brick red again.

"But what of the ship named after him?" Hitler continued and belched, again without appearing to notice.

Cautiously, on her stomach, ears flat against her skull in fearful anticipation, the Alsatian bitch Blondi started to crawl out of range. She knew, apparently, what was soon to come.

"She is regarded as the pride of the English navy," Canaris answered. "And indeed, she is a fine ship."

Hitler waved his hand impatiently and Canaris speeded up his explanation, suppressing his inner annoyance. Like all officers engaged in his type of work, he loved the oblique approach. He hated to have to state facts plainly and swiftly. Still, Hitler was the chief. Not only that.

He held the power of life and death over his subjects. "She gained her reputation in the twenties with overseas cruises, showing the flag across the British Empire or being engaged in goodwill cruises to North and South America. But she *had* – and *has* – a fatal weakness."

"It is?"

"She was designed as a battle-cruiser. She sails at a top speed of thirty-two knots. She can deliver an impressive weight of shell. But, *mein Führer*, she hasn't got the armour to withstand the kind of firepower that – say – the *Bismarck* could bring to bear on her – and you will remember, *mein Führer*, that forty per cent of the *Bismarck*'s displacement is made up of her armour."

"In short," Hitler concluded, proud as always of his ability to absorb, understand and use statistics, even those that concerned a navy that he didn't particularly like, "the *Bismarck* can give *and* take punishment?"

"*Genau, mein Führer*," Raeder butted in proudly, as if he personally had been responsible for the *Bismarck*'s performance.

Hitler was thoughtful for a moment, then he said, beating Raeder to it, "So this is the ship – the pride of the English navy – that we intend to knock out?"

They nodded in unison.

"But, gentlemen," Hitler protested, holding out his arms hugely, as if he were addressing a party rally at the annual Nuremberg meetings, "how can we be sure that this paragon of the English will be there and take up the challenge when our own fleet sails to do battle?" Then he had it. "You mean the fat lady, Canaris . . . the one with the ability to raise the spirits?"

Slowly and apparently reluctantly, almost as if he did not wish to impart this secret information even to the Führer, Canaris replied, "Yes, you are right, sir."

Hitler smiled and, raising himself excitedly, snapped, "I knew it . . . I knew that was the surprise you were going to spring on us, Canaris."

In his triumph that he had caught the head of his Secret Service out, he forgot himself. His bottom erupted in a tremendous burst of wind. The huge fart caught even Martin Bormann by surprise. Trying to get out of the way, he stumbled over a cowering Blondi and sprawled full length, his normally ruddy features turning a ghastly green as that noxious wave overtook him.

A Message from the Other Side

The package was big and clumsily wrapped. Instead of tape to seal the old envelope, which was being used for the third or fourth time to judge by the varied stamps and cancellations, the Australian had got the post office people to stick it up with odds and ends of stamp paper. And someone had added – as further protection against the package opening – a piece of twine, wrapped around a couple of times like people used to do when I was a kid more than half a century ago.

Surprisingly enough it was correctly addressed – *completely*, down to the local postcode; and – surprise, surprise – the sender had got an 'esquire' on my name, and got it right, too. It wasn't the kind of sloppy usage you receive even from solicitors these days, such as 'D.E. Harding, Esq', but the really one hundred per cent formula of 'Duncan Edward Harding, Esq.'

Everything was explained a few minutes later after I'd managed to get the bloody thing opened, had read the first couple of lines and had recognised the spiky, shaky handwriting for what it was – that of an old man – an Englishman, naturally – who had probably learnt how to address a letter of that kind at his prep school before the Second World War.

"Dear Mr Harding, I have been advised by our national association of ex-naval servicemen of your interest in a certain wartime subject," the first sentence ran in that old man's old-fashioned style.

> By birth I am not an Australian but an Englishman from the Bath area and during the war I was a junior officer in Naval Intelligence (under Lt Commander Ian Fleming, the author of James Bond who as you know was in the same service) . . .

I sighed. The old man's writing, the mention of the fact that he was born in Bath and the name-dropping of James Bond's creator all told me one thing. I was in for a lot of long-winded pomposity from the old fart. I sighed again and looked out of the window. It was still bloody raining and at this particular moment the letter and the rest of whatever the package contained were the only leads that I possessed. I'd drawn blanks with all the old chaps of the ship's associations and even the editor of the *Navy News*, who was usually so obliging in such matters, had been of no help. Perhaps the fact that the 'man who had known Ian Fleming' (as I was beginning to call the new Australian in my mind) had lived in Oz so long might have rubbed off. Despite his prose and all the rest of it, it was possible that he would be more forthcoming.

Another sigh and I bent my head to the letter once more, screwing up my eyes in the fading winter light, with the sea thundering outside, and read on.

> It wasn't that I was on duty when I first came across the woman – far from it. In fact I was on leave. I'd been blitzed in Portsmouth – 'Pompey' we used to call it in those far-off days – and I'd cadged a lift to Plymouth. Out of the frying pan into the fire, one might say . . .

"One might," I said to myself, "you silly old arsehole." Like most lonely people and would-be writers (remember this, as a writer you're on your own, mate. Forget the glamour. It's all toil, sweat and tears all on your ownsome, and piles from too much sitting if you're unlucky) I talk to myself.

"But I won't bore you with too many details," he'd written, as I read on.

> When you get to my age your hand aches with the effort of too much writing. So I've decided to make it simpler for me – and I hope you. I'm enclosing a little piece I did for the *Alice Springs Advertiser*. It was about time the local TV did a repeat of Shute's *A Town Called Alice* and they were interested, for a time, in the Second World War . . .

I skipped the rest. I could guess it'd be pretty much the same as the beginning of the letter . . . more bull. Instead I opened the old newspaper carefully. The date was June 1990 and the headline, if you can call it that, read: 'The Spy Who Spied On Spies – A Strange Carry-On In Wartime Britain'.

I grinned at that 'Carry-On'. What with the main title and that wording, you could have expected Sid James' lecherous old face beaming out at you from the unfolded page or Barbara Windsor exhibiting her undeniable assets in one of those movies of the same name which keep appearing on our television screens, week in and week out.

Instead of those well-known comedians, I was confronted with a badly blurred picture of that old-fashioned warship that had been bothering me ever since I allowed my publisher to talk me into the book over one of his celebrated liquid lunches. He might be tight with his pennies as far as authors' advances go (but then I guess all authors say that) but he certainly doesn't stint on his lunches. It had been the Gay Hussar, full of the usual Labour politicians busy at the place's celebrated trough. But despite the 'names', the Gay Hussar's waiters had been particularly deferential to Sir. They should. My publisher usually left a lot of money in the restaurant.

Yes, there she was, looking as powerful and somehow sinister in a lean rakish manner as she must have looked back in 1918 when taking part in a war that was already finishing. I'd got a lead at last!

The man who'd known Ian Fleming's first few sentences, as carried in that obscure Australian newspaper, probably now defunct, confirmed that it was not only a lead, but one that was going to guide me down the path that I had already visualised for myself when my publisher had first dangled the project under my nose over a fiery paprika goulash, washed down with expensive Tokay.

> In the winter of 1940–41, as an active officer of the Royal Navy's Intelligence Service, I was instrumental in bringing to book a woman, who ought, in some people's opinion, to have been shot as a German spy. I have no hard evidence now (nor even had then, for that matter) that she was. But it seemed to me that it was an amazing coincidence that a mere two months after she made her prediction, that great ship was hit by the Huns and by some apparent fluke, though we later learned it wasn't a fluke at all, went straight to the bottom of the sea, taking with her the whole of her crew – near two thousand of her poor chaps. Only three survived, more dead than alive . . .

I stopped there. I felt my heart race. It's something like the flood of adrenalin when your blood's up, or perhaps after a hit of whatever crappy drugs people shoot, but that's the feeling for a professional writer when he finds a lead. And I thought my new Australian, Lt Timothy de Vere Smythe (he would be called 'de Vere Smythe' – that name must have gone down like a bomb in Pom-hating Oz) had just given me that lead because there, halfway down the newspaper clipping, I'd caught a glimpse of that fat pudgy face raised on Scotch porridge – and probably Scotch whisky later on. There was no mistaking her. I'd known about her virtually from the start of my investigations but I'd given up hope of ever finding out any more about her. The whole bad business was so long ago, amid the confusion of wartime, with records in the UK being destroyed left, right and centre by Goering's Luftwaffe.

But there she was under that cliché of a title, 'The Spy Who Spied On Spies'. One didn't need a crystal ball to figure out who our tame ex-officer in the Royal Navy had been spying upon – Madame Clarissa Campbell, once known in the halls of the North of England as 'Florrie Future'. She was the spy he had seen involved with, that was for sure. But how had he known she was a spy?

I looked at the bottle of Scotch. Should I? I decided not to. What I was now going to read slowly and carefully should be stimulation enough. I settled myself in my chair more comfortably. Outside the wind howled and the sea thrashed, the shingle slithering back and forth noiselessly. But I was no longer listening. I was preparing myself to slip back into that long-forgotten world of England at bay, circa 1940–41. That would provide all the intoxication I needed now . . .

Five

De Vere Smythe needed a change of underclothing, a stiff drink and, if he were exceedingly lucky, a nice nubile blonde in bed with him in the large double room he had managed to book for himself at a moment's notice with surprising ease for packed wartime Plymouth.

But once he had emerged from the station into the snowbound darkening street, he knew why it had been so easy. The city was virtually empty. It was obvious that the Huns had been to Plymouth quite recently. There was still smoke drifting over the city centre and here and there Civil Defence men in their blue battledress and white helmets were picking away half-heartedly at fresh ruins, looking – without too much hope – for the last bodies.

De Vere paused and looked at the green-glowing dial of his watch. What should he do next? Get cleaned up? Or should he chance his arm and hope that his uniform might win him a double whisky in the first pub he came to? Landlords were notoriously cagey with their spirits when it came to strangers, even if the stranger was prepared to pay over the odds. They hid the damned stuff beneath the bar as if every drop was exceedingly precious. All they'd give you, if you didn't persist, was the usual 'gnat's piss', as the matelots called it – mild and bitter.

Despite de Vere's gloomy predictions, he struck lucky in the first pub that he went into. The landlord looked at his weak, white-faced features, took in the soiled stiff white collar and the rings of the 'Wavy Navy' on his tunic and said, "Got a nice bit of Scotch if you fancy, sir. Just got it in from my supplier." He touched his long nose, heavy with blackheads, significantly.

De Vere jumped at the chance. The pub was run down, had not been painted for years and had sawdust on the floor. It was obviously working class, but the promise of Scotch convinced him to stay.

"Rather," he said in the affected upper-class accent he had learned at his prep school, "do give me a large Scotch, please."

"Coming right up, sir. That'll be three and six."

The price was steep, but de Vere didn't mind. He needed the drink. Besides, the only other occupant of the saloon bar, a woman – dressed in a black suit, surprisingly enough, with peroxided hair – was definitely giving him the eye via the big fly-blown Victorian mirror behind the bar. She was obviously a 'lady of the night', as he preferred to call prostitutes, but she was decently dressed and she was in the saloon bar where drinks cost a penny more than in the other, public, one.

He gave his drink a squirt of soda and raised his glass in toast to the whore looking at him in the mirror. She did not need a second invitation. She was over like a shot, uncurling her legs to reveal that above her black silk stockings she was wearing no knickers and saying in what she apparently thought was a seductive voice, "I'll have a gin, if it's all right with you, duckie."

It was.

"Thus it was that I met the unfortunate but decent widow woman who unwittingly involved me in the whole strange business," he had written some fifty years later for that obscure Australian newspaper. "For I took pity on her and her grief for her lost sailor husband and one thing just led to another . . ."

It certainly had done, but not – naturally – exactly as the former junior officer of the Wavy Navy described it to his readers in far-off Oz.

They had agreed on a pound. It had been money well spent. She hadn't laid down off-putting ground rules as so many of the whores he had had dealings with usually did. He could touch her. He didn't need to wear a french letter. If he wanted to squeeze her breasts from underneath her bra it wouldn't be extra and, delight of delights, it'd only cost an extra half-crown to see her totally naked save for her black stockings and high heels in the freezing cold of the little flat to which she had taken him after the 'gin-and-it'.

It was then that she made the offer which, after some rapid mental arithmetic, he accepted hastily. If he agreed to feed the gas fire and paid her another 'two nicker' he could spend the night and have her as often as he wished. He jumped at the chance. It would be cheaper than going to one of the hotels near the station where they didn't ask too many questions, but where you still had to go through the silly rigmarole of pretending to be married, signing the register and giving the receptionist a ten-bob bribe.

She had only one condition. She wanted a little treat, if he were prepared to pay the half-crown each involved. "I mean," she said, pulling a fresh pair of black-market stockings on to her shapely legs, "it's what yer'd pay if you took me to the pictures, ain't it? Besides, Madame Clarissa's more spooky and exciting." She shivered. "She don't half put the wind up me, I can tell you."

He nodded, only half listening to her chat, concentrating on her near-naked body, warmed by the gas fire now hissing merrily at the foot of the bed. He'd put a full shilling in the meter to ensure that she remained naked as long as possible.

"When do you want to go?" he heard himself ask, gaze fixed hypnotically on the lovely breasts with their erect dark-coloured nipples. It was a hundred times better than any picture he'd ever fantasised over in *Health and Strength*.

"I thought we'd go and have some fish and taties in the cafe next to the fish shop at the corner. They're cheap and afterwards we'll go to her first séance at seven. She likes to start early. She doesn't want drunken matelots – you'd be surprised how many sailors from the fleet she gets – coming wandering in from the boozers causing trouble."

"Yes . . . damn nuisance, drunken sailors," he mumbled obediently, hardly aware what she was talking about.

It was only when she was nearly dressed and was dabbing *Soir de Paris* – "Comes straight from Paris," she boasted, though Paris had been in German hands ever since the summer – all over her upper body and behind her ears that he became aware of what she had been saying. "Séances," he said, looking at her quizzically. "Why do you go to séances, I mean, it's not like . . ." He let his voice trail away to nothing, unable to really put his thoughts into words.

She looked at him. For the first time her powdered, prettyish face revealed something about the real woman hidden by the professionally pleasing look of the street whore. "Because of my Bill . . ." She bit her bottom lip. "He went down with *Barham*, you remember?"

He nodded. Even de Vere's tiny middle-class prissy mind realised that he was witnessing some great emotion – one that he would never experience in his nice, tidy, orderly lifetime.

"She predicted the ship would go down, you know. She's very clever like that and a lot of us sailors' widows in Pompey, Plymouth and Poole and other places around here like to go to her now and again and see how our chaps are getting on—" she hesitated, as if she half wondered if he would laugh at the words she would use "—on *the other side*."

De Vere didn't laugh. Nor did he comment on the subject as they ate in the little cafe filled with the smoke of red-hot lard and the sharp odour of malt vinegar, listening to her babble on.

"Course, some people sez fish an' taties taste best out of paper, eatin' 'em with yer fingers. But I prefer 'em on a plate with knife and fork and best bread and butter . . ."

He wasn't really listening. His mind was still trying to deal with what she had said while she had been dabbing herself with the cheap scent, about the HMS *Barham*, that old Great War battleship that this 'Madame Clarissa', whoever she was, had predicted would 'go down'.

How would the old fake have known that? De Vere Smythe regarded all that business with Ouija boards, séances and 'voices from the other side' in the same light as reading tea leaves and gypsies looking into crystal balls: something for poorly educated working-class housewives and dotty old widows who were so senile they'd believe any damn thing.

But as they 'linked up', as Mavis called it, and set off for 'Madame Clarissa's Parlour', he kept his thoughts to himself. After all, when they got back and she got stuck into the half-bottle of Gordon's gin he'd bought under the counter from the knowing barman with a conspiratorial wink, he'd roger her again. There was no use upsetting her now, however stupid and silly her belief in the 'powers' of this fake medium was.

Lt Commander Ian Fleming of Naval Intelligence was in a foul mood. He'd gone with his chief, Vice-Admiral Godfrey, to meet 'C', otherwise known as Major-General Menzies, head of the MI6 organisation, at White's. He'd done his duty as a good staff officer should, and returned to the Admiralty to pick up the young Wren officer who, he'd confidently expected, would provide his night's sexual excitement for him, only to discover that some counter-jumper bounder of a civil servant had detailed her to drive him to see the PM at his country place at Chequers.

"Sorry, old boy," the airy answer to his angry query had come back over the scrambler phone in Godfrey's office, "hush-hush and all that, you know. Some sort of a flap at Chequers. Couldn't have sent anyone from the lower decks. Wouldn't have looked good and all that. Tootle-pip." And that had been that. The phone had gone dead.

But that had not been all. He'd been landed with the night watch in Room Thirty-Nine as well. He'd protested he'd done night duty only the previous week to no avail. The commander in charge, a regular, who had a down on Wavy Navy officers, had snapped with an air of finality, "This is not civvy street, Fleming. When you receive an order, you don't discuss it. You carry it out. If you have any complaints, you go through channels *afterwards*. Now carry on, Fleming, will you."

Fleming had 'carried on'. There was a flap on which concerned the Royal Navy and it seemed whatever he did, he couldn't find out anything about it. Twice he'd been up to the signal station on the roof of the Admiralty, with the flashes of the anti-aircraft guns ripping the night sky apart in slashes of angry scarlet, but the signallers had nothing to report. The Huns were raiding London, as usual – they had been doing so for the last four months – and tonight they were having a go at the south-western naval ports as well. But that was about it. Nothing of world-shaking importance as far as he could ascertain.

So the future creator of James Bond sat by the big marble fireplace, hugging the meagre flame – coal was running out again – polishing his well-manicured nails with his buffer and chain-smoking the gold-ringed cigarettes he had made specially in a shop off Bond Street, telling himself morosely at regular intervals that life was bloody shitty really – even considering it was wartime.

Thus engaged, he was startled by the sudden urgent ringing of the red-painted duty phone. It was the one that the Admiralty exchange had to give priority to and which members of Naval Intelligence only used in matters of urgency – save Fleming who often gave that number to his current 'popsy'. Hurriedly he reached for it, his bad mood forgotten immediately. Whatever it was, that phone always signalled excitement, beneath or outside the sheets.

A prissy voice answered which he could hardly recognise until the speaker gave his name – "Lieutenant de Vere Smythe here, sir" – and then he gave an inward groan at the information. It was that inferior middle-class twat of a former grammar-school teacher Smythe.

"Yes," he answered testily. "Where's the fire at this bloody time of the night?" For it was already approaching midnight and after twenty-three hundred hours, Room Thirty-Nine rarely got any more signals from Bletchley. Hitler's admirals, it seemed, went to bed with the chickens.

Smythe gave a faint chuckle. "Speaking of fires, sir, there really are some. We're being bombed again."

"Good for you, Lieutenant," Fleming said coldly, using the damned schoolteacher's rank to put him well and truly in his place. "Get on with it. I haven't all the time in the world, you know. We're busy here."

"Yes sir . . . sorry sir. I wouldn't have bothered you till morning, sir. But she's moving on, sir, and I really do think we should take action against her before she does any more damage. I—"

"For Chrissake, man," Fleming exploded, for he had a short fuse at the best of times and Smythe seemed to be suffering from verbal diarrhoea. "Get on with it, will you?"

"It's the woman . . . A kind of fake medium I just went to see some hour or so back. I didn't want to go because I can honestly say I think such people are crooks, right from the very start, sir. In addition—"

"Smythe!" Fleming cut him off, voice icy and full of upper-class menace.

Smythe understood. Fleming could hear him gasp audibly at the other end of the line before stuttering, "Sir . . . I think I've discovered a spy, my first in counter-intelligence – and a naval one."

"What in thunder do you mean, man?" Fleming snarled. He'd heard Smythe well enough, but the idea that the ex-grammar-school teacher of foreign languages could really have uncovered a spy was beyond belief. Why, the man couldn't find his way out of a bloody paper bag!

"Sir . . . a *German* spy. I'm sure of it." Hurriedly the junior officer filled Fleming in, while the latter's agile, inventive brain raced. He could see what the other man was getting at. There certainly seemed to be something funny about this Clarissa woman and the way she attracted gabby naval widows and dotty mums to her so-called séances. It was worth looking at it – and it would certainly be a feather in his cap if he could pull something off down there in Plymouth. He knew he had plenty of enemies in the Admiralty, who thought of him as Admiral Godfrey's spoiled pet who was working a cushy number here in London. It'd be one in the ruddy eye for such folk if he really could unmask a genuine German agent.

"Listen, Smythe," he snapped urgently, as soon as the latter had finished his stuttered, excited explanation. "As soon as I can find the assistant watch-keeper, I'm getting a staff car and coming to see you. Do what you can to secure your end and see this Madam Clarissa, or whatever she's called, doesn't do a bunk. I want to speak to her. Get it?"

"Got it."

"Right, then do it." With that Fleming slammed the phone down hard. Ten minutes later he was gone, with the assistant watch-keeper still struggling into his clothes further down the corridor and the phone in Room Thirty-Nine ringing its merry head off – for reasons which wouldn't be explained till it was all too late . . .

Six

The shabby drifter passed the main fleet anchorage and started to run in between the islands of Fara and Flotta. On the bridge of the battered old craft, its single stack belching thick black smoke, the skipper eyed the bare purple hills of Hoy directly ahead. It was still the early hours of the morning, but in these northern climes dawn came early. Indeed, at this time of the year it never really seemed to get dark properly.

Next to him, Oberleutnant Hartung of the Regiment Brandenburg said in English – Canaris had ordered them to speak English as a precaution all the time, even when they were with their comrades from the special Secret Service regiment – "That's Lyness . . . to your front, sir." He indicated an untidy straggle of huts and oil tanks in the distance. Above it was the neat white cross of the naval cemetery.

"Yes, Hartung," the skipper, who spoke better English, answered. "The cemetery tells me. In there are buried the dead of the 1916 battle, English and our own people. Plus those of the High Sea Fleet who died after the—" "—business of 1918." The tough-looking commando officer completed the sentence for the naval officer. He knew that the navy people didn't like to talk about the surrender of the German High Sea Fleet to the victorious Tommies after the Great War.

The skipper nodded and concentrated on steering a straight course down the shipping lane, which was cleared of mines daily. All the same, his mind lay on the task ahead. To him it seemed almost a suicide mission, venturing like this into the heart of the enemy's greatest naval anchorage, Scapa Flow, trying to find out the information that the people in the *Tirpitzufer* 'God Box' – Canaris' headquarters – wanted, and then trying to make a run for it before the tea-drinking Tommies woke up to the fact that they had been caught with their knickers down.

Still, he told himself, they had an even chance of getting away with it. Their cover was good. The battered Norwegian drifter from Trondheim had been part of the enemy's 'Shetland Bus', which carried supplies and agents back and forth between the two countries, before the Secret Service had seized it, complete with codes, recognition signals and so on. It had got them this far without even being seriously challenged. But their luck wouldn't hold out for ever, he knew that. Recognition signals were changed regularly at odd intervals. At any rate, he'd have to be on his guard. Once the balloon went up, he'd do a bunk and shit on the fine gentlemen of the God Box.

They chugged ever closer to their objective. To starboard the skipper could now see the destroyer's anchorage. It was busy. There were destroyers there, plus a fleet auxiliary and what looked like a couple of coasters. That pleased the young, tough-looking German captain. His own craft wouldn't be too out of place, he told himself, in this massive naval anchorage.

He flung a fleeting glance to the north. There he could just make out the bottom of the German battle-cruiser *Derfflinger* of the scuttled Imperial German Fleet, which the Tommies had razed just before the outbreak of war. His face hardened. It reminded him of his duty to that old navy, stabbed in the back by the Jews and Reds back home in 1918. That kind of abject surrender would never happen again. German pride and achievement wouldn't allow it. Despite the danger of this daring mission, he felt a growing sense of purpose. He'd see the Brandenburgers through, come what may. He didn't know what the champagne pissers of the God Box in Berlin were up to. It didn't matter. The success of this mission did.

Time passed, but despite the slowness of the captured Norwegian craft and the monotony of that dreary landscape, the men on deck, both army and navy, were not lulled into a sense of false security. Indeed, the atmosphere was electric with restrained tension as the Brandenburgers waited for the orders to go into action. They all knew the danger they were in. Dressed in British Army uniform, they'd be shot out of hand if the Tommies captured them. But that didn't seem to worry the Brandenburgers particularly. Most of them had been through the same sort of thing, disguised as Polish, Belgian and Dutch soldiers in the invasions of those countries in the winter and spring of 1939–1940. Their concern was for the success of the mission. Although they didn't understand its aim fully, they had all been impressed by the little admiral's final words to them before they had flown off from Berlin-Tempelhof.

"Soldiers – comrades," Canaris had declared, his voice, for that secretive man, quite emotional for a few moments, "you have heard these words before, I know. *Germany's fate depends on the success of your mission* . . . But I salute you, Brandenburgers, for this time those words are true." With that he had touched his gloved hand to his battered cap and turned without another word, his shoulders bent, as if abruptly bowed with sudden emotion.

Now the gaze of the men on the bridge, which was open, attempted to penetrate the keen wind, which made their eyes water, and find the target. Here, with a bit of luck, they would find what their masters wanted of them and be back to the little Norwegian ship before the Tommies tumbled to the fact that anything untoward was happening. After all, why should the English expect any trouble inside this formidable naval base? It had been nearly two years since the submarine commander Prien had penetrated the anchorage with his U-boat and daringly sunk the British battleship the *Royal Oak*. Thereafter no other German vessel had attempted to do the same; it had been regarded as virtually impossible after that 'black Saturday', as the English had called it.

"*There*." Hartung cut the tense silence of the bridge. He pointed. "Longhope!"

He was right. There was Longhope, five miles inside

the fiord that ran into Hoy, recognisable by the old-fashioned silhouette of the *Iron Duke*, the partly demilitarised warship with two of her turrets removed. They had arrived!

Now things happened fast. It had all been planned at Bergen two days before. The skipper and the engineer worked on the ancient engines. It wasn't very difficult. As the engineer exclaimed sourly, "Shit . . . shit . . . no decent German bumboat would tolerate an engine like this."

Within five minutes they had the machines clattering and panting, puffing out great clouds of evil black smoke as if they were on their last legs. Slowly the drifter started to slow to a halt and, in that same instant, the rubber dinghy containing the half-dozen Brandenburgers in British Home Guard uniform set off from the lee side, from which point they couldn't be seen from the little island hamlet, on their way to Longhope.

The mission was underway and while he posed on the open bridge, going through the motions of a very angry skipper for the benefit of any Tommy watching through a glass, the German captain started to count off the minutes. The next hour, before the watch boat would lift anchor and come to check what was going on with the shabby Norwegian craft, was to be vital. As he whispered out of the side of his mouth to the grumpy ancient engineer, as if the Tommies were already listening to them, "This is it, Heini – march or croak, eh?"

The latter's puffy face lit up in a craggy smile as he pulled out his flatman and offered the anxious skipper a snort. "Well, sir, at least we can make a handsome corpse."

The skipper smiled wanly and accepted the bottle.

Hartung was careful but unconcerned now. Ice water seemed to be running through his veins. He told himself he'd been through it all before. In his mind he echoed the old engineer's phrase, '*marschieren oder krepieren*' – march or croak. If he was going to die, well, there it was. If he wasn't, well, good luck to him. He'd live – to die another day, as he surely would in the long war he suspected was to come. In the meantime he'd get drunk, feed his face with the best grub he could afford and undoubtedly get his ashes raked a couple of times by some whore or other.

Now he watched, eyes narrowed to slits against the icy wind, as the hamlet came closer and closer. He knew the place contained no civilians to speak of. The place was strictly naval – hence the Home Guard uniform, which might prevent the sailors asking too many awkward questions. Not that there'd be many of *them*, either. As the intelligence officer who had briefed them had declared, "Men, you'll find there are more seals sunbathing on the beaches of that arsehole of the world than human beings. They say the poor shits stationed there write love letters to the local sheep." The sally had raised a laugh, but not much of one. For the men had realised for the first time just how far from home they were being asked to go to carry out their dangerous mission. During all the other missions they had carried out in the last two years of total war, they had been able to walk home if things had gone wrong. Not on this one. It would be too far even to swim. Besides, the arctic temperature of those northern waters would probably kill them, if they attempted to do so, within minutes.

A quarter of an hour later the engine turned off and the dinghy ground to a halt in the soft sand of the inner bay. There was no sound save that of the curlews they had disturbed and, somewhere far off, the baaing of sheep like the cries of lost children. Hartung nodded and grasped the Browning Light machine gun of Great War vintage he was carrying – Intelligence thought it might have been the type the Americans had supplied to the Home Guard – and jumped into the knee-deep water. It was freezing. He repressed a gasp by an effort of will. Behind him the other five men did the same, while the corporal in charge of the smoke discharger, who would remain behind to cover the retreat if necessary, secured the rubber craft against the soft lap-lap of the icy wavelets.

Almost noiselessly they moved forward and breasted the sandy rise. Hartung flashed a look to left and right. Nothing moved. Over in the handful of rough, tumbledown shanties, smoke curled in a thin grey whirl from one of the stovepipe chimneys. Not even a dog barked. *If they have hounds in this arsehole of the world*, he told himself contemptuously and placed his hand, fingers splayed outwards, on the top of what he called his 'pisspot helmet', that of the English Home Guard. It was the infantry signal for 'advance'.

Dutifully his men followed him. Veterans that they were, they needed no orders. They spread out, crouched low, fingers on the triggers of their weapons, ready for anything. Hartung nodded his approval. They were good boys.

Metre by metre they crept forward. They passed the first of the shanties. He felt the wall in passing. It was ice-cold and not a sound came from the place. It was empty and had been so for long enough. That pleased him. Perhaps this was going to go off without trouble after all. He had told the young skipper of the drifter, "I have a feeling that the clock's in the pisspot and we'll be up to our hooters in shit once we get ashore, Oberleutnant."

Now, it seemed he had been wrong. Not even the clock had fallen into the pisspot so far. *Prima*!

They pushed on, starting to feel their way from cover to cover down a steep incline that led to their objective, the jetty where the lighters from the great ships, dim grey outlines in the far distance, were anchored in Scapa Flow. It was here that the little craft offloaded the men on leave and those going off sick and took on board fresh supplies for the crews on the water.

Many of the lighters were manned by half-naval and half-civilian crews, Hartung knew that from the Intelligence briefing, and all the storemen were civvies. So in the case of showdown, he didn't expect much trouble from the Tommies; most of them were probably unarmed. All the same, Intelligence had picked this ungodly hour for the reconnaissance because the big shots in the God Box assumed most of the Tommies would still be in their bunks for another hour at least.

Hartung hoped they were right, though the stomach-churning smell of frying bacon coming from one of the tin shanties next to the jetty told him that some, at least, of the Tommies were awake. He prayed that they'd be too busy frying that disgusting breakfast fodder of theirs – it wasn't natural to be scoffing fried food at this time of the morning – to take a look outside and spot the intruders.

Unfortunately for Hauptmann Hartung, his forecast was to be proved badly wrong.

Five minutes passed in tense, nervous excitement. Now they were on the jetty itself. Hartung gave a whispered order and the men straightened up. Now they looked, he hoped, like a Home Guard squad out on a boring early-morning routine patrol before they could return to their normal daily jobs. He felt this was the right way to attract as little attention as possible to themselves.

While his men took on the expressions of bored part-time soldiers killing time before they went off duty out of the freezing wind, Hartung's keen blue-eyed gaze took in the wooden uprights with the names of the ships placarded upon them as the spots where the ships' lighters would tie up ready to take on stores. To Hartung it seemed a gross lack of security. But then, he told himself, the Tommies obviously didn't expect any enemy to penetrate so far into the greatest naval base of their empire.

Moving his lips as he did so, Hartung read the names of the British ships, telling himself that if he were a real spy he'd be able now to assess the strength of the whole British Home Fleet from the neatly printed official signs giving the names of the ships the lighters supplied.

Suddenly, almost startlingly – although he had naturally expected to find it there; Intelligence had told him he should – there it was. These simple four letters of the great ship's name. He had found that she was there, virtually as easily as clicking his fingers.

"*Grosse Kacke am Christbaum*!" he cursed to himself with joy. "I've got it!"

For a brief moment he savoured his triumph, his hard-weathered face lighted up with joy. Then he became strictly professional once more, telling himself it was the fool who hesitated who got his balls caught up in the wringer. It was time to go while they were winning. He spun.

"Klemenz," he began, addressing the NCO closest to him, "*Los, hauen wir ab*!"

It was that same instant that a sharp angry challenge came from the door of the corrugated iron shed to their right; stabbed into their beings like the blade of a sharp knife. "Halt . . . who goes there?"

Hartung spun round.

An angry, helmeted face was staring at them. But it wasn't that which caught his attention. It was the long rifle with its old-fashioned bayonet which the sailor sentry was pointing in their direction which did.

Hartung reacted instinctively. He knew he had to. He brought up the silenced pistol which he had kept concealed all the while and fired low. The pistol jerked in his big fist. A puff of smoke, a soft plop and suddenly the sailor was going down, a look of total astonishment on his face, a red patch beginning to spread across the front of his greatcoat – and, in that last dying moment as he fought against falling to the ground and death, his forefinger, curled around the trigger of his Lee Enfield, jerked backwards.

The rifle exploded with what seemed to Hartung to be a tremendous crack of thunder. Then they were running back up the jetty to the hidden dinghy and rifle shots were ringing out on all sides, joined an instant later by the dreary dirge of the air raid sirens sounding the alert. They had been rumbled. Now it really was 'march or croak'.

Seven

The Spitfires had gone.

The drifter had proved too slow for them. At 300 miles an hour they had come zooming in at wave-top, machine guns chattering frantically – and had overshot the German craft by yards. Their slugs had lashed the grey-green water to a white fury quite without purpose. They had come in a couple of times more, while the skipper on the open bridge, sweating heavily despite the freezing cold, had dodged and zigzagged desperately. Then they had given up. Obviously their fuel had begun to give out and they had departed, disappearing into the ever-thickening cloud for their bases on the Scottish mainland.

For a while, the young skipper had hung limply at the wheel, his hands trembling helplessly. Hauptmann Hartung had said something from below, his hands red with blood, a shell dressing unwrapped and ready to apply to the wound of one of his men. But he hadn't been able to take in whatever the Brandenburg officer said. Besides, he was attempting to regain his nerve. The Tommies would be back. He knew that with the certainty of a vision.

The Brandenburgers had managed to get away, save one, Hartung had gasped as he had clambered over the side. He had been killed outright by a burst of machine gun fire. But that hadn't been the end of it. Indeed, within what had seemed only minutes all hell had been let loose. Everywhere sirens had begun to wail their dread warning. On the land, signal flares had shot alarmingly into grey sky. Signal lamps had blinked on and off between the great ships. Even anti-aircraft searchlights had been switched on over Flotta as if the Tommies thought they were being raided from the air.

But the young German skipper had been more concerned with the motor boat protecting one of the booms which had taken up the chase immediately. Going all out, a white bone in her teeth, curved prow standing right out of the water, she had narrowed the distance between herself and the civilian craft at an alarming speed. Even when she had been out of range, her quick-firer on the forward deck had started to spit flame. Tracer shells had zipped towards the German vessel in a lethal morse. Naturally they had fallen short, as the skipper had zigzagged desperately, great white spouts of whirling water erupting on both sides of her stern buffeting her from side to side, as if she had been punched by some gigantic invisible fist.

However, Intelligence had provided the bold intruders with some protection for such an eventuality as this sudden chase. The young skipper knew it was time to use the rough-and-ready device which the gentlemen of the God Box had provided. He snapped out of his battle-shocked reverie and shouted, "Obermaat – *jetzt los . . . DALLI, DALLI, MENSCH*!"

The grizzled old chief petty officer at the stern needed no urging. As he had told his mates in the petty officers' mess, "I don't fancy spending the shitting war scoffing English corned beef, drinking that shitting tea and playing the five-fingered widow in some Tommy cage, mates." The twenty-six-year-old skipper saw the danger quicker than the 'Old Man'.

With a grunt, he heaved the first of the tiny mines overboard. Immediately he followed it by another – and yet another. Suddenly the bubbling white wake of the drifter was filled with bobbing lethal metal eggs.

"For what we are now about to receive," the old salt gasped cheerfully as he shoved the last of the mines overboard, "may the Good Lord make us truly thankful." Then he waited.

He hadn't had long to do so. At the very last moment the skipper of the Tommy motor boat had spotted the deadly mines. Frantically he had swung his wheel to port. Too late! The sharp prow had struck the first of them in the fleeing drifter's wake. There was a thick throaty crump. The motor boat stopped abruptly, as if it had run into a brick wall. Next moment, its prow rose into the air in a ball of flame and a second later bits and pieces of man and metal were flying heavenwards. The happily brutalised Obermaat chuckled and crooned the old phrase, "Roll on death, mates, and let's have a fuck at the angels . . ."

That had been half an hour ago and with the suddenness of the northern climes, a thick white woolly fog had come rolling in and covered the Germans' flight, until the Spitfires had found a 'window' and come zooming down for their abortive strike. But now, as the almost exhausted skipper tried to concentrate on the course home to the safety of Bergen on the Norwegian coast, that window in the fog persisted. Indeed, it seemed to the harassed young officer that it followed the drifter as it headed eastwards. "For Chrissake," he hissed to himself angrily more than once, "will you bloody well go away."

But the window in the fog stubbornly refused to do his bidding.

In the distance, the big white bulk of a Sunderland flying boat from the Tommies' Coastal Command was coming ever closer, approaching with relentless determination. The old Obermaat spat out a stream of tobacco juice into the foam sea at the drifter's stern, crossed himself in mock solemnity and muttered to himself, "Heaven help a sailor on a shitty night like this." Then he thrust his skinny shoulder against the butt of the vessel's anti-aircraft gun. There was going to be trouble . . .

"Trouble; you can bet yer bottom dollar, Fleming, there's going to be trouble." Godfrey's irate voice crackled across the radio waves as the big staff Humber roared through the weak dawn light towards Plymouth and the waiting de Vere Smythe. There were silent flickering pink flames on the horizon to indicate the naval port had suffered yet another enemy coastal blitz. But Fleming, holding on with one hand behind the Wren and gripping the earphone tightly to his left ear with the other, had no eye for the fires. His whole being was concentrated on the surprising news that the Chief of Naval Intelligence was relaying from a still sleeping Chequers.

"The PM's gone to bed in a furious temper. He wants a report first thing in the morning when he wakes up. Northern Command is screaming bloody murder and my piles are playing me up like merry hell."

Under normal circumstances Fleming would have made one of his customary flippant remarks, especially about the piles. Now, however, the Lieutenant Commander thought it wiser to remain very professional and attentive. He said, "But what exactly happened at Scapa Flow, sir?"

"Nothing in one way," came back the surprising answer, but before Fleming had time to comment, Admiral Godfrey cried, "but on the other hand, all sorts of strange things did occur. The Hun landed there for one thing. Only one very small party, but they definitely came ashore. We found one of the cheeky buggers – only unfortunately, he'd been shot through the heart by some bloody Navy marksman. And I always thought matelots couldn't bloody well shoot straight."

"Anything?" Fleming cried above the furious squeal of rubber as the Wren driver took a corner far too fast, still whistling that damned jingle through her front teeth like a street-corner errand boy: "I've got spurs that jingle-jangle-jingle as I go riding merrily along . . ." Fleming would have dearly liked to have told her what to do with her spurs, but he thought better of it. She was in charge of the big car, after all.

"Anything that could give us a clue?" he repeated at the top of his voice, as the Wren took the car back up to seventy once more, whizzing down the blacked out village street.

"Just that the Jerry stiff was wearing a German tunic beneath the Home Guard blouse and it bore the Brandenburg armband on the right sleeve."

Fleming whistled softly. Now that really was something for the books, he told himself. Old Admiral Canaris' house troops.

Godfrey must have heard the whistle, for he shouted from the other end, "Yes, I know what you mean. Canaris wouldn't use his elite for anything in the nature of a common-or-garden commando raid. There's more to it than that."

"But what about the plane or ship which brought the Brandenburgers to Scapa Flow?" Fleming butted in, intrigued despite the Wren's crazy and highly dangerous style of driving.

"Ship, Ian," Godfrey answered. "Coastal Command's spotted it and one of their Sunderland flying boats is ready to go into the attack. But that's it. If the Hun craft gives the Sunderland the slip, we've had it. There's thick fog up there – too much for our surface ships. The Admiralty's not prepared to risk anything bigger than a torpedo boat, especially under present circumstances, until we can bloody well tell them what's going on. As if *we* damn well knew," Godfrey ended bitterly.

"Take your point, sir. But what do you want me to do? Should I continue to Plymouth or should I scrub the meeting with de Vere Smythe and hie myself tootsweet up to Scapa?"

"Not just yet. See what you can find out from that impossible counter-jumper Smythe. Report to me at zero eight hundred hours. Then I'll decide. Somehow" – Godfrey hesitated – "I have a funny feeling about this whole strange business . . ." He dropped his normally somewhat booming voice, acquired on the quarterdeck of the battle-cruiser he had commanded before 1939, and said, almost as if he were talking to himself, "There's a connection . . . I'm damn sure there's a connection."

"Between what, sir?" Fleming enquired, puzzled. He had always taken Godfrey for a straight character with no doubts: a plain-speaking sailor of the old school.

Godfrey didn't answer directly. Instead he said, "Continue with your present assignment, Ian, as I've said, and then we'll see." The connection went dead and as the big boxlike staff car raced on and on, Fleming sat for quite a while with the dead earphones of the wireless receiver in his hands, wondering what was going on and what the old Admiral had meant by saying that he was 'damn sure there was a connection'. A connection between *what*?

He could find no logical answer to that particular puzzling question and in the end he took a sip of the single malt whisky he always kept in his silver pocket flask, settled down more comfortably in the back seat and, closing his eyes, attempted to sleep till they reached Plymouth and the new problems that awaited him there.

Eight

"Er, well, sir, I'd say it was a pretty typical sort of a crowd that you'd find attending that kind of mumbo-jumbo. Mostly women" – de Vere Smythe never could refrain from expressing his middle-class snobbery – "of the lower orders, naturally."

Lower orders! Fleming, a snob of a different kind himself, groaned inwardly at the expression. But he said nothing aloud. Outside, the bombed city was settling down and a loudspeaker truck from Civil Defence was cruising by at a snail's pace, announcing, "Lists of casualties are now being posted at the Central Library . . . Those who have lost their homes should report this afternoon at the Guildhall for information . . . Ration cards which have been lost or destroyed will be replaced at . . ."

"A couple of middle-aged ladies, you know, sir, knitting and twin sets, and half a dozen matelots at the back looking a bit sheepish, as if they didn't really like being seen there. Not that they could be, really. Right from the very start, the lights were kept pretty dim. And it was nothing to do with the blackout. *He* obviously wanted to keep it that way."

"Who?"

"The organiser."

"What did he look like?"

"Big, surly-looking chap, about ten years younger than Madame Clarissa," de Vere answered, obviously enjoying the question-and-answer session – as if he thought himself doing a bloody Doctor Watson to my Sherlock Holmes, Fleming couldn't help telling himself sourly.

"Think he might be her boyfriend," de Vere continued. "That sort of thing."

"All right, when everyone had coughed up their entrance fee and had settled down, what happened next?" Fleming asked.

"Not much out of the ordinary, sir. The sort of thing you might have found at the WVS or the Mothers' Union. A lot of old – and young – biddies gossiping away about nothing. After a while, though – I hardly noticed it at first – there was music."

"Music?"

"Yes. Soft and mysterious somehow. I knew the tune, but for the life of me I can't remember the title of the piece now. Very soothing, though, almost soporific. I felt my eyelids blink a couple of times, I can tell you. I thought I was going to fall asleep." De Vere smiled faintly at the memory and told himself he'd had good reason for feeling tired – nay, exhausted would have been a better word. First there had been the session in Mavis' bedroom and then, lo and behold, in that crowded, hot, fetid atmosphere she had reached her naughty little fingers in underneath the greatcoat he'd folded over his lap – it had been so warm that he'd taken it off almost immediately – opened his flies and pulled his thing out of his pants. Nothing like that had happened to him before. A woman playing with his thing in a public place, utterly without shame. He had been so shocked – and, he had to admit it, tremendously excited, too – that he hadn't attempted to stop her.

So, while some silly old biddy next to him waffled on about how difficult it was to get offal these days, though it wasn't rationed, she'd been pulling at his thing for all she was worth and he could feel himself shaking and glowing with heat, knowing that in a minute, if she didn't stop that delightful torment, he'd be spraying all over her cunning dear hand.

"And?" Fleming demanded harshly, killing that delightful memory immediately.

"Oh, well, Madame Clarissa appeared from behind a curtain at the back of the room. The end of the place was lit by a dim red light so it was pretty difficult to make her out properly. But she was wearing a large robe – she's a large woman – that was a bit like a bell-tent."

"Was she wearing head covering too?" Fleming asked eagerly. "Also very loose?"

Smythe looked at his senior, surprised. "Yes. How did you know?"

Fleming indulged him. "Old trick with these dodgy mediums. The loose clothes can conceal things. They can also be got out of quickly and the medium can emerge wearing a totally different outfit for a while. In other words, the loose robe may hide a second person – from the other side." He emphasised the words cynically.

"Crikey!" Smythe was so awed that he reverted to the working-class slang of his youth: a fact that Fleming, the old Etonian snob, noted immediately.

"Well, then the chap in charge said that Madame was going to go into a trance in the chair at the back on a kind of little stage – again, that red light made it difficult to see much – and that we were to keep quiet and say nothing until she was 'under'."

"I'd put her bloody well under," Fleming said grimly. "The damned traitor." By now he had made up his mind about Madame Clarissa.

Outside a middle-aged warden, the tears streaming down his honest, hard-working face, was carrying the body of a little child like some broken doll, exhibiting her to the silent crowd as he stumbled across the smoking brick rubble to the ambulance. Was he asking for someone to identify her? Or was he exhibiting her limp broken body like this, with her dangling little legs, as an expression of man's inhumanity to man? Fleming cursed beneath his breath. He was a cynical, uncaring man normally, concerned solely with his own personal pleasures and career. But this hurt. Someone had to be hurt in return – and it might as well be Madame Clarissa, if he could find the fat cow in time.

"Get on with it," he said urgently.

"It was a bit eerie, I must admit," Smythe continued. "She said something in a kind of gibberish, then she began swaying back and forth as if she were in the throes of a fit, all sorts of rubbish coming from her mouth. For a few moments I could have sworn she was cussing like a trooper – all sorts of vile words. Then suddenly, very suddenly – indeed, she gave me and the rest of the audience quite a start –

she stopped her writhing and trembling. She sat like that for what seemed an age. You could have heard a pin drop . . ."

It had been then that Mavis had stopped playing with his penis, so rigid by that stage that it hurt him physically. He would have dearly loved to have begged her to finish him off then and there, damn what people might think. But he didn't. The atmosphere in the tight, smelly room was like that of a church – a church in which the congregation was about to witness a miracle.

"It was then, sir – I know you might not believe this, but I *did* see it with my own eyes – that a sort of white cloud seemed to develop in front of Madame Clarissa. I know that the light was bad, but I saw it – and so did everybody else – and slowly, very slowly, the cloud began to form into what I can only call a rough-and-ready" – he paused and even now, hours after the event, he could feel the icy finger of fear trace its way slowly down the small of his back and make the hairs at the back of his head stand up – "*human figure.*"

Fleming was unimpressed. Before the war he had been an avid reader of the thriller writer Denis Wheatley; he knew all about spiritualism and such things. "Ectoplasm," he announced, "probably a large, shaped bunch of cotton wool she'd hidden behind that robe you mention. It would have been the ideal hiding place for it. And then?"

"Once we'd got over the shock, she – or the, er, ectoplasm; I couldn't really make out which – started talking. At first it was a lot of mumbo-jumbo. You know: *Uncle Joe is calling from the other side . . . Auntie May is feeling lonely . . . Is there anyone here tonight who'd like to reply?*"

"And of course there was," Fleming interjected.

"Yes; they were all a bit shocked or dazed, but once Madame Clarissa told 'em all was well they seemed pleased enough."

"Well, they got their money's worth. That's what they went there for in the first place."

"I suppose so, sir. But then it got even funnier – I mean, she did."

"How do you mean?"

"Well, she started speaking in a man's voice—"

"A man's voice?"

"Yes, sir. But that wasn't all. It was a tough, real down to earth sort of thing. You know, like the way that one of those old three stripeys of the lower deck talk – one of those who never acknowledges that he's in the company of women and talks like he does in his division – all 'bloody' and 'bastid' – and even worse, if you'll forgive my French." Smythe was plainly embarrassed. He even went red.

Fleming didn't seem to notice. He leaned forward and rapped urgently, "You mean like a matelot?" Before Smythe could answer, he followed with a swift "And what sort of questions did this – er – man ask?"

"You know that too, sir," Smythe said, surprised, then he saw the look in his superior's eyes and continued with a hasty, "Well, sir, leading questions, I'd call 'em."

"How leading?"

"For instance, he asked a stoker what his ship was – just like that. Then to top it all, he asked him whether he was bunkered up, meaning—"

"Meaning, he'd – er – she'd know whether his ship was about to sail!"

"That's what I thought, too." He was going to say more, but he could see from the look on Fleming's broken-nosed face that he was thinking hard and didn't want to be disturbed.

Outside the sweepers had arrived from the council, looking very like Royal Marines in the tall pith helmets they wore. They engaged themselves in sweeping away the broken glass and brick rubble. The city was being patched up and restored to normal until the next raid came – and it would come, Smythe knew that. They always did. Hun air raids had become part and parcel of everyday living in Britain these days. There seemed no end to them.

Finally Fleming broke his heavy brooding silence. "All right; I think we can assume that she is a spy. It is imperative that we arrest her. There's something very funny going on at Scapa, which I'll tell you about later. It might well be that this Madame Clarissa of yours has something to do with the events up there. The best way to find out is to grill her. Where is she, Lieutenant Smythe?"

Smythe looked miserable. He hung his head like a shamed schoolboy. "When the sirens sounded, sir, the air warden came in shrilling his whistle, crying 'everybody into the shelters'. You know how ruddy officious they can be – and there wasn't even a shelter, anyway . . . Before I could do anything, sir, the whole lot of them had disappeared. Later I checked her hotel."

"Yes?"

"She'd gone – and left no forwarding address. Why should she? After all . . ." The explanation died on his lips. He could see that Lieutenant-Commander Fleming wasn't listening. Besides, he could feel a strange burning sensation in his penis. He had experienced it an hour or so before when he had gone to the latrine to pee. Idly he wondered what it was.

"It's obvious she's on no theatre or music hall circuit now," Fleming said slowly and softly, as if musing to himself. "That might be too dangerous. If she had a fixed timetable she could be picked up at any time. All the same, she's travelling. But where?"

"Sir." Smythe cleared his throat and half held up his hand like a timid schoolboy asking some frightening beak, armed with a cane and quick to use it, if he might be excused.

After some time, Fleming deigned to notice him. "Yes?" he snapped impatiently.

"If I may be so bold, sir—"

"You may." But irony was wasted on Smythe.

"This Madame Clarissa . . . she works with sailors."

"So?"

"Well, the place where she'll find sailors is a port – a big naval port. As we know, she's been to Pompey and now Plymouth—"

"She'd never be able to get to Scapa," Fleming snapped, seeing the way that the other man was going. "It's out of bounds for civvies."

"I know, sir, but there are other naval bases which feed drafts and the like to Scapa for the Home Fleet up there. If she wanted to find out about our ships up there, she'd go to one of those places to pump the matelots for info."

"Of course," Fleming cried excitedly. His voice dropped. "But why did you think it was that place – and the ships up there – that this Madame Clarissa of yours is interested in, Smythe?" He stared hard at the other officer's weak pale face.

"That place?"

"Scapa Flow, Smythe," Fleming snapped.

Smythe's mouth dropped open with surprise. "I say, sir," he managed to gasp, his face suddenly frightened, his mind racing at the realisation he had just come to. "It must be catching, sir."

"What?"

"This seeing in the future stuff . . ." He looked earnestly at his superior's arrogant face. "Do . . . d'yer think I'm *psychic*, sir?"

Harding Waxes Poetic

I was bloody stymied!

Again I seemed to have come to a dead end in this half-century-old business of the *Hood.* Mr *sodding* de Vere Smythe had turned out to be a loser. He had whetted my appetite but when it came down to cases, he hadn't produced the grub. Perhaps they're all like that in Oz. It's all that sitting in the sun on the beach in funny hats drinking their disgusting 'bevvies'.

He had finished the letter accompanying 'my piece' from the bloody provincial Aussie rag with, 'I'm afraid I couldn't pursue the matter any further at the time. Lt Commander Fleming, who, as you know, departed for the other side' – God, he was beginning to start to sound like a bloody table-rapper himself – 'a long time ago now, did instigate a search for the missing Madame Clarissa, but as to whatever he may or may not have discovered then . . .'

I breathed out with exasperation. Didn't the little creep waffle! *He'd* never get a contract for a book from my publisher, that well-known patron of the Gay Hussar, I can tell you. He'd never be able to afford a book of the length that de Vere Smythe would produce. At a penny a word, it would bankrupt him. And that would be the end of crawling waiters, *paprika gulyas* and bottles of the finest Tokay. It'd be McDonald's after that . . .

'You see,' my correspondent had gone on, 'I was taken quite ill at the time from some sort of abdominal complaint. They shipped me straight off to the Haslar' – he meant the great wartime hospital at Portsmouth – 'and I never heard about the end of the affair with Madame Clarissa. It was, after all, very hush-hush . . .'

The words blurred. I looked out of the cottage window and I frowned at the cold remorseless North Sea and the drizzle. I remembered the burning sensation he'd mentioned and hoped that Mavis, that obliging lady of the night, had given him a nice juicy dose of the clap as a souvenir. It couldn't have happened to a nicer guy.

I smiled at my blurred reflection in the steamed-over window pane. In those days they didn't prescribe penicillin as a cure for the clap. So probably de Vere Smythe had had to suffer quite a while in the Haslar with his 'social disease', as they called VD in those far-off days.

My smile vanished and I frowned at myself. De Vere Smythe's troubles with sex and its after-effects didn't help me one bit. As for Fleming, he was not only dead, but the information he *had* left behind regarding his wartime Intelligence work was totally unreliable. How the hell did he get away with it? He travelled everywhere, rode the gravy train first class and as far as I could see never produced one solid contribution to British victory in World War Two during his whole six-year naval career. But then, look at the success of 007, as played by a former Scottish milkman, and an easy-going chap with warts who went to my old Catholic school in Leeds . . .

I digress. None of this took me one iota closer to what really happened to the *Hood*. How was I now going to get rid of that image of the old lady in her husband's boots running shrieking down that passage so long ago: 'The *Hood* . . . my son . . .'

Even now I can wake up sweating, heart beating like a bloody trip-hammer, hands trembling – and it's not the booze – when I recall that childhood memory. *She* deserves an explanation, if nothing else.

Outside the rain was beating a murderous tattoo at the window. I pretended I didn't notice. I had to concentrate. What did I know? *Bugger all, matey*, a coarse voice from the past sneered at the back of my mind. I ignored the voice and concentrated even harder.

I knew the facts – and damn few they were, too. The MOD wasn't coming across. Kew wasn't releasing the relevant documents. OK, that meant the Admiralty – and, naturally, the Government – had something to hide. What? How was it that the *Hood*, once the greatest ship in the world, was sunk so quickly? A matter of five minutes and she was gone, taking nearly two thousand poor souls with her. Such things happen in warfare, happen all the time – but not with such apparent ease. So what was so special about the way HMS *Hood* was sunk by the Germans in 1941?

A lot of questions and so few answers . . .

I must have sat there for quite a long time, pondering the ancient mystery. And wasted time means lost money for an underpaid hack writer.

In my type of book I rarely get a chance to quote the Bard. But he is handy. He's got a quote for everything and he's easier to remember than the Bible. What had he said about time? 'I wasted Time – and now doth Time waste me', or something of the sort. Exactly.

The quotation put the old brain into third gear. (These days it'd never make fourth without the gearbox blowing up.)

Who knows everything, can find out everything in the late nineties? Who's smarter and more efficient than the CIA – MI6 – MI5 – Bundesverfassungschutz, et cetera, et cetera, all bundled into one? Why, the British Press of course. With those magnificent cheque books of theirs, they can open virtually any door with a neat signature – at the bottom of a suitably large amount of the readies, of course. Those fools who govern us keep getting caught with their knickers down about their ankles because they haven't reckoned with that yet; they still think we live in the time of Queen Victoria.

So who did I know in the gutter press who could point me in the right direction? I mean, most tabloid hacks, as bright as they are, don't even know what they had for breakfast, liquid or otherwise, the previous day.

Then I had it. *Horace the Obit.* Horace would know – and if he didn't, he'd bloody well tell me where to find out.

I reached out for the black book and the phone and prepared for a long siege at the door of British Telecom. For a change I was happy, the woman in the boots temporarily forgotten . . .

Nine

Admiral Lutjens and Captain Lindemann were arguing. Even through the steel walls of Lindemann's cabin, Oberfahnrich Klaus von Kadowitz could hear them, as he waited next to the immaculate Marine sentry, together with Obermaat Hansen. He frowned. He didn't like to hear senior officers raising their voices, especially when there were men from the lower decks present. It wasn't good for morale, and he guessed that within the hour, the buzz about the two big cheeses being engaged in a slanging match would be doing the rounds of the *Prinz Eugen*. He looked at Hansen, but his rough, ruddy, drunkard's face revealed nothing, save perhaps a little look of joy at the cadet officer's discomfort. Instinctively, Klaus touched the new black enamel of the Wound Medal which decorated his chest now. It did show he had seen some action – even if it was only in an air raid – and had shed his blood for the Fatherland.

"I don't like it, Herr Admiral . . . I don't like it one little bit," he could hear the skipper Lindemann saying. Even the typical sound of the great ship, the low regular whirr and hum of the auxiliary machinery, couldn't drown their voices. Lutjens' reply, however, remained inaudible. Klaus's frown deepened. What in three devils' names could the Fleet's two most senior officers be arguing about? They commanded the most powerful ships in the world. Admittedly the Tommies outnumbered them collectively, but individually they were more than a match for anything the enemy could put in the field.

"We can safely assume that the Tommies will spot the *Bismarck*'s entry into the conflict in the North Atlantic once we reach Norway. As you know, we'll sail from Bergen with a fake convoy. Thereafter our two ships, *Bismarck* and *Eugen*, will break away for the action to come."

Lindemann nodded. His face revealed nothing of his doubts, only his resentment. It expressed his feeling that he was not able to represent his own doubts fully enough. He knew Lutjens didn't like Raeder's plans any more than he did. But Lutjens was out for glory; he'd carry out the plan in the knowledge that the Führer would reward him for doing so. Hitler always liked his commanders to barrel ahead without asking awkward questions.

"Now we must understand this," Lutjens continued quite severely, ignoring the look on the captain's face. "We can be sure that the Tommies are fully informed of our firepower and range of action, especially that of the *Bismarck*, our flagship."

Lindemann nodded, but said nothing.

"So they will throw in everything they've got, including the *Hood*, as Canaris has informed us. Well –" he hesitated, as if even he was not quite sure of himself and the outcome of the battle to come, – "come what may we must return with a victory or –" he hesitated again momentarily – "not at all."

Lindemann had expected the comment. He didn't like it. He had never liked, in all his career, these black-and-white statements of the more unthinking naval officers. Their rigid logic lacked finesse, and he had already prepared his counter-argument. "Herr Admiral, with your permission, I don't think we should look at the matter quite like that. There are not just two alternatives."

Lutjens gave him a sharp look. Outside he could make out the rumble of the tugs as they prepared to tow the *Prinz Eugen* out into the channel. He'd have to be leaving soon. "Pray continue," he said coldly.

"A victory we must have – to please the Führer. But let it be a limited one, and not one that is foolhardy and risks our two capital ships. As you know, Admiral, we're aiming at the *Hood*. Fine. We sink her and we have our great victory. Thereafter we make a run for it."

"I don't like that phrase."

Lindemann ignored the comment. If Lutjens wanted to be a hero, so be it. But he personally had no ambitions in that direction, especially if the glory was going to come posthumously. "In my opinion," he said quickly, as the first of the tugs nudged the side of the *Prinz Eugen* and sent the glasses on the tray shaking, "we can have our victory *and* save our ships from damage and possible destruction, if we're quick enough. In and out before the Tommies can gather their whole fleet and set about blasting our craft out of the water. After all, Herr Admiral," he reminded a stony-faced Lutjens, "the *Hood* will probably be the first on the scene, with her speed. She can outspeed the rest of the English fleet by at least eight or nine knots."

Lutjens humoured the red-faced captain with a nod. "I see . . . and?"

"And this. We keep this business secret as long as possible. Why should the English know that we're in Bergen? Why shouldn't they find out where we are much later, when their aircraft patrols finally pick us up? Then they'll send the *Hood* at top speed to intercept us." He paused for his punchline. "We'll have her on our own, Herr Admiral, and she won't have a chance in hell – not with our combined firepower."

Lutjens considered and then reached for his cap, as if he couldn't believe that his subordinate could do anything about the situation as it stood – after all, it had been planned at the very top, at the *Tirpitzufer*. He snapped gruffly, "And how, *mein lieber* Lindemann, will you ensure that we keep this business a secret 'as long as possible', as you phrase it? After all, we are sailing through one of the most busy of inland waterways, the Baltic."

Lindemann was ready for the question. "As you know, Admiral, the neutral Swedes have been warned to run for port now. They can guess what is going on, but they won't know. But there will be some of their skippers, the ones with the little boats that do all the contraband running between Sweden, Lübeck, Wismar and the like, who'll stay out in the Baltic. Anything they pick up, they'll sell to the Tommies' agents in Stockholm. They, Herr Admiral, will be the ones, if we allow them to do so, who pass on the information about the *Bismarck* and the *Prinz Eugen*. They are the ones, too, that we will – er – eradicate if necessary."

Lutjens looked at the *Eugen*'s skipper as if he had just cursed the Führer himself. "*Eradicate*?" He caught himself in time. He slapped his cap on to his shaven head and rose to his feet. "Do as you wish, Captain Lindemann. I for one don't want to know."

Lindemann stood to attention. Lutjens pressed his hand, seeing through his subordinate as if he were made of glass. "I shall see you in Bergen, Lindemann." Without another word he passed from the cabin and through the waiting sailors, all standing stiffly to attention in the companionway, staring at some distant horizon known only to themselves.

Hansen wrinkled his nose as if he had just smelled an unpleasant odour and Klaus von Kadowitz, loyal as he was, understood why the sailors called the Admiral '*der schwarze Teufel*' behind his back. He had no heart for his men. He would sent them all to hell without a moment's hesitation.

A minute later, the duty officer called them in and Captain Lindemann began to explain to Klaus and Obermaat Hansen what he wanted from them. Without ever being aware of it, the young officer-cadet, the hard-bitten petty officer and the score of young sailors under their command had become part of the greatest security and counter-intelligence operation ever prepared by Admiral Canaris.

* * *

Operation Bismarck, as it was code-named, had been planned with unparalleled thoroughness. Involving naval, army and counter-intelligence units, it began on that evening of May nineteenth from the Baltic through Bergen right up to the Artic Circle.

Infantry units were shipped in regimental strength to Bergen. Fake convoys sailed to and fro up the Norwegian coast. Minesweeping flotillas were everywhere, apparently sweeping areas where there hadn't seen a mine since the outbreak of war nearly two years before. Infantry and naval marines moved right up to Norway's remote border with Russia.

In Oslo, Canaris' counter-intelligence agents let the Norwegian spies signal what was going on in their area, though even the Norwegians couldn't make head nor tail of all this hectic activity. The Abwehr would pounce on the Norwegians on the morrow and close down their networks. Thereafter there would be total silence from Norway, presumably leaving the English more confused about what was going on than ever.

But still there was that problem of the inner sea, the Baltic. Here there was no hope of confusing the enemy, Canaris knew that. It was for that reason that he had suggested to the *Prinz Eugen*'s skipper, rather than to the Fleet Commander, Lutjens, that he should, as he had put it in that delicate manner of his, 'take special measures . . . even if they could be messy'.

The *Prinz Eugen*'s skipper knew, as did Hansen and even a reluctant Klaus, what that 'messy' meant. In his own inimical fashion, the old salt laid it on the line. "We croak 'em, Oberfahnrich. No two ways about it. If we suspect the Swedish saucehounds, it's a quick knock on the back of the turnip" – he meant skull – "and heave-ho, m'hearties – over the frigging side!"

They were sitting in the little bridge of the armoured motor boat which had been allotted to them for their task in the Baltic, watching the tugs pull the majestic bulk of the *Bismarck* through the evening mist so that it appeared like a ghost ship sliding mysteriously and silently on its mission of death. "Fine ship," Klaus said almost dreamily as he sipped his scalding hot coffee.

"Ay, that she is," Hansen agreed, his red swollen nose savouring the delightful odour of real bean coffee well laced with a hundred millilitres of strong rum. "You know, Oberfahnrich, I saw the Grand High Fleet sail out of Kiel to meet the Tommies at what they call the Battle of Jutland back in 1916. Snotty-nosed kid of fifteen at the time. Grand sight they were with the bands playing, the flags flying and even them bloody red dockies cheering 'em; social democrat to the man they were, too. And then . . ." He shrugged and stopped.

Klaus waited and, when nothing came, asked a little uncertainly, "And what then, Chiefie?"

"Not so many of 'em came back – and what did, didn't look so grand any more. We never left harbour again after that until the Tommies ordered us to sail to the surrender at Scapa Flow."

Klaus forced a grin. "A real ray of sunshine you are, Obermaat. That won't happen to us, I can tell you. We won't let it. After all, Chiefie, we have the finest, strongest and most modern ships in the world, you know." His chest swelled with pride. "This is a different Germany from the days when you were a kid. The whole nation's behind us now, Chiefie."

Obermaat Hansen was not convinced. Abruptly his good mood vanished.

With the enthusiasm and one hundred per cent confidence of youth, Klaus tried to reassure the dubious old salt. "Look at her." He indicated the *Bismarck* slowly disappearing into the mist. "She's all of forty-five thousand tons displacement. She carries eighty-nine guns of all calibres, her big guns sighted and aimed within a metre by radar – a helluva lot faster than those of the Tommies. As far as her armour is concerned, she has a nickel-chrome-steel torpedo belt right round her hull." He smiled confidently at the surly petty officer. "Hansen, you know and I know that there isn't a torpedo in the world powerful enough to smash through that torpedo belt. Hell, man, she's virtually unsinkable."

Hansen didn't reply. He continued to sip his coffee and rum, saying nothing, lost, it seemed, in his own thoughts – and they weren't pleasant.

Oberfahnrich Klaus von Kadowitz gave up on him. He sighed and said, "All right, Obermaat, I'm going below. You take over the con till we're out into the Baltic. *Klar*?"

"*Klar*, Herr Oberfahnrich." Hansen came to an approximation of attention, mug held at his side.

Klaus touched his fingers to his cap, battered in the approved fashion by dint of much hard work in the secrecy of his tiny cabin so that it would lend him the look of a veteran. He clattered down the companionway to go below deck. But before he did so, he flashed a final look upwards.

Hansen had put his mug down and was holding the wheel now. But Klaus could see he wasn't paying too much attention to the con. His eyes were fixed on some further point than the area immediately in front of him, in the wake of the tugs and the *Bismarck*. It was as if he were looking into another – and not so rosy – world, known only to him.

Idly Klaus wondered what it could be. Hansen, he told himself, didn't look the type given to introspection. Then he shook his head as if physically dismissing the matter and opened the door into the tiny wardroom and its thick fug, his mind already racing excitedly at the prospect of the great adventure to come.

Ten

At first light, the fog came drifting in from the land. At first it was nothing more than a few faint grey wisps. They curled themselves like a soft silent cat around the motor launch, almost unnoticed.

On the deck the handful of young ratings went about their early morning duties without seeing it, emptying the slops from the night, throwing overboard the waste from the tiny galley, checking the 20mm Bofors mounted on the forward deck and the twin Spandaus behind the little bridge.

But slowly the mist thickened. It brought with it a freezing, bone-chilling cold, more intensive than normal for the Baltic in early spring. When it was time for the on-duty watch to do their morning 'physical jerks', they did so in their heavy sea-going gear and hobnailed winter boots and at the end a couple of the usual comics found on board every ship waltzed together in mock solemnity, stomping on the metal deck. But as the cold grew more intense, even the young men's high spirits deserted them and they went about their duties in an almost sullen, brooding lethargy. As Hansen grumbled to Klaus von Kadowitz, "It'll frigging well snow next, you just watch,

Oberfahnrich, you just watch!" And he was right. Half an hour later, as the last smudge of what had once been the Danish island of Rugen disappeared on the horizon, the first gentle flakes of snow came drifting down.

On the bridge, Klaus cursed. This was his first independent command and an important one at that. Now the fog and the lightly falling snow could only make his task more difficult. The Swedes running contraband in and out of the German Baltic ports would know this coast like the back of their hands; they'd know where to hide even under ordinary conditions. Now the weather conditions would make it even more difficult for a novice like himself to spot them.

At his side Hansen broke his silence and said, as if he could read the young skipper's mind, "Not to worry, Oberfahnrich. Those *Svenskas* are greedy swine. They're after our money and they're after the Tommies' cash. Neutral, my arse!" He spat contemptuously on the floor of the bridge, a habit which Klaus thought wouldn't be too well regarded in the higher circles of the German Kriegsmarine. "They're in this shitting business only for this." He made the gesture of counting money with his forefinger and thumb. "So, bad weather or not, they'll stay out at sea as long as they can without running for the shelter of the land. If we can stay out, them Swedish slime-shitters will, too. If it's gonna pay them to spot the *Bismarck* and our *Prinz Eugen*, they'll stay out, believe you me, Oberfahnrich . . ."

It was about noon, just after the off-duty watch had consumed their usual thick pea-soup and 'dead men's toes', otherwise known as sausages, that the lookout on the prow, tied into his little circle of steel railing to protect against being washed overboard, cried, "Object . . . port bow, sir!"

The sharp announcement broke into Klaus's reverie as he smoked somewhat moodily on the bridge, watching the fog roll in, wet, sad and sound-deadening. He stared at the lookout, muffled in his leather Joppe and thick fur hat, peering through his glasses trying to penetrate the grey fluffy damp gloom. "Where?" he called.

"Green one-zero, sir." The lookout amplified his original announcement.

Klaus von Kadowitz turned into the direction of the bearing and focused his glasses. Next to him Hansen waited, but said nothing. For what seemed a long time he saw nothing, then slowly and silently, almost in a sinister fashion, a clumsy, lumbering shape crept into the twin glittering circles of calibrated glass and, for an instant, he caught a fleeting glimpse of a blue and yellow flag painted on the slow craft's rusting side.

Hansen followed his gaze. "Got a nice big neutral flag painted on her side, has she?" he asked, drinker's voice full of cynical contempt.

"Well, she's a Swede – that's for sure."

"And what's one of those Swedish slime-shitters doing in the middle of nowhere, hove-to in weather like this, instead of going about her business of making green moss?" He meant money.

Klaus knew what the cynical petty officer – who smelled strongly of hard booze once more, as he usually did at regular intervals during the working day when he allowed himself 'one behind the collar stud', as he phrased it – meant. The Swedes must have spotted the *Bismarck*. Now they were waiting for the great ship's escort to follow. That meant they were waiting for the *Prinz Eugen* and the destroyers. He didn't need a crystal ball to realise that he was in the presence of the Swedes – who were selling info to the Tommies.

Hansen read his thoughts. "It's them, isn't it, Oberfahnrich?"

"Yes," Klaus agreed slowly, as the frightening realisation started to dawn upon him that if he was right, he was going to have to do something about it.

The skipper had made his instructions quite clear. "If you find them, von Kadowitz," he had rasped, his thin-lipped mouth worked as if by rusty tight steel springs, "you must not hesitate. It will have to be a *Nacht und Nebel* action. Is that clear? There are to be no tell-tale survivors."

Nacht und Nebel. The customary police phrase now rang through the innermost recesses of his brain alarmingly, echoing and re-echoing as if it would never end. 'Night and Fog' – a puzzling phrase for a very simple – and very *final* – operation.

"Well, sir?" Hansen asked easily, as the young skipper lowered his glasses, face crestfallen at the knowledge of what he must soon do. "When do we begin to tango?"

Obviously there was no doubt in the petty officer's mind, either about the ship in the fog off their bow or what would soon have to be done with it. For him the matter was already decided.

"Do you think we ought to give them a chance?"

Klaus commenced, but the look on Hansen's tough, drunkard's face told him he was wasting his time.

"They wouldn't give us a frigging chance in hell. They'd sell us down the river, Oberfahnrich, in zero-comma-nothing seconds!" he said roughly.

Klaus bit his bottom lip, plagued with doubts. He knew what the skipper would want him to do. He knew, too, that Hansen had no doubts whatsoever about the course he must now take. Yet still he was not certain. He had never attempted to kill anyone, even though he had been in the service since he had volunteered straight from high school in 1940, as soon as he had been old enough to apply for an officer's commission. All the same, to decide to kill someone in this cold-blooded, clinical fashion when not a single shot had been fired at him was hard, very hard.

Hansen realised Klaus's indecision, for he spoke, breaking the sudden heavy silence, his voice not so gruff as it was usually. "Don't take on, sir," he said. "It happens to all of us once . . . the first time. But it's got to be done and when you've done it once, you go on doing it." He hesitated and, for an instant, Klaus could sense the old salt's inner warmth and humanity beneath that normal exterior of swaggering boozer's toughness. "It's almost like a habit . . . you don't even seem to be doing it. In the end it's just something you do because you're told to. It—" He broke off abruptly as if he had realised he had said enough already. Now the decision was up to the tall handsome aristocratic officer-cadet facing him, his gaze worried and anxious.

"You're telling me," Klaus von Kadowitz said after a moment, the only sound the steady throb of the motor boat's engine at slow speed, "to use your own pretty phrase, Hansen, it's either piss or get off the pot?" He forced a tight-lipped smile.

"Something like that, sir."

"*Gemeinnutz vor Eigennutz,*" Klaus muttered as if to himself.

Hansen waited, saying nothing, his eyes fixed once more on the dark object bobbing up and down on the horizon, unsuspecting and trapped already, though her crew did not yet know it.

"All right." Klaus made his decision. "*Beide Motoren voraus* . . . half speed. We don't want to alert the Swedes just yet."

"*Beide Motoren voraus.*" Hansen almost whispered the young skipper's instruction down to the waiting engine-room artificer below.

Almost instantly the two powerful engines throbbed into half power. It was like a highly strung thoroughbred being released from the trap. The motor boat's prow rose from the water. A small white bone appeared at her sharp knifelike bow. She surged forward, gathering speed at every monent. Automatically Klaus grabbed a stanchion to prevent himself from being knocked over against the side of the tiny bridge.

Hansen handed over the con to Klaus. "If it's all right with you, sir, I'll take care of the peashooter." He meant the 20mm and Klaus knew instinctively why he had made the offer. He was volunteering to take over the dirty work of opening fire on the unsuspecting Swedes.

He forced a grin, though he had never felt less like

smiling in the whole of his young life. "You've got a heart of gold, Obermaat."

"And an arse full of piles," the latter answered somewhat obscurely. Then he was gone and Klaus was left alone with his thoughts. They were not, it must be said, very happy ones . . .

Two hundred miles away at the other side of the Baltic, the middle-aged Royal Navy captain masquerading as a British naval attaché waited impatiently down in the bowels of the cellar which housed the British Legation's secret radio station.

Despite his outward calm, the middle-aged professional sailor, now turned temporary diplomat, was nervous, even a little flustered. Time and time again he looked at the well-shaven neck of Sparks, the naval rating who acted as his secret signaller, as if anticipating that he might spring into action at any moment. But each time he was disappointed. Grumpily he eased his ring round his tight starched white collar. Dammit, he was beginning to sweat now. At this rate, with this damned Swedish super steam heat – the Swedes did love to spoil themselves, considering they were supposedly the descendants of the hardy Vikings – he'd be stinking like a pig by lunchtime.

For days now Captain Denham of Naval Intelligence had known there was some kind of flap going on at the other side of the Baltic in Nazi Germany. He had been too long at this funny sort of war-in-the-shadows not to be able to smell a flap when there was one. It was the same at the nearby German Legation in Stockholm. The Hun diplomats had refused all invitations for the last week or so and had virtually disappeared from the capital's social scene. He could guess why. They'd been ordered to do so from Berlin. All the same, he hadn't the foggiest what the bloody flap was about.

Still, he had guessed it would come within the area covered by the office of the naval attaché. One clue to that fact was that the pro-German Swedish naval intelligence service was watching him once more. As he had remarked the night before to his opposite number in the army, "Carruthers, dammit all, I found one of the Swede buggers trailing me into the gents at the International Club this lunchtime. I mean, people will begin to talk." The military attaché had guffawed in that horselike manner of his – indeed, he did look a bit like a clapped-out cavalry mount – and Denham had joined in. But in reality it had been no laughing matter. Swedish Intelligence didn't trail diplomats unless they were worried what the latter might find out.

But what could they be worrying about? Captain Denham pursed his lips, which were dry for some reason – perhaps it was the general mood of nervousness at the Embassy – and considered the matter. Naturally, the less the British knew about Swedish shipments of ball bearings and other strategic materials to the Huns, the better pleased the Swedes were. The same applied regarding the case of the neutral Swedes allowing the Germans to use their railway networks to transport the vital iron ore from Occupied Norway to the ice-free Swedish Baltic ports to the Reich.

Yet somehow, sweating it out in that hot underground

cellar, Captain Denham thought what was happening now had nothing to do with the supply of material for the German war machine. It was something else, something more directly connected with the conduct of the war.

Now, as he waited, he prayed and hoped that his tame Swedish contraband runners out in the Baltic off the German coast, palms well greased with British gold, might provide him with an answer to his problems.

He was just considering whether he should light another cigarette from the glowing stub of the one that he had about finished when the back of the radio operator's neck stiffened. He forgot the cigarette instantly. "Got something, Sparks?" he barked urgently.

Instead of answering, the smart young radioman fiddled with his dials with one hand, clapping his earphones closer to his ears with the other as if he were finding the reception difficult.

Denham swallowed hard. He leaned forward tensely. This was it, he told himself. He waited, fighting back his almost overwhelming desire to question the radio operator, who was now scribbling down figures urgently with his left hand, while adjusting the controls of his receiver with his right – a skilled trick that only very experienced 'sparks' could manage.

Finally Captain Denham could contain his curiosity no longer. The *Gustavus Adolphus*, the old Swedish contraband coaster that worked for British Intelligence, never used code – the old tub's rough-and-ready crew wouldn't be up to that. But whoever Sparks was receiving was using code. So who was it? That was the question he posed to the operator during a brief break while Sparks turned the page of his message pad.

Sparks, keen-eyed and flushed with excitement himself, looked across at Denham, still listening to the signal, saying, "No names have been given – only a code signal for the name of the ship in question, sir. But I can make an educated guess."

"Who?"

"I think I can recognise the operator's hand . . . I don't know what—"

"For Chrissake, man," Denham almost screamed at the operator. "*Who*?"

"I think – no, I'm certain, sir, it's the chief operator from the *Gotland*."

"You mean the Swedish cruiser?"

"I do, sir."

For what seemed an age Denham stared at the young rating, his flushed excited face in what seemed to be total disbelief. Then, as calmly as he could, he said, "Sparks, please give me the message. I'll start decoding it, the best I can, *now*."

Numbly the rating handed the message pad over, while Captain Denham started to fumble in his tunic for his glasses. He didn't yet know the meaning of the encoded message which they had inadvertently picked up from the neutral Swedish cruiser, but what he did know was that the message was so erratic and jumbled, the operator who had sent it must have been drunk, mad, or frightened out of his wits.

Eleven

The motor launch had glided the last couple of hundred metres towards the anchored Swedish freighter, her outline barely glimpsed through the rolling morning mist. Even her riding lights had been extinguished – something which contravened the maritime navigational code, Klaus von Kadowitz knew. It was obvious the unknown Swedish skipper had done so in order to conceal the position of his ship. The knowledge strengthened the young officer-cadet's belief that the Swedes were up to no good.

Metre by metre they had come closer to the rusty old coaster, with the crew of the motor boat, tense with expectancy, holding their weapons. Hansen was taking no chances with those 'treacherous Swedish slime-shitters' and had ordered the men to arm themselves – in hands that were damp with sweat despite the dawn cold. When they had been within fifty metres or so of the Swedish ship's stern, Klaus had begun to feel they were going to take her by surprise. He reasoned that the Swedish lookouts would be up on the forward deck, watching for the passing of the *Prinz Eugen* and her attendant destroyers.

But the young officer-cadet had been proved wrong.

Suddenly – startlingly – an angry voice had challenged them in Swedish from somewhere to the stern. For a moment on the tiny bridge he and Hansen had been paralysed, unable to act, wondering what the challenge in Swedish had meant.

Hansen recovered first. He cried in his rough North German accent, "German Navy. Identify yourself!"

Now it was the turn of the Swedes to be surprised. But when the original voice replied and they caught a glimpse of a broad, bearded face peering down at them through the rolling wet mist, the answer was definitely defiant.

"*Hau doch ab, Mensch*!" the Swede cried in good German. "These are international waters—"

"And this is a German machine gun." Hansen cut him short. "Try this on for frigging collar size." He pressed the trigger of the Schmeisser machine pistol clutched to his side.

The little machine gun leapt into angry life. Suddenly the damp air was full of the stink of burnt cordite. Tracer zipped lethally towards the Swedish ship. The Swede cursed and ducked. A pattern of holes was stitched along the plates where his big head had just been seen. Bits of gleaming shattered metal showered his ducked shoulders. "Now then," Hansen yelled, voice no longer so angry. "Are yer frigging well gonna talk turkey, you frigging arse with ears?"

Just for a moment Klaus thought the 'arse with ears' might. But he was mistaken.

Plop! With a sudden hush, a flare hissed into the grey sky. It traversed the length of the little motor boat in a green-glowing curve. *Whoosh*! It exploded.

Instantly they were bathed in a green-glowing, eerie, unnatural light. Hansen cursed and Klaus shielded his eyes against the abrupt blinding glare of that incandescent flame that hovered above them momentarily like some strange angel.

"What in three devils' name—" he began.

The Swede – later Klaus discovered that it was the contraband runner's skipper – cut him off. "Now you can see who you're talking to, eh?" Before Klaus had a chance to object, the angry Swede beat him to it with, "A neutral Swedish ship, going about her business in international waters—"

"Yeah, you neutral ape turd." Hansen's voice was filled with real anger. "Selling out honest German sailors' lives for them precious Swedish kroner of yourn."

The Swedish skipper ignored the interruption. "I've already signalled the Swedish cruiser *Gotland*. She'll be on her way here soon. Then you'll cop it, sailor boy." There was no denying the sneer in the Swede's voice as he recognised Klaus von Kadowitz as the skipper of the little German Navy boat. "If I was you, I'd pick up me hindlegs in me hands and make a run for it before our boys in blue come and blow you German pigs out of the water." He turned at the rush of heavy boots running from amidships. At least a dozen sailors were coming towards him, all armed with some sort of weapon. "Perhaps, though, we might do it ourselves," he added. "Bunch of shitting kids like you, still wet behind the spoons . . . Easy as falling off a frigging log."

Hansen, angry beyond all measure, pressed the trigger of the machine gun, which he held in those steam-shovel paws of his as if it were a child's toy. It burst into crazy life. This time he aimed to kill.

Behind the contemptuous bearded figure of the Swedish skipper, a crew member was hit. A series of blood-stained buttonholes had been suddenly stitched across his chest. He screamed, high and hysterical, and his shotgun clattered to the deck. Madly he clawed the air in his dying frenzy. It was as if he were attempting to climb the rungs of an invisible ladder, his eyes fixed pleadingly on the heavens. But on this cold foggy morning in the Baltic, God was looking the other way. Next instant the man fell face forward on to the blood-slickened deck. He was dead before he slammed into it.

Almost immediately all hell had broken loose. The Swedes had opened fire at once. A ragged, but potentially lethal volley swept the little boat bobbing up and down on the wavelets below.

A young signaller cursed angrily. Almost as if in surprise that it was happening to him, he stared in shocked silence for a moment at his shattered arm, the bone gleaming like polished white ivory through the gory scarlet mess of torn flesh. Then he fell.

That seemed to be the signal for the German crew to react. Klaus barked an urgent signal down to the engine-room artificer and the motor boat surged forward once more. As he tossed the little wheel from one side to the other with crazed energy, the slugs striking the sea water on both sides of her, the young sailors began to fire back, Hansen yelling wildly, "That's it, you bunch o' cardboard seamen! Kick 'em in the bollocks. Slap 'em in the chops. Show them Swedish slime-shitters what *real* Germans are like!"

And that was what the 'real' Germans did. Klaus ignored the slug which shattered the glass protective screen of the bridge, showering him with glass shards. His blood was up. He was carried away by the wild, mad, unreasoning primeval urge of mortal combat. Later he could have sworn that he had been laughing almost hysterically all the while like a man demented.

He slammed the boat against the hull of the coaster just near the forward ladder. "*Los, Männer*," he cried, "board her!"

"Get your frigging pansy arses outta a sling," Hansen snarled and ripped off another wild burst. A Swedish seaman trying to emerge from the forward deck hatch went down screaming, arms flailing in the air in his absolute unbearable agony, what looked like a handful of strawberry jam spilling down his shattered face.

The men needed no urging. As Hansen covered them, standing legs astride on the swaying deck, firing controlled bursts to left and right like some cowboy gunslinger in a Hollywood western, they scrambled up the ladder. They jostled each other for a foothold and hit the deck up top. They fired, wildly cheering all the while like a bunch of excited kids suddenly released from school after a boring day.

The Swedes tried to press forward. Hansen didn't give them a chance. He kept firing, holding them at bay, while at the quick-firer the two ratings brought the gun round frantically, training her on the Swedish ship's superstructure and bridge.

Klaus realised it was time to act. Soon his youngsters would begin to take casualties. He couldn't wait for that. He grabbed the loudhailer and shook off the shattered glass shards urgently. He pressed the power button and the instrument came to life with a hollow boom.

"Now listen to this . . . now listen to this," he cried through the instrument, using the traditional German Navy formula, the boom drowning out the angry snap and crackle of the small-arms battle raging on the deck above him. "Cease firing immediately . . . Cease firing and nothing will happen to you . . . Cease—" His words ended in a yelp of pain as a slug struck the base of the loudhailer.

The power went immediately. The electric shock swept up his arm rapidly, painfully. "Dammit!" he yelled in exasperation and, drawing his own pistol, fired six shots rapidly and without aim at the coaster's bridge.

That did it. It seemed to be the last signal – an unspoken command – for Hansen. He rose to his feet. Ignoring the slugs stitching a crazy pattern of sudden death at his flying feet, he raced forward. "Follow me . . . follow me," he yelled, using the traditional formula. "Follow me – *the captain's got an hole in his arse*!"

They followed, whether the statement was true or not, and five minutes later it was all over, with the young men, chests heaving still as if they had just run a great race, their eyes sparkling and bulging wildly as if they were drugged, racing through the ship, plundering and destroying, cramming their mouths full of good Swedish chocolate, thrusting looted American cigarettes into the pockets of their reefer jackets – for a while absolutely out of control.

It was then that Hansen discovered the women: the one still crouched over the radio transmitter sending as if her life depended upon it; the other, blonde and beautiful, but obviously very drunk, hiding behind the bunk in the radio shack, drinking straight out of a litre bottle of potent *aquavit*.

The sight stopped him in his tracks. "*Phew*," he breathed, pushing his helmet back from his red puckered brow, "as I frigging live and breathe!" Suddenly he registered the sight of the woman hunched above the transmitter. He slammed the butt of his Schmeisser down on the top of the radio. It shattered, its valves snapped and the transmitter died with a short electronic moan. The operator began to sob as if her very heart was broken.

It was thus that Klaus von Kadowitz discovered them a few moments later, grouped there as if frozen for eternity like third-rate players at the end of a fourth-rate melodrama. For a moment he was tempted to ask what was going on. Then he thought better of it. It was quite clear what had happened here.

For what seemed an eternity, all remained silent save for the sound of the operator crying, while the beautiful blonde stared up at him from her useless hiding place, bottle still raised to her full lips. Then Hansen said, "What are we going to do with them, sir?"

"How do you mean, Obermaat."

Hansen licked his lips thoughtfully. "God, it's a waste. But—"

"D'you mean . . ." Klaus blurted out, aghast. The full

realisation of what Hansen was saying hit him with an almost physical blow.

"Well, it's obvious, sir, isn't it?"

"Obvious – I do—" But before he could finish the objection which had sprung to his lips instantly, the one who had been crying looked up and said thickly in German, "What will you do with us?"

Hansen tapped the butt of his machine pistol significantly. The two woman started. They knew what the gesture meant well enough. Hansen spoke a moment later and made it even clearer. "Dead men tell no tales, sir," he said in a low voice.

"*No*!" The blonde spoke at last. "Please no, gentlemen."

Hansen ignored her, though it was hard to do so. *Holy mackerel*, a little voice at the back of his head whispered, *she's worth a sin – or two*. He silenced the voice. "We've got to do something, sir."

"No," Klaus said sternly. "It wouldn't be honourable, would it. They're women, after all."

"*Honourable*?" Hansen sneered. "What does that matter in war? You wait, sir – I've seen it all before in the old war. Before this little lot is over, they'll be killing men, women and kids by the thousand – the hundred thousand – and they won't give a wet fart about it."

"You're wrong – and even if you were right, which you aren't, it does not matter to me," Klaus von Kadowitz said sternly. "We do it my way, whatever the outcome."

"The big shots up top won't like it, sir."

Klaus ignored the interruption. "They go in the boats – the women first. Then we open the seacocks. That'll give our people the time they need, you know, and it will give them a chance to reach the coast safely."

"As you say, sir," Hansen said easily. He jerked his machine pistol at the two women. "All right, ladies. Follow me."

As if in a trance they followed him, but both glanced significantly at Klaus as they brushed by him and went up top.

The boy didn't seem to notice. He was too concerned with his own thoughts. Perhaps even then, still 'wet behind the spoons' as Hansen would have put it, he realised that this was the last time; from now onwards he would have no further chance to indulge himself in what could only be called a conscience. The good, innocent days were over for him.

Twelve

Admiral Tovey of the Home Fleet was worried. The tall, rangy admiral with the big nose looked around the circle of his staff officers, hurriedly flown into Scapa this very dawn, and announced in as calm a voice as he could muster, "Gentlemen, I think I can safely say that the balloon is about to go up in northern waters."

If he had expected an excited reaction to his announcement, Sir John Tovey would have been disappointed. His staff officers were all seasoned old salts – they had been used to 'the balloon going up' ever since September 1939 – which now seemed another age. Besides, they were tired. Most of them, save those permanently stationed in Scapa, had been rushing around on fact-finding missions to Portsmouth, Plymouth, Tilbury, Bristol, Harwich, Hull and all the other naval ports, trying to ascertain the readiness of Britain's hard-pressed navy. They were simply worn out.

Admiral Tovey acknowledged the fact with a slight smile and the words, "I know you're knackered, gentlemen; arranging those damned Atlantic convoys month in and month out has knocked the stuffing out of the best of us." He gave a little sigh, something unusual in such a stiff, old-fashioned officer. "But I'm afraid it's once more into the breach – what nonsense Shakespeare wrote. After all, the PM's breathing hard and fierce down my neck."

Some of them obliged their chief with a faint laugh, tired as they were.

It pleased him for a moment, and then his long face hardened and he got down to business. "Well, gentlemen, if our suspicions are correct, at least our troubles will be large ones, instead of worrying about freighters that should have long gone to the knacker's yard and their cargoes of Spam. With luck we're going to add to the glorious tradition of the Senior Service." He frowned. "But I must confess that luck is going to have to play a large role in the drama which I think will soon be performed on our very own doorstep." He paused for effect, then he let them have it as if he were ordering a tremendous broadside from one of the armoured giants that were stationed, antiquated as they were, at Scapa. "We think the *Bismarck* – and perhaps the *Prinz Eugen*, too – are coming out."

"Great balls of fire!" the skipper of the *Norfolk* exclaimed above the sudden excited buzz occasioned by Tovey's announcement. "This is going to be some party, sir!"

Tovey looked grim. "It's going to be no walk-over, Bob," he warned. "We know little about the *Bismarck* – we didn't expect her to complete her running-in so soon – but we do know this. She is, our experts believe, the most powerful ship in the world. All we've got to touch her is a superiority in numbers. So . . ." he let his words sink in for a moment and watched as the smile and enthusiasm vanished from the face of the *Norfolk*'s skipper as quickly as they had appeared, "that's why you are here. To inform me of how many ships we are able to put to sea ready for battle within the next forty-eight hours."

"We've got that amount of time, sir?" someone asked from the back of the group of senior officers. Tovey thought it was the captain of the brand new *Prince of Wales*.

"Yes, I think so. The first indication of her position has come via Godfrey of Naval Intelligence through his chap in Stockholm – Denham. Early this morning there seems to have been some sort of a shindig between a German craft and one of our spy ships run by Denham. We guess the business is connected with an attempt by the *Bismarck* to sail the Baltic."

"And her objective, Sir John?" someone else asked.

"Search me," he answered a little helplessly. "But we can make an educated guess." He turned to the big map which covered one wall of his office and reached for the pointer with a practised hand.

"Incident reported by Denham in Stockholm reckoned to be about *here* at zero seven hundred hours . . . just off Travemünde."

They nodded their heads. All of them had studied the Baltic, in which German fleets had lurked ever since the Prussian Navy had been founded back in the middle of the nineteenth century, right back from their days as midshipmen at Dartmouth. They knew the inland sea well.

"So I don't have to tell you how long it would take the *Bismarck*, travelling at convoy speed and in shallow coastal waters, to reach, say, Bergen *here*." Again he tapped the map with his pointer. "So what does that mean to us?"

He answered his own question. "We have some thirty-six hours or so before she sails on the tide from Bergen, heading" – he stopped short and shrugged – "God knows where. But we'll come to that problem when we have to deal with it. First things first."

"As soon as we locate the *Bismarck*, we try to delay her for as long as possible?" Commander Rotherham of Coastal Reconnaissance, the lowest-ranking officer among all the brass, dared to comment when no one else reacted.

Tovey wasn't offended. "Exactly, Rotherham. Good point. We will be unable to assemble *all* our forces to meet the *Bismarck* – and *sink* her," he added, irony suddenly in his voice, "within thirty-six hours. So we must delay her. Coastal Command is already out looking for her."

"And then, sir?" the skipper of the *Norfolk* ventured.

"Then we send in the Swordfish." He forced a smile. "The old stringbags."

Inwardly Rotherham groaned. The torpedo biplanes were hopelessly obsolete. Loaded with a two-ton torpedo, it took the biplane all its power to reach a speed of one hundred knots an hour. The 'stringbags', as the Fleet Air Army pilots called their old-fashioned planes affectionately, were easy targets for even the slowest of the enemy's fighters. The attack on the *Bismarck* – unless they caught the most powerful ship at sea by surprise – would be a suicide mission.

Tovey caught the younger officer's look of dismay at

his announcement about the 'stringbags', but he didn't comment. He couldn't. It wasn't navy policy. Besides, if he forced himself to consider the deficiencies of the Royal Navy due to the parsimony of pre-war governments, he'd probably shoot himself. There were deficiencies everywhere. Even the pride of the fleet, the *Hood*, was a problem—

He stopped himself short mentally. That was a secret, a great state secret. He would not even allow himself to *think* about HMS *Hood*. But aloud he said, "Now we come to the *Hood*."

The faces of the assembled officers brightened. They were all proud of the great battle cruiser which had been the world's largest warship until the German battleship, the bloody *Bismarck*, had come along. Still, all of them believed firmly that the *Hood* could still outfight the German ship that was nearly a quarter of a century younger than she was.

"Naturally the *Hood* is going to be our first line of attack," Tovey said with more confidence than he really felt. "She'll get on the scene of the action faster than any other of our ships and she'll be able to hold the *Bismarck* – and more – until the Home Fleet arrives."

"Here, here . . . well said, sir." There were murmurs of agreement on all sides and Tovey's lean face lit up momentarily as he told himself that when it came down to it, these senior officers, all normally as temperamental as a lot of opera divas, would rally around the flag loyally.

"But a word of warning. We can't let the *Hood* tackle the Hun for too long without support." Tovey's smile vanished. "I expect every man here, whether in a sea command or on the beach in a staff function, to do his utmost to hasten the gathering of the fleet. That is absolutely vital."

A few of the attendant officers looked mystified. Why should the fleet commander be so concerned that HMS *Hood* not be left alone too long in the coming fight with the *Bismarck*? Surely the great battle-cruiser could match the Hun shot for shot! But they didn't comment on the little mystery. Instead they snapped to attention, as if they would be expected to leave to carry out Tovey's orders immediately.

They were not mistaken. A minute or two later Tovey said, urgent and imperative, "You know what to do, gentlemen. Please go and do it – and don't leave the *Hood* out there too long, I beg you." With that he bent his head over the papers on his desk, as if the men were no longer there.

A few shuffled their feet. One or two put on their caps and saluted a little hesitantly, while the rest waited uncertainly. But when they realised the Admiral was going to say no more to them, they started to file out.

In the bay, the 'stringbags' were lining up on the flight deck of the force's sole aircraft carrier, engines already started, flares begining to shoot into the grey northern sky from the bridge, as they prepared for take-off and the suicidal strike to come.

Beyond, the Sunderland flying boats of Coastal Command were waddling out to sea, all four engines blasting away, a wide white wake of boiling water following them. It was the second reconnaissance flight – the first had already been airborne for thirty minutes.

On the fleet itself men were smartly moving through the controlled chaos of the littered deck. All the hundred and one precautions and preparations for the battle to come were being made, with Marine buglers sounding off, petty officers shrilling their whistles and red-faced deck officers and petty officers crying orders at the matelots, while everywhere gulls were diving and rising, screaming shrilly as if in protest against all the noise and activity.

Tovey watched, sucking his ugly false teeth as he did so. He had seen it all before, many times, even as long ago as the Battle of Jutland back in 1916. But never had he felt this strange sensation of foreboding, even fear, which now sent a cold finger of apprehension tracing its way down his spine. Something was going to go wrong, he knew it in his very bones. But what?

Thirteen

Klaus von Kadowitz was in a quandary. The Swedish crew had obeyed his instructions without difficulty, though with much cursing. They had gathered their wounded and gone over to the boats while the excited young German sailors had opened the coaster's seacocks and then come back up to the deck, once more looting and wrecking as they did so.

The women, however, were different. They had refused to take their chances with the male crew members. The pretty blonde had protested in her good German, "But Herr Officer, we'll drown. They won't" – she meant the male crew members – "do anything for us. They don't like us."

"It's only a matter of, say, ten to twelve sea miles to Travemünde," Klaus had urged them, "and the wind is favourable. You won't even need to row, ladies. It'll blow you in."

But the 'ladies' had not been convinced.

Klaus knew he had to make a decision about the women soon. He couldn't be caught here, with a neutral ship sinking only metres away and the crew in their little boats not yet disappeared into the drifting fog that lay low over the still surface of the water. It could cause an international incident. When they had their victory later, and had swept the Tommies from the northern seas, as the *Bismarck* and the *Prinz Eugen* surely would, it wouldn't matter. But what in three devils' name was he going to do *now*?

The young sailors, gulping down their stolen Swedish chocolate and brandishing the looted bottles of beer and *aquavit*, which he'd allow them to drink later, were already beginning to man the boats which would bring them back to their own ship. Meanwhile the two women continued to sob, their shoulders heaving like two pathetic, broken-hearted little girls. "Heaven, arse and cloudburst," Klaus told himself angrily, "what a shitting mess. Why should I be shitting well landed with it?"

There was no answer to that particular overwhelming question. Even if there had been, there was no time left to deal with it, for now the young lookout in his little steel cage on the foredeck was crying in alarm, "*Aircraft* . . . coming in fast," and even before they were identified and the twin Spandaus behind him had hissed in high-pitched hysterical fury, Klaus knew they were English. The great break-out into the Baltic had been spotted already.

The next five minutes were hell. The great four-engined flying boats came zooming in all out. They seemed fearless. With their prop-wash thrashing the sea in their wake into a frothy white fury, they attacked at mast height, only ascending in the same instant that they dropped their bombs, with Hansen, too drunk to realise the danger, crying, "Now they're shitting steel on us poor sailor boys . . . what a shitting life."

But the 'poor sailor boys' were fighting back desperately. Behind the bridge, now peppered and splintered to matchwood with the flying shrapnel, the two gunners fired for all they were worth. They were no longer afraid. The crazy fury of battle had seized them. As they spun their air-cooled Spandaus, the brassy, smoking cartridge cases splattering down in a metallic rain at their feet, they shrieked and shouted, cursing fluently, obscenely, their one aim in life to strike back and punish those who were punishing them so cruelly.

A great wedge of gleaming silver shrapnel came hissing the length of the craft. It sliced and hacked at all before it. The radio mast came tumbling down in a mess of angry blue sparks. A dinghy went over the side and the compressed gas pumped into it exploded in a ball of fire, searing the length of the starboard side. Paint blistered and popped and great scabs appeared suddenly like the symptoms of some loathsome skin disease.

The left Spandau ceased firing. Klaus flung a look upwards. A headless corpse was lolling there, held upright by the steel retainer ring. Thick scarlet blood welled up in obscene bubbles from the severed neck. In the scuppers a head, complete with helmet, rolled slowly to a stop like a football abandoned by some careless child.

Klaus felt the hot bile well up inside his throat. He couldn't help himself. He choked and spluttered. In the next instant he bent and a thick, sickening stew poured from his gaping mouth.

"That's right, Oberfahnrich," Hansen yelled with drunken exuberance. "Get them cookies up . . . the best for yer. Spew 'em up, sir."

When Klaus von Kadowitz raised himself again weakly, gasping for breath, his heart beating furiously, the first Sunderland was coughing and spluttering on a westbound course, dark and dangerous smoke pouring from her feathered starboard engine.

He shook his head and wished next moment he hadn't. A stabbing pain – like that made by a red-hot poker, it seemed – thrust into the back of his right eye. He gave a little yelp of pain. This time he shook his head more gently. The red mist cleared and now he could see normally. Cautiously he looked at the departing Tommy flying boat and then around him.

Hansen was leaning weakly against the bulkhead. He stared with a look of total disbelief at the shattered bottle of schnapps below him. It was as if he were unable to comprehend that such a tragedy should have happened to him. Klaus began to give a weak grin.

It died almost instantly as he gazed at the two Swedish women. They were still clinging to each other in total despair. But now their contorted features were set, frozen in a parody of great emotion for all time.

"Oh, God in heaven," Klaus gasped, carried away by the shock of that terrible vision. "They're . . . they're both dead!"

Hansen pulled himself from the bulkhead and dropped the remains of the shattered bottle to the deck with a clatter. His voice was no longer so hard and unyielding. Instead he kept his voice deliberately low. "You'll get used to it, Oberfahnrich . . . We all do – and if we don't," he added tonelessly, as if he were stating a simple truth, "we go mad . . ." Then his voice resumed its normal harsh urgent manner. "The second bastard's coming in – to starboard." Already the remaining machine gun had taken up the challenge and a white-and-red tracer was beginning to arc its way in a lethal morse towards the approaching Sunderland. "I think we ought to get under way. Like this we're frigging sitting ducks—"

"Engine room," Klaus von Kadowitz was already shouting down the voice-pipe to the engineer rating below, "both ahead. *Volle Fahrt voraus*!" He braced himself for the shock.

It came in the very next moment, the twin engines thundering into full power. The little craft shuddered violently like a thoroughbred dog waiting to be let off the leash. The nose tilted upwards. In the same instant that the great Sunderland came roaring in, dragging its evil black shadow behind it across the surface of the sea, its machine guns chattering sudden death, the motor boat shot forward. Behind its flying wave, the first enemy bombs started to explode purposelessly. On the deck, the two women, clasped in each other's arms like star-crossed lovers, stiffened in the cold sea air. For ever afterwards, the image of the two nameless foreign women would symbolise for Klaus von Kadowitz the absolute futility of war, which knew no victories, only personal defeats . . .

They ran into Hamburg harbour that night, limping past the familiar lightship *Elbe Eins*, struggling with ever-decreasing power down the long haul of the River Elbe. Finally they saw the badly blacked-out docks ahead and, with thcir bomb-damaged engines gone altogether, came gliding noiselessly to a stop at the great port's civilian

Landungsbrüke where a greatly surprised middle-aged policeman with a well-nourished paunch drew his service pistol and demanded to see their identity cards. This gave the survivors their first hollow weary laugh since they had left Danzig in what now seemed another age.

But their sense of humour vanished when Klaus and Hansen, weary, dirty and as bloody as they were, were summoned to the great port's famous Hotel Vierjahreszeiten to meet a certain Kapitän *zur See* Wichmann. He even sent a gleaming Horch staff car, complete with yeoman chauffeur and tin flag on the bonnet, to fetch them through the blacked-out streets to the hotel on the Innenalster, Hamburg's great inland lake.

The reception attendants stared at the two dirty, unshaven, bloody apparitions from the fighting front as if they were creatures from another world. It was the same with the elegantly uniformed senior officers – a few of whom carried swords, of all things, in the midst of total war – and their bejewelled ladies who sauntered in and out leaving behind them the sound of dance music, the popping of champagne corks and high-pitched tipsy girlish laughter. Obviously Hamburg's *Prominenz* were holding the usual May Ball – and were lacking none of the trimmings, including bowls of what Hansen whispered was 'frigging shoe-polish' and which Klaus knew was real caviare.

"One law for the shitting rich and another for the poor," Hansen commented out of the side of his mouth as he watched an elderly admiral feasting his eyes on the delightful low-cut cleavage of a girl half his age, his knuckles white as he gripped the hilt of his sword. "Get a load of him, for instance. He's going get a heart attack if he keeps on looking down her dress like that."

"Knock it off, Hansen," Klaus hissed urgently out of the side of his mouth. "This looks like the big cheese coming our way now." He gave a slight nod of his head at the officer now approaching them, one that, in his shabby naval uniform and tarnished gold rings, looked slightly out of place in that glittering assembly. But there was no denying the keenness of the officer's eyes, which almost seemed to spring from his pale intellectual's face, so unlike the ruddy, well-fed ones of the other naval officers and their young mistresses, who passed to and fro bearing their glasses of vintage French champagne that everyone who was anyone drank these days.

"Oberfahnrich von Kadowitz; Obermaat Hansen," Captain Wichmann snapped without any preamble, "report."

"Oberfahnrich . . . *zur Stelle*!" Hastily Klaus rapped out the standard, long-winded formula, standing stiffly to attention.

Wichmann nodded his approval. He relaxed a little. "Obermaat," he ordered Hansen, "go over to the buffet, help yourself to drinks and food for ten minutes, then come back with a drink for the officer. I wish to talk to him alone."

Hansen was so taken aback by the no-nonsense order that he didn't even attempt one of his usual bloody-minded objections. Besides, one of the girls behind the buffet counter, in her short black silk frock and tiny white frilly apron, was definitely giving him what he regarded as a 'come-hithcr' look – and she really did have 'bedroom eyes'. He hastened away to try his luck not only with the buffet, but with the delectable young blonde running it.

Wichmann waited till he was out of earshot, then took Klaus to one side and said without any further details, "As you have probably guessed, Oberfahnrich, I'm Abwehr, Branch Hamburg and Bremen."

"Yes, sir," Klaus answered, flustered. He hadn't guessed anything of the sort. Now he wondered why such an important person as this local chief of intelligence was talking to a lowly ensign. Wichmann soon enlightened him.

"Now what has this got to do with you?" Wichmann proceeded. "I shall tell you. When you reach Bergen tomorrow" – *tomorrow*? Klaus queried to himself. *With our shot-up motor boat we won't reach Norway by then, or the day after for that matter* – "you will have the ear of Admiral Lutjens for five minutes or so. He'll want to know the details of the air attack on your craft. It will be important to him. Now," he continued, without giving Klaus a chance to ask questions. He flashed a glance at the buffet. It looked as if Obermaat Hansen was wasting no time. He was bent close to the blonde barmaid, his gaze fixed firmly on the neckline of her low-cut dress, busily engaged in some ploy, presumably sexual, of his own. "From your point of view and perspective I am an important man. After all, I am a four-ringer." He meant his captain's four gold stripes. "In fact, I am only a very little fish in a big pond. And you'll have the ear of the admiral . . . I won't."

"I'm confused, sir," Klaus confessed a little helplessly.

"Bear with me and I'll enlighten you."

"Sir."

At the heavily laden table covered with delicacies brought from everywhere in the German-occupied New Europe, the like of which Klaus hadn't seen for years, Hansen was rubbing his horny palm down the maid's silken flank suggestively.

"I want the admiral warned. As you have already guessed, British Intelligence is on to us. That Swedish drifter and crew were in the Tommies' pay. Their report was followed up by the aerial attack on your own boat."

Klaus nodded his agreement. The pale-faced Abwehr officer was beginning to interest him.

"Somewhere, another aerial attack is imminent. We have that from our agents in—" He stopped just in time and again Klaus was impressed. Did Wichmann mean agents in England? He thought the pale-faced spymaster with the brilliant eyes did.

"Suffice it to say this, von Kadowitz. The English now know roughly what's afoot here in Germany – and they are taking corresponding measures."

"But what do you want me to say to Admiral Lutjens, if he sees me?" Klaus finally managed to pose his overwhelming question. "Is it about these serial attacks?"

"Yes. But more, Ensign," Wichmann snapped. "Tell him, in view of what Intelligence here knows about the English reactions, that we suggest he limits himself to a fast hit-and-run attack on their battle-cruiser, the *Hood*."

Klaus was impressed. The Abwehr knew that the Tommies' greatest ship would take part in their defensive measures. He told himself that they must have spies in every naval port in the length of the little island. "And that's it, sir?"

"No, not quite." Wichmann flashed a look to left and right as if he was afraid he might be overheard. But the foyer was now empty and, in the sudden silence as the orchestra took a break, there was no sound.

Wichmann leaned closer and Klaus caught a whiff of the captain's discreet eau de cologne. "You fly to Bergen from Hamburg-Fuhlsbuttel tomorrow at dawn by naval courier. As soon as you are admitted to the admiral's presence and are allowed to talk, Ensign, tell him this." He leaned even closer and whispered his vital information concerning the *Hood* into Klaus's ear.

Harding and Horace

"Russian generals take over," Horace the Obit cried in mock despair, slapping the *Daily Mail*'s headline for the benefit of the bored barman waiting to serve us at the Oporto. "Christ, I can see it all coming again. Gas masks, and Vera Lynn warbling – excuse me, *Dame* Vera Lynn *singing* – 'We'll Meet Again'. There'll even be dried eggs, courtesy of the People of the Free United States." He dropped the tabloid on the bar as if he were sick of the world, couldn't stand it anymore.

Behind the counter the barman said, "More grog, Cap'n?"

"Yes, more grog," Horace the Obit said, perking up immediately at the mention of his favourite subject – booze.

For a moment I watched him from the open door of the Shaftesbury Avenue pub which Horace still frequents through habit and in hope that he might meet a 'kindred soul' – of what type, literary or otherwise, I have never dared to ask.

He is very old now, though he didn't realise it or show it. He is still a star reporter interviewing 'Fabian of the Yard', Freddie Mills and the like. But he's very bald and his hearing isn't too good, especially when he doesn't particularly want to hear, which is most of the time. "The world stopped for me in 1969, a vintage year, laddie," he booms when in the mood. "By God, wasn't I spreading it around in those days! Now I live in the past."

I smiled at the memory of that – and of some of the things he had written since he had been demoted from the front page to the obits. Who else but Horace could have written of some poor old fart who had passed away, 'He was a well-known street-corner writer of short stories, who spent his last thirty years on a street corner in South Shields, carrying a knuckle-duster in his right-hand pocket to protect himself from would-be marauding Scots from just over the nearby border'? Who else could have written that as an opening paragraph, especially with that well-observed 'right-hand pocket'? He might have made it up, but who would have thought so after that particular detail?

But, however much of an old-style mountebank that Horace is, and however much he is given to large G and Ts, large scotches, large rums, indeed anything strong and large, he is a mine of information on people, his knowledge gained through the Fleet Street old-boy network, huge domestic history tomes, and his work 'tarting up' (as he phrases it) the contributions of the other anonymous obituarists with whom he works for the 'pound-notish' papers (yet another of his creations). For that reason I was visiting 'HQ', as he calls the Oporto pub, just in case he could tell me something about the *Hood* and its mysterious sudden demise.

I was not to be disappointed – well, not totally. After the usual palaver – "What's happened to old Leo? Things are not the same since he doesn't have his own outfit. The Oporto's gone to the dogs. They'll be having actors in here next. Lot of old queens," plus naturally another 'large 'un', the first of many – he got down to business.

He knew about the *Hood*, of course. Of *course.* (Horace tends to repeat himself for emphasis – an old cheap novelist's trick.) And he did. At one time or another, he had actually interviewed Viscount Hood, a descendant of Admiral Samuel Hood, whose exploits had inspired Nelson and given the name to that great, tragic ship.

"Hood had actually been at the launch of the *Hood* as a four-year-old," Horace explained. "Said his main memory of that day was being allowed three puddings to mark the occasion. Good memory, what, Duncan."

I didn't mention that it was Horace's memory that was good. How he manages it after having pickled that particular organ in various 'large ones' for nearly half a century I don't know. But he does; he has a better sense of recall than some top-notch Jap computer.

"Do you think the Viscount would know anything of use?" I asked, watching him pour another four pounds or so of my publisher's pitiful advance down that undoubtedly scarlet gullet of his.

"Dead," he retorted with a gasp and a satisfied yet direct smirk. I nodded to the man behind the bar. Whisky flowed, coins of the realm changed hands and we were ready for the next round of the Memory Game.

"One thing, however—"

"About Viscount Hood?"

"Yes . . . and don't be too eager, Duncan. It's unseemly in a writer," he chided me in that grand fashion of his which he adopts when the 'large ones' start to rise above what Horace the Obit calls 'that celebrated plimsoll line'. And here he always points to the left of his ample belly, where he wrongly supposes his poor old battered liver to be located.

"Yes, of course, Horace," I said, looking suitably chastened. "But—"

"He always followed the career of the *Hood*, you know. He even served on her as a midshipman. But when war came he went into destroyers and on to the staff of some admiral based in the Med. He happened to be married to the *Hood*'s captain's American half-sister, of course."

"Of course," I echoed, again admiring Horace's talent for slipping in these little nuggets, dredged up from some remote seam of his memory, which might have some value or might not. It depended, as always with Horace, on how you wished to interpret his statements.

"But I did gather, when I interviewed him in his old age, that the Viscount wasn't too happy about the fate of the *Hood*."

"Understandable, Horace. After all, he had a close association with a ship that was connected with his family and his distinguished ancestor." I looked at his bland fat face. No emotion showed on it. His lips had suddenly clamped firmly together like those of a truculent small boy resisting the efforts of his mother to force cod-liver oil or some other bitter but life-enhancing potion between them.

I nodded. The barman put down the *Daily Telegraph*, poured another large one without my asking for it and, pushing it towards me, returned to the *Court Circular*.

"Ta very much," Horace said cheekily.

I beamed, pleased. The lips were unsealed.

He looked at me, suddenly solemn and quite serious – for Horace. His eyes were now bloodshot, but not clouded. Indeed, one could have said they were remarkably sharp and keen for such an old toper – and as Horace often said of himself, 'a bullshitter of the premier class'.

"Your publisher has obviously commissioned you to do a mud-raker. With luck you might make *Panorama* – or even *Timewatch*. He has, hasn't he? Small advance – and big royalties, if you're lucky." He cocked his head to one side knowingly.

"Something like that, Horace," I agreed. I wasn't prepared to give too much away. When the need for large numbers of 'big 'uns' was upon him, Horace knew no shame. He'd flog his own granny to the devil.

"Intrinsically the story is priceless. Great defeat, followed by equally great victory of our chaps – brave fellows one and all." I thought that in his new enthusiasm, he might well burst into 'Hearts of oak are our men . . . steady boys, steady'. But he didn't. Instead he continued with, "Seeing off the Bismarck several hours later; an eye for an eye, what." He licked his lips pointedly.

I nodded to the man behind the bar, who sighed and, remaining seated, reached up. For one heart-stopping moment he looked as if he might be about to pass over a bottle and let Horace help himself. Thereafter my advance from the gent in the Gay Hussar would have decreased very rapidly indeed. Fortunately he merely filled up a brand new glass to save himself fetching the old one and shoved it along the bar.

He held up four fingers wordlessly. Another four readies had vanished. I sighed and hoped he'd finish what he had to tell me soon. Otherwise I'd be solving the mystery of the poor old *Hood* for nothing.

"I looked at it myself once, you know," Horace continued after wetting his whistle yet once more. "I got as far as you have probably got – I must say, I prefer the American 'gotten' here—"

"Oh, do move along, Horace," I protested.

"Well, as I said, I reached the point where the *Bismarck* knocked the *Hood* out so easily – even though the *Hood* was pretty well protected by additional armour which had been added to her over the years. So what had happened?" He answered his own question. "Was it the torpedo tubes at her sides, near to the waterline, both armed with torpedoes which were ready for firing when the *Bismarck*'s shells hit her? Did those torpedoes explode and send the ship and all the poor devils aboard her to kingdom come? Or was it the extra ammo that some people maintain was stacked on her deck at the time of sailing? Those, my dear Harding, might well be rational explanations. But," – he was almost purring now – "reality is a bit of a bore and can, at times, be downright dangerous, don't you think, Duncan?"

I didn't rise to the bait. I was running out of money – and patience – rapidly. One more 'big one' and that was his lot, *Hood* mystery be damned!

"So what do you think happened, Horace?" I put it to him directly. "Why did she sink so rapidly, after perhaps two salvoes from the *Bismarck*'s heavy guns?"

He looked at his almost empty whisky glass and then thought perhaps he had been bribed enough.

"Why did she sink so rapidly?" he echoed, chin raised like that of some great thinker waiting to be immortalised in marble by the sculptor. "Well, I shall tell you. I shall reveal it to you, dear Duncan, the great secret gained by sleuth from a paragon of the admiralty in the course of a long, hard drinking session at the United Services."

I could have shaken him. But I didn't. He'd last a few more minutes in his present state before he had to stagger off to the bogs. He'd have time enough to reveal all. So I waited on tenterhooks.

"It was the metal."

"*Metal*?"

"Yes." Suddenly Horace the Obit belched rather loudly and clutched his stomach as if in pain.

"Metal—" I began and then thought better of it. Horace was rising to his feet, bent slightly and still clutching his stomach. "Wind?" I enquired.

"More like a bloody tornado . . . on its way . . . old bean," he gasped, as if it took an effort of sheer willpower to get every phrase out. "I'm afraid I must leave you . . ." He farted now, long, loud and not totally unmusical.

The barman stepped back hastily and cried indignantly, "Hey, none of that, man! It ain't allowed in here."

"*Hospital*?" I cut his protest short, but I could see his point. His honest face was turning a very peculiar shade of green. Perhaps he was still not used to the noxious gases that elderly men release into the atmosphere while under the influence of the demon drink.

"No, you silly sod," Horace gasped. "To the loo . . . I must bid you adieu—"

He never completed the sentence. Instead, his lips clenched tightly together, his hand gripping his belly, he stumbled to the Operto's bathroom.

"Cirrhosis of the liver causing reflux," I said aloud to no one in particular.

The barman looked very worried. His hand reached out instinctively for his favourite tipple, rum. "Is it catching, Mr Harding?" he asked, hurriedly unscrewing the cap with trembling fingers.

"Not for a long while," I reassured him. "Give Horace – when he emerges – my best, please."

He shook his head and poured himself a stiff grog. "Not till all that green smoke he made clears. Now *that* is real dangerous." With that he tossed off the neat rum in one gulp. Then he shuddered.

Outside there was the usual long line of impatient taxi drivers waiting to turn left past the Oporto, hoping to catch the unwary and unsteady as they emerged from the doors of HQ. I saw Leo. He waved. I waved. "Ships that pass in the night," I mouthed at him, knowing the roar of the traffic would drown any attempt to exchange the usual civilities.

"Tin ear," he mouthed back and headed for 'headquarters'.

"Stimulating conversation," I replied, but already he had vanished inside to conduct those important affairs which engage the day of us city chaps, leaving me to dodge a taxi driver engaged in one of his usual midday kamikaze attacks and to wonder what Horace the Obit had meant by 'metal'.

Fourteen

Hamburg-Fuhlsbuttel Airport was empty, save for a few lumbering Auntie Jues, as the troops called the three-engined Junkers 52 transport planes. Hansen and Klaus both knew there was a red alert in place, but the fighters patrolling the Baltic and Denmark Straits on the lookout for English air attackers were already in position. And no one, it was reasoned by the Hamburg Flak District, would attack the city and its airport, not at this time of the morning anyway. As the flight controller had pointed out earlier when he had allotted them their seats in the Bergen-bound plane, "The Tommies will be drinking that awful tea of theirs still."

"Flyboy," Hansen had sneered when he had been out of earshot. "What does that rear-echelon stallion know about the Tommies?" He had spat contemptuously into the dust outside the flight control building, though without his usual energetic emphasis; apparently he was too weak. As he had remarked to Klaus during the long journey from the Hotel Vierjahreszeiten through the suburbs, along the Sachsenwald and towards the airport, "God in heaven, Oberfahnrich, first I had so much ink in me fountain pen that I didn't know who to write to first. Then she had me going at it in bed like a frigging fiddler's elbow." He had sighed as if sorely troubled. "I swear she's shagged me impotent now."

Klaus had laughed. "I'm sure you'll get over it, Obermaat," he had commented.

"At my age, you've got to be careful . . . things happen," Hansen had hinted darkly. "You've got to be a bit careful about throwing it about too much; it could snap." And he had lapsed into a brooding silence as he considered that terrible fate.

But he'd cheered up at the airport, where the fat kitchen-bull had laid on such a spread for them that the other passengers, mostly officers, had stared across enviously. There'd been Bauernfrühstück, Stinkkäse – a whole heap of it – and real Bohnenkaffee, as much as they could drink, with a whispered offer of a schnapps for those who fancied the fiery liquor. Hansen, naturally, did and he had drunk half a bottle of best Steinhager in a matter of minutes, maintaining it was the only thing that might still be able to "put lead in me limp pencil, sir."

Whether it had or not, Hansen was a happy man by the time Klaus saw no less a person than Kapitän *zur See* Wichmann descend from his Horch and come striding purposefully across the tarmac towards the building, where Hansen was now busy finishing the last of the Steinhager.

"Look at that," Klaus exclaimed, surprised. "Wonder what the Captain wants at this time of the morning?"

Hansen followed the direction of Klaus's finger with glazed eyes. "Perhaps he wants to kiss us goodbye,

Oberfahnrich," he suggested. "The big shots are pretty good at getting rid of hairy-arsed old hares like us – me – so that they can die safe and sound in their little beds."

Klaus ignored the comment. Wichmann looked both purposeful and yet harassed, as if something other than duty was driving him. The young officer-cadet wondered why and concluded after a few moments that Wichmann had probably forgotten something important enough to come out here at this hour to tell them. It was only later that Klaus von Kadowitz realised that people like Wichmann forget nothing. Kapitän *zur See* Wichmann of the Abwehr had had this final fleeting meeting planned all along, but it had to be done in the fashion of Intelligence services all over the world. Nothing could be done directly; the oblique fashion, or so it seemed to Klaus, was the Abwehr's chosen means of passing on orders.

"Glad I caught you, von Kadowitz," Wichmann panted. "Thought I'd come to wish you well and remind you of the importance of your mission to Admiral Lutjens."

"Thank you, sir," Klaus answered, a little overwhelmed. Full captains in the Kriegsmarine didn't normally see off humble officer-cadets at this hour of the morning.

Next to him Hansen cleared his throat quietly. Klaus thought he knew why. The veteran skirt-chaser was warning him. There was something strange going on.

On the field, the pilots of the antiquated 'Auntie Jues' were warming up the three engines noisily. The air was suddenly full of the cloying stench of petrol. Wichmann raised his voice against the sudden roar. "They say there's a great deal of enemy air activity – they obviously know we're up to something – over the Denmark Strait and Southern Norway. As a result we have to be very careful."

"Do you think we might get a parachute, Captain?" Hansen asked.

Irony was wasted on Captain Wichmann this dawn. He shot the big, red-faced petty officer a stern look and said to Klaus, "If anything goes wrong . . . you know, I hate to paint the devil on the wall, but if you're shot down, I make you personally responsible for the security of what I've told you – and this." Like a conjuror producing a white rabbit out of a black top hat at an excited kids' Christmas party, Wichmann pulled a small, carefully wrapped and sealed package from his tunic pocket and pressed it into a surprised Klaus's hands. "I almost forgot this last night at the Vierjahreszeiten," he said, avoiding, for some reason known only to himself, looking at the younger man with those cool, calculating eyes of his.

Klaus felt the weight of the parcel. It seemed heavy for its size. But he didn't comment, save to say, "Will I have any trouble with security, sir?" He nodded in the direction of the helmeted Luftwaffe soldier guarding the plane.

"No; it's just a piece of metal, that's all, Oberfahnrich. Besides, the head of my service, Admiral Canaris, has taken it up with the Luftwaffe personally. Everything is in order." He clicked to attention and raised his gloved hand to the peak of his cap. "*Hals und Beinbruch*," he said, keen gaze now taking in Klaus's face as if he might never see it again. "Do your duty. Report to the Admiral, as ordered. Guard that package with your life." His voice softened a little and the hand raised to the braided peak trembled slightly. "I envy you, young von Kadowitz." With that he turned and made his way back to the waiting car, his driver already gunning the engine, as if the two of them were in a hurry to get away from the little airfield for reasons known only to themselves.

"Funny one, that," Hansen said without much interest as they droned their way slowly up the Schleswig-Holstein peninsula, getting nearer to the old border between the Reich and the now-occupied Denmark. Within the hour they'd be approaching Bergen Field and the meeting with Admiral Lutjens, something that Klaus was not particularly looking forward to. After all, meetings between full admiral fleet commanders and humble officer-cadets still waiting to be commissioned were not very common.

"How do you mean?" Klaus asked, although he knew full well what the old boozer next to him in the hard leather and canvas seat meant.

"Coming to see us off like that. For a minute or two I thought I was for the jump-hooter right down hard in the brown matter – on account of that girl last night. I forgot to ask how old she was. Besides, one never asks a lady her age, does one, sir."

"One does not," Klaus mocked him, and added, "No, it was very strange indeed that he should come out like that."

Hansen tapped the end of his pock-marked, bulbous nose and closed one eye knowingly. "Wooden eye sleep not," he intoned, the customary phrase indicating that one should be always on guard.

Klaus nodded and closed his eyes as if to signal he wanted some peace. In reality he did. He hadn't slept much and now the monotonous drone of the engines was beginning to have a soporific effect. But he couldn't fall asleep. His mind was riven by the events and happenings of the last twenty-four hours and now this new problem which Wichmann had occasioned. There was something fishy going on; he knew that just as well as the permanently suspicious Obermaat Hansen, who was now beginning to snore loudly as if he hadn't a care in the world, did. But what was it . . . ?

A hundred miles further north, the little decoy convoy was beating its way forward at a snail's pace. The mixed group of German and Norwegian coastal freighters, all part of the great deception operation, were fighting a powerful icy head wind coming straight down from the Arctic Circle. Daylight had come later than was normal at this time of the year. A pale yellow sun peered over the heaving grey-green horizon, lying there as if exhausted and lacking the energy to rise any further. Every now and again the ships were buffeted by squalls of rain which turned into momentary snow flurries. It was a grey day in the grey part of a long war.

But the old salts, both Norwegian and German, who were manning the ancient, red-rusted ships, didn't mind particularly. It was now only hours before they ran into harbour. They hoped that, till then at least, the overcast weather and the squalls of sleet, snow and rain would keep the Tommy bombers off their backs, for the commodore in charge of the little convoy had already received a signal that English planes were cruising about looking for targets of opportunity. They preferred not to be those opportunities. As the middle-aged commodore remarked to his Number One, "Heinz, we're going to be the sacrificial lamb – without the mint sauce. Let the Tommies blow us out of the water and then they'll go home out of gas and honour satisfied. Old Lutjens in that fancy *Bismarck* of his will then live to fight another day."

His Number One, a sensitive soul, had made no comment. He now sat in the stinking lavatories, praying hard, while above him on the deck the red-faced, drippy-nosed deck hands discussed their chances in what was surely to come.

The commodore's gloomy prognosis was one shared by Admiral Lutjens, as that doomed officer sat in his state cabin on the *Bismarck*, reading the latest signals and reports from the radio room. To his mind they were encouraging. In the main it was clear that the Tommies were collecting their fleet. They had already sent out their reconnaissance planes – the attack in the Baltic proved that – and their antiquated torpedo planes were somewhere over the sea between Scotland and Norway, too.

He drew on the long thin cigar which he allowed himself in moments of tension to soothe his nerves and told himself that everything was going to plan. If the Tommy dive-bombers could be diverted to Convoy 21, currently sailing north at eight knots towards the Norwegian coast, he would be a happy man. They would waste their torpedoes on the totally unimportant coastal freighters, their cargoes useless ballast, and fly back to Scapa. It would be in the intervening period, before the Tommies could refuel and rearm the Swordfish and get them airborne once more, that he would sail with the *Bismarck*, the *Prinz Eugen* and their attendant escorts. It would be the ideal 'window' for him to leave Bergen and disappear into the wild wastes of the northern seas. Then his major problem would be to locate the *Hood*, sink the 'Pride of the British Navy', as the Tommy press called the great ship and show a clean pair of heels to their fleet in the dash back to the safety of the French port of Brest.

He leaned back in his padded leather chair and breathed out a stream of smoke, the very picture of a contented executive in complete charge of his affairs a man for whom nothing could go wrong.

Outside the men prepared for what was to come, while further off double sentries, helmeted and with rifles slung over their shoulders, patrolled Bergen docks keeping the Norwegians as far away as was possible from the ships. Those who actually worked on the docks were members of the Quisling party, headed by the pro-German Vidkun Quisling. They, like many of their fellows, were loyal to their new masters.

Admiral Lutjens grinned at the thought. But he did feel a sense of pride, too. Germany, the one-time pariah of Europe after her defeat in the Great War, was the master of the Continent once more, admired and supported by those many Europeans who believed in the 'New Order', introduced by the Führer, which was sweeping away that old decadent Europe with its rich Jews and their decadent, allegedly democratic politicoes. As if democracy had ever worked!

It was at that moment that Admiral Lutjens, soon to die 'honourably' in battle, had his dishonourable idea. It was probably the thought of Europe and the New Order, plus the consideration of the futility of democracy, that brought it to fruition. But it came to him, complete and without any loose ends. Even as he picked up the internal phone and asked for the signals officer, he knew it would work – and speed up the arrival of that window he needed.

When the Chief Signals Officer answered, Lutjens wasted no time. "Please dispatch this signal as an 'immediate'," he barked in that no-nonsense manner of his.

"Herr Admiral?"

"Signal Commodore commanding Convoy 21 *stop* please report your position at once *stop* plus estimated time of arrival Bergan *stop* Lutjens *stop*."

He could hear the signals officer gasp slightly at the other end of the line. "I'll have to use our top-level cipher on this one, sir. It'll take at least an hour to encode."

"*Immediate*!"

"But if we use our normal signals code, sir, the Tommies'll crack it before you can blink an eyelid. If you'll forgive the expression."

"*Immediate*," Lutjens barked once more in a voice that brooked no opposition. He waited no longer. Slamming the phone down, he took another puff of his cigar. Soon the Tommies would know the position of the convoy and attack. They'd sink the lot, probably. But they wouldn't be too proud of the fact when they learned the nationality of the ships involved. It might well be another small-scale Mers-El-Kebir. At all events, it would be the window he and his fleet needed.

He grinned at his reflection in the mirror opposite. He was well pleased with himself.

At this point he had a little over fifty hours to live.

Fifteen

"Oslo," the second pilot said and pointed through the little square porthole to their right.

Hansen and Klaus bent forward and peered through the grey gloom. Beyond the stretch of dark green sullen sea there was the capital of the occupied country.

"The pilot's keeping well clear of the place," the second pilot, a handsome young officer with an enviable chestful of medals who looked even younger than Klaus, explained. "This morning everyone, including our own flak down there, has an itchy finger. He's not chancing getting a piece of home-made Krupp steel up his worthy senior lieutenant's arse."

Klaus laughed shortly, but Hansen, his head throbbing now from the night before, said sullenly, "What they frigging well filling their pants for? The Tommies'll still be waking up at this time, eating that egg-and-bacon muck of theirs. Fancy scoffing that kind of fodder at this time of the morning." He grunted and bent his head as if he were about to fall asleep again.

However, that wasn't to be. The second pilot straightened up as the Norwegian capital slipped away behind them and they headed out to sea once more. "The senior pilot's not risking flying over land. We're sticking to the briny. So he suggests you look beneath the seats and find those parachutes. I'll get the turret gunner to show you how to put 'em on in an emergency."

Hansen blanched. Klaus had never seen a man go so pale as the tough old salt. "Parachutes," he gasped. "Frig that for a frigging tale! I'm not gonna trust my luck to some old woman's knicker silk, Lieutenant."

The young officer shrugged carelessly. "Suit yourself, old house. If we have to bale out, you can stay behind and practise your driving." He laughed uproariously at his own humour and swayed and jolted his way back along the gangway to the cockpit, leaving Hansen to stare at his slim back aghast and open-mouthed as if he couldn't believe what he had just heard.

Klaus bent, grunted and tugged out the chute. He looked at it curiously. It was the first he had ever seen at close quarters. Indeed, this was the first flight he had taken.

For a while he stared at the gadget, wondering what it would be like to launch oneself into space attached to a square of 'knicker silk'. Hansen, for his part, didn't move. He seemed frozen to his seat, not even speaking. Klaus thought he had been struck dumb at the prospect of the parachute jump. That cheered him a little. *He* was not scared at the prospect, just bewildered.

But, scared or bewildered, the navy men did not have long to reflect on the problem, for they had hardly left the land again when the senior pilot's voice came over the address system in a harsh metallic monotone to state: "Starboard . . . it looks as if we might be in trouble. Get those chutes on, will you—" The rest of his announcement was drowned by the sudden hammering of the turret machine gun. Smoking brass cartridge cases started to cascade on to the deck in a bright golden stream.

The two men flashed a look to starboard. Set in two stark black Vs, about eighteen biplanes were progressing steadily towards the east, the heavy torpedoes slung beneath their undercarriages clearly visible even at that distance. But it wasn't the enemy torpedo bombers which were worrying the senior pilot. It was the two white-painted Sunderland flying boats that were flying almost parallel to the slow, lumbering Auntie Ju, coming in from both sides, their turret machine guns chattering frantically, sending white tracer hurrying towards the trapped German transport like glowing golf balls which increased in speed and intensity by the moment.

"Christ on a Christmas tree!" Hansen gasped, finding his speech at last. "The buckteethed Tommy barnshitters have got us with our dong in the wringer. How in three devils' name do I get into this shitting parachute?"

"Shut—" Klaus began. He never finished his command. His words were drowned out by the thwack of slugs repeatedly striking the fuselage to his right and above his head. There was the sudden acrid smell of burnt cordite and the plane was filled with bitter fumes that set Hansen off coughing. Next instant, the turret gunner came stumbling towards them, his hand clasped to the red gory mess of his face in horror, crying thickly, "I'm blind . . . comrades, I'm blind . . . oh, do please help me!" He stumbled and fell full length on the metal deck. He was already dead, the blood from his shattered face forming a pool.

Hansen pulled himself together. He turned the gunner over. "It's all right, mate, he gasped. "Don't worry. We'll see you're all—"

The words died on his lips with a stifled cry of horror. Where the man's eyes had been were now two suppurating empty pink holes. The burst from the attacker's machine gun had ripped his eyes out. Gently, for such a hard man, Obermaat Hansen let the dead man sink back on to his face, hiding that terrible wound.

Klaus was seized by a terrible burning rage. It was as if suddenly an emotional dam had burst within him and released a torrent of violent rage. He sprang to his feet, the danger, and the parachute that might save him if the worst came to the worst, forgotten. He stepped over the dead gunner.

"Where you going, sir?"

Klaus ignored Hansen. He swung himself upwards and into the gunner's turret seat in one and the same motion. He grabbed the butt of the Spandau and tapped the two drums of ammunition, one to each side of the deadly air-cooled machine gun. They were full and fixed tight. "Good," he said to no one in particular, while below Hansen still called, wondering what he was up to.

He peered along the length of the barrel and through the ring sight. The big white Sunderland was turning in a slow clumsy circle, its engines ejecting white smoke, clearly visible against the icy grey sky. He tucked the barrel more firmly into his right shoulder, one eye closed, jaw clenched pugnaciously. There was icy-cold murder in his young heart now. "Come on, you cruel swine," he hissed softly, staring at the great white four-engined seaplane, "come to Daddy."

The Tommy obliged. He had completed his slow turn now, engines feathered slightly before he gave them full power. All four roared mightily. The pilot, glimpsed as a white blur in the cockpit, poured on the power. He felt he had crippled the Junkers and its defensive ability now that the upper turret had been shattered and the gunner knocked out.

Klaus let him think so. He didn't dare miss. He'd let the great flying boat come as close as it could and then he'd let the engines have all that was stored in those twin magazines.

On and on the Sunderland came. It seemed to fill the whole horizon. The two planes were on a collision course. The German senior pilot was unable to take the defensive, since the Sunderland flying to port was just waiting for the lumbering, slow-moving Junkers transport to break in that direction and run straight into the enemy plane's full firepower. He'd blast the Junkers right out of the sky.

Klaus waited. He felt no fear, just a tense burning rage. Out of the corner of his eye he could see the enemy biplanes falling out of the sky, directing their torpedoes to a group of ships below. They wreathed the sky in deadly puffballs of flak. But the British sailed through that killing barrage unscathed. They were going in, come what may.

Klaus dismissed the planes and their target. The Sunderland was within firing range.

He tensed. "For what we are about to receive, let the

Good Lord make us truly thankful," he intoned in the same sombre way that Hansen and the other old hares would have done in a similar situation. He felt a cold trickle of sweat trace its way slowly down into the small of his back. It was almost the moment of truth.

The Sunderland shuddered. Smoke erupted from her turrets. Tracer arced gracefully towards the trapped Junkers, gathering speed with every instant. The fuselage trembled. Bits of metal and fabric flew everywhere. The Tommy gunners' aim was good. Still Klaus waited. He wouldn't get a second chance, he knew that. The other Sunderland would join in if this one failed to down the Junkers now.

Klaus von Kadowitz felt – as so many of his ancestors must have felt in all those battles they had fought for Germany – Fehrbellin, Jeng, Sedan, Langemarck and all the rest – that his personal fate no longer mattered. It was a question of doing something for the German race and the German Fatherland. If he had to die in the next few minutes then he would do so gladly, as had all the young men of his family who had done so before him. It would be an honour.

He took aim, controlling his breathing as he had been taught even as a youngster in short pants. "Lead 'em into it, little Klaus," his grandfather, the old Herr Baron, had always quavered in those long ago pheasant shoots, as he had squatted on his shooting stick, silver flask of some fiery liquor or other in his ancient, spotted hand. "Lead 'em in."

He did so. The plane grew ever larger. Surely he could not miss now? His knuckles whitened as he put the first pressure on the trigger. The world was exploding in front of him – a great white roaring mass, splattered with the crimson spurts of cherry-red flame of the hissing machine guns.

"*Jetzt . . . los . . . FEUER!*" the old Herr Baron's voice cried in his ears.

He pressed the trigger. The butt slammed back against his right shoulder, and he yelped with pain. The detonation slapped him wetly about the face. Madly the machine gun chattered. Empty cartridge cases cascaded to his feet. And then, before his eyes, as seen in some slow-motion movie, the attacking Sunderland started to disintegrate. Great chunks of metal flew left and right. Huge gaps were rent in the fabric. The cockpit shattered into a gleaming spider's web of cracked perspex. An engine stalled – and another. The plane's nose tilted. Frantically the pilot fought to keep control.

Klaus fired again. He felt no compassion – no mercy. This was war. The first magazine fell dead. Still the stricken plane came on. In a moment it would smash into the side of the Auntie Ju.

Madly Klaus fired off the other magazine. The Sunderland halted in mid-air. It was as if it had run into an invisible wall. Klaus tensed. A head-on smash seemed inevitable. But it was not to be. In the very same instant that the Spandau went dead and Klaus dropped the useless weapon, the Sunderland fell from the sky.

He gasped with shock, as if someone had just smashed a tremendous blow into the pit of his stomach. A white blur passed before his eyes as a parachute came hurling across his front. It failed to open. It carried an airman – minus his head – and was followed by another.

This time the escapee was alive, but he was screaming in silent agony, his face contorted beneath the leather flying helmet as the greedy blue flames licked higher and higher about his defenceless body. Then the great plane went into its final dive, with Klaus slumped on the littered deck, choking and sobbing, the nauseating bile running unheeded down his chin, his shoulders heaving in great gasps, while Hansen patted him like an overwrought, anxious mother, crying, "It's all right, Oberfahnrich . . . it's all right . . ."

Sixteen

Now alarm bells were ringing all over Europe. From Murmansk to Munich and from Cracow to Calais, everywhere there was hectic, even feverish activity. Telephones rang. Teleprinters clattered. Secret messages were encoded and decoded on the German Enigma. All seemed controlled chaos as officers and officials of half a dozen nations – those at war and those still neutral – discussed, decided and put into operation hurried plans for what was soon to come.

In fact hardly one of those concerned, outside of Germany's Admiralty on the *Tirpitzufer*, knew what was really afoot. But all *did* know that Hitler's *Kriegsmarine* was beginning its biggest and boldest operation since the outbreak of war nearly two years before. Even the Reich's 1940 sea invasion of Norway paled in comparison.

In the Kremlin the brutal dictator brooded while his officials brought ever more alarming messages about the Fritzes' activities close to the country's Arctic circle border with German-occupied Norway. The highest ranking commissars came and went on tiptoe, afraid to risk the wrath of 'Old Leather Face', as they called the pock-marked dictator Stalin behind his back.

For his part, Stalin sat slumped in his great thronelike chair, puffing at his pipe moodily, wondering if Churchill's latest warnings that Germany was about to invade Soviet Russia were merely provocations after all. This new massing of German troops in the Arctic could mean there was an attack coming from that direction on the key Russian port of Murmansk. What was he to do?

Others were in a similar quandary. Admiral Raeder of the German Navy was worried, too. He knew he was fighting the greatest navy in the world, the British, whose tradition went back five hundred years or more. The English Royal Navy had fought and, in the end, beaten every power in Continental Europe at some time or other. It had done the same with the old German Imperial Navy back in 1916. After the Battle of Jutland, as the English called it, the German High Sea Fleet had only once ventured to sea again: to surrender to the triumphant English.

Now, although the German ships were far superior to those antiquated British vessels, most of them dating back to the old war, the Tommies did have the expertise.

What if he lost the *Bismarck*? The Führer would never tolerate that. It would mean the end of the German High Sea Fleet, his pride and joy. The Führer would mothball his capital ships to avoid any further losses and hand over the war at sea to Admiral Doenitz and his damned U-boats. That ruthless bastard felt no allegiance to the navy as a whole. His main concern was the advancement of Karl Doenitz and his 'blue boys', as he called his sub-crews. *God*, he worried, head in hands, old-fashioned stiff collar already beginning to wilt in the steamy heat of his office, *I could be on the damned retired list – or worse – within the week.*

The Führer was worried too. But not about the *Bismarck*. Up in his 'Eagle's Nest' in the Bavarian-Austrian Alps, the 'Watzmann', Germany's second highest peak, still capped with snow, which glistened and sparkled delightfully in the May sunshine, he was more concerned about the land campaign in Russia soon to come. Still, he did find some time for the reports of his naval adjutants. In between conference after conference he received them in the huge tea-room, sipping his peppermint tea, nibbling the sweet cakes he adored and farting all the while – for he no longer noticed the routine noxious explosions that came from his well-padded rear end any more; they had become too frequent and common. He listened to the adjutants' hasty latest summaries – "You have exactly sixty seconds, Herr Kapitän!" – and then dismissed them with an airy, "Just bring me victory at sea . . . that is all I am concerned about, my dear fellow." With his tail between his legs the messenger would disappear and Hitler would call to his mistress Eva Braun, concealed as usual behind one of the Gobelins, "What ponderous fellows these naval officers are. Still, they'll do the job. Now, what about a nice kiss for poor old Uncle Adolf." And she would fling herself into his outstretched arms with a squeal of joy at being allowed to be visible for a moment and hug him hugely.

For a moment or two the dictator, farting more excitedly now, and his mistress, in her Bavarian peasant dress, looked the picture of German middle-class joy. As the Führer often proclaimed in those halcyon days of victory, "What a blessing it is to be German and alive this glorious 1941!"

Churchill, a thousand miles away in London, was not so sanguine. He knew as much as he needed to know about the movements of the *Bismarck* and her escorts. It was not very cheering news: the world's newest and most powerful ships were being pitted against the world's oldest, though still powerful, ships of the King's Senior Service. Still, he was confident in the British Navy and her sailors. The days of 'rum, buggery and the lash', upon which he had always maintained the Royal Navy's reputation rested, were over. But the sailors were as good as they had always been back to the day of Horatio Nelson himself, though he had his doubts about the abilities of some of his admirals.

As he told his opposite number on Capitol Hill, President Roosevelt, a naval enthusiast like himself, over the transatlantic scrambler phone that May day, "The Hun has gotten" – he preferred the American usage; after all, he was half American himself – "too big for his boots, my dear Mr President. We shall beat them, despite the *Bismarck*; you have my word on it."

Roosevelt, no friend of the British Empire but still desirous of bringing neutral America into the war in order to defeat the German dictator, sounded a word of warning. "Let there be no defeat, Winston, come what may. It would only confirm those damned America Firsters of ours that the US would do better by keeping its nose out of a foreign war in Europe."

Churchill was ebullient as ever. "Never fear, Mr President, we shall win. You will take Uncle Sam to war yet. Lafayette we're here – *again*," he quipped, then, with one of his typical little poisoned barbs, "Then you will undoubtedly set about dismantling the British Empire." He chuckled at his own humour.

Roosevelt didn't laugh, but the men of HMS *Hood* did. They filed aboard the ship in their divisions, tugging at their caps under the wary eyes of their petty officers, laughing, making the usual old jokes about the 'lifers', as they called the former; young and happy, as if they were going on some pleasant outing, a gentle cruise perhaps, instead of possibly to their deaths. But then they were mostly 'HO' – 'hostilities only', young men who would serve for the duration of the war; men who didn't yet realise they would be facing not only the current enemy but that timeless one who confronted all sailors throughout the ages – the sea itself. Not until it was too late would they learn that the sea was the navy's most implacable foe: one that would show no mercy upon them once it had them in its grip.

"Look lively, lads," the petty officers urged, as they assembled in their divisions to listen to the skipper in due course. "Get them caps on at a regulation angle . . . move that fag from behind yer lug, Martin, or yer feet won't touch the ground . . . You there; you're on the rattle if you keep grinning at me like a pregnant penguin . . ."

It was customary banter that they had heard time and time again ever since they had joined the great sleek battle-cruiser, 'the pride o' the British Navy – and you remember it, mate, if yer don't want to lack a set of front teeth,' as they were wont to threaten in the dockside pubs they frequented on shore leave. But now the two thousand men who made up the crew were hearing it for the very last time. Those cocky boys, some as young as sixteen, were on their way to a rendezvous with death – and they went laughing.

Admiral Holland, the *Hood*'s skipper, wasted no words on the vast assembly as he addressed his crew for the last time. He wasn't a man given to unnecessary eloquence, even on occasions such as this. He stood there in front of his mike, hands stuffed into the pockets of his 'warm', a dyed-blue duffle coat, and barked, "You've heard the rumours by this time, I know. Well, they're true."

Next to him, his Number One frowned at the suddenly animated, excited faces of the young matelots as if warning them not to start chattering. The skipper wouldn't like it.

Holland didn't even seem to notice. He continued with: "We're after the *Bismarck*. The whole fleet is. We've been given the honour—" he paused in a dramatic manner quite unusual in such an austure man "—of leading that fleet."

Holland let the crew absorb the information, then snapped through the microphone, voice made even more harsh and metallic, "We shall be covered by an escort of six destroyers as far as the Denmark Straits. To the van there'll be the cruisers *Suffolk* and *Norfolk*. We'll be accompanied at some time in the next few hours by the *Prince of Wales*."

Someone gave a fat juicy wet raspberry but, although his Number One frowned severely, Holland let the sign of contempt pass. He knew of the rivalry between the crews of the *Hood* and the fleet's newest battleship.

Naturally he liked them to think the *Hood* the superior ship.

"As you can see, we will be well protected for most of this sortie. However" – his voice hardened once more – "when we find the *Bismarck*, we will take over and take the brunt of the action. It is our right – and, naturally, privilege – as the Senior Service's most important ship."

"Hear, hear," one of the teenage midshipmen cried enthusiastically, carried away by the excitement. Automatically the Master-at-Arms opened his book and took the blushing offender's name and rank. He'd be on the 'rattle' before this day was out. (In fact, he wouldn't. The fifteen-year-old youth would die with the rest.)

The admiral spoke a few more words, mostly dry-as-dust details of the sortie to come. Most of his speech didn't register. His excited young sailors were too concerned with the battle in the offing.

It was the same with the veteran 'three-stripeys' and petty officers, who had seen it all before. Some of the older ones had even fought at Jutland. They wanted to survive, and already their minds were working out the details of that problem. Some decided that they'd change into clean underwear. That way if they were hit, dirty cloth, which brought gangrene and other infections, wouldn't be forced into their wounds. Others concluded they wouldn't eat the traditional hearty meal before action stations. An empty gut was a good gut when you were wounded: again, it ensured that you cut out infection. Some told themselves they'd put a metal shaving mirror in their breast pocket. They'd all heard of the matelot who had been saved by the mirror when struck by shrapnel. (It had always happened to a bloke in another division.) A few prayed – but not many.

Admiral Holland muttered a few more words until his Number One nudged him and said, "Met coming through. Down in your cabin now, sir."

That did it. The weather forecast for the next few hours was vital. He had to hear it immediately; it might occasion him to change his plans. "Remember Nelson's words, men," he said with an air of finality. "England expects every man to do his duty."

It was trite, overused and something of a comic phrase to the more irreverent of the young 'HO' men. Still it stirred them with memories of another, more patriotic age, when men were not so cynical. Here and there they squared their shoulders, heads raised, chins stuck out defiantly like a recruiting poster of the ideal sailor, full of 'Jolly Jack Tar' and 'Hearts of Oak are our Men'.

Then the petty officers were trilling their pipes the marine buglers blowing their horns, the officers shouting orders against the wind and the sailors were marching away to their duty stations, with the admiral watching them for a moment. Observing him, his Number One was shocked to see tears in the Old Man's eyes. It took his very breath away. In all their long service together he had never seen the admiral give way to any emotion whatsoever. What was going on in the Old Man's mind at this particular moment? he asked himself, and decided that one day, when all this was over, he'd make it his duty to find out.

He never would. Like all the rest on the May morning,

with the fog rolling like a grey spectre across the flat sullen sea, he would soon rest in three hundred fathoms off the coast of Greenland.

Admiral Holland shook his head like a man trying to wake from a heavy sleep.

"Well?" he demanded of his Number One.

His second-in-command gave a little smile. "Fog, sir. Air reconnaissance couldn't get through as far as the Norwegian coast. But that's to the good, sir. Cloud as low as two hundred feet and the Norwegian coast blanketed in fog. Ideal cover for us, sir." He beamed at the admiral.

His smile went unanswered. It was as if Holland was preoccupied with other, more remote matters than the fog this day . . .

An hour later, the great ship sailed. In the old days, when she had sailed to show the flag at some other part of that great British Empire upon which schoolteachers maintained the sun never set, there had been cheering crowds, schoolkids waving cloth flags from Woolworths and marines, all sparkling brass and blancoed white accoutrements, coming to the 'present' with their bands blaring 'There's Something about a Sailor' and all the other popular ditties of the time.

Now the *Hood* sailed in secret, accompanied by the dour, eerie wail of a boy piper from the training battalion of the Black Watch, detailed to play alone and on the heights by his irate pipe-major. But even the boy, who would be killed at El Alamein, piping his battalion through Rommel's minefields to the assault, was moved by the sight of that great ship stealing silently away into the fog. Putting his heart into it and trying to avoid those elementary mistakes that had so angered old Sandy, the pipe-major, he piped that wistful tune that had sent so many of Scotland's sons away to die in some foreign field. "Will ye no come back again . . ."

Out in the loch, the great ship vanished into the fog.

Insomnia

Why I always pick a hotel in Southampton Row when I stay the night in town is beyond me. I have known for years that the damned street is one long noise twenty-four hours a day. But I always stay there. Possibly the proximity of the place to Bloomsbury – and, naturally, HQ at the Oporto pub is the explanation for my unfortunate choice. Or perhaps some long ago nostalgia. I remember marching as a seventeen-year-old with hundreds of other reinforcements, five and six abreast, laden with rifles, helmets, field service marching orders, filling the whole of the fog-bound street that winter over half a century ago, just, I suppose, as my father and grandfather had done before me. I came back. My old grandpa, who I never knew, didn't.

All I know, whatever my stupid reason for staying there, is that it was a damn fool thing to do. Even with the skinful I'd imbibed with Horace the Obit, I couldn't get off to sleep. The noise was dreadful as usual – police sirens, screaming drunks and the homeless being evicted from doorways, and sundry foreign tourists. I was still awake and angry at my failure to sleep at two in the morning, with the reflection of some whirling police car light flashing on and off in neon blue warning on the wall of my bedroom.

At three, tossing and turning in the bed which had seemingly overnight developed a rocky surface at my most sensitive spots, I was still mulling over the mystery of the poor old *Hood*. My brain raced furiously, considering the various possibilities, while a hard little voice at the back of my mind was urging cynically, What the fuck do people care now? It was a different time. The people were different. Write anything you like – that'll satisfy the publisher. Think of that bloody piss poor advance. Knock it off, Dunc, and frigging well go to sleep, won't yer?

But it wasn't as easy as that. When I've got my teeth – what's left of them, that is – into something, I don't let go easily. Hack that I may be, I still have some professional pride, and there was a mystery here that I'd dearly love to solve. Naturally I could accept the traditional solution – that the *Bismarck*'s gunners had gotten lucky that May day so long ago, had hit the *Hood* in some particularly vulnerable spot and had done for her in that way. But if that was true, why wouldn't Kew release the documents for free use by writers and by the general public interested in such matters?

Or take the Ministry of Defence. Why were they so bloody cagey at this distance of time? What concern was that ancient battle-cruiser to them? The sinking of the *Hood* was merely a footnote in the long six-year history of World War Two. At the best, it presented part of the case for halting the construction of battleships, which were no proof against aerial bombs or huge shells which could penetrate their poorly armoured upper decks. The loss of the *Prince of Wales*, sunk by Japanese bombers seven months later, should have been the final coffin nail. After all, she had been Britain's most modern battleship afloat at that time.

No, it had to be something else – something which still had relevance to the time in which we lived. Perhaps it was connected with politics? Political parties and prominent politicians still try to cover up their misdeeds and failings long after the event; and the successors in power continue to do so even when the people concerned are long dead.

For instance, I told myself, why are the papers concerned with the kidnapping of the two British Secret Service bosses by the SS in Holland back in November 1939 still kept under lock and key at Kew? What possible security breach could occur now, in the year 2000, if their contents were revealed? After all, the main participants have long since passed away – decades ago, in fact. But even now Kew sits on the papers of the Venlo Affair and will continue to do so till the year 2015, seventy-five years after the event.

But what politicians that sit in Westminster today would have any interest in the fate of the *Hood*? And what was that 'metal' old drunken Horace the Obit had mentioned before his hasty departure for the loo at the Oporto? If it had been of real interest – and could be connected to some current politico or his party – wouldn't Horace, with his eye for the main chance, have sold the story himself? Horace knows only one loyalty – that to the money which would buy him the strong waters that will keep him going till his raddled leathern liver solves his financial problems once and for all.

Outside two drunken Irishmen, perhaps ejected from the foyer at Euston in some pre-dawn police raid, were shouting at each other in the slurred toothless tones of professional meths drinkers. "Fight for frigging de Valera, that's what me old dad did," one of them was maintaining doggedly. "Old Dev, God bless him, knew a fighter when he saw one . . ." They rolled away, taking with them that remote figure of de Valera, and a kind of pre-dawn silence settled over Southampton Row.

I sighed and then yawned. Suddenly I felt I could finally sleep and thought that I'd better bloody well get on with it now. An hour at the most and the place would be noisy as ever. I thumped the pillow, took a last swallow of my whisky and closed my eyes. I didn't pray. What's the use? I dreamt of York . . .

In the days of the *Hood*, York was not the tourist town it is today. It was a forgotten, dirty old place where the last event of any importance to happen to the ancient city had been its siege and capture by the Roundheads back in 1664. Now, the streets where we played as kids have long vanished. The local university has eaten up the farms and smallholdings and the like which edged right up to the city walls in that May of 1941. It has all changed, in short – but not for the better, places never do.

These days when I walk about the place, the street names are naturally still familiar, but the streets themselves aren't. They are peopled with ghosts for me – the 'Mad Major', a supposed First World War shell-shock victim, who saluted lampposts and pillar boxes, but who was sane enough to be the local illegal bookie's lookout; the old gaffer with a beard down to his knees who rode a penny farthing twice as big as himself with surprising agility for such an old man; the 'basket case', the ex-officer with no arms and no legs, pushed around by his former batman in what looked like a long, shallow basket on wheels . . . They're all still there and will continue to remain there till I snuff it myself. Then they'll be finally dead.

And every time I go up March Street and stare up at the noble outline of the Minster to my front, the only thing of beauty in that tourist city, then and now, I remember her particular ghost. It has been with me nearly sixty years now, fifty of those spent in climes far away from that shabby provincial Yorkshire city – so I should remember that one, shouldn't I?

I can even remember the weather that May day when it happened. So you can guess the impression that her appearance, as she burst shrieking into March Street, must have made upon me. We were squatting in the dust, as kids always do, at some sort of loose end – what, I've forgotten now. Next to us the old printing works, with their German machines dating back to the previous century, were clattering away, providing the only sound save that of Old Abie, the rag-and-bone man, crying, "Any old rags, any old bones." If you were mug enough you'd give him the bits and pieces which brought good prices in rationed wartime England and get a gold fish back in return.

Then it happened.

A boy in blue uniform with cycle clips and a leather

pouch in which he carried the feared telegrams had hardly rested his red Post Office bicycle against the wall of the passage that led from March Street to the woman's house when she came running out, waving the message from the Admiralty.

She was screaming already, her iron-grey hair escaping from the steel curlers she wore, and her face was contorted by a kind of hysteria that I'd never seen before and which was frightening to behold. Indeed, Derek R, who would be killed in action in Normandy two years later with the Fusiliers, snorted, "Heck, the old cowbag's gone barmy." He must have been terribly frightened, too, to have uttered such a terrible word as 'cowbag'. In those days, boys swore very modestly.

There she stood in that dirty apron and oversized, laceless men's boots, waving the telegram like a flag, crying for her lost son. He had not been one of the three survivors of the nearly two thousand of his shipmates who had gone down with the *Hood*.

I can't remember her exact words now; too much water has passed under the bridge since then. But I have a strong impression that she railed against her fate that muggy overcast May afternoon while we stared at her in open-mouthed, shocked wonder. In those days, only mad women were allowed to have hysterics in public, especially if they were working-class. Hysterics and 'carrying on', as it was called, were only allowed for middle-class and rich females.

Afterwards, when the other women had ushered her inside with bribes of tea and the like, I thought about the matter in a boy's sort of way, trying to make sense of her hysteria about something which had happened so far away. In those days there were tragedies happening every day. Men, women and children were dying by their scores, hundreds, thousands, tens of thousands all the time.

I couldn't even remember what her son looked like, save that I vaguely recollected a cap tilted at the back of his mass of cropped curly hair and a broad grin . . . oh yes, plus a gas mask in a canvas haversack slung across a navy blue chest. But in those days all sailors looked like that: cocky, grinning, caps at the back of their heads in a definitely non-regulation manner.

It was that 'kiss me quick' look; the way the sailors attracted the 'judies': Jolly Jack Tar, living for the day and bugger tomorrow. They were men without a care, blind to the cruel Nature that would face them soon enough, so it was, 'You'll get no promotion this side of the ocean, so cheer up my lads, fuck 'em all!' That was their style, doomed men destined for a watery grave.

In the end, all I could remember in the evening of that day when we read in a skimpy *Yorkshire Evening Press* the first details of the great battle being waged out at sea was that distraught mother's scream: that primeval cry of protest against a cruel fate which had deprived a widow woman of her single consolation for a hard, unrewarding life. Her son was now resting at the bottom of three hundred fathoms of icy water with nearly two thousand of his comrades.

I woke with a start. For one wild moment I thought I heard the stamp of hobnailed boots, hundreds of them, echoing and re-echoing in the stone chasm of

Southampton Row, heading for their appointment with destiny. But I was mistaken. The rattle of empty milk crates and the sudden drone of an electric motor told me otherwise. It was the local co-op dairyman delivering the hotel's morning milk for those who would soon be about, wanting their full English breakfasts and pots of tea, ready to go out money-grubbing for yet another day.

I tried to relax, feeling my heart beating fast, a little frighteningly. I could have done with a stiff drink. But it was only six in the morning and the mini-bar was empty. In an hour I'd sneak downstairs for an early breakfast – the very thought made me want to puke – and see if I could find a mini-bar with a miniature bottle – or anything alcoholic for that matter – still left in it.

I calmed myself and watched the sky over London flush from a dirty white to a soft pink, indicating that the sun had risen somewhere or other to the east. The Chinese say the sun brings enlightenment – or is it the Japanese? I don't know, but it does not bring yours truly very much in the way of a solution to the problem that had been bugging me ever since I had been conned into taking on the bloody book in the Gay Hussar. What a bloody silly name for a restaurant these days!

Still, it had to be solved. I owed it to the old woman with the men's boots. It was as simple as that.

I looked at my watch in the dirty white light. Six twenty. Good. I'd have a shower, shave and the usual. I'd be finished by ten to seven. By then the maids would be yawning, and beginning to think of rattling the cutlery to waken their guests. By then I'd be downstairs and, having found the mini-bottle, be in the nearest lav savouring it and watching my hands begin to stop shaking. I started to feel happier.

Seventeen

Admiral Lutjens drew closer and closer to the enemy. Now and again through the rolling, billowing low fog he could catch a glimpse of the English squadron through his glasses. He knew Raeder, acting as the Führer's mouthpiece, had ordered he should avoid battle if possible. But with the English so close – and, by what his lookouts could make out, made up of an inferior force – it would be an insult to the Kriegsmarine if he made a run for it now. How would he go down in the history of the German Navy, which had so few traditions as it was?

Lutjens made his decision, while all around his officers waited, pretending to focus on the barely-to-be-seen enemy ships and identify them for the admiral. "Give permission to fire," he said simply, his harsh narrow face underneath the cropped black hair revealing nothing.

"Permission to fire," the senior staff officer cried. "I repeat—"

"Sir," the most junior officer, the one with the keenest eyesight compared to the middle-aged officers, whose vanity wouldn't allow them to wear glasses, cut in excitedly, "It's the *Hood*!"

"What?" Lutjens demanded. "Are you sure?"

"Yes, sir," the young Leutnant *zur See* said. "There's no mistaking her. She fits the recognition table exactly, Herr Admiral."

Lutjens' doubts fled. With what he knew now, he felt he could achieve a great victory with perhaps no cost at all to his own two capital ships. He did some quick thinking. "Run the permission to fire signal flags," he snapped, as his excited staff officers focused their glasses rapidly on the dim grey shape on the heaving, green-and-white flecked horizon while others worked out ranges and completed complicated calculations in their heads. All were animated by a frenetic mental energy. None of them had ever engaged in a battle contest such as this. If they won, it would be a tremendous victory for the German Navy, the Third Reich and Europe's New Order. Even Lutjens, not a demonstrative man under normal circumstances, told himself, brain racing furiously, Destroy the *Hood* and it will be an unparalleled signal that Britain's Rule of the Seven Seas is nearing its end. Once that takes place, it may well mean the demise of the British Empire itself.

He flashed a glance at the green-glowing, complicated dial of his gold chronometer, presented to him by the Führer himself. He noted the time very carefully. It was, in Central European Time, zero five hundred hours and fifty-two minutes. "Eight minutes to six on a May morning," he muttered to himself, awed a little by his own thoughts, "the end of the British Empire . . ."

"They're running up the 'open fire' flags on the *Bismarck*'s yard-arm," Hansen yelled in Klaus's ear above the thunder of the waves and the pounding of the *Prinz Eugen*'s engines going full out. He pointed to the battleflags beginning to run up their own ship's yard-arm in response.

Klaus felt a sudden emptiness in his stomach. It wasn't fear. Later he explained it to himself as the result of an overwhelming realisation that at this moment his young life was being changed by external factors over which he had absolutely no control. The change would be irrevocable. He would never be the same again.

"What are we going to do?" he asked himself – and Hansen.

They had reported to the admiral on the *Bismarck* and had then been shipped across to the *Eugen*. But their skipper had insisted they shouldn't return to their normal duty stations. He had declared them 'super-cargo', men with no job to carry out. Why, they didn't know. All that Hansen could say was, "It's something to do with that little box of metal you gave him, Ensign. I'd swear on it." And with that a puzzled Klaus had to be content.

Now Hansen, answered his somewhat plaintive question with, "Keep our frigging turnips" – he meant heads – "down, I'd suggest, Ensign. I think we've been frigging heroes enough for the time being, don't you?"

Wordlessly Klaus nodded. He supposed they had. In all his young life he had never undergone so many traumatic experiences in such a short time as he had done in these last few days. The dead Swedish women, the slaughter in the Baltic and all the rest of it, a lifetime of experience packed into a few hours.

Hansen opened his mouth to say something, but didn't.

Instead he stood there on the sea-lashed swaying steel deck of the *Prinz Eugen* with his mouth open a little stupidly. On the horizon bright red lights had blinked abruptly on, off, and then on again. For what seemed an age he appeared not to comprehend what they signified until finally he burst out almost as if with indignation, "Heaven, arse and cloudburst – the buck-teethed Tommies – they're – *firing* at us, Ensign!"

Holland focused his glasses. Down below the smoke from B Turret was drifting away, carried by the stern wind. The *Hood*, not the most stable of gun platforms at the best of times, was going all out. Holland was not taking chances. He wasn't slowing down to enable the gunnery officers to carry out a better 'shoot'.

Next to him his officers tensed. This was it. The first with the most would win this battle: all of them knew that.

Holland counted off the final three seconds before the great fifteen-inch shells from the *Hood* detonated, praying they'd find their target, in this case the *Bismarck*'s running mate, the *Prinz Eugen*. His strategy was simple. Damage the *Eugen* and she'd turn and attempt to get back to Bergen. En route the 'stringbags' would be able to deal with her at their leisure, whatever the cost in pilots and planes. That would leave the *Bismarck*, deprived of her support and the massive firepower of the *Eugen*. With luck the *Hood* would be able to see off the Hun battleship. If she couldn't, there'd be others to assist once the *Bismarck* started to make a run for it – which inevitably she would, he knew that implicitly.

"They're on target!" someone yelled.

"There they blow!" another cried on the bridge.

Glued to his glasses, Admiral Holland watched as the first shell exploded to starboard of the *Bismarck*, the target. The knuckles of the hand holding his binoculars whitened, the only sign of his frustration.

The second shell raised a huge spout of water between the *Bismarck* and the *Prinz Eugen*. Then it happened. The third shell struck home. A burst of blood-red flame, obscured a moment later by a huge cloud of whirling grey-brown smoke, and the *Prinz Eugen*'s radio masts came tumbling down in a frenzy of blue angry sparks. "We've hit her," Holland heard himself shouting. "We've hit the *Eugen*!"

"Bloody hell," an officer said in awe. "The *Eugen*'s bloody well slowing down, chaps. Oh my holy Christ, this is going to be some party after all . . ."

The scream rang out. It pierced even the roar of the explosion and the sudden hush of flame. Klaus shivered, as if with a sudden fever. "What in three devils' name—"

The cry died on his lips. A figure, one hand held in front of it like that of a blind man searching his way, appeared out of the smoky gloom, his body riddled with shrapnel wounds, the bloody gore flecked with smashed white bone that had been a human face dripping down the shattered skull like molten red sealing wax.

Klaus reeled back, hand held in front of his mouth. Hot sickening bile swept up in a flood from his throat. He retched. Next moment he spewed down the front of his uniform while before him that terrible apparition, glimpsed as through a shimmering red haze, trembled, reacted, failed and fell flat on that ruined face. A squelch, a nauseating squelch, and what remained of the dead man's features burst open like piece of overripe fruit.

Hastily Hansen grasped the reeling ensign. "Hold on, for God's sake, hold on!" he roared over the hollow boom of the guns. "Tuck in yer eggs and squeeze the cheeks of yer arse together, Oberfahnrich, it'll keep them in place." He flung a glance at the sailor lying in the pool of steaming red gore. "He's dead. *His* problems are over, poor shiteheap."

Hansen's rough-and-ready attempts to soothe Klaus worked. Weakly he shoved away the Obermaat's hands. "Thanks," he said thickly, his mouth sour with green bile. "Thanks for looking after me. I'll be all right now."

Hansen let go. "Nothing's too good for the boys in the service," he replied, using the current motto, his brick-red, tough face cynical once more. "I've got a flatman, Oberfahnrich, if yer fancy a snort behind yer collar stud. It'll put hairs on yer manly chest."

Klaus declined in the same instant that there was another whoosh like the sound a midnight express going all out makes when it roars through a deserted station. The two men ducked instinctively.

The great shell from the *Hood* exploded just to port. A huge wave of icy cold water swept across the upper deck, flooding it knee deep for a moment. Great gleaming shards of red-hot metal scythed through the rigging, bowling men over everywhere. A head complete with flak helmet rolled like an abandoned kids' football into the scuppers. Another rating was propelled screaming over the side, as if he had just taken a tremendous punch in the chest.

In an instant all was chaos again. Men were screaming on all sides. Someone yelled, "Mates . . . help me . . . I can't see . . . honest, I can't see." Fire control parties ran back and forth, reeling out their lines, while angry, red-faced control officers rapped out their orders, slipping and sliding on the blood-slickened deck.

Klaus pulled himself together. "Hansen, we've got to do something, do you hear. We can't just stand around like this."

Hansen forced a grin. "Don't worry, sir. Our time of standing around like spare dildoes in a convent'll soon be over. Don't you fret – the frigging war'll soon be coming our—"

His words were drowned out by the fire of the *Prinz Eugen*'s main battery. A great hot wave of compressed air swept the length of the debris-and-dead-littered main deck.

Automatically Hansen opened his mouth. The Old Hare knew that if he didn't, his eardrums might well be burst. Next to him, Klaus, in the shelter of a door, clung desperately to a stanchion as that tremendous blast of hot air plucked and ripped at his hold, trying to sweep him with it. It hit him about the face like a blow from a flabby wet fist. He gasped for breath, choking crazily like an ancient asthmatic in the throes of a final attack. On the deck in front of him the dead rating with the horribly shattered face was picked up by that great whirling tornado and swept away over the side as if he had never even existed.

Behind, the vanished detonation of those three massive cannons firing simultaneously left Klaus and Hansen panting and gasping weakly, hardly daring to believe their luck. They had survived! They were still alive!

They were the only ones. Those unfortunates who had been unable to find a solid hold had disappeared. The main deck had been swept as clean as it would have been before a ceremonial visit by the Führer himself. Nothing remained of the dead and the debris. All had gone.

Hansen broke the momentary heavy brooding silence. "God Almighty," he quavered in a shaky voice, for even the tough old mate was awed, "you can't hardly believe it, Ensign. All . . . all . . ." Suddenly he raised a knobbly fist that looked like a small steam shovel and waved it threateningly at the shell-pocked bridge. "You swine – you rotten swine . . . you got us into this. Like you did in the frigging old war. But you'll pay for it. I swear, if it's the last thing you do on this frigging earth, you'll pay for it." His whole body was shaking with rage now, his eyes bulging wildly out of his head like those of a man demented. Again he waved his fist at the unseen officers and skipper high above him on the bridge. "You'll pay, you bastards."

"*Hansen.*" Klaus grabbed roughly at him and forced that upraised arm down with more strength than he thought he was capable of. "They'll put you before a firing squad."

"I don't frigging care!" Hansen cried, his face contorted bitterly. "Why do they make poor old sailormen go through this misery? First in 1916 and again right now. Let the bastards shoot me. Ain't that what they're doing now, Ensign?" He stared at Klaus with those wild eyes of his as if demanding some kind of justice, understanding.

But Klaus von Kadowitz had no time for such luxuries on this cruel May day. All he knew was that he had to save Hansen from himself. He brought back his other fist and then punched it forward. It caught the petty officer squarely on the jaw. His head clicked and his eyeballs rolled back to show the whites. Next moment his legs started to give way beneath him like those of a newly born foal. Klaus caught him before he hit the steel deck. Gently he lowered the tough old petty officer the rest of the way.

Above them the turrets prepared to fire again, the battle pennants fluttering merrily up the yard-arm. Admiral Lutjens and his little fleet were going in for the kill.

Eighteen

Admiral Holland watched as the shells landed all around the *Prinz Eugen*. He knew that every second was precious. Yet for a moment or two he seemed paralysed, as if he were watching the battle in some cinema, settled down in a plush warm seat, really unconcerned about its outcome; as if it were happening to someone else.

Suddenly, for some reason he couldn't explain, he remembered that other May in 1916 when the buzz had run round the Home Fleet that 'the Huns are coming out'. He'd had a grandstand view of the Battle of Jutland, thrilled by that awesome spectacle. Later he had read that Churchill had felt that 'we could have lost the war in an afternoon'. Out at sea watching the battle, a sixteen-year-old midshipman at the time, he had told himself that they *were* losing it.

The German gunners had been better, their marksmanship and cannon had been superior and there had been something wrong with the British ships. What had Admiral Beatty snapped to his flag captain that day, with the *Invincible* sinking before his gaze? 'Chatfield, there seems to be something bloody wrong with our bloody ships today.'

Now, still in this self-induced trance, unable to act or react to the Germans only a handful of miles away, he knew there was still something wrong with the British battlewagons – in particular his own. It wasn't that they were all veterans, save the *Prince of Wales*, dating back to the Old War. It was their construction and the successive refits since the victorious end of that war, which had been aimed at making them match the most modern of German and Japanese fleets. The refits hadn't worked. The government hadn't been prepared to spend the money needed on Britain's traditional and most powerful weapon, the mainstay of the Empire, the Royal Navy. Now the supreme test had come. Could Britain still 'lose the war in an afternoon', as Churchill had recorded? Should he take the *Hood*, with her fatal flaw, out of the battle now while there was still time? They'd probably dismiss him from his command, perhaps even court-martial him, if he did. But what did he matter in the light of this momentuous issue? Holland wrung his hands in that classic gesture of despair and overwhelming doubt. God in heaven, what should he do?

But already that decision was being made for him. Five miles away, sixty-four German seamen – brawny and muscular for the most part, as gunners usually are – laboured in each turret of the four mounted on the *Bismarck*. Two hundred and fifty-six men, pale, sweaty-faced, their eyes flickering and their lips dried and cracked as if they hadn't drunk for a long time, prepared to open fire on the *Hood*.

On the bridge Admiral Lutjens waited for his chief

gunnery officer to report. He had already discussed the barrage on the *Hood* with the latter. The gunners knew exactly where to aim. Four times since she had been launched, the *Hood* had been refitted. Each time the Tommies had reinforced her superstructure with yet more armour. They had already begun to realise how ineffective their old capital ships were against aircraft and modern guns. But each time they had made the same fatal mistake, about which – thanks to Canaris – he now knew. Soon it would be up to the chief gunnery officer to make use of that secret information.

Admiral Lutjens forced a wintry smile. Around him his staff officers nudged each other knowingly. It was rare to see that hard, inflexible man smile. The Old Man was up to something, that was for sure.

In the four turrets the gunners waited, their guns loaded now. The call to action would come at any moment.

"Sir . . . *sir*!" The chief gunnery officer's urgent cry woke Admiral Holland out of his self-induced reverie. He shook his head, hard, whistled down the tube and answered, voice perfectly normal once more, totally in control again, "Guns?"

"We're mistaking the target, Admiral. We're hitting the weaker vessel."

"What do you mean, Guns?" Holland demanded.

"I think we're concentrating on the *Prinz Eugen* instead—" His urgent cry was drowned by the thunder of a great salvo striking the *Prince of Wales* half a mile away. The navy's newest battleship reeled and Vice-Admiral Holland knew she must have suffered serious damage. He flashed up his glasses, ignoring

Guns for a moment. Around him his staff officers tensed as signals started to fly back and forth between the two great ships.

"Bridge hit," someone read off the aldis lamp signal, as a yeoman on the *Prince of Wales* clicked his machine on and off. "Shambles . . . severe casualties . . . Captain Leach and . . . Chief Yeoman of Signals . . . only survivors . . . Turrets still operational . . ." As if to confirm the signal, cherry-red flame speckled the thick smoke rising from the bent, twisted, wrecked bridge. A turret had crackled into action once more.

The sight galvanised Holland into renewed action. "What did you say, Guns?"

"Wrong target, sir. We're going for the *Prinz Eugen.*"

"Switch targets to the *Bismarck,*" Holland rasped urgently. "Now!" They should not have continued to attack the *Prinz Eugen* for so long.

"But sir, we're having trouble – technical trouble."

Holland could have groaned out loud, but he knew a successful commander never reveals his feelings to his subordinates. Instead he barked, "What? Quick!"

"Breakdowns, sir. We didn't have time enough to work them up after the last refit."

Refit! The word stabbed Holland in the heart. It was the same old thing. It was the failing that successive captains of the *Hood* must have heard time and time again over the last quarter of a century of the ship's life.

"Don't worry, sir," Guns reassured him urgently. "We've still got the workmen on board. I'm getting them cracking on the problem tootsweet. For dockies they're good lads. They're going all out. But they are civvies." He raised his voice and tried to cheer the Admiral up. "God knows, sir, what the unions'll say about all this. You know how bolshy they are at the—"

"Get to it. Fire with what you've got, Guns."

"Yessir." The tube went dead.

Time was running out fast. The *Hood* had eight more minutes to live . . .

The *Prinz Eugen*'s guns roared. The grey sky was ripped apart by their elemental fury. One . . . two . . . three huge spouts of whirling water flailed upwards. The men on the *Eugen*'s bridge caught their breath. None of the Tommies could survive that elemental fury, that lethal maelstrom of deadly steel and fire.

Collectively they gasped. A lone destroyer, rocked by the shells from side to side, was coming straight at the 19,000-ton battleship. Time and time again, her ragged, shrapnel-torn masts seemed to touch the very water. But she remained stubbornly afloat, intent on her mission of death.

The side machine guns and light 20mm quick-firers took up the new challenge. A solid wall of white fire erupted on the *Prinz Eugen*'s starboard side. No one, it seemed, could live through that murderous fire. The lone destroyer disappeared into the smoke of battle. But no! There she was again, smoke pouring furiously from her twin funnels, reeling drunkenly from side to side as she was buffeted relentlessly by that terrific rate of fire. It lashed her as if to her doom, time and time again. But still she survived, as if by magic, though she sank visibly as she did so.

Clasped together like orphans in the storm, soaked with the foam and the great splashes of sea water that were thrown over the side of the *Prinz Eugen*, Hansen and Klaus stared in disbelief at their puny attackers. "Only madmen can do anything like that," Klaus roared, eyes full of the tragedy in the making, the sea water streaming down his face like bitter salt tears.

"They're half dead already," Hansen roared back in a voice that Klaus could hardly recognise. "It ain't human . . . *Himmelherrje*, how in God's name do they survive?"

But perhaps even God was no longer capable of logical thought that terrible May. Perhaps He wasn't even thinking; had given up on these mad creatures below who knew no sense, no reason, carried away as they were by that crazy unreasoning anti-logic of total war.

Now the destroyer, smoke pouring from her wrecked aft bow, losing speed visibly, was only a matter of a couple of hundred metres away. Even without realising it logically, Klaus von Kadowitz knew the Tommy was going to ram the mighty battleship. It would achieve nothing, save perhaps to slow the *Prinz Eugen* down a few knots. But it would be a last symbol of defiance. The Tommies, under that polite, calm exterior of theirs, were tough, obstinate bastards. They didn't give up.

So he let what had to happen happen. What could he do about it anyway? All around, all those except for the gunners, who continued to blast away in elemental fury, ripping great chunks of metal from the doomed craft, tearing her apart visibly, did the same. They watched with hypnotised fascination.

Now Klaus could see everything about her with utter clarity: the fallen masts, the shattered bridge, the shrapnel-torn funnels, the dead lying everywhere like bundles of abandoned soaked rags. It was as if a ghost ship from one of the ancient Nordic sagas was advancing on the *Prinz Eugen* out of exact revenge for some unknown age-old slight.

Then it happened.

Frustrated beyond all measure, the gunnery officer in charge of the deck bellowed through his phone to the score of gun-layers crouched the length of the *Prinz Eugen* and sweating, despite the icy cold, "Full salvo . . . FIRE AT WILL!"

The gunners, up to their ankles in empty shell cases, cartridge cases piled up to left and right, abandoned machine gun belts thrown in heaps like nests of curled snakes, needed no urging. They were afraid and exhausted. If they were going to die, then let it happen. If they weren't, then they wanted to destroy the bastard stubborn Tommy *now* – get the ordeal over with at last.

They took final aim. All rules learned on the musketry ranges so long before were thrown to the winds. They were out to kill – destroy – tear apart – completely destruct. Make this dying nemesis disappear at last. The whole side of the *Prinz Eugen* facing the Tommy destroyer, towering up above the dying craft like a mighty steel cliff, erupted. In an instant all was a mass of brilliant white and fiery red. Nothing could survive such an inhumane hail of fire.

But the Tommy ship, stopped in its tracks by that tremendous barrage, sinking rapidly, but without a single soul attempting to save himself, had one last trick to pull. She would be unable to ram the *Prinz Eugen* now, but there remained to her one final card. Her torpedoes!

Klaus saw it first. The flurry of bubbles. It was followed by the momentary silver gleam of the first torpedo speeding away from the dying craft.

"Enemy torpedo . . . starboard . . . bearing . . ." His voice trailed away to nothing. He couldn't be heard over that tremendous ear-splitting volume of fire.

Hansen heard, however. He grabbed Klaus even tighter. His fingers dug into the younger man's arm cruelly as the sweat, mixed with spray, streamed down his desperate scarlet face. It was the moment before Obermaat Hansen died. It was a moment that Klaus would remember for the rest of his life. Hansen's lips were moving. Was he saying a prayer? Or, more probably, was he cursing his fate? Klaus von Kadowitz never found out . . .

The torpedo slammed into the side of the *Prinz Eugen* the very next instant. The world exploded. Klaus felt Hansen wrenched from his arms and whirled into outer space by that great howling wind. Then he was gone – they all were. He was alone in a great howling red world, with the light vanishing rapidly and the enormous echoing roar that seemed to go on for ever and ever . . .

Nineteen

The *Prinz Eugen*'s second salvo came falling out of the flaming, smoke-filled sky. This time the shells didn't miss. The *Hood*'s main mast was hit. It came tumbling down in a mess of sparking wires and crumbling metal. Shrapnel hissed across the deck. Men were scythed down everywhere. Still the great battle-cruiser plunged on at top speed, apparently unaffected.

The second shell from the *Eugen* did it, however. On the deck, piled high because they had arrived too late and there was no immediate stowage available, the new, secret anti-aircraft shells exploded with a roar. Almost immediately a furious blaze broke out. The wind had sent a great blowtorch of all-consuming flame the whole length of that tremendous deck.

It was the target the *Bismarck* needed. Against that flame her major target, the *Hood*, was clearly outlined in stark detail. Lutjens didn't hesitate. He knew where to strike and there could be no excuse for the gunners: they simply couldn't miss, could they?

Swiftly Fire Control made their calculations. They relayed them to an impatient Lutjens, who was going to have the honour of issuing the decisive fire order himself. He'd go down in history after all. He looked at his reflection in the glass of the bridge proudly. Yes, he would be remembered as the officer who sank the *Hood*, the Pride of the English Navy.

Next moment he reeled, and just prevented himself from falling by grabbing a stanchion at the very last second. The *Bismarck* had been hit. Next to him a thick steaming stream of crimson blood was pouring on to the chart table from the tube. Around the chart table, the officers slumped back in their little chairs, unconscious or dead. The Tommies were fighting back. Now it was going to be a duel to the death.

Shaking his head, Lutjens, not realising that his white cap had gone and there was a thin stream of blood edging its way down the left side of his hard face, started to call out the fire order the best he could. The crew of the *Hood* had less than five minutes to live . . .

Through his glasses Lutjens surveyed the ship. Her captain was reacting. So far she had been able to use only half her firing power; her aft turrets were unable to fire. Now her skipper had brought her round and was beginning to fire on Lutjens' own flagship. He narrowed his gaze against the hell of flying steel and smoke to his front.

Every minute was now vital, the German commander told himself. The longer he was engaged in this battle, the more time the Tommies had to bring up the rest of their superior numbers. Once he had dealt with the *Hood*, he'd make a run for it. No one would question his decision after that particular triumph. For seconds he considered how to deal the *Hood* her death blow. Then he had it.

He knew now the state of the *Hood*'s armour in general and the fatal weakness of her steel deck. All that was needed was a single shell to penetrate that deck as far as the main magazine below. "In that moment," he said half aloud, while his officers stared at the trickle of blood as if mesmerised and waited for the admiral to make his final decision, "she'll be finished." The exploding magazine would blow her apart.

He made his decision. "Elevate A and B," he commanded. "Maximum height . . . plunging fire . . . two salvoes." He relaxed, the spirit seeming to flow from his lean hard body as if someone had opened an unseen tap. He had done all he could. Now everything depended upon the *Bismarck*'s gunners – and the rapacity and sloppiness of those English shipyard owners and their trade union officials of so long ago. "Carry on," he said – and that was that. He had made his last decision.

The great shells – one, two, three – plunged with devastating impact through the deck, igniting the anti-aircraft shells. The *Hood* commenced trembling – violently, frighteningly. The men caught by this strange movement trembled too. They looked as if they had been caught by some strange medieval plague, one of those which made men and women twitch, cry, engage in a parody of a leaping dance in the streets for no apparent reason. What was it?

On the cruiser *Norfolk* they viewed the sudden transformation of the sky – grey to violet, and then to grey once more – with bewilderment, too. What was going on? What was happening to the *Hood*?

The next instant they started to find out. Suddenly, startlingly, the grey sky turned to flame. The *Hood* gave a violent shudder. It was like that of some wild animal of the forest, caught by the hunter's bullet and taken by surprise as its hindlegs began to weaken and it started to fall for no apparent reason.

There was a hellish boom. Abruptly the *Hood* was shrouded by thick billowing smoke which reached higher and higher into the grey sky. Behind, there were gouts of vivid flame and a frightening trembling once more. The *Hood* began to come apart. The watchers gaped, open-mouthed and stupid in disbelief. Surely . . . not the *Hood*? their contorted faces seemed to say.

She was racked by yet another explosion. There was the ear-splitting grinding of metal being torn apart by force. Like some great whale surfacing for air, the whole of her bow rose higher and higher. Tiny figures slid from it. A man dived from a shattered derrick. He missed his aim, hit the deck like a sack of wet cement and burst open. Very faintly the watchers could, by straining their ears, hear the faint cries for *help*, *mercy*, *mother*!

Abruptly the bow plunged down again. A spout of whirling white water appeared as the bow started to sink. More and more panic-stricken ratings flung themselves into the freezing, killing water. They wouldn't last more than a couple of minutes. Now the men of the *Hood* were beginning to die by the score, the hundred, the thousand. All hope had vanished.

On the *Norfolk* the watchers turned their heads, eyes filled with tears. They could bear to observe the tragedy no longer. Their shipmates, men they had trained with, drunk with, visited brothels with in the Middle East and the China Seas, were dying only a mile or two away – and there was absolutely nothing they could do about it.

Another German salvo thundered. Again the *Norfolk*'s officers forced themselves to raise their binoculars to view the tragedy taking place before them. But there was no explosion. What had gone wrong? Were the Hun shells dud? Was the *Hood* going to be allowed to go to her watery grave in a final peace?

It was not to be. Admiral Lutjens had ensured his final order had been carried out to the letter. This time the *Hood* must go – and go for good. Then, not to put too fine a point on it, the *Bismarck* would flee for her very life.

"*Look*!" a young officer on the bridge of the *Norfolk* howled – a cry like the elemental one of some wild animal caught in a trap and in extremis. "For God's sake – LOOK!"

A violent sheet of purple flame shot hundreds of feet high. There was a tremendous crash which sent great combers heading towards the watching cruiser. Over forty-two thousand tons of defective steel, which had been the Pride of the British Navy's greatest secret – and her undoing – flew through the air. It all happened so fast that the men on the bridge of the *Norfolk* could hardly follow it.

Molten, red-hot metal started to shower the sea. It boiled in crazy fury. It set the oil leaking from the shattered tanks afire. Swiftly the tide of burning, flaming oil swept forward, engulfing the men attempting to brave the freezing water, catching up with the best swimmers and those on Carley floats in an instant. They screamed, as they too were turned into flaming torches: poor pathetic creatures, who screamed and pleaded with God for mercy in their last few seconds alive. But there was no mercy from the grey unfeeling heavens. God was – on this day – looking the other way.

A vast cloud of thick black smoke now arose.

It gave those silent men on the bridge of the *Norfolk* a moment's respite from the horror. But they appeared mesmerised. They didn't move. They didn't speak. They were like cheap actors frozen into position at the close of a final act in some third-rate melodrama . . .

On the *Bismarck*, the victor, the crew went wild with joy. A wave of overwhelming ecstatic joy swept through the great battleship as deck after deck, right down to the engine room, learned of their triumph. Men embraced. Officers shook hands and fell on each other's shoulders like men who had not seen each other for years.

Momentarily the iron discipline of the Kriegsmarine broke down. Those who possessed illegal flatmen on duty broke them out and started toasting the victory. Others ran wildly, aimlessly, up and down the steel passages, shouting, yelling, punching shipmates heartily in the ribs. "Good old *Bismarck*!" they yelled, beside themselves with joy. "I knew she'd do it. That'll learn that drunken sot Churchill. Now he can go and stick his cigar up his own fat arse . . ."

Men started to sing. Others, already drunk on illegal schnapps and crazed exuberance, danced clumsily together while their comrades cheered, made obscene gestures, blew them wet kisses and maintained they were going to their bunks to "fetch up the vaseline, dreamboat!"

Up on the deck where they had watched the end of the *Hood* – for that pillar of smoke had now vanished to reveal an empty sea where the English ship had been – they cheered and cried, "*Heim zur Mutter, Jungs* . . . Parades and as much tin as you can carry on yer frigging heroic chest, mate. Flowers; girls; yes, girls being thrown at yer as if it's Christmas every frigging day . . . Oh, you frigging heroes, what a homecoming it's gonna be. *Heim zur Mutter, Jungs*!"

For his part, Admiral Lutjens no longer shared the joy of his crew. The triumph was over almost as soon as he had felt it at the disappearance of the *Hood*. The fate of the great enemy ship had made him realise that the same one could overtake the *Bismarck*, too.

At six thirty-two a.m., at the moment of his victory, he had signalled Raeder in Berlin: 'Have sunk battle-cruiser, probably *Hood*. Another battleship damaged and in retreat. Two heavy cruisers are shadowing us. Fleet Commander.'

Half an hour later, at five past seven, his moment of exhilaration vanished to be replaced by one of despondency and foreboding. He signalled his chief once more. By this time his sense of triumph at his great victory over the English had vanished totally. The message was sombre. It read:

1. Engine Room Four out of action.
2. Port stoke-hold leaking, but can be held. Bows leaking severely.

3. Cannot make more than eighteen knots.
4. Two enemy radio scanners observed.
5. Intend to run to St Nazaire. No loss of men.

Fleet Commander.

The crazy intoxication of victory was over. Cold reality took over as the admiral realised what was now to come. The English wouldn't give up; they never did. The Tommies had long memories. They had been temporarily defeated – but now their admirals, their governors and, above all, their people would demand revenge at all costs. He had to escape while there was still time – or else . . . But the doomed Admiral Lutjens dare not think that tremendous, overwhelming thought to its logical conclusion.

Majestically the *Bismarck* sailed on to her own fate. Behind her she left the sea empty, tossing back and forth in that green, cold immensity, save for the mass of floating debris – and the lone man from the *Hood* on the Carley rubber float, sobbing as if his very heart was broken.

Envoi

The mood in the Gay Hussar was sombre that lunchtime. Outside the sky over London was leaden and threatening. There was a hint of snow in the air. People walked by hunched against the cold. Newspaper sellers huddled in front of braziers next to the meths drinkers. Their posters read 'Euro Crashes . . . EC Panic Measures!'

Just inside the door, Lord Longford was talking earnestly at the small 'single' table to some unfortunate. Closer to the centre of the inner room, a well-known ex-Labour cabinet minister, huddled in a camel-hair coat for some reason, was complaining bitterly to a publishing gent that the tenth volume of his memoirs of a working-class boyhood in Yorkshire wasn't selling well. It was the same as usual except that the plaque commemorating the old Seventy-Eight Division belonging to the 'Hungarian' from Dewsbury who had founded the Gay Hussar was missing. It had been the last link with the place's past save for the *gulyas*, hot, steaming and full of chunks of pork and beef, that my publisher was tucking into heartily.

He was making one of his fleeting visits to the UK –

he followed the MCC cricket around the world for most of the season – and he enjoyed what he called 'typical English grub'. Obviously he'd never been into a typical English McDonald's.

"So you solved the mystery in the end, Duncan," he said, reaching for the red wine – Tokay, naturally. "The mystery of what really happened to HMS *Hood*."

"I suppose so," I answered hesitantly. I wasn't quite sure I had. But it didn't really matter now, did it? All that mattered was to build a small and transitory memorial in words to these dead men of so long ago.

The publisher took my answer for agreement. "Splendid," he said, spearing another big chunk of soft pork, the thick gravy dripping from it – rather nauseatingly, in my opinion. "Our readers do like their 'faction' to be accurate, you know, Duncan. They're an eagle-eyed lot. They know their Mark Ones from their Mark Twos. You can't fool our chaps." He swallowed the pork chunk and beamed at me, as if he were exceedingly proud of 'our' readers. "It's like at cricket, you know. These modern umpires would get away with murder if it weren't for the old hands who watch them like hawks. Naturally they know their rule books – and *Wisden* – back to front. So—"

"Surprisingly enough," I cut in rudely – I am not one bit interested in cricket; the only thing I have noticed about it, since the day I gratefully turned in my pads when I left school, is that the players seem to wear a lot of make-up now, which certainly wasn't in when I was habitually bowled out for a duck – "I found what I suppose you'd call the last piece of the jigsaw here in London. It was when I was here to see Horace the Obit—"

"Who?" my publisher asked, removing some tough meat fragments from his excellent capped teeth – after all, *he* can afford good teeth, can't he? "Who did you say?"

"Please forget it. It doesn't matter. But I chanced upon him—"

"This Horace chap?"

"*No*, the last piece of the jigsaw – at King's Cross just before setting off for the North."

"Oh, the North," he echoed dully, as if I'd mentioned I'd been setting off for an expedition to the Arctic Circle. "Headingly's in the North, isn't it?"

I ignored the reference to the well-known Leeds cricket ground and said, "I could see he was blind even before he spoke. It was the patch he was wearing on his right sleeve together with the white cane."

My publisher had already lost interest, and was searching for another piece of pork to spear with his fork. Obviously it was a task that took a great deal of care and concentration, even for a publisher whose readers were skilled enough to know all about Mark Ones and Mark Twos.

The foreigner was tall, handsome in an old-fashioned way, wearing his hair sleeked back rather like Prince Philip and those other survivors of the old German aristocracy. His guide was much younger and looking worried, as if he were concerned that the old man wearing the yellow patch of the war-blinded on his sleeve might not make it on his own in a very crowded King's Cross.

The foreigner didn't seem one bit concerned, on the other hand. He kept patting his guide's hand reassuringly and whispering, "*Schon gut, schon gut. Ich schaff' das schon, altes Haus. Schon gut . . .*"

I didn't discover his profession – *vocation* might be a better word – until he had entered the carriage, said, "*Guten Abend*," to everyone in an old-fashioned German manner and sat down opposite me, asking in English, "I can smoke?"

"*Ja, Sie können rauchen, Herr Pfaffer*," I answered, showing off as usual and addressing him as 'pastor', for that seemed to be what he was. At least, he was wearing the German Lutheran equivalent of the dog-collar black sweater with a tieless white shirt, its long lapels hanging over the edge of the pullover.

His face lit up – it made him look at least ten years younger – and he bowed stiffly, again in that old-fashioned German style, saying, "Klaus von Kadowitz. *Ich fahre nach Hull . . . Seemanns Mission, verstehen Sie?*"

"The ice had been broken," I told my publisher, "and by an amazing coincidence I'd met an eyewitness, dressed as a German clergyman, nearly sixty years after the event."

My publisher wasn't particularly impressed. Like all Londoners and ex-public schoolboys, he had spent long years being trained not to show surprise – just, as you might phrase it, qualified and somewhat reserved interest.

"I say," he commented, savouring his latest piece of pork, "that was quite a turn up for the books, eh. Jolly interesting." He got down to what he called his 'vittles' once more. "What happened then, Duncan?"

I hesitated. What was the use?

But just then Leo came through the door, leaning on an elegant silver-topped cane and looking more like the Squire of Stroud than ever. He gave me an encouraging smile and shrugged. It meant 'Soldier on, old chap. It might never happen' or something of that sort. He sat down and I turned back to my publisher and my account of this strange, totally unexpected meeting at King's Cross and what followed after that.

"You see, he was some kind of travelling pastor, whose job it was to visit German seaman's missions abroad. He was on his way to the one at Hull, just outside King George's Dock, where the ferries to Holland and Belgium go from." I knew the detail didn't interest my publisher one bit – nothing north of the Wash ever did – but I felt constrained to put him in the picture. Authors are expected to put in the details; it's part of their job. "He'd hold a service there, distribute a few Bibles, have a beer to be matey and one of the chaps, console some poor miserable sod whose wife had left him—"

My publisher pushed away his plate and started eyeing the dessert trolley, hoping, presumably, there'd be some of those overly rich and creamy Austro-Hungarian *torten*, which old-fashioned Continentals – and English people – still eat in this weight-conscious age.

I repressed a sigh, waved to Leo, who was saying goodbye to Lord Longford, and added, "Just outside

Peterborough, when we'd broken the ice and he knew what I was writing, he told me about the *Prinz Eugen* and the metal. It was the secret revealed at last . . ."

By now Klaus von Kadowitz knew he was blind. One Ball, his fellow patient in the surgical ward, had tried hard to get him to see more than a shadowy outline. He'd crept back and forth from his bed, tenderly holding the wad of bandages which protected his remaining testicle – he'd lost the other, and nearly his life, in the freezing sea after the *Bismarck* had been sent to the bottom by the Tommies – urging Klaus to shout when he could see his outline. But in the end, when Oberschwester Klara had severely ordered One Ball back to the bed with the blood-filled chamberpot beneath it, they had conceded that the explosion which had killed Obermaat Hansen had virtually blinded him.

"Don't worry, Klaus," One Ball had repeatedly tried to console him during those first bitter days after that overwhelming realisation. Plenty of girls ready to oblige wounded war heroes like us."

In later years when he was studying theology at Kiel University, Klaus had often thought of One Ball, who had been killed two years later during the great week-long raids on Hamburg in 1943. One Ball had seen him through the worst time. He had made Klaus come to terms with his horrific injury and made him realise that he still had a life in front of him. Indeed, it had turned out to be a long, happy one with a loving wife – that same Oberschwester Klara, who had seemed to be so strict – and a supportive ministry out in the Frisian Islands, where they understood the ways of men who had once gone out to sea.

Some time that summer, One Ball proclaimed quite happily, "Listen, Klaus, the big shots are coming to hang medals on our manly breasts." He had lowered his voice as if he were imparting a state secret to Klaus, sitting on the white chair near the open window of the ward, enjoying the summer sun's rays on his face. "The buzz among the nurses is that the Führer *himself* is coming – and the ceremony is going to be filmed for posterity by the Deutsche Wochenschau! *Now* what do you say to that, Old House? Klaus, old friend, we've hit the jackpot!"

They hadn't. All the same, the Führer did appear, as the rumour had said he would. He didn't stay long. He had never liked the northern ports. But Admiral Raeder had convinced him that he had to travel from the new Russian front, which was now his primary interest, to boost the morale of the navy after the sinking of the *Bismarck*. So he went through his usual act for the cameras of the Deutsche Wochenschau: a smile, a serious look, the production of the Iron Cross, a close-up of him bending down over the wounded hero in his blue-and-white striped hospital pyjamas, the medal pinned on, the hand clasped, a pat on the cheek and on to the next hero who had spent his blood for 'Folk, Fatherland and Führer'.

"I received the same treatment," the pastor confided to me as we sped through Peterborough heading north. "Iron Cross, First Class – lost it years ago. Nazi medals are not much prized in post-war Germany," Pastor von Kadowitz added with a wry grin on his old face. "Plus I got one of his three standard phrases for the wounded. In my case it was, 'Keep your ears stiff, Ensign,' and then he was gone with his entourage stamping after him, all heavy boots and clanking swords and medals and poor old One Ball moaning, 'For God's sake, *doucement*, *doucement* . . . all that shitting stamping makes my shitting afflicted appendage ache!' He smiled softly at me. "Poor chap, he never did learn to moderate his language once he was a civvie again."

I reflected a moment or two. How strange. Here was a man who had received a medal for bravery from the arch-tyrant himself, sitting among unsuspecting Standard Class passengers, snoring, reading the latest Jilly Cooper – God bless her – or eating Great Northern Railways' excellent – if expensive – tuna-and-cress sandwiches. Funny old world, there was no denying it.

"Afterwards, when the Führer had gone," he had continued, "Grand Admiral Raeder, no less, had made an appearance to see me *personally*."

"The head of the German Navy?"

"The same."

Suddenly I realised that I was on the verge of an explanation for the great mystery of the *Hood*. I don't know how or why. I just knew it . . . like a vision. I tensed and waited.

"He exchanged the usual civilities for a political sailor – which he was – but," Klaus von Kadowitz explained, "I felt he was visiting me because he really felt something for me and – I hope – all the rest of us who had suffered in the *Bismarck* fiasco. You know he was a stiff, unbending sort of person with that old-fashioned manner and uniform of his. But I sensed he wanted to explain why I'd lost—" He didn't finish the sentence, but I knew what he meant.

"Go on," I urged.

"Well, to cut a long story short, Mr Harding, he produced a lump of metal. It was from the *Hood*, he explained. Naturally I couldn't see it. So he handed it to me and said, 'Feel it, Oberfahnrich.' "

"And?"

"I did so . . . quite puzzled, wondering why he had broken away from the Führer's party to see me and give me a piece of metal from the *Hood*. It meant nothing to me until he commanded, 'Feel it again and tell me what the surface of the rough edge feels like.' "

"And what had it felt like?" I interjected, leaning forward urgently, realising that I was now almost at the end of the trail.

Even in the eminently level-headed environment of the Gay Hussar I wasn't altogether able to contain the note of excitement in my voice and my publisher exclaimed with the fake enthusiasm of a boy from a good school who had been trained always to repress his feelings, "I say, how jolly exciting!" He dipped his cake fork into the Sachertorte almost as if with regret that he was destroying that beautiful balance of cream and cake. "Go on, Duncan."

"Well, according to the German pastor, it was not only rough but porous and pitted." I groped hurriedly for a simile to make my meaning quite clear. "You know, a bit like those Aero chocolate bars made by Rowntrees in the old days."

"They still make them, Duncan. Now and again I indulge. Memories of school and all that." He slid his cake fork once more into the crumbling edifice of that Austrian concoction before it tumbled down in complete ruin.

"So the *Hood*'s armour had been virtually worthless. The Pride of the British Navy – even the British Empire – had been based on a ship which successive governments in the twenties and thirties – naturally with the connivance of the factory owners and labour union bosses; they didn't want to blow the whistle and lose jobs for their members during the Depression – had shored up with cheap, inferior steel – no match for that being turned out by Germany's Ruhr Barons." I took a hasty sip of my wine, feeling myself flush even more.

Across the way, Leo waved his fork at me. Was it a warning?

With a flourish, my publisher finished the last of his torte and gave a contented sigh. "Makes a good punchline," he commented, as if he were suddenly very tired. "Mind you, this is not fact but fiction you're writing, Duncan. But it's a nice symbol. A crumbling Empire protects itself with a great ship that is crumbling as well. Not bad." He cocked his head to one side in that chirpy manner of his which he uses to make clear to his authors that he is assessing them. "What of the Jerry?"

"You mean the pastor . . . Klaus von Kadowitz?"

"Yes." He had dropped his gaze and was staring at the satellite TV cricket schedules which he carried around with him all the time. His interest had vanished already.

I shrugged. "He changed at Doncaster," I answered baldly. After all, what did it matter? Nothing much does.

Five minutes later we'd shaken hands, he'd muttered something about looking forward to the 'latest opus' and that a cheque was 'in the post' – they always are, aren't they – and hurried off, presumably to watch cricket from Brisbane or somewhere or other.

Leo saw me rise to follow. He signalled, 'A snifter for the Road to the Isles?' He meant Yorkshire. He was a Yorkshireman himself, but he always made out that Yorkshire was some remote province that could only be reached by dog sledge and huskies.

I nodded.

Leo's 'snifters' usually come in triple glasses. But it didn't matter much. They could pour me into the three o'clock for Aberdeen at King's Cross. It's usually full of drunken Scots anyway. One more lush wouldn't be noticed.

We toasted. Leo signalled discreetly for another. He was the most generous of publishers I've ever known, and I've known the breed now ever since I wrote my first book as an undergraduate. "Why do you do it, Duncan?"

"You mean novels?"

"Yes; they're not of importance. It's not like your non-fiction."

I shrugged. "Search me, Leo." I used the phrase of my youth. "Perhaps you can say things in novels that you can't in non-fiction."

The second snifter arrived. It looked even bigger. Leo raised his glass in toast.

I swallowed it in a gulp. "Let me say this, Leo," I said, swaying slightly as I rose.

"Say on, old friend Duncan."

"Someone's got to write books for women in pinnies, who lost sons in wars long forgotten."

"Here's to women in pinnies – whatever they are." Leo drained the rest of his snifter.

I ignored my old friend. "Women who wear men's boots cut at the side on account of their corns."

"Very obscure, Duncan. But I'm sure you know what you're talking about."

I wasn't offended. No one ever can be with Leo. Besides, I must have sounded an awful 'arse with ears', as the unlamented late Obermaat Hansen might have said.

"Bye," I said and staggered outside, leaving my old friend mystified. I started waving frantically for a taxi – I usually do after a 'publisher's lunch', which ends by being very liquid. I prayed I'd find one which would deliver me to King's Cross and the 'Road to the Isles'. On the morrow I'd begin another epic . . .

SINK THE BISMARCK

"War is not an adventure. It is a disease. It is like typhus."

Antoine de Saint-Exupéry, 1943

Letter to the Author, June 2000

The 'Hollies' Nursing Home,
Collingwood

22 June 2000

Dear Mr. Harding,

I have read your book Sink the Hood (Severn House) with some interest.

I know it is based on fact, though appearing as as novel. I feel, therefore, that you will be interested in some additional factual detail, with regard to the ship the poor old Hood was chasing, the German battleship, the Bismarck.

Perhaps you would like to come up here from Portsmouth at your earliest convenience to discuss the matter with me. I am prepared to pay your fare - the standard rail fare to Reading, where you will have to change and take the bus. If you possess a motor car, I shall pay your mileage.

I should be pleased to receive an early reply.

Yours faithfully,

Horatio Savage
Vice-admiral, RN (ret)

P.S. Bring sandwiches: the food is terrible here. I am housebound and cannot take you out to lunch. Don't worry about the 'grog'; fortunately, I am well supplied. H.S.

P.P.S. See note on 'Gestapo Müller', me and Bismarck.

The Savage Statement

The place stank of piss.

As I got out of my old Renault, I could smell it right off. There was no mistaking the odour – that diseased brown piss of sick old folks. Mind you, the home looked attractive enough from the entrance. Tidy garden, heavy with tea roses, polished steps and a brass plate, which announced:

THE HOLLIES NURSING HOME
Prop. Mrs Hakewill-Smythe, SRN
Founded 1998
All Facilities

Still you could not miss the smell of piss. But then all such places stink like that, don't they?

I paused at the door, with its customary security buttons, and thought about the complexities of getting in and out of houses in the modern world. Anyone would think we permanently under siege. But then again perhaps we are. Hurriedly I swallowed the rest of my Polo mint. Perhaps it would remove the smell of the pint of beer I'd just imbibed at the local pub. I didn't want to offend "Prop. Mrs Hakewill-Smythe, SRN", did I? At least *I* wasn't going to smell.

Then I tapped in the code. A click. The door swung open and I was able to see into the lobby.

The old ladies sitting there didn't turn. Instead they

slumped in their stained Parker-Knolls, old hairy jaws quivering as they babbled with their toothless gums of some happier past world. Still they were sane enough to realise that they had to be near that outer door. Their crazy old, worn brains could still reason that it was their last link with the real world.

"The Prop.", Mrs Hakewill-Smythe SRN, received me personally. She was blonde and brassy. Her fat body was enclosed in an expensive blue silk frock *à la* Queen Mother, the shape of the corset below clearly revealed by the silk. She smiled warmly, all capped teeth – at the fees she charged she could afford them! – but her bright eyes were smart and calculating like a cash register. "Ah! Mr Harding, the writer," she gushed, taking my hand. Her accent was definitely *not* "Mrs Hakewill-Smythe"; it was more "Smith out of North London". But she had learned the business. "Mr Harding, the writer" showed that. She knew how to flatter the paying customers and their friends. "Here to see the dear Admiral. I'll show you to his domicile myself." She flashed a look at the slovenly care assistant in the cheap nylon apron, carrying a bedpan. The girl got the message. She disappeared instantly into the lavatory.

She took my hand, as if I were one of her patients and I could smell her discreet, but expensive perfume. Her fees *were* higher than most, so that she was able to afford such things, I told myself, as I listened to her professional chatter. "We're very proud of the Admiral here, you know . . . One of that bulldog breed who saved us back in 1940 when dear old Winnie knew we were fighting with our backs to the wall, eh, Mr Harding?"

I nodded. Mrs Hakewill-Smythe, if she'd have been alive then, I thought, would have probably been fighting her war on her back not against a wall. I doubted that very strongly.

"Mind you, our dear Admiral is still a bit of a rogue, Mr Harding. Typical old seadog with a wandering hand." She gave her acquired silvery, middle-class laugh and added, "But I hope you won't put that in when you write your article for the *Gazette*, will you, Mr Harding?"

"No," I assured her, "I won't put that in the *Gazette*," though what the *Gazette* was, I hadn't the foggiest idea.

We paused before one of the doors at the far end of the corridor, presumably reserved for the male residents of the "Hollies".

She knocked.

The response came immediately, as if whoever was in the room had been expecting a visit. "Enter." The voice was that of an old man, but it was alert and swift.

Mrs Hakewill-Smythe tugged her blue frock down more tightly at the rump, where it was riding up above the corset. She put on her professional smile and entered, "Your visitor, the writer Mr Duncan Harding." She spread out her right hand gracefully like a head waiter ushering a special guest, who tipped well, to a particularly good seat in a restaurant.

The Admiral – Vice-Admiral Horatio Savage, DSC, MC, to be exact, sat upright in his wheelchair and glared at the "Prop". "All right. Thank you." He held up a hand urging Mrs Hakewill-Smythe to stay put. Instead, though, she crossed the bare room, as if she wished to plump up his back cushion. "I'm all right," he snapped icily, and I could see that the crusty old bird had long seen through her. As he told me later, "With that old trout, I lock up everything of value, Harding. God knows what she'll do with my stuff when I snuff it. But then it won't matter. I've got no one to leave it to after all, what?"

"Now," he said when she asked if he needed anything, "another bottle of grog for the two of us and have one of your skivvies clean out the commode, will you. It smells worse than a knocking shop in here. Thank you. You can go."

Surprisingly enough the "Prop", who looked as if she could be a real tartar under other circumstances, went, still giving the cranky old man with the hard angular face and square jaw her fake smile.

Five minutes later the two of us were sharing a bottle of "grog", warm and without ice, which turned out to be the cheapest kind of rum from the local supermarket. The Vice-Admiral remarked, "Real paint-stripper, Harding, but it puts a bit o' fire in an old fart like me, and makes a man forget this bloody prison and its bloody pong."

I told myself, he was "Savage" by name and savage by nature. I took another drink of that fearsome cheap rum, wondering how my guts could survive and waited, too, for his first reference to the letter he had sent me the previous week. It was that which had brought me to the "Hollies", this smelly last resting place for the country's OAPs. But I guessed I would have to wait till the old boy in the wheelchair was good and ready. Old and frail he might be, but Vice-Admiral Horatio Savage would want to stay in command until he no longer had the breath to command.

In the end, after we (read "he") had consumed half a bottle of that dreadful fire-water, the opening came from him, "Well what do you think of my Gestapo Müller business and naturally its connection with the *Bismarck?*"

Unfortunately at that moment, I was just in the process of allowing the smallest possible amount of rum to pass down into my innards when his question caught me by surprise and started me off into a series of hacking coughs. He watched my face turn scarlet – eyes blinded by tears – with apparent surprise, saying, "Weak as gnat's piss, really. Must have gone down the wrong hole. But keep it down to a dull roar, Harding – the coughing I mean – or they'll be in here like a flash with their bedpans and bloody down-boy pills. Well?"

In the end, I summoned up enough breath to wheeze, "I . . . I thought your letter very interesting and . . . and . . . quite a surprise."

Vice-Admiral Savage smiled thinly, revealing that he still had his own teeth at least, and said, "Thought the old boy was probably barmy too, I'll be bound. You asked yourself no doubt, when did they let that one out of the funny farm. What?" He laughed.

I didn't. I simply didn't have the strength. Instead, in an attempt to make conversation and prevent him from offering me some more of his "gnat's piss," I said, "You must remember that my book – the one you referred to in your letter, Admiral – was fiction, or at the best faction. You know, a mixture of fact and fiction."

He nodded, his hard blue eyes sizing me up, as if he was wondering whether I was the right type for what he wanted. Was I just what he would have undoubtedly called a "bloody scribbler"?

"I understand, Harding. All the same I thought you did a good job on the poor old *Hood*, even if it was mostly fiction, as you point out."

I liked that. Show me an author who wouldn't. So I said, "That's kind of you, Admiral, and I must admit that I was intrigued about your reference to the head of the Gestapo – Heinrich Müller."

"A hard-looking Hun bastard," the Admiral said half to himself.

"And the fate of the German battleship *Bismarck*." I paused and hoped he wouldn't reach for the Happy Islander rum again. "I must confess to you, though,

Admiral, it is a bit far-fetched. A Gestapo chief using you to help sink the *Bismarck*!"

"Stranger things have happened at sea, as they say, Harding. Besides after the war, Gestapo Müller disappeared. They caught all the rest, including that swine Eichmann, but not Müller. And as you probably know, he is still wanted as a war criminal, though he'd be a hundred years old now, if he were still alive." He eyed the half-empty bottle significantly, and I shook my head hastily but the next moment wished I hadn't; I'd got a headache from the damned paint-stripper already. "But naturally he had his reasons. Müller was working for the Reds, of course." Savage continued. "He thought the future lay in the Peasants' and Workers' Paradise, ha, ha and bugger old Hitler."

Savage had one of the defects of old age. He was a bit garrulous and found it difficult to stick to the point. Still what he had to say was definitely interesting. It *would* give a new dimension to the old proud story of the sinking of the *Bismarck*. So I said, "What exactly do you feel you could contribute to any retelling of the *Bismarck* saga, Admiral?"

Later I realised I had been a bit cruel to the old dog by behaving in that rather dogmatic, no-nonsense manner. Admiral Savage was not really interested in rewriting the history of a famous sea battle. His driving force was a more personal one: a question of betrayal and counter-betrayal, a love won and a love lost. A point in time about which a person can say, "Here my life changed irrevocably!"

Savage took his time. His eyes took on a faraway look. It was as if he were viewing scenes from long, long ago that only he could visualise. Then he said, "Harding, I'd like to tell you my history so that it isn't lost for ever."

Suddenly his bottom lip quivered. That worried me. It

is a character weakness of mine, but I hate embarrassing, sentimental moments. He pulled himself together and went on, "All the people I once knew are dead, you know, and once your friends are dead, you are dead too. Your memory vanishes with them." He cleared his throat gruffly and this time I accepted his rum without demur.

With his wrinkled hand, covered with the brown liver spots of old age, he indicated his bedroom with its commode, spare bedpan and row after row of pillboxes on the dresser, as if the place said it all. He wanted to go out leaving behind more than that.

"So, Harding," his voice picked up, "write my story." It wasn't a request; it was an order. I didn't know it then, but it would be the last order that Vice-Admiral Horatio Savage, DSC, MC would ever give . . .

BOOK ONE

The Savage Escape

One

"Time . . . Ready to go?" The dispatcher hissed.

The young sub-lieutenant, his face ashen and glazed with sweat, nodded his head. Outside there was no sound save that of the steady tread of the sentry's steel-shod boots beyond the main gate. Naval POW camp Wesertimke Marlag was asleep. Or so it seemed.

The young naval officer grabbed his bundle, whispered hoarsely, "The Navy's here, chaps," and moved closer to the door. Behind him the rest of his stick did the same.

The officer next to the dispatcher, muffled up in a dark duffle coat, thrust the skeleton key carefully into the lock. It was made of a pilchard tin-opener. He grunted, testing the lock carefully. If the key broke, that would mean the end of three months' hard graft and short rations. "Harry the Horse", the camp's senior naval officer, tensely gripped his unlit pipe between his big yellow teeth that gave him his nickname. His knuckles whitened. Fervently, he prayed that the key would hold up.

It did. The old door opened with a rusty click. "Good show, Mallory," he said to the man with the key. All right, let's get this little show on the road, chaps."

Now things started to move fast. The door was pushed open further. The days of secretly lubricating it with the oil from sardine cans paid off. It hardly made a sound, letting in a rush of icy-cold winter air. The senior naval officer shivered – and it wasn't just with cold.

Outside the blackout was perfect. Not a light showed.

Even the drunks who had left the *Offizierskasino* an hour ago had been careful. They had turned everything off and checked the blackout curtains and shutters before staggering off into the night.

"*Number one – GO.*" The dispatcher hissed fervently.

"Good home run, Charley," the others whispered. Then the young officer with the bundle was stumbling through the door and running at an awkward crouch. The rest of the stick caught one final glimpse of him, then the door was closed once more and all they could hear was the soft crunch of his boots, muffled with socks, flying across the hard surface of the frozen snow. The great escape from Wesertimke had commenced.

Now Harry the Horse began his countdown. The others hardly dared breathe. In the masked yellow light cast by the single electric bulb of the hut, the senior naval officer looked down the line of the escapers. They were all equally pale-faced, strained, tense, save one – Savage.

Lieutenant-Commander Horatio Savage's hard, emaciated face showed no emotion save bold impatient determination. Harry the Horse nodded, as if confirming something to himself. It was typical of the man. He never displayed his emotions. For Savage feelings were a weakness.

Harry the Horse's frown deepened even more. He wondered if he had done right in allowing Savage to go out with the first stick. He knew that Lieutenant-Commander Savage was a dangerous man. If anything went wrong, he had long realised, the younger man wouldn't hesitate to kill. He had been in the bag since his corvette had been sunk off Dunkirk the previous year and he had been eating his heart out ever since trying to get back into the war. Savage would now let nothing stop him in achieving that aim. He was not just escaping the boredom, the sexless stink of the fetid overcrowded huts, with their odour of piss buckets and human misery. Savage was escaping to fight once again come what may. That made him a dangerous man, a very dangerous one indeed.

The dispatcher went into action again now. Outside, all was silent. It was obvious the young officer had sneaked safely through the perimeter fence. Swiftly, one by one, with thirty second intervals between each man, the others of the stick slipped through the door and into the dangerous world of the Third Reich beyond. And no one really knew what the feared German secret police would do to an escaper: these Gestapo men were a law unto themselves.

Now the stick was almost through. It was Savage's turn. Harry the Horse cleared his throat. Although he outranked Savage by two rings, he always found it awkward, decidedly awkward, to talk to the man. "Savage, I know you'll make a go of it if anyone can."

Savage didn't respond. The senior naval officer thought, "Damn your eyes, Savage, have the decency to look interested." But Savage's mind was concentrated solely on the task ahead. Twice he'd been out and he'd suffered a beating and a month in the "cooler" on bread and water for his pains. This time he'd sworn that he was never coming back. He knew that like an article of faith. Harry the Horse tried again. "Do your best for the chaps when they're on the outside. They need all the help they can get, Savage . . . and you're an old hand at this lark," his voice trailed away. The other man wasn't even listening.

Savage wasn't. He was looking for the last time at the squalor of the hut in which he had spent the last year of his life. His sharp, emaciated face wrinkled in disgust. Bearded, scruffy officers snoozing or reading books by the flickering light of candles. Others frying spam in homemade pans. A Canadian officer running a lighter down the seams of his dirty shirt, trying to kill the lice eggs hidden there. Losers – the lot of them.

They had already made their separate peace with the Huns. Now they'd sit out the war, with correspondence courses, amateur dramatics and, if they were fit enough, a little furtive groping of one another in the dirty stinking latrines. That was their war. They'd have precious little to tell their offspring about their role in the great conflict. But they'd survive for what it was worth.

"Ready, number eight." The dispatcher's urgent whisper cut into his reverie.

Savage was wide awake, alert, ready to go in an instant. "Ready," he hissed back. "OPEN."

"In like Flynn," the Canadian killing the lice quipped.

Savage shot him a nasty look. Next moment he was through the door, bundle over his shoulder, his right hand tightly gripping the homemade knife he'd placed in his tunic pocket. He was off.

Outside, he paused momentarily. Naturally he knew the vital importance of getting away swiftly, but as the Huns said, *Eile mit Weile* – hurry slowly. Never make any rash moves that might result in disaster. He grew accustomed to the darkness, covering the perimeter wire at the same time, moving his gaze from one stork-legged tower to the other. They were manned, of course. With a machine-gunner and searchlight operative. But there was no sign of the Huns. They had heard nothing. They were probably sheltering from the icy wind behind the wooden parapet, enjoying a crafty "spit and a draw", as his matelots on the corvette had used to say before those damned Stukas had scuppered them at frigging Dunkirk.

All clear.

On the other side of the compound he could hear the faint sounds of the others making their way across the frozen snow and under the wire. There was no mistaking the twang of wire being cut. He grinned. It wasn't a pleasant sight. It wasn't intended to be. Savage knew that they were fools. Soon or later the Germans in the watch-towers would catch on. Then the "Hitler saws", as the Hun guards called their lethal spandau machine guns, would burst into angry life. There wouldn't be many escapers who'd survive that first salvo. No, that wasn't a route he intended to go down, as desperate as he was to escape. No sir.

He darted forward once more. Crouched low, he crossed the snow like some menacing evil shadow. The stench of the latrines hit him in the face like a physical blow. There was nothing that smelled so terrible as an eighty-seater "thunderbox". He gasped involuntarily. But there was no turning back now. Time was of the essence.

Hurriedly, he worked himself down the corridor between the tightly packed stinking stalls. Here, promptly at eight hundred hours every dawn, a shift of four score men went in, paper in their hands and, gasping wretchedly, completed their task, with the impatient guards yelling all the time, "*Los . . . los menschenkinder . . . scheisse' doch schneller . . . LOS!*"

He reached his own usual "thunderbox". In the camp, life was so routine and boring that people even picked their own "bogs". Quickly he dropped his bundle. He raised the wooden seat. Next he pulled out the stinking enamel bucket within, to reveal the dirty concrete floor below.

Hurriedly he swept away the dirt. He found the finger holes he had prepared weeks before. He stuck his outstretched fingers into them like some old gaffer in white flannels playing bowls on an English summer lawn might do and grunted. The slab came up easily. Below there was a narrow tunnel and a current of cold, if foul, air emerged. Savage's harsh face relaxed momentarily into the suspicion of a grin. Everything was working out as he had planned. It had taken him three months of hard secret graft – even his fellow inmates, of the POW cage, weren't privy to this – to prepare his escape route. But it was worth it. Now he was completely on his own; no one else to take care of – worry about – save himself.

He dropped into the narrow pit with ease. His nostrils filled once more with the damp mildewed smell of the old, long disused sanitation tunnel. Somewhere beyond, in the darkness, he could hear the scampering of rats – the only creatures still alive in the place. To the end of his days, he told himself, as he prepared to move on, he'd never forget the claustrophobic horror of this place. Now he was kissing it goodbye.

On hands and knees, dragging his bundle behind him with a length of packing-case twine from the Red Cross parcels attached to his belt, he crawled down the pitch-black passage. For fifty yards, as he well knew, it ran slightly downwards. When it reached the edge of the line of thunderboxes, it would turn right. There it would be a little lighter. Perhaps there might even be a candle glowing, to guide him. He hoped there would. Hardly able to contain himself after so many months of waiting, he pushed on.

Scraping his head and shoulders against the edge of the tunnel – occasionally setting off heart-stopping showers of dirt that he prayed wouldn't turn into a major fall – he came closer and closer to his objective. Suddenly he swung round the bend – and stopped dead, heart beating furiously.

A great grey rat, standing on its hind legs, faced him, outlined in the flickering yellow light of a homemade candle. It was preening its whiskers, displaying wickedly sharp deadly teeth, staring at him fixedly, as if it intended to go for his face the very next instant.

Savage waited. He knew what was coming. It did. The rat left its perch. It sprang lightly on to his tense rigid body. The loathsome creature slithered the length of his head. He could have screamed out loud. But he didn't. Even underground, the guard, some fifty metres above, might hear him. The rat took its time. It crawled down his neck and slowly the length of his back. Finally it disappeared, leaving him sick and nauseous, ready to puke at a moment's notice.

He pulled himself together. With his right hand, now shaking like a leaf, he seized the candle that others had placed there for him – at a price naturally. Those Aussie bastards never did anything for a pom without a price. He pushed through the final soil wall and there he was "Mad Dog Doogan", the Vanishing Aussie.

He grinned happily at the lieutenant-commander with his toothless gums. "Hello, mate," the big man said cheerfully, as if they met like this, in the middle of the night, all the time, "doin' a walkabout, cobber?"

Savage was in no mood for happy chats. "Shut it, you bloody Aussie madman. Couldn't you have got rid of that bloody rat? Frightened the life out of me!"

"Could have, mate. But I was saving it for my brekker. Make good tucker, rats do, if yer—"

"Let's not waste, time," Savage said interrupting the easy-going Australian. "You've got your pay. Let's see you start working, and get me out of this bloody place."

"Right yer are. Off we go."

Knowing that the pommy was in no mood for banter, the big Australian "ghost", as his type were called, turned awkwardly and, then, like the half-rat that he had become, started back down his own tunnel, heading for the spot they had picked outside the perimeter wire, well away from where the other POWs, "kriegies" were now going out.

Five minutes later the two of them were crouched outside the wire – shivering in the chill wind that came straight from the North Sea – eyeing the velvet sky studded with its remote unfeeling stars. Hastily Savage took his bearings. Next to him the Aussie was waiting – obviously for a tip of some kind.

"Where yer going now?" he asked finally when Savage didn't say anything.

"South," Savage lied glibly. "Heading for Holland and then through one of the networks that will take me to Spain."

"Yer," the Aussie said, spitting the words from his toothless mouth. "That seems the best way. I'd take it."

Inside Savage laughed hollowly and furtively searched his bag for a sock he had filled with damp earth. The Australian wouldn't lift a finger to escape. He'd sit it out till it was all over and go back to "Oz", as he called his native country, to live off the state – and the beer he could "win" with his tall tales of the "big war".

"Yer'll be off, cobber?" the Australian asked. There was a wheedling tone in his voice now. Savage thought he sounded like a cheap waiter hovering around his customers for a tip. "I'll pray for you this night when I get back to my hidey-hole."

"That's decent of you," Savage said, irony in his voice, but he knew irony was wasted on the other man. "I certainly do appreciate all you've done for me over the last weeks." He fumbled inside his bag as if he were searching for some goodie to give the Australian.

"Think nothing of it, cobber. You might not be an Aussie, but you're a good bloke and we are comrades-in-arms after all, though you are—"

His sentence came to an abrupt end as Savage hit him hard right in the centre of the forehead with the sand-filled sock. Without a single sound, the Australian "ghost" reeled back into the hole from which they had just emerged.

Savage laughed harshly. "See yer down under after the war, cobber," he snarled, with a poor imitation of the man's Australian accent. Then he was going, heading for the snow-heavy woods beyond the camp. He was out . . . out . . . OUT!

Two

The Tommy bomber was dying in the sky!

Its starboard engine was shattered, greedy little blue flames licking about the still prop. Its port engine was going full out, as the pilot desperately tried to keep the English bomber in the sky. Below the fleet at Wilhelmshaven mercilessly peppered the sky around it with flak. The spy plane was not going to escape, the *Kriegsmarine* was going to see to that. Black puffs of smoke exploded all around it. Tracer – red, green and yellow – zipped back and forth lethally. Even at that height, the two observers on the quay could see the shreds of gleaming metal, ripped off the stricken plane, floating down to the sea like frozen silver leaves.

Fregattenkapitan Feuchtner grinned, without malice. Indeed he felt sorry for the lone Tommy pilot who had braved the anchorage of the German fleet so boldly – and so foolishly. "He ain't got a chance in hell, *Standartenführer*," he said to his undersized companion, apparently in no way awed by the presence of one of the most feared men in the Third Reich.

Gestapo Müller, small, shaven-headed and insignificant, even in the smart uniform of a senior Gestapo official, nodded a little nervously. He wasn't afraid, of course. He'd been a bomber pilot in the old war himself; he knew the drill. But he didn't like the sea and the people who sailed it. These men from the north of Germany were all "sow Prussians" – and communist to boot. The coast, the sea and the sailors always made him feel uneasy; he was always happy back in his native mountainous Bavaria. "He's trying to feather the other prop," he began to explain to his naval escort, but broke off abruptly.

Suddenly the cadence of the remaining engine had changed to a despairing whine. He knew what that meant. The pilot had failed. He had! The nose tilted down. Thick black smoke started to pour from the "good" engine. She was preparing for her last dive – to her doom.

"There she frigging well goes," the young lieutenant-commander yelled exuberantly.

Now the Wellington seemed to stand on its nose momentarily. Suddenly, startingly, a sheet of flame seared the length of the plane like that of a gigantic blowtorch. A wing fell off and came twirling to the waves below. Then, after what seemed an eternity but might only have been a second, it fell out of the sky like a stone. Next instant it had plunged into the winter sea. Wild white foaming water erupted in a furious geyser. A mushroom of steam shot up. A second later, all that marked the passing of the Tommy bomber was a swirl of oil spreading steadily across the anchorage, on and on until eternity.

Fregattenkapitan Feuchtner crossed himself in mock modesty.

Gestapo Müller frowned. Once he had been a fervent Catholic in his native Munich; he still didn't like that sort of ungodliness.

Feuchtner saw the look on the Gestapo boss's face and it wasn't very pleasant. Hastily he said, "He deserved it, but I wished the pilot well – on the other side, *Standartenführer*."

Gestapo Müller did not seem to be listening to his explanation. Instead he said, "Is it always like this here in Wilhelmshaven?"

Feuchtner nodded and wondered why their guest had asked such a question. After all, he supposed that the Gestapo chief was only at this remote northern naval base – so far away from the Berlin Secret Police HQ – by chance. "Yes," he answered almost casually, "the Tommies try to keep a permanent eye on our surface fleet. They can't do much about Admiral Doenitz's U-boats." He meant the admiral who commanded Germany's deadly underwater fleet, which had already brought the damned Tommies almost down to their knees. "But they can do a lot about our surface ships. Once they are spotted by the Tommies heaving anchor, there'd be all hell to pay on the other side of the pond. The Tommies would pull out all the stops."

Gestapo Müller's heavy-jawed face, with those curious, shifting eyes of his, which made even the hard-boiled lieutenant-commander feel a little uneasy, revealed nothing. He nodded carefully, as if he were storing up the information he had just received for further use.

Feuchtner gave a little shrug. It was no skin off his nose, was it? He'd probably never see the Gestapo chief ever again after this day. Not that he wanted to do anyway. "The Tommies might not be too bright in the upper storey, Standartenführer, but they're damned persistent, that's for sure." He tugged his tie into place above the Knight's Cross of which he was so proud. "I suppose, sir, we'd better move off. The Grand Admiral frowns upon lateness, sir."

"Yes, of course," Gestapo Müller agreed easily. At the back of his shaven head, a malicious little voice sneered, "Who in three devils' name gives a shit about the – er – Grand Admiral?" And of course, Gestapo Müller was right. In his profession, nothing or nobody counted. He only needed to snap his fingers and the most important people in the land would disappear without trace . . .

"Stillgestanden."

The big open shed echoed and re-echoed with that tremendous command bellowed through the public address system. One hundred pairs of boots stamped to attention as one. The seagulls, disturbed in their roosts, flew away cawing in hoarse protest. Ourside the naval sentries paused momentarily in their beat and then carried on, sealing the shed off from big ears. Müller nodded his approval. At least these sow Prussians knew how to maintain security. The thought pleased him. It made his life easier. He relaxed a little, that is as much as he ever did. On the dias, fringed with the black and white iron-crossed flags of the old Imperial Navy, Grand Admiral Raeder waited before saying in his soft, old man's voice, "Gentlemen, stand at ease – please."

There was the usual outbreak of coughing, shuffling of feet, clearing of throats and indeed the barely concealed noise of officers breaking wind. Gestapo Müller's face took on a momentary look of scorn. Ex-NCO that he was, he had never lost his contempt for these officers and gentlemen – "monocle Fritzes," as his fellow ex-NCO, Adolf Hitler called them. Just like any ordinary mortal, he told himself, *they* didn't shit through the ribs either.

Raeder cleared his throat. In a reedy voice that went with his old-fashioned sword and wing-collar, he announced, "Comrades, I don't need to tell you that our friends in the Army and Air Force have achieved tremendous successes in the last few months. The press and radio have been full of their exploits. Perhaps too much so," he allowed himself a tight-lipped smirk.

Next to Gestapo Müller and Feuchtner, a young officer whispered, "As long as the damned Navy runs on wheels it'll never hit the headlines." Feuchtner laughed softly as he recognised the old pun on Raeder's name and the surface fleet.

"But I think the time has come, gentlemen," Raeder continued, "for you, officers of the fleet, to share some of that glory. Most of Admiral Doenitz's young men have already cured their throatache," he meant won the Knight's Cross of the Iron Cross, the decoration which was worn around the neck and throat, "and I feel that some of *you* should be cured from that same affliction – *soon*!" He beamed at his assembled officers.

It was a look which was returned with enthusiasm. The U-boat officers had become like film stars in these last few months after their tremendous victories against the Tommies in the North Atlantic. It was said that they could have any woman they wished; even titled ladies offered them their bodies – by post. It was a status which many of those present this cold morning in Wilhelmshaven would have liked to achieve, too.

"What of the surface navy, people are asking," Raeder continued. "What role have the big ships played in the war thus far, the man-in-the-street demands. As far as the average folk – comrade – goes, gentlemen, they think we are sitting on our fat blue bottoms doing exactly – *nothing*!"

Gestapo Müller listened carefully. He noted Raeder's points, realising, although he knew little of the subject, that the old Admiral was jealous of the success of the much younger Doenitz and his U-boats. For Doenitz, who had the Führer's ear, was the future. He, Raeder, was the past.

As Müller listened, he wasn't quite clear to what use he could put the information he was now gaining, but somehow he realised he would eventually profit from it. For the time being, however, he was here to check the security of the surface fleet and its anchorage in Wilhelmshaven.

"Naturally," Raeder concluded five minutes later, "I don't want to discuss operations here and now, comrades. It would hardly be the place to do so. But I can assure you that they are in full swing. Suffice to say," he paused significantly, as if to let his listeners know that what he was about to say was the reason for his coming her from his Berlin HQ to talk to them on this cold overcast day, "you can confidently anticipate that you will be engaged in ops before the winter is over. And they won't be low-key, you may be sure of that. The day of the surface fleet is nigh." He raised his liver-spotted old hand to the gold-braided cap – automatically Müller, the long-time cop noted the hand shook – as if saluting them. "Comrades, I already wish you good hunting." And with that the pep talk was over. The loudspeakers boomed. The officers sprang to attention. A little wearily, assisted by his goldbraided adjutants, the Grand Admiral descended from the dias and the air was abruptly filled with the brass-heavy bombastic march so popular that year. "*Wir fahren gegen Enger-land . . .*"

Müller frowned. One should never count one's chickens before they hatched, he told himself. Next moment he dismissed the thought as Feuchtner took his arm in that happy-go-lucky manner of his, saying, "The Grand Admiral's having a piss-up. Might as well get the free sauce, '*Standartenführer*,' eh?"

The *Standartenführer* allowed himself to be persuaded . . .

"*Lieber Herr Standartenführer*," Raeder said affably, using the wrong form of address for an SS officer, which made Müller think that the old shit might have been overindulging, "how good of you to come."

Müller mumbled something and wished he had a good glass of Munich beer in his hand instead of the champagne piss these officers and gents were drinking, bringing up their glass to the third button of their tunics, as regulations prescribed, clicking their heels and toasting each other.

"You've checked out the situation thoroughly, I mean the security business?"

"*My* people have, *Herr Grossadmiral*," Müller corrected him.

"And?"

"On the whole, good. There are a few weaknesses, but I am sure that we can take care of them without too much difficulty. There are still plenty of communists in our northern ports."

"Damned red swine. Should have shot the lot of 'em back in '33 when the Führer first took control," Raeder said hotly, cheeks flushing, as if the presence of potential communist spies and saboteurs was a personal affront. "Thank God, with your recent experience of the Red Orchestra traitors, *Standartenführer*, you know how to deal with vermin of that nature."

For some reason that Feuchtner, who was standing close by, couldn't fathom, Müller's sallow brooding face flushed for an instance.

"Yes, I suppose so," Müller said, a little grudgingly. "But is there, Grand Admiral, something that I ought to know in addition?" He had long sensed, ever since he had arrived at this particular Prussian arsehole-of-the-world from Berlin, that he hadn't been told everything.

Raeder hesitated.

A naval steward, the back of his white jacket now soaked black with sweat, clicked his heels and presented his silver tray laden with flutes of French champagne. "*Champus, Herr Grossadmiral*?"

Impatiently Raeder waved him away. He flashed a look to left and right like a man who saw danger in every shadow. "Yes. I suppose there is, Müller. That is why the Führer himself asked me to request your expert services."

Müller forced his face not to reveal his contempt at the statement. All of them, even commanders-in-chief like Raeder, could not refrain from showing off with the Führer's shitting name. It was a kind of magic key, they thought, which would open all doors. But one day even Hitler would have his downfall. Then no one would dare boast that he had had the approval of the Führer for his undertakings, whatever they were.

"You see, Müller, we are going to start our own blitzkrieg on the sea. We have waited long enough. I know we are not ready, but one can never be fully ready – *ever*. If we don't do something soon, the Führer will lose patience with us completely. He'll have the surface fleet mothballed and leave the war at sea to Doenitz's U-boats and that will be the end of the real German Navy."

Müller nodded in that wooden cop's fashion of his, his broad peasant face revealing nothing. In fact his mind was racing electrically. He had just been informed of a great secret, one that might affect the whole future course of the war. He had suspected all along that he had been called here for more than a routine security check-up. Now he knew he was right. Security was only a factor in the great plan soon to be put into operation.

Raeder must have been feeling his "*champus*", for he added in an excited whisper, "They're all going out – the *Prinz Eugen* . . . the *Bismarck* . . . the *Tirpitz*, perhaps even the *Scharnhorst*, if we can get her seaworthy in time." The Grand Admiral's raddled old face glowed suddenly with almost youthful enthusiasm. "It is nearly a quarter of a century now," he continued, "since the terrible ignominy of Scapa Flow. Now the time has come for the German Navy to take its revenge. This time the Tommies will pay the butcher's bill in the blood of their sailors." He paused, chest heaving as if he had just run a race, staring hard at the policeman.

Müller opened his mouth, as if to ask another question, as cops always did. They never grew sick of asking questions. But he wasn't fated to ask that overwhelming question which would have made life a lot easier for him later. Instead a tall, burly civilian elbowed his way past Feuchtner, almost making him drop his glass of champagne, and hissed to Müller, "Chief, I've got an important message for . . . straight from HQ."

Raeder looked angrily at the civilian, who had Gestapo written all over him, from his cheap cigar (unlit) to his mouthful of gold teeth and ankle-length creaking leather coat. The civilian stared him out. He was "Secret State Police" wasn't he? The brass didn't impress him. He was a law unto himself.

Müller forgot Raeder immediately. Again, in the fashion of cops, he took his aide and steered him out of earshot and, when he was sure that there was no one listening, snapped. *"Los . . . raus mit der Sprache."*

The aide didn't waste any time. "Top priority call from Berlin, *Standartenführer*. Officer courier only. The—"

"Yes, yes," Müller cut him impatiently. "Forget the crap. Where's the fire?"

"Everywhere, sir. Over half a hundred Tommy POWs have escaped from Wesertimke. Just down the road from Wilhelmshaven. The Führer's hit the ceiling. You've got to get them back *now*."

"Then?"

"The other cop stuck out a forefinger like a hairy pork sausage and jerked it back and forth, as if he were pulling the trigger of a pistol. *"That!"*

Three

The sudden shriek of the siren woke Savage with a start. It was muted a little by the thick wooden wall of the barge's hold, but it was there all right. The escaper shook his head – hard. Yes, he wasn't dreaming. It was a siren all right and the shriek it made was accompanied by the steady, but urgent throb of engines. A second later, he realised he was in trouble by the metallically distorted command. "*Achtung* . . .*Achtung* . . . *Wasserschutzpolizei*!"

"Blast and bloody damn," he cursed, his heart missing a beat. It was the Hun river police.

Swiftly he squirmed out of his makeshift burrow beyond the pile of metal scrap for Hamburg's factories and clambered towards the hatch cover. Gingerly, he opened it and peered out.

A fat slattern of a woman in a man's sailor cap and boots was standing there, hands on hips, staring down at what he guessed would be the police launch below. By the look on the woman's fat face, he could guess, the cops weren't particularly welcome. He knew why. There'd be contraband aboard bound for the great port's black market. Next moment, he heard the heavy clatter of seaboots mounting the ladder fixed to the side of the Elbe barge and knew that the police were coming aboard to search the ancient craft.

Savage cast a quick look to the opposite bank of the great river away from the still hidden police launch. There, the sandy bank was covered in dense firs, their tops still wreathed in a powder of white snow. It would provide an excellent place to hide. But he'd never make it. The police, still on the launch, would undoubtedly spot the swimmer before he got that far. If he was going to make a break for it, it had to be the nearside bank. But there was still that little runt – he guessed he was the slattern woman's lover or husband. He'd spot him going over the side and shout to the men in the police launch below. It would be an obvious tactic in order to take the pressure off him and prevent the cops from searching for the barge's hidden black market wares.

Savage bit his bottom lip. What was he going to do? He hadn't come this far to get caught now. Somehow, he would have to cause a diversion and do a swift bunk while the cops were occupied elsewhere. But what?

Then he had it.

Gingerly he dropped back into the open hold. He picked up the two precious packets of camp tobacco; that was his currency, the way he'd buy himself aboard a neutral Swedish freighter at Lubeck, as was his plan. He reached the deck again. In that same instant a big red-faced policeman came over the side, pistol held in his free hand.

Savage knew why immediately. They weren't looking for black market goodies; the river police were looking for him. He didn't hesitate. Taking one of the packages, he slung it with all his strength at the slatternly woman. She yelled with surprise. But she recovered swiftly. He saw her grab the precious tobacco, worth a small fortune in the black market district around Hamburg's Dammtor Station, at the same moment that the big policeman yelled a command. It was just the distraction he needed.

In a racing dive like the one that had habitually won him the 100-yard swimming race at Dartmouth, he was over the side and racing all out for the opposite bank, blind to everything but the overwhelming knowledge that he was fighting for his very life.

The towpath and bank loomed up in front of him: a stretch of frozen white Elbe sand, a shabby church and a clutter of medieval half-timbered houses with fishing nets hanging outside to be repaired or dried.

"*Halt*," a harsh angry voice commanded behind him. "*Halt oder ich schiesse, Mensch.*"

Savage, going all out, ignored the command. Behind him the engines of the police launch burst into noisy life. The slovenly woman yelled something, but Savage couldn't make it out. He thought afterwards that she had shouted. "Give 'em one in the kisser, brave boy . . . Fuck 'em."

The cigarette diversion must have worked, because someone was refusing to hurry to cast off the line attaching the launch to the barge. Savage plunged on desperately.

He slammed into the steep slippery bank. A shot rang out. He ignored it. The slug howled off the cobbles a foot or two away in a shower of furious red sparks. Still he kept going, clambering up the bank for all he was worth.

The cop was rattled. He fired again. This time he was even wider. Below the launch, freed at last though a little alarmed and out of control, Savage had managed to knock the river policeman off his aim yet even more. Savage didn't give him time to recover. He sprang on to the towpath and started running, scattering river water everywhere. A woman, pushing a pram like a wickerwork basket on wheels, came towards him. She screamed. Savage didn't hesitate. He punched her brutally. She fell backwards, revealing her naked thighs and patched bloomers. The basket pram wobbled and went slowly over the side towards the river, the hidden baby inside screaming its head off furiously. Savage didn't even hear.

Suddenly he skidded to a halt. A man was standing in the field to his right. He was wearing a green Loden coat and a hat with a feather sticking out of it. He looked like some small-time farmer enjoying a day off, decked out in his rustic finery – and he was carrying shotgun crooked over his right shoulder!

For one long instant the two men confronted each other. Savage watched the kaleidoscope of emotions – shock, fear, determination, anger – flash across the German's honest, ruddy face. The farmer pulled the shotgun off his shoulder. He fired. One . . . two . . . both barrels.

The twin muzzles erupted in blasts of scarlet flame. Vicious little lead pellets whizzed everywhere. Savage yelped with pain. He had been hit everywhere. He did the only thing available to him. He dived back into the icy water. Next moment he was swimming for his life while the farmer, frantically to reload his shotgun before Savage got away, was yelling frantically, "Over here . . . the shit's here . . ."

By now Savage was beyond caring. He was determined never to go into the bag again. He'd rather die. He felt himself possessed of that old red blinding rage, which had been his downfall in the past. All of a sudden, though, he spotted a way out. A kind of culvert, a dark stone chamber on the side of the bank. The flags worn by the river and time, covered with slippery dark-green moss. Just as a burst of machine gun fire scythed the surface of the water, Savage dived. Above him the slugs whipped the river into an angry, wide whirlpool. He went down further. His flailing hands hit and caught on to a big square-shaped stone. He'd found the entrance to the chamber. Next moment, he was clambering inside and, slipping and slithering, he was moving deeper and deeper into the darkness, heavy with the stench of centuries.

Flame erupted behind him like a blossoming scarlet bloom. The noise of the chattering machine pistol blasting away was ear-splitting. Slugs howled off the ancient flags everywhere. Savage, gasping frantically, breath croaking through leathern lungs like that of an ancient asthmatic, slipped round the bend in the tunnel just in time.

"I can hear him," someone cried excitedly.

"Put a sock in it, arse-with-ears," another voice shouted angrily. "We'll never hear the shit if you kick up that racket."

Savage didn't hear. With the last of his ebbing strength, he ran on blindly. Now he was solely intent in putting as much space as possible between himself and his pursuers. On and on he blundered, gasping for breath. All around him in the stinking half-darkness, there was a confusion of pipes and tubes. All were covered with an ugly white dripping fungus. The slime of generations seemed to be covering them.

Behind him, magnified tenfold by the hollow tunnel, he could hear the clatter of heavy boots. They were still after him. Desperately he twisted and turned. In and out of high-roofed chambers, the slime-green walls rushing by in a crazed phantasmagoria.

He felt like screaming. Would they never give up? Madly he tried to keep control of himself. But he was weakening fast. He felt hot tears of self-pity fill his eyes.

Abruptly his feet went from beneath him. There was no saving himself. He was in space without a hold. Screaming, now in absolute panic, he found himself falling . . . falling . . . falling.

With a hellish splash he hit the pit filled with water far below. He went under, desperately fighting for breath. For a moment he panicked, terrified he was going to drown, nostrils filled with the stench of long stagnant water. But only for a moment. He broke surface, splashing frantically, to realise that he had fallen into some kind of long-abandoned drainage ditch.

With an effort of sheer naked willpower, he calmed himself. He floundered on the surface, taking stock of his circumstances. He struck out for the side. It seemed miles away. His arms sought the reassurance of a solid object. Just when he thought he was going to go under once more, his nails rasped against rough, worked stone. It was the side. With the last of his strength he held on. In that same moment as he took hold, the crunch of heavy nailed boots came level with him, high above his dripping head.

He took a deep breath. He ducked his head beneath the green scum, which parted and then closed above him almost instantly. The sound of the boots stopped. There was a faint mumble of distorted voices. A beam from a torch flashed down the pit. It swept across the surface of the green scum. Beneath it Savage could see the faint glow. He held his breath, ears pounding. With one hand he held on to the side of the pit, body motionless. The beam seemed to hover above him for an age. He knew his breath wouldn't hold out much longer. His lungs were bursting. Now red and silver stars were beginning to explode inside his head. He screamed out within himself for the beam to move on. When it seemed he couldn't last any longer, it did. The boots vanished.

He forced himself to count to five. Next moment he broke the surface with a great splash, gasping for air, breathing in the noxious foul-smelling substance in great grateful gulps. But there was triumph on his soaked, emaciated face. For the time, he had thrown off his pursuers once again. The Hun bastards still hadn't got him . . .

* * *

A hundred miles away, in the prison block at Hamburg's Altona Jail, Müller watched with seeming boredom the interrogation of the recaptured escaper from the Wesertimke Camp. He was a mere boy, fair-haired and blue-eyed – a perfect Nordic type, Müller couldn't help thinking – who didn't look old enough to have been shot down as a bomber pilot and taken prisoner. Now the boy was at the end of his tether. His right eye was blackened and through his torn shirt, Müller could see the bruised darkened flesh where he had been routinely roughed up by his captors. For the boy, it must have come as a shock to have been beaten up like that, but the average continental, Müller knew, expected the punishment for having caused the Secret Police trouble; it was standard operating procedure.

Müller continued to smoke moodily, while the interrogators' questions were translated into English for the benefit of the prisoner, who didn't speak much German. In the corner, the female secretary with the good legs typed his answers. It was all a great bore. Besides, he had realised within five minutes that the Tommy kid would be of no use for his purpose. First of all, he wasn't even British Navy. Still, dutiful cop, as he was, the head of the Gestapo listened.

At the POW camp, they had planned the great escape for months. The original intention, according to the prisoner, had been to send out over a hundred men. In the end the planners had reduced the number of escapers to fifty. To simplify papers and other items of escape, the Tommy planners had decided on three escape routes and destinations: the nearest was over the border into occupied Holland where the escaper would make contact with "the Dutch Resistance".

Müller had allowed himself a hollow, cynical laugh at that, as the crestfallen boy's answer had been translated.

Most of the Dutch did as they were told, glad of full employment and full bellies now ensured by the German war industries working all out in their "conquered" homeland. Indeed so many Dutch were now so taken by their supposed "occupiers" that they had volunteered to form a whole SS division. As for the "resistance", it was made up of work-shy individuals, petty crooks and adventurers on the make.

Then there was the escape route south and the Tommies' conviction that they would be received with open arms once they had crossed from the Reich into the neutral "Home of the Cuckoo Clock". Again, they were mistaken. For the Swiss, venal as they were, would sell their own grandmother for money. They had their "little francs", as they called their currency, for hearts. Besides the Swiss sold over sixty per cent of their exports to the Reich and were major supporters of Hitler's war industry. They were not going to risk such financial gains for the sake of a couple of escaped Tommy POWs who were still wet behind the ears in that naive English manner of theirs.

Müller took out his cheap working man's cigar, one of the makes that he favoured, and looked at the spittle-damp end, as if he could see something important there. No, he concluded, it would be the naval types he wanted: those who were heading for Lubeck and Wismar and the other small Baltic ports that traded with neutral Sweden. There he'd find the kind of Englishman he needed to carry out the plan he had begun to formulate in his devious peasant mind ever since that old fart, Raeder, had told him about the break-out and attack of Germany's surface fleet. This pathetic fly boy was useless as far as he was concerned.

Outside, the music in the *Reeperbahn* had commenced. Hamburg's pleasure area, home of pimps, pros and prosperous black marketeers, was frowned upon in the great port's more respectable quarters. How could such a disgraceful place be allowed when Germany's sons were dying in their hundreds at the front? This is what the good honest National Socialist citizens snorted. But Naval High Command knew that such a place had to exist for the pleasures of its sailors on leave. They were risking their lives, too, daily, fighting the Tommies – and there were no brothels on board ship. Hence the *Reeperbahn*, a couple of kilometres of sordid, cheap, quick thrills for sailors with too much pay in their wallets and easily excitable tools in their trousers!

Slowly the noise started to rise. It came at a good time, Müller told himself, swinging his legs off the table of the little makeshift interrogation room. It'd drown any noise the boy made when he was liquidated. He squashed out his cigar in the over-flowing ashtray and nodded to the *Scharführer*, a brutal-faced thug, who was doing the actual interrogation. "Get rid of the interpreter," he said softly.

The secretary paused, hands in the air, and looked at him and then back at the boy. Suddenly Müller thought she had a soft look on her middle-aged mug. Typical, he told himself. Women were no good for this kind of job.

The boy looked puzzled. He had expected the relentless interrogation from the ugly-faced thug to continue. Why had it stopped so abruptly? Surely they wanted to get more out of him. They knew he hadn't finished "singing like a yellow canary", as the interpreter had translated the SS man's contemptuous phrase.

Müller didn't enlighten the kid. He couldn't speak English anyway. Still he felt sorry for the young Tommy. It was not that he was a soft touch. Not as the head of the Gestapo. It was simply because the kid was like so many he had watched being questioned in his twenty-odd years of police service. They never woke up to the fact that this was the end of the road; they had said their last words, smoked their last "lung torpedo", taken their last few breaths. There was nothing more. They were dead men already. That was the sad bit. Their life had come to an end and they didn't even know it.

He waited till the interpreter and the secretary, with the nice legs, filed by him and then he nodded to the *Scharführer*, who would carry out the execution. Why bother with a trial? It would be a waste of money. The outcome would be the same. The *Scharführer* nodded back his understanding, while the kid watched the silent interchange in bewilderment.

Müller picked up his cap with its gleaming skull-and-crossbones silver badge. He passed out into the busy street, barely acknowledging the salutes of the two fat, middle-aged policemen standing there in their black leather helmets. Things were livening up in the crowded street. There were sailors and whores everywhere, grinning professionally, haggling in street corners, dragging off already drunken young gobs to their rooms to dance a quick "mattress polka" at ten marks a go. "Nothing too good for our boys in the service," they chortled, as they lifted their skirts to show their fat dimpled naked arses.

But Gestapo Müller saw hardly anything of this. His mind and mind's eye were elsewhere. He knew what he had to do. Moscow had been overjoyed, according to his control, when he had passed on to Beria – the head of the dreaded Russian secret police – the information he had received from Grand Admiral Raeder. But how was he going to carry out the plan he and his control had formulated without risking his own nesk? It had to be foolproof. Russia hadn't won the war by a long chalk.

Indeed she hadn't really entered it. At the moment Hitler and his Third Reich dominated most of Europe. For the time being he had to be careful, exceedingly careful. If anything went wrong, even the long arm of the NKVD wouldn't be able to save him.

There was a pause in the roll and drumbeat of the great Dutch organ outside the Moulin Rouge, a strange sudden – somehow awesome – silence, broken only by the snap of a single shot like that of a dry twig cracking underfoot in a summer forest. Müller knew instinctively what it was: the *Scharführer* blowing the back of the Tommy kid's head off in the prison courtyard.

An instant later the merry clatter of the Dutch organ started up again and Müller continued walking – even the drunks getting out of his way, for the little man with the enormous, shaven head and the dark sinister eyes had Gestapo written all over him. And no one, drunk or otherwise, wanted to fall foul of the Secret State Police.

Four

Every pace was sheer agony. The sudden snow came down in blinding white sheets. Desperately, he cleared the wet flakes from his face and eyes time and time again. But the wind continued to rage. Ever anew it whipped the snow against his frozen, wolfish features. Shivering almost uncontrollably, Savage carried on. Now it was only by sheer effort and determination that he was able to place one foot in front of the other in the ankle-deep snow.

At first he had been glad of the unseasonable snowstorm. He guessed it would throw the police off his tracks ever since he had left the River Elbe and began heading north-east towards Lubeck. But now the constant snow, beating down in silent fury as if some god up on high was determined to bury him beneath it, had turned into a nightmare. More than once he had been tempted to simply throw himself down in its soft whiteness and sleep . . . perhaps for ever.

But he had always caught himself just in time. Through gritted teeth he had snarled, "No, you Hun bastards . . . you won't get me . . . I won't die . . . Do you hear me? I *won't*!" The words were torn from his mouth by the wind, but the challenge remained. He was going to keep on. *He had to.* And Savage did. He slogged across the seemingly endless North German plain, fighting the merciless snow-heavy wind, a pathetic little creature lost in that howling wilderness.

At two o'clock that afternoon, he knew he couldn't go

on. With the sky as black as night and the snow still falling in solid sheets, he took shelter in a small grove of firs that made up the boundary of some side road. Here he tried to take stock of his position.

His camp-made compass – a razorblade magnetised in a light socket and a piece of stiff cardboard from one of the Swiss Red Cross parcels, paid for by the British taxpayer – functioned perfectly. He was still well on course on the left bank of the Elbe, heading for the two bridges crossing the river eastwards at Lauenburg. Here it would be his intention to cross the river by the railway bridge, which he guessed wouldn't be guarded, and head north-east for the Baltic coast, some fifty or so kilometres away.

It was then that he looked down at his "civvies": a dyed black battledress suit, which had been stained with printer's ink. Now the ink had run and was patchy from the effects of the sewage in the conduit. In this outfit, as it was now, he knew he'd stand out like a sore thumb once he got among the Germans again. And he knew, too, that sooner or later he'd have to mingle with them when he reached the Baltic searching for a Swedish ship. Besides the whole damn outfit stank to high heavens. "No, old man," he said softly to himself in the manner of lonely – or mad – people who speak to themselves a lot, "you've got to get yerself some other clobber . . . and you've got to get out of this blasted freezing snow before your goolies drop off."

That particularly terrible thought gave him a new burst of energy. If he moved closer to the river somewhere to his right, he'd be bound to find inhabited places; there were always houses close to a river, especially one which was a major trade route as the Elbe was. There, there would be clothes. But would he be able to buy them with the marks stuffed into his breast pocket, the result of months spent bribing guards by means of his cigarette ration? He doubted it. He had an uneasy feeling that the Huns had clothing coupons just as the folk back home did. Money wouldn't be very useful then. He bit his cracked chapped lip and winced at the sudden pain. There was only one other alternative. His hand slid into his trouser pocket and felt the cold lethal hardness of the jack-knife that rested there. If there was no other way, well . . .

An hour later, the fugitive spotted the yellow gleam of a petroleum lamp shining through the scraggy, snow-heavy firs to his right. He paused wearily. He wiped the wet snowflakes from his face to get a better view.

It was a typical red brick-and-wattle construction of the area. Low and long, it had yellow dried tobacco leaves drying under its eaves and, from the building towards the end of the dwelling area there, with steam rising from the tiny open window slats, came the warm animal smell of cows. It was obviously a small, one-family farm with both the humans and the animals living under the same roof.

The thought of warmth and hot food made Savage shiver with anticipation. All the same he forced himself to watch the lonely little farm for a solid half-hour while the snow fell softly and, sadly, muting the sound of the cows. It was occupied, he could see that. There was thick blue wood smoke coming from the main chimney and there were tracks, already disappearing quickly in the snow, around the main door. But how many people were there in the place? He couldn't even guess. All he could surmise was that such a small farm wouldn't be able to support more than a farmer and his wife, plus one of the Polish or French prisoners-of-war being hired out by the local *Kreisleiter* as a labourer.

In the end, after he had seen nothing move for nearly three quarters of an hour, with his body turning to ice as he crouched there, he decided it was now or never. Soon it would be dark and he didn't want to be surprised in the act by some latecomer arriving at the house after work or such like. It was time to go,

Cautiously, open jack-knife clutched to his right hip, he moved through the snow, grateful that it muffled any sound he might make as he passed through the open gate and advanced upon the old farm. Foot by foot he crept ever closer. There was no sound save the hiss of the snowstorm and the wind in the skeletal trees. Inside the house nothing stirred. No one had even moved to put up the blackout, though perhaps in this remote area, they didn't worry about such things.

Suddenly there was a low growl, accompanied by the rattle of a chain to his right. "A bloody dog," he cursed.

Behind the barn a dog of some kind was presumably tied up and, despite the snowstorm, it had obviously scented him. In half a minute it would begin barking and sounding the alarm. There was no time for further caution. He had to act *now*!

Throwing all caution to the wind, panting hard, as if he were running a great race, he flung open the door, knife held aloft, ready to plunge it into the body of anyone who attempted to oppose him.

Sitting next to the great tiled oven which reached to the ceiling, the old crone dropped her knitting in panic. Her bent hand flew to her scraggy, veined throat.

Savage was taking no chances. Even if her yellowed teeth bulged from her trembling lips in abject fear, he advanced upon her. Meaningless words tumbled from her quavering mouth.

"Listen," he cried in his best German. "You scream . . . I kill . . . *Verstanden*?" He slashed the air viciously with his knife to make his meaning clear. The saliva of fear started to trickle in streams from her wrinkled hairy chin. "*Verstanden*?" he rasped again.

The old woman didn't trust herself to speak. She nodded her head rapidly. Savage relaxed and lowered the knife.

"Other men . . . women here?" he queried.

The old crone pulled herself together. She understood that the stranger wasn't going to slit her skinny throat after all. She shook her head and managed to croak, "*Nee.*"

Savage gave her a fake smile and, very slowly and deliberately, while she watched, hypnotised, he closed the jack-knife and carefully put it in his pocket. Now he placed both hands deliberately on the warm tiles of the *Kachelofen*. It was another gesture to show the crone that he intended her no harm, if she behaved herself. "*Hunger,*" he said loudly, as if he were talking to an idiot . . . "*Essen . . . bitte . . .*"

She understood. She rose with an audible creak of ancient bones. Still terrified, she smoothed her way past this soaked, unshaven intruder and fled into the kitchen. Moments later he watched through the open door as she held a great round loaf of dark bread – "a wheel", the Huns called it – to her weak breast and sliced off the chunks, while in front of her on the wooden stove, the salt bacon lumps sizzled nicely.

For the first time since he had escaped from the camp, Lieutenant-Commander Savage smiled. "Thank God for old Adolf," he muttered to himself, "he certainly taught the female of the species where her place is – in the kitchen."

So it was that for a while Savage, at peace at last, lounged outside the open kitchen door, watching the old crone and sniffing the delightful smells coming from the old iron, wood-burning stove with mouthwatering anticipation.

But only for so long . . .

Despite the howl of the wind, Savage heard the steps crunching slowly over the frozen snow of the little patch that led up to the door. There was someone coming. Suddenly he was one hundred per cent alert, the adrenalin surging through his tired body. He flashed a look at the woman. She had heard nothing. She was devoting herself whole-heartedly to the task of frying his chunks of *Speck* and the *Bratkartoffeln* which she had mixed with the pieces of salt bacon. Obviously she wasn't expecting anyone at this time. Otherwise her brain, old as it was, would have been prepared for someone coming and she would have recognised the sound already. So who was it?

Savage didn't know. All he knew was that the approaching footsteps spelled danger.

He grabbed for his knife, thought better of it and, glancing around, wildly, spotted one of those great paddles German housewives used to beat their carpets. That would do. One blow from that and there would be no dangerous grappling with whomever was now approaching the door. He'd be out like a light with a bit of luck. Then when he had dealt with the unknown visitor, he could decide what to do next. Taking a deep breath, he grasped the wooden paddle more firmly.

The footsteps halted. He heard the scraping, once twice. The visitor was clearing the snow away from his feet on the old-fashioned scraper. Savage held his breath. The door was beginning to open. "*Oma*," a cheerful, rather light voice called, "*Ich bin . . .*"

Savage raised the beater. His hand felt wet with sweat.

"Granny," the voice called again. In the kitchen the old woman turned, a sudden beam on her wrinkled old face. "*Ach, du bist—*"

Savage caught a glimpse of a slim body muffled in an old Polish Army greatcoat and surmounted by a pretty glowing face. But even before the old crone could complete her welcome, the beater came slamming down and the woman was reeling against the wall, face suddenly pale with shock, her silk blonde hair abruptly turning red with blood . . .

Five

"*Here the shitehawks come agen,*" the *Obermaat* yelled above the sudden roar of massed plane engines. "*Off port bow . . . green five-O . . . Lead 'em into it, yer bunch of frigging candy asses . . . Look lively now!*"

Standing on the deck next to Rear Admiral Doenitz, head of the submarine service, Grand Admiral Raeder shook his head, as if he couldn't believe his own ears. "How coarse these new sailors have become, Doenitz," he said severely. "In my days, any petty officer using that kind of language would be behind Swedish curtains," he meant the bars of a jail, "very quickly indeed." He shook his greying head once again.

"*Jawohl, Herr Grossadmiral,*" Doenitz answered dutifully, though in fact, he had nothing but contempt for his superior and his old-fashioned attitude. He didn't give a damn how much his U-boat boys cursed, damned and fornicated, as long as they continued sending plenty of Tommy ships to the bottom of the sea.

The Tommy bombers were coming in at the usual height, which the flak concentrated upon without much difficulty. As Doenitz told himself, the English were methodical, pedantic creatures; they always stuck to the same sort of tactics. Now the ship's anti-aircraft guns were rounding away with routine precision throwing up a lethal chain-mesh of shot and shell in front of the first V of Wellington bombers. Still, as routine as they were, the Tommy pilots were brave fools; they kept on coming.

Down below the *Obermaat* in charge of the quadruple twenty millimetre flak cannons – blasting away at a tremendous rate so that the tracer shells seemed to be shooting upwards in a solid wall of white fury – was yelling above the hellish racket, "Hit the buggers, or by the Great Whore of Buxtehudem where the dogs piss through their ribs, I'll take the vaseline to your pansy asses this very night. If it's the last frigging thing I do, I swear I will!"

Doenitz's cold, calculating face cracked into a grin again. That particular *Obermaat* would be losing his "stars" in zero, comma, nothing, if he kept swearing like that in front of Grand Admiral Raeder. The old naval chief was like some virginal well-born old maid. Next moment the grin disappeared from Doenitz's face almost as soon as it had appeared.

The Tommies were trying a new tactic. Under the cover of the approaching V of Wellington bombers, on which the ship's anti-aircraft artillery was concentrating all its fire, three old-fashioned biplanes had appeared from the smoke of battle. They were coming in at seatop level. Their propellors lashed the sea below into a white fury, as they swerved from side to side, laden down as they were with a great two-ton torpedo fixed beneath their undercarriage.

"Swordfish!" Raeder breathed. "I thought the English Navy had withdrawn them from service because last year's fiasco up north." He meant the battle for Norway.

"Doesn't look like it, sir," Doenitz said, face set and sombre now. Although his love affair with his U-boats was almost all-embracing, he *was* a member of the German Navy; and he knew these obsolete British planes could inflict tremendous damage on even these most modern of German ships, especially if they got lucky with their damned all-powerful "tin fish".

Raeder knew it, too. He turned and, with surprising

energy for such an old pedantic officer, he yelled to his orderly, "Lieutenant, at the double. Get the gunner officer. Switch flak on to those damned flying canvas bags."

"Sir." The young elegant officer immediately flew across the ship's deck, littered with battle debris, towards the ladder that led up to the gunnery officer's control room, as if the Devil himself were at his heels. To starboard the old-fashioned British planes, wave-hopping now, came on with grim determination . . .

"Well," Commander Jensen asked, as "Pox" waddled into the wardroom, totally unconcerned by the English attack, "how's Old Wheels" – he meant Raeder – "getting on? After all, he's not used to having all this Tommy shit flung at him."

"Pox", otherwise Surgeon-Lieutenant von Mauz, one of the great ship's doctors, said, "Shitty." He sat down abruptly and helped himself to one of the bottles of schnapps on the silver tray right beneath the forbidding gaze of the Führer, who, as every one knew, hated alcohol. He pulled put the cork with his excellent teeth and poured himself a stiff peg. "*Prost*," he said to himself, and downed the fiery liquid in one go. He gasped and said, "That hit the frigging spot."

Commander Jensen affected concern and disapproval, "I say, Doctor," he intoned, "It's not yet zero ten hundred hours. Bit early for the old fire-water, isn't it?"

"My guts can't tell the time," the bespectacled Pox replied sourly.

Jensen smiled sympathetically. He could understand how the MO felt. He was responsible for the VD rate on board the ship. It was an unenviable position. There were two certainties in the life of the average sailor in the German Navy: he was going to get drunk and he was going to get a dose. It was the nature of the beast and all the threats and punishments in this world couldn't stop either eventuality. "Siff rate gone up again?" he enquired politely. He took a sip of his coffee.

Despite the Führer's forbidding gaze, Pox helped himself to another stiff drink. "No, it's that arse-with-ears Doenitz."

"Tut, tut," Jensen admonished him. "Not our beloved U-boat Führer."

"Yes, he's talking to Old Wheels ten to the dozen. They don't even seem to notice the Tommies dropping square eggs on their heads."

"So?"

"So," Pox answered hotly, "He's trying to put one over on Old Wheels. You know, Doenitz and those U-boats of his. He thinks that the sun shines out of the arse of his submariners. It's the only war he knows and if we get shafted in his attempts to give them the premier place in the sea war, then it's hard shit for us."

"My dear Pox," Commander Jensen said with apparent ease, but all the same his handsome face looked worried, "your years of looking at the diseased sexual organs of generations of naughty sailors have coarsened you, old chap. But be that as it may, what can we do about it—"

But before the MO could answer that particular question, a burning biplane came flashing by the nearest porthole, trailing a scarlet, searing flame behind it. An instant later the whole great ship rocked like a child's toy ship on a lake, as it exploded, torpedo and all, sending the two officers sliding the length of the wardroom, accompanied by breaking bottles and glasses. Up above Grand Admiral Raeder desperately clung on to the rail, as the ship heaved and wallowed, debris flying everywhere, with the severed Tommy pilot's head racing across the sky in front of him, complete with leather helmet and severed wireless leads.

Next to Raeder the much younger and more agile Doenitz recovered swiftly, saying a little breathlessly,

"I think we've cured that particular Tommy flyboy's headache for him – *permanently*."

Raeder watched as the head struck the water, bounced a couple of times and then vanished. He said severely, "He was some mother's son, I shouldn't doubt."

"Old fart," an angry voice at the back of Doenitz's shaven head rasped in sudden anger, "why does he frigging well moralise to me?" He remembered the Führer's words to him the last time he had attended one of his conferences at his mountain fastness in the remote Bavarian Alps. "Doenitz," the leader had intoned solemnly, "I wish all my soldiers were like your 'Blue Boys'" – he had meant Doenitz's submariners – "as tough as Krupp steel, as fast as greyhounds and hard as leather. This nation will go under unless it is more ruthless, purposeful and murderous than its opponents." And then he had added something *sotto voce* so that the other brass present couldn't hear, "My eye, Doenitz, rests very favourably on you and your command – it may well be that I shall call upon you sooner than you think."

Doenitz had long learned to distrust the veiled promises of great men, but he had thought that the Führer had been making him an offer, that if Raeder failed with his surface ships, he would take over with his "Blue Boys" and start a campaign of unrestricted warfare, which he had long advocated and which would finally bring the damned buck-teethed English down to their knees where they had long damned well belonged.

Another obsolete British torpedo bomber had come winging in through the drifting anti-aircraft smoke, specked with cherry-red spurts of exploding shells. It, too, was flying at wave-level, dragging its prop wash behind it. Doenitz flung up his binoculars, the look of the hunter suddenly on his lean hard face. He could see the face of the pilot and then that of the observer slide noiselessly into the gleaming calibrated rings of the glass. They were set and determined: the look of two men doomed to a sudden death.

Doenitz felt no pity. Indeed he was animated by the opposite: a feeling burning rage. How dare the Tommies dare attack Germany's ships like this at their home anchorage. They deserved to die – and soon.

They did. The gunners concentrated all their fire on the lone, slow plane. They knew if that enormous torpedo hit them, they were done for. Now they poured a murderous hail of hot steel on the plane, as it came in on its final ride of death. At that range, they simply could not miss.

Great chunks of metal started to fly from the Swordfish's fuselage. The rigging went. The wings flapping almost out of control. Desperately, his face contorted under the leather helmet, the young pilot fought to keep the stricken plane from plunging into the sea. "What a brave young fool," Raeder said, as if to himself, as he adjusted the setting of his glasses. "Why doesn't he jump for it, while he still has time?"

Doenitz's face flushed with anger. God, Raeder was already in his dotage. When did you win a war by having pity on your enemies. *Hate* – that was the name of the game. You had to hate your enemy with every damned fibre of your body. It was the only way.

Now the plane was beginning to burn. Greedy little blue flames were beginning to lick up about the fuselage. Smoke, white and thick, was already pouring from the engine. It was only a matter of moments. Nothing could save the Tommy plane. But would the pilot be able to loose his torpedo before his Swordfish went totally out of control and dropped into the sea? Doenitz felt himself start to sweat heavily. His hands gripping the binoculars abruptly turned into white-knuckled claws. He was suddenly panting as if he were running a great race. He gasped. He's doing it!

The pilot was. In his dying moments, he had thrown all concern about the safety of himself and his observer to the winds. Slowly he was hand cranking the torpedo, jammed a little between the wheels of the shattered undercarriage, down and down so that he was then in a position to fire it – and at that range, he couldn't possibly miss.

But now his luck had run out. Just as he had cleared the wheels with his torpedo, the *Obermaat* with the "loose, filthy tongue," as Raeder had snapped, pulled off a feat which would earn him the Iron Cross, First Class, from the Führer himself, though he would never live to receive it personally from that quarter. Under his direction, a massive burst of nearly 1,000 twenty millimetre cannon shells from the quadruple flak gun slammed straight into the stricken plane. It disappeared in an instant. One minute it was there; the next it wasn't. All that remained of it was the patter of shattered metal striking the surface of the sea for a few moments like a heavy tropical downpour. And then all was silent . . .

Five minutes later it was all over. The ship's sirens were sounding the all-clear. Fire control parties in their heavy fire-proof suits looking like creatures from an alien planet rushed back and forth; while on the quays the ambulance from Wilhelmshaven's naval hospital rushed to the scene of the bombing, sirens shrieking their urgent warning.

Slowly, thoughtfully, automatically dodging the battle debris which now littered the once spotless deck of the great ship, the two admirals walked back to their quarters, deep frowns on both their faces. Jensen, watching them from the open door of the wardroom, said to "Pox", "They look like some of your patients, who have just been told they've got a full house, gon and siff."

Pox ignored the dig. Instead he said, "Look at Doenitz. The cunning bugger's up to something – you can see that on his shitting Polack face."

Jensen eyed the U-boat commander with his high Slavic cheekbones and sharp features, telling himself Doenitz's mouth always seemed to be worked by a tight steel spring. Yes, he concluded that the younger Admiral did have a Polish look about him. "Wonder what they're talking about, Pox?" he asked.

"Nothing good for Old Wheels, you can bet your bottom dollar on that," the little MO replied. "Doenitz is up to his old tricks. Sooner or later he's gonna find the right tack and then Old Wheels will be out on his neck and we big ship folk will be out there with him." He shivered dramatically. "Fancy being a medic in one of Doenitz's subs."

Like so many other big ship sailors, Jensen was terrified at the thought of being posted to Doenitz's underwater tin cans. "We've got to do something about it," he said after a few moments of watching the two admirals disappear towards their own state rooms.

"What?"

"Well, like trying to stop Doenitz talking Old Wheels into doing something which will spell the end – or mothballing the surface fleet."

"What, for instance?" Pox asked bluntly, suddenly remembering that in an hour's time he had to administer what the sailors called the "umbrella" to half a dozen unfortunates.

"How do I know?" Jensen blurted out in sudden worriedy irritation. "Am I Jesus? Do I walk on water? All I know is that Doenitz is up to no shitting good."

And Commander Karl Jensen was right. Doenitz had plans. And they didn't bode well for Grand Admiral Raeder and his surface ships.

Six

Gestapo Müller was angry. Not in that flushed, loud-mouthed excitable manner he used both to frighten and impress prisoners. Now his anger was a low-key burn that no one else but he might have noticed. But this kind of anger in a man of his nature, and with the vast power he commanded, was of a much more deadly kind. It was that type of rage that, in the past, had impelled him to order the destruction of whole villages and the systematic slaughter of their helpless populations. And, as usual with Gestapo Müller, this slow burning rage had been occasioned by very small and relatively unimportant matters.

Two hours before he had felt the need for sexual relief. It was a problem of no great momentum. But in his peasant fashion, he felt that one satiation of this physical need would ensure great mental ability. So it was that he turned to the senior officers' brothel located in a fine old turn-of-the-century house overlooking the harbour.

It had been a bad mistake. Right from the start he had realised that he had been unwelcome there, although he was prepared to pay for the services offered instead of trying to avoid payment like most Gestapo officers did, who traded on their fearsome reputation to get what they wanted.

The other officers, drinking and smoking their cigars, occasionally glancing at the racked newspapers while they waited their turn to be called upstairs, ignored him and even the Madam, big bosomy and blousy treated him like some village yokel who had wandered into her "establishment" by mistake.

The whore she had allotted him – "very much your type, *Standartenführer*" she had assured him, "a good hard-working girl, ready to put her heart into it" – had turned out to be disappointing.

She had been fat, flabby with pendulous breasts, the nipples painted bright red and hanging down to her belly folds of lard. Even as she prepared to slump into the untidy stained bed with him, she had continued eating her chocolates, as if her very life depended upon it, licking her nicotine-stained fingers after every supposedly delicate bite. As Müller had loosened his trousers belt, he had told himself grimly, "This is going to be like climbing shitting Mount Everest without the shitting oxygen." And his description of the act hadn't proved far wrong.

In the end, the whore had promised a "free go" next time "when you're in better mood, *Standartenführer*" but had obstinately refused to return to him even part of the agreed-upon price. The Gestapo had obviously cut no ice with her. She had called after him as he had slunk somewhat shamefacedly down the stairs, avoiding the looks of the place's other clients, "You can't expect a working girl to do the impossible, after all, *Standartenführer*," and he could see from the expression on the others' faces that they had supposed he had demanded some impossible perversion from the whore. Even as he had hurried to his waiting staff car, his ears were burning as he imagined what they were already relating *sotto voce* to their fellows.

But the unfortunate incident with the local whore palled in Müller's mind in comparison with the other item which occasioned his rage this dark winter's afternoon. It was really a failing on his own part and Gestapo Müller, who had been a professional cop since he was nineteen, hated to slip up on the job.

He knew that he had slipped up badly in the matter of the escaped POWs, when Eichmann, of all people, telephoned him from the Gestapo HQ in Prinz Albrecht Strasse, Berlin, to point out that the Führer had called personally. Eichmann, the only senior officer present, had taken the phone call and had been on the receiving end of the leader's wrath when the latter had discovered that there were still so many escapers at liberty.

According to Eichmann, who Müller thought was a typical Austrian lightweight with a head full of crazy ideas like his countryman, Hitler, the Führer had snorted, "Do you expect me to tell you damned policemen your own job? Haven't I got enough problems on my hands running a war, Eichmann?"

Eichmann, petrified at speaking to the Führer personally – Müller had guessed he'd probably been standing to attention as he had held the phone – had mumbled something and had waited apprehensively.

He had related Hitler's words to his boss, Müller. "The Führer said, 'the matter is quite simple. It only needs a bit of common sense to round these Tommy criminals up within twenty-four hours at the most'."

Müller had been inclined to interrupt his subordinate, but then he thought better of it – could he trust Eichmann? – and had held his peace.

"The Führer said, 'it's a matter of organising the checks and controls on specific points where one could expect the escapers to appear as they make their way to their various objectives. Seal off the area purposefully and logically, instead of wasting men and time in mass searches . . .'" Eichmann had continued relating the leader's words, ending with that undeniable threat that the Austrian blowhard, Hitler, always used when thwarted, "If Müller can't do it, then he'd better let someone else take his place who can." And with that he had slammed down the phone in one of those blind rages of his, leaving Eichmann trembling with fear and "heiling" a dead phone for all he was worth.

Still, an angry Müller told himself as he stared out of the big picture window, the Führer was right for a change – he had never paid even lip-service to Hitler's supposed infallibity. There had to be a simple way of ensuring that his unsuspecting Tommy escapers walked right into the net he was preparing for them – and quickly at that.

He turned from the window and strode over to the map of the Baltic area which covered the entire wall behind him. Right from the first instant he could see that anyone moving eastwards from the POW camp at Wesertimke and heading for the Baltic ports and the ships which linked them with neutral Sweden was faced with a major barrier – the natural one of the River Elbe.

Müller frowned and peered a little short-sightedly at the map, trying to make out the bridges which spanned the great waterway in the upper part of the Elbe. Naturally Hamburg looked the easiest option. But only at first sight. There, there were several bridges running from west to east. But anyone trying to reach them would be confronted by the task of covering the length of Germany's second greatest city, full of police, informers and soldiers on duty. Hamburg was out.

The Baltic, 1941

Müller posed there thoughtfully. Outside, despite the weather, a group of half-naked recruits to the *Kriegsmarine* were being put through their paces by a typically sadistic instructor. He was making a right sow out of them.

"Up . . . up," he cried and when the recruits were running, he was already bellowing, "down . . . down," making them slam to the snowy, slushy ground so that their soaked training uniforms became even wetter. Müller knew the drill; he had been through it himself as a young soldier back in the First World War. Soon they'd be unable to get up, lying there in the dirt panting and exhausted. Then the instructor would approach – with majestic slowness – and shore his big boot in the small of their skinny backs and force their faces into the muck.

Müller, who had tortured more people than he cared to remember in the course of his long career with the police, didn't like it – he didn't like it one bit. It was part of a system, that of the "monocle Fritzes", which he hated and which, in part, had made him take the dangerous course he had now embarked upon.

Abruptly he dismissed the pathetic recruits and their sadistic taskmaster and concentrated on the job at hand. Again he peered short-sightedly at the big map. No, Hamburg was out, he told himself, and the fugitive wouldn't have the resources and energy to try out the minor bridges along the Elbe which ran through Germany till it reached the sea. He'd have to go for the bridges between – say – Magdeburg in the south up to those below Hamburg around Geesthacht and Lauenburg. Here there was not only a road bridge but a railway bridge, carrying the main line from Berlin to Hamburg.

He tugged at the end of his big nose thoughtfully. Apart from the Hamburg bridges, those at Lauenburg were the ones closest to the camp at Wesertimke, from which the damned Tommies had escaped and caused all the panic. Was Geesthacht-Lauenburg, the point where he should concentrate his forces? Thereafter anyone on the run would have half a dozen Baltic ports to choose from and that would make his task very much more difficult. What was he to do?

Outside the instructor had finished with making sows of the trainees – for this day. He was shouting, "When we move off, you shitting asparagus Tarzans, I want a song to impress the CO. And none of yer shitting lame-assed singing. I want yer shouting off the words, as if you frigging well belonged to the frigging *Leibstandarte*." He meant the premier SS regiment, the Adolf Hitler bodyguard regiment. "Now then a song – One, two, three . . . '*Auf der Heide bluht ein Roselein . . . und das heisst Erika . . .*'"

They joined in. Without enthusiasm. Müller watched them go, trailing dripping water behind them, no strength left in their young bodies. Cannon fodder, he told himself, just rotten old cannon fodder, boys doomed to die young before they had even begun to live.

Then he dismissed them, as if they had never even existed, to concentrate on his current tasks. He scribbled out his orders, which were to be sent out immediately to all Gestapo stations along the line of the Elbe up to Hamburg. His local men would, in their turn, alert the uniformed cops, plus the battalions responsible for the country's internal security in that region. By midday, Müller reasoned, as he scribbled furiously in that tiny, almost illegible handwriting of his, the whole area would be standing by at red alert. The Tommies – he wanted to catch them alive – wouldn't stand a chance now.

By eleven that morning, Müller's rage had passed and he was feeling quite pleased with himself. Things were proceeding smoothly and according to plan. By tomorrow evening he'd be returning home to Berlin to his pious Roman Catholic wife and his very *un-pious* secretary-mistress. He smiled coldly at the thought. One way or another, it was going to be an enjoyable weekend.

But just as he was about to get carried away by these thoughts, there was an urgent knock at his door and even before he could call "*Herein*", Milz, his personal assistant burst in, face red and excited, eyes bulging from beneath his bottle-lensed nickel glasses. "*Standartenführer* . . . *Standartenführer* . . . important news!"

Müller held up his hands for peace, snapping. "Hold your horses, Milz. Now get your breath back and tell me what's so important."

The little man gulped and swallowing his own spit, he said, "Just come in from our man at Raeder's HQ. You know, sir, that big *Oberkommissar* who drinks so much . . . Barthels or what—"

"Get on with it, *please*, Milz."

"*Jawohl, Standartenführer* . . . sorry. Well, sir, Barthels has just called from across the bay. The High Sea Fleet is to pull out first tide tomorrow morning. Zero six hundred hours to be exact."

"What?"

"Thought you'd be surprised, *Standartenführer*. I nearly popped out of my pants, if you'll forgive the phrase, when I heard it."

"But where . . . where is the fleet going?" Müller stuttered.

"Barthels doesn't know exactly, but the buzz at Old Wheels' HQ is that it's bound for further up the Baltic – Danzig to be exact."

"*Danzig*," Müller echoed, totally confused now. "But why Danzig, for God's sake?"

But the pop-eyed little Gestapo man had no answer to that particular, overwhelming question . . .

BOOK TWO

Enter James Bond

One

Dawn.

Silent and sinister, the British submarine sailed at periscope depth into the shallows. This was the most dangerous part of the whole mission: the penetration of the Baltic.

One arm hanging over the periscope, battered cap stuck at the back of his head, Lieutenant de Vere turned the instrument through its 360 degrees slowly and carefully. Watching him in the fetid, green-glowing area of the control compartment, any uninitiated observer might have thought the submarine's skipper was terribly complacent and nonchalant – in the best British public school fashion. But de Vere was anything but. At the side of his pale face a nerve was ticking electrically, out of control and his breath was coming in fast, frightened gasps. For he knew better than most – he had carried out this death-defying mission more than once – just how dangerous the situation was. One slip, one wrong move and he and his crew might well be "sitting on a frigging cloud learning to play a frigging harp, with St Peter leading the frigging orchestra."

A satisfied de Vere turned the periscope to survey the block ship anchored to their front. In the sun's thin rays of the new day, it was outlined a stark black, rocking slightly as it rode at anchor. It might well have been abandoned, its crew long gone, leaving it to grow ever more rusty. But the young sub-skipper knew that wasn't the case.

Down below, men like themselves would be busy at

their instruments, listening and checking, alert for the slightest indication that some unauthorised intruder was attempting to penetrate the Baltic and the anchorage of the German surface fleet beyond. One signal from the rusty old tub, which creaked alarmingly every time it was hit by a wave and the whole of northern Germany – airforce and fleet – would be alerted. Then all hell would be let loose and HMS *Defiant* would be easy meat in these shallow waters. Soon the posh accent of the BBC's radio announcer would be intoning, "The Admiralty regrets to announce that one of His Majesty's submarines is reported missing, presumed lost at sea . . ."

Swiftly de Vere dismissed that unpleasant thought and ordered softly, "Tube . . . down ten."

Carruthers, de Vere's number one, responded immediately. There was a hiss of compressed air and the shining steel periscope slid down until its head and the gleaming circle of calibrated glass protruded just above the dirty brown water of the entrance to the Baltic.

Now slowly and silently, praying that the head of the periscope was not making too much of a tell-tale white ripple, de Vere steered the submarine slowly by the block ship. Time seemed to move on leaden feet. Over and over again, he cast a glance through the scope at the German guard ship. But nothing moved there, save a thin trickle of smoke now coming from her stack. It indicated that the cook was in his galley preparing the crew's breakfast. That reassured the young officer; it was perfectly normal. "All shipshape and Bristol fashion?" his number one asked.

De Vere, arms hung over the periscope, nodded, "Yes. Only I wish they'd put out some buoys to indicate the channel."

"Mines?" his second-in-command uttered the dread word.

"Yes, mines," the skipper answered, forcing himself to

fight against superstition. He didn't want to join all the other average submariners in their rows to avoid words that could bring upon disaster if spoken aloud. Nor was he going to indulge himself in all the other talismans of the submarine service – teddies, silk stockings, lucky rabbits' feet and all the rest of the junk with which his men hoped to ward off doom. Constant alertness was the only answer.

They ploughed on. Now they were beginning to leave the rusty old tub behind them. To the east, the sky was getting brighter. That was good. He reasoned that decent weather would bring the crab and shrimp fishermen out from Emden and Cuxhaven and the other coastal fishing ports. An unarmed fishing boat on its own, manned by a couple of crew, would be just what he needed.

Again time crept by leadenly. Now that they had left the block ship behind and that there were no other signs of danger in the vicinity, the crew began to relax. Here and there men whistled tonelessly as they carried out their duties. Back in the crews' cramped quarters the smell of bangers tempted the men. Sausages, even navy issue "pussers", always cheered the boys up, de Vere, still at the periscope, told himself. There might even be a fried egg thrown in. Now *that* would be a real treat!

Suddenly, startlingly, he caught his breath at a noise. It was very faint, but there was no mistaking it. Metal grating against metal. Instantly a cold finger of fear traced its way down the small of de Vere's hunched back.

For a moment he thought his imagination was playing tricks upon him. But when that dread sound came again and a look of fear flashed across his number one's ashen face, he knew it wasn't. He reacted immediately. "Stop engines." he hissed.

Number one echoed the order urgently.

The engines died. The sub's pace stopped almost

immediately. But the terrible sound didn't go away. Now, instead of the grating of metal on metal, there was a soft steel knocking noise on the hull. De Vere knew what it was, but it was for Chalky White to put the name of the sound into words. "Christ," he hissed, "a chained mine!"

The start of fear at the announcement was almost tangible. Instantly all eyes were focused on the young skipper. De Vere was as afraid as the rest, though. There was little even a skipper could do in such a situation.

They had run into a minefield; with mines – rather than floating loose as they might do in an enemy war zone, their acoustics activated and propelling them towards enemy vessels – anchored at regular depths to prevent any intruder penetrating the position. With a loose mine, a cool-headed skipper might stand a chance. But with a tethered mine, the submarine commander had to rely upon blind luck. There was no way he could deal with the mine from within the sub. He could only sail on at the lowest possible speed, hoping that if the sub's hull struck one of the mine's horns, it would do so gently, failing to activate the charge which would rip the guts out of the under-water craft.

Number one looked at de Vere's face, now grey with fear. De Vere pulled himself together, "Well, at least we'll all make handsome corpses," he said, suddenly smiling, though he had never felt less like smiling in all his life. "All right, we can't go back really, so let's go forward. Number one. Both ahead – dead slow."

Chalky White, the crew's cockney comedian, broke the tension by crossing himself and intoning solemnly in a gravelike voice, "For what we are about to receive, may the good Lord make us truly thankful."

De Vere could have kissed him.

Slowly, very slowly, with every man tensed for the

explosion that could come at any moment and send the submarine to the bottom of the channel for ever, the craft pressed on. Desperately, nerves tingling electrically, de Vere pressed his eyes to the periscope, turning up the amplifier so that his range was magnified and enhanced, searching for the first sign of those deadly infernal machines that he and his crew passionately despised.

But luck was on their side.

For an instant, he couldn't believe his own eyes. Then he knew that he wasn't seeing things. He had run right into a small fleet of fishing boats, the typical shrimping craft of the Frisian coast: small, with red sails, trawling the customary lopsided net behind them. But that wasn't all. The half a dozen or so boats were heading straight for him into the minefield and it was clear that they weren't going to stop when they came level with the block ship. They were going to proceed even further out.

De Vere reacted immediately, realising instantly that he could use the German small craft to his own advantage. "Stop engines," he commanded. Then he shouted, "Down periscope."

"What?" His number two commenced.

De Vere held up his hand for immediate silence. "Silent running," he hissed urgently. "Every man on listening watch. A group of Hun fishing boats—" He didn't finish his words. For he could already hear the steady hard throb-throb of ancient engines approaching over his head. The Huns were almost on top of them . . .

"We want a body, Lieutenant," the Flag Officer at Harwich had announced, as if he made statements of that nature every day. "More than one, if possible."

"Yes sir, I understand," de Vere had replied, though of course he hadn't understood one tiny little bit. Two hours before, just after entering the naval docks, at Harwich, with not a kill to his name after a two-week patrol in the Atlantic and North Sea, he had been summoned to go straight off to the Admiral's HQ. As he shaved off his pathetic beard and struggled into his uniform, he had told himself that he was in for a rocket. This was the second fighting patrol from which he had returned without a "kill" to his name. They might even give him the boot, he thought, and send him down south for further training. Such things did happen. Christ, they might even keep him at HQ!

But the Flag Officer, very grand, whose broad chest was heavy with the ribbons of the Old War, had soon enlightened him that he was being sent on another mission almost immediately. "Refuel, re-victual and give the men a twenty-four hour shore leave – local – before you set off again, my lad," the Flag Officer had said.

"Yes sir," de Vere had managed to stutter. "All a bit sudden, if I may say so, sir."

"You may, de Vere," the other officer in the room had said in his booming hail-fellow-well-met fashion. "But the signal's just come in from the Admiralty and I think I know who's behind their Lordships on this one," he lowered that overloud voice of his, "Winnie himself," he confided.

The submarine commander had been impressed. Churchill, the Prime Minister was well known for poking his nose into service affairs – a lot of officers disliked him on that account – but the younger ranks knew that "Winnie" only did so when he saw slackness and slowness in seizing an opportunity to hurt the Hun.

"Naturally you'll want to know where the fire is, de Vere?"

He had nodded numbly, still too confused by the reference to Churchill to be able to think straight.

"I'll tell you. We've gone and lost the bloody Hun

surface fleet." The Flag Officer had looked through the spume-dirtied window of his office at the estuary – packed with destroyers and cruisers – as if he half expected the German fleet to come sailing up at any moment. "Careless, you might admit. It was all the fault of those Brylcreem boys of the RAF. But no matter. We've lost 'em and you're gonna find 'em again for us."

"Me, sir?" de Vere had stuttered.

"Yes, you sir." the Flag Officer had snapped back, adding swiftly, as if time were of the essence, "We want bodies, de Vere – and you're getting those bodies for us. After all, yours is the only sub available with such a shallow draught . . ."

Later Lieutenant de Vere told himself that he hadn't been picked to enter the Baltic because HMS *Defiant* had such a shallow draught. No, he'd been selected because if anyone was expendable, it was de Vere's *Defiant*, the only sub in the command which hadn't yet made a kill . . .

De Vere took one last glance through the periscope at the little fishing fleet. In the rear craft, the one he had already selected in his mind, a bearded fellow was throwing fish bits overboard. All about him the gulls cawed and pleaded in a flapping, whirling angry cloud of white. Then the periscope was down and, at the hydrophones, the operators tensed, ready to pick up the sounds from above. De Vere started to count the minutes.

In the submarine, all was silent save for the soft hum of the electric generators which powered the lighting. The men were tense. Their faces seemed to be greased, as if with oil. At their desk the two hydrophone operators seemed to be the only crew members to be alive, as they moved, clamping their earphones more tightly to their shaven skulls, delicately adjusting their instruments. But the crew no longer needed their services to warn the boat that the German fishing craft were approaching. They could hear the steady throb of their props as they grew ever closer.

Now de Vere's mind raced at full speed, as he thought out his plan. He'd position the *Defiant* between the block ship and the little fleet, using the fishing boats as protection in the hope that the block ship wouldn't open fire in case its shells struck then. Then he'd surface, grab the "bodies" and do a crash dive. For in these shallows – where a submarine was always clearly outlined from the air – the *Defiant* wouldn't stand much chance if there were an aerial attack. Everything now depended upon split-second timing and the *Defiant*'s ability to do a quick bunk. His plan firm, de Vere started to issue his orders to his number one.

At the desks, the leading seaman in charge of the hydrophones sang out – "Screws directly ahead, sir . . . bearing . . ." – startling de Vere a little.

De Vere was no longer listening. He started to count the seconds as the screws' swishing noise started to fade and then he rapped, "Up periscope." The operation was on.

Two

All hell was let loose.

The fishermen hadn't been fooled. As soon as the sub had surfaced, they had reacted. With surprising speed for middle-aged men, laden down with heavy clothing and bad weather gear. Almost as soon as de Vere's number one, armed, with – of all things – a naval cutlass, started to swing himself over the side of the fishing boat, followed by Chalky White, toting a Thompson sub-machine gun, the bigger of the two Germans had grabbed an old-fashioned flare gun and, even before the number one had been able to warn him against retaliating in his pathetic German, the fisherman had fired it off.

It had exploded over their heads, In an instant they had been bathed in a glowing blood-red light. Chalky White hadn't hesitated. He pressed the trigger of his Tommy gun. The Germans who had fired the flare, shrieked. Blood erupted from what seemed to be a series of red buttonholes, stitched across the front of their chests. Next moment, arms flailing wildly, one of the Germans had gone over the side. He didn't come up. And the other German raised his arms in surrender.

Just in time. The block ship had understood the situation instantly. Tracers zipped across the intervening distance in a lethal morse. Slugs howled off the submarine's hull like heavy tropical rain on a tin roof. Chalky White slammed the butt of his weapon into the German's back. The man nearly fell into the clutches of the *Defiant*'s waiting sailors. An instant later, its klaxon making an ear-splitting sound, the submarine was performing a crash dive just as the block ship's heavy guns opened up . . .

The alarm was raised all over the north of Germany. At HQ they had almost immediately tumbled to what the Tommies were about. One didn't send a submarine to snatch the crew of a humble Cuxhaven fishing boat, did one? The Tommies were after bigger fish and the submarine had to be stopped before it got back to its base to report. And the staff at Wilhelmshaven Naval HQ knew that the submariners on the run wouldn't break radio silence during their flight across the North Sea; they wouldn't reach their base if they did.

All air bases from Jever on the Frisian coast to Fuhlsbuttel, just outside Hamburg were put on red alert. Everywhere, the search planes took to the air. All coastal shipping off occupied Holland and Norway to the north were ordered out. From the German naval bases at Texel, Zeebrügge and Calais, the coastal craft, sub-chasers, mine-sweepers, E-boats – anything that could be sent to sea swiftly – were alerted for immediate operational duty. It seemed as if the whole of the German Forces were now working to knock out one obsolescent British submarine . . .

While the kidnapped German fisherman slept in a makeshift bunk between the aft torpedo tubes, drugged to the world – for he had refused to settle down and had been getting on the crew's already taut nerves – de Vere steered a course for home. Already Harwich had offered its congratulations – HQ had picked up the German signals about the kidnapping – and had warned de Vere that from now on he had to keep total radio silence: the Huns were out gunning for him everywhere.

It was clear from the hydrophone operators' readings that Harwich had been right. The operators had been picking up enemy ships all the time, while they had stuck close to the occupied Dutch Frisian islands. The radio operator had reported similar findings. "The air waves are full of Jerry messages, sir," he had informed a pale, anxious de Vere in his broad Yorkshire accent. "Yon buggers are out to get us. We're gonna have to be reet jammy to dodge the squareheads this time, sir."

Silently de Vere agreed. They *were* going to have to be "reet jammy". Still he kept on doggedly, encouraged by the efforts of his young crew. Though their nerves stretched to the limit de Vere knew his "matelots" wouldn't let him down.

They had just left the Dutch territorial waters off the island of Texel, happy that no one at that great German naval base had picked them up, when the leading hand, hydrophone operator lifted up one earphone and reported urgently that "Bridge, we've got a contact!"

Swiftly de Vere nodded to his number one to take over and bound to where the pale-faced sweat-lathered operator was again listening intently, trying to pick up more details of the strange screws.

De Vere waited, biting his bottom lip, for he would have dearly loved to ask what the operator had heard. But he forced himself to bide his time. While he waited he flung a glance at the depth meter. One hundred and ten! Deep, but not deep enough.

"There you are, sir," the operator announced, as if he had achieved some fearsome but personal triumph. "It's a Jerry."

De Vere didn't argue. Only a Hun would be in these waters and even if it weren't a naval vessel, it would be under German control. He reacted immediately. "Stop both," he commanded quietly. "Silent running. No noise. Let's listen."

The crew needed no urging. They froze at their posts, hardly daring to breathe.

The cat-and-mouse game had commenced. The side which kept its cool, its nerve the longest would win. Thus they waited as the sound of the screws above grew louder and louder. But strangely enough, as that sound rose to a crescendo, a dull menacing thunder, all that de Vere seemed to hear was the steady drip-drip of a minor leak somewhere in the bulkhead.

"Large vessel," the operator hissed. "Twin set of screws. Bearing a red seven-five. Could be a destroyer."

De Vere cursed inwardly. If it was a seven-five, they were in for trouble. But his tense young face revealed nothing to the crew who were watching him intently. For, although he wasn't the best submarine commander in the world, he had learned one thing since he had taken over his own command: panic in a sub under attack starts at the top with the skipper.

Now the screws were almost directly above. De Vere was sweating freely. He could feel the back of his old school soccer shirt, which he wore on patrols, damp with sweat. For he knew what would come now if they had been spotted and somehow he thought they had. The enemy would have no mercy. They'd drop a diamond pattern of depth charges. If they exploded close enough to the old *Defiant*, she'd twist and groan as if the hull were being wrung like some washerwoman wringing out her laundry.

Thereafter the pressure waves would force the deck plates to jump. Glass dials would splinter. Glass would zip through the boat frighteningly – lethally. Packing and gaskets would fracture. Water would start trickling in. You'd pray fervently that it would not turn into a flood. For you wouldn't dare to start the pumps because they'd give away your position on the seabed.

Then you'd sit at the bottom. You'd be lathered in sweat. You'd gasp for breath like some poor old asthmatic fart in the throes of a final attack. The air would get fouler by the minute. The men would become snappy and ill-tempered. The whole vile atmosphere of the trapped sub would become even worse. And so the litany of horrors would escalate. De Vere forced a weary smile. No wonder most submarine skippers ended up drunks – or in the looney bin.

The screws were drowning out every other sound, even that of the squeaking bulkhead. Fast turbines. De Vere recognised the whine. A destroyer – or destroyers – moving at speed.

Noiselessly de Vere began to count. To time the crossing of the sub by the craft above. Would the enemy ship miss them. Forcing him to measure out the timing, he went on . . . *three . . . four . . . five . . . six . . .*

Wildly, he grabbed for a stanchion, as the depth charges exploded all about the *Defiant*. It was buffeted from side to side like a toy boat, as if struck by a gigantic fist. The lights went out. Next moment they flickered back on again to reveal a scene of absolute chaos. The whole interior of the boat was in total confusion. But the crew had no time to concern themselves with the mess. There were more depth charges coming down.

Again the *Defiant* was slammed back and forth effortlessly. Dials popped. Plates sprang leaks. One of the batteries was flooded. Suddenly noxious biting gas started to escape into the hull. Men started to cough furiously. But there was no end to the torture. More and more of the deadly high explosive eggs came floating down to explode all about the *Defiant*. She lurched alarmingly. She began to sink. For one terrible moment, de Vere thought she was going down for good. But to everyone's surprise, she righted herself and remained there, trembling, it seemed, like some drenched frightened dog just pulled out of a stream and saved from an early death.

And then the screws had gone. At their desks, the hydrophone operators slumped, heads bent, temporarily exhausted. They were the only ones to move. The rest remained as they were, as if they were already dead, frozen into a grotesque waxwork of death for eternity. But all were listening . . . listening . . . listening. Was that it? Or were their torturers not satisfied? Would they come back for another run of depth charging: one that could only spell the doom of the *Defiant*?

"*Na und*?" Raeder demanded. Behind, holding the telephone attachment, Doenitz listened for the staff officer's reply. For him it was a matter of total unconcern. One way or the other Raeder was going to have to lose his capital ships and make way for his, Doenitz's war winners: his "grey wolves", the underwater killers of the U-boat Service.

The staff officer hesitated. "We can't be sure, *Herr Grossadmiral*," he answered Raeder's query hesitantly. "You never can be in these matters—"

"Don't play me for a damned fool, Commander," Raeder interrupted the officer at the other end of the line with, for him, unaccustomed rudeness. Doenitz told himself Old Wheels was losing his nerve." I know about such things. Any tell-tale signs of a sinking? You know, Commander – oil slick, bodies, bits of clothing, etc?"

Still the man at the other end was hesitant. Waiting for his answer, an equally impatient Doenitz told himself, "Come on, man, piss or get off the pot, won't you?"

Finally the staff officer spoke. "We think, *Herr Grossadmiral*, that the attack *must* have been successful. There has been no radio traffic between the submarine and the English authorities, which is unusual for the English who foolishly tend to give their position away by—"

"Get on with it," Raeder said gruffly.

"Sorry, sir. Most importantly, the English have not alerted any of their forward air force bases in Scotland, which they do when they feel there is a need to give protection and cover to one of their vessels which is damaged or in danger." His voice trailed away to nothing, as if he had said all he was going to say.

Raeder flashed Doenitz a look of enquiry. Doenitz considered for a moment. The staff officer, pompous fool as he seemed to be over the phone, had a case. The English were not observing standard operating procedure when one of their boats was in trouble. He nodded to indicate that he felt that the Tommy sub had been sunk.

Raeder hesitated briefly. For a change and for such an old man, Doenitz couldn't help thinking, he made his decision quickly. "All right, Commander," he snapped, "let's assume that the English submarine has been sunk. For the time being the English will be working blind. But I want maximum effort on radio traffic and naval shipping movements on the island. Anything suspicious, especially at Scapa Flow," Raeder meant the home of the Royal Navy's Home Fleet "and I want to know immediately. *Klar*?"

"*Klar, Herr Grossadmiral*," the answer came promptly.

"All right, that's it for the time being."

With a clearly audible sigh of relief, the Commander at the other end put the phone down and Raeder, turning to Doenitz, asked, "Well, do you think I did the right thing, Doenitz?"

"Yes," Doenitz answered without the slightest hesitation. After all, things were going according to his plan. When things went wrong, the Führer wouldn't blame him.

Old Wheels would be the one who'd get the Führer's thickest cigar."

Raeder frowned, his mind seemingly elsewhere. "So the Fleet will assemble at Danzig," he said after a few moments of reflection." We won't have much time. The Führer won't give us much time. Naturally." He laughed a little bitterly. "But when has the Führer had much time for our surface fleet?"

Doenitz didn't comment.

Raeder went on with, "So, as soon as the weather provides the cover we need, our ships will make a run for the enemy. Once we're out of the Baltic and into the open sea, I don't think our vessels can be stopped. The English might out-number us, but we have the fastest, most modern and most powerful ships in the whole world. Theirs are the outmoded products of the Old War." Raeder beamed with sudden pride at the other admiral.

Doenitz allowed him his moment of pride. Raeder's days were numbered. Let him live in his dream world for a little longer. "Yes, *Herr Grossadmiral*," he answered dutifully, but without conviction. "As long as we can keep the Tommies unaware of our intentions until you are clear of the Baltic narrows, I think, sir, that you will win a battle that will make the name of the new German High Sea Fleet ring round the world, and," he added, with a certain underlining malice, "please the Führer as well."

"Yes, yes," Raeder said hurriedly, his smile vanishing. "That is vital . . . we must keep the Führer happy, must we not?"

Thus, they parted, the past and the future. Raeder would achieve his great victory, but in the end it would turn to ashes, just as Doenitz had predicted. And Gestapo Müller, watching them from his temporary office in the old German Hansa town of Danzig, told himself, as the two officers parted to their waiting staff cars, that they were both already ghosts: symbols of Hitler's vaunted "1,000-Year Reich", which wouldn't last out the decade.

Three

"Elena," the old crone had cried as her visitor had fallen to the floor next to the door, revealing a mass of gold-blonde hair. Suddenly, the old lady's fear vanished. She turned on Savage, her face flushed with anger. "You are a bad one, Englishman!" she shrieked, wagging her long dirty forefinger at him furiously. Behind her the frying pan started to smoke blue. A smell of burning permeated the air. "Why did you do that? Englishman, you will never have any luck in this world, striking women like that," she stared down at the startled young woman in a long grey Polish greatcoat that couldn't quite hide her shapely figure. "You are accursed . . ."

Savage had hardly been able to understand the angry flow of words. But he had experienced a *frisson* of fear. He couldn't understand why. But there had been something uncanny about the old woman as she had stood, rheumy old eyes blazing, her outstretched talon trembling like some medieval witch's in a fairy-tale.

"*Matka*," the blonde woman on the floor said, raising herself and holding out one hand towards the furious old crone one as if attempting to calm her, "*Dobje . . . dobje . . . je dobje . . .*"

When Savage had first arrived at Wesertimke POW camp, there had been a few captive Polish naval officers and Savage had recognised the sound of the Slavic language, though he didn't understand the meaning of the words. The realisation surprised him and he soon forgot the fear that the crone had occasioned a moment before.

The old woman was of Polish origin herself, one of those labelled contemptuously by their fellow Germans as "*Wasserpolacken*", water Poles: a mixture of German and Pole, from the former border area between the two countries. The crone – Olga Schmidt – had lost her husband in the first months of the war and had continued to keep farming with the aid of her teenage son. He had now been called up by the *Wehrmacht* and, in his place, she had been given Elena Warzawa, a former student from the capital, Warsaw, whose name she bore. They had struck up a relationship which went much further than that of mistress and maid. Indeed, as Elena had eventually told Savage in her hesitant mixture of German and school English, "She is like *Oma* . . . grandmother, you say . . . I look for her . . . she look for me . . . Understand . . . *Verstanden*?"

"*Verstanden*," he had agreed.

And over the next few days, as Savage's suspicions about the two women had weakened, he had begun to understand a lot about the disparate pair: the old one had lost her "Emil", as she called her dead husband who had been lost in the September 1939 campaign against Poland; and Elena had paid the price of defeat. She had been transported from her middle-class home in the Polish capital to this run-down, remote farmhouse to become, as far as the local Nazis were concerned, little more than a third-class citizen, a slave labourer and Slavic sub-human, who any German could use – and abuse – in any way he or she preferred. Her beautiful body no longer belonged to her, but to the Nazi state, which had a right to it until that body no longer functioned. As Elena had once said bitterly to Savage, "I . . . animal . . . just animal." And he had known all too well what she had meant.

Savage and Elena became lovers.

The crone usually went to bed with the chickens, as she phrased it. The girl, Elena, usually read on, trying to improve her German till her eyes closed and she fell asleep. Savage, for his part, found sleep difficult. The old woman and Elena worked hard all day, trying to keep the farm going on their labour. But Savage had been ordered by the Polish girl not to show himself during daylight hours. The result was that he wasn't as physically tired as they were.

So, one day it was with a sudden start that Savage heard the soft creak on the rickety wooden ladder which led up to the straw-filled barn above the pigs in which he slept. Had he been discovered? Hurriedly he made a grab for the sawn-off pick-handle, his only weapon; for a moment he felt as he had done when he had escaped from the PO camp, vowing to himself that he wouldn't be taken again without putting up a fight.

He lay there tensely, besides his makeshift bunk in the straw, a primitive weapon gripped in a hand that was now sweaty and hot. The footsteps, soft and hesitant, came ever nearer. Savage held his breath, ready to spring forward and deal with the intruder – whoever he was – the moment his head appeared above the trap that led into the loft.

Abruptly, he relaxed. In the yellow glare of a storm lantern, her face was revealed, framed by that lovely blonde hair, hanging loose now. During the daylight hours when she worked outside, Elena kept her hair tightly concealed beneath an old workman's cap so that, from a distance, she looked like another man to any inquisitive German male. Her figure, too, was clearly visible beneath the old crone's thin, well-worn nightgown. "You!" he exclaimed.

She smiled at him a little nervously with those excellent white teeth of hers, "Who you think?"

Savage, normally so taut and unsmiling, now grinned at her words. Yes, who could he have expected? Certainly not the old crone. "Come," he ordered and, dropping his weapon, indicated that she should sit on the blanket spread out over the rough hay and straw.

She hesitated. But only for a moment. She sat down a little carelessly. He caught a glimpse of inner thigh and the golden fuzz above. His heartbeat quickened. He had almost forgotten what it was like to go with a woman. He felt himself go red. But if Elena noticed, she made no comment. Instead she said, "Come closer, it is cold here."

He did so. The heat from the body, naked beneath the thin shift, seemed almost too hot to bear. He shivered and she snuggled even closer to him, so that he could feel the warm curve of her left breast close to him, so much so that his heart began racing once more. He felt it was moving so fast that it might well burst out of his ribcage at any moment.

Thus they crouched there in the barn, with the wind howling outside and the rats scrabbling in the shadows, both wreathed in a strange tense silence, the lantern casting their shadow in magnified distortion on the sloping wall, trembling and flickering as the wind caught the candle's flame the lantern.

Words came slowly . . . with difficulty. Language was not only the problem; the strangeness of the situation – two strangers thrown up by the tide of war and having to resolve a personal conflict – was also against them.

But in the end, it was not the words that solved their dilemma – it was action. Suddenly without explanation, they felt into each other's arms with a kind of sob of mutual relief. He could feel Elena's heart beating furiously underneath the thin worn material. She, for her part, ran her work-worn fingers through his cropped hair, as if she were feeling the head of a beloved child, sobbing – tears of passion, joy, relief . . .

Later, much later, he told her his plans, as best he could. He knew he could trust her implicitly. After all, she had sacrificed her virginal body to him, giving all of herself, without hesitation, demands or reservations. Never before in his life had he ever experienced a woman who could be so sensual, so passionate and, yet, at the same time, so innocent.

She listened intently, head cocked to one side, hair askew, as if she was concentrating her whole being on his tale, not wishing to miss a single word. When Savage had finished telling Elena of his plans, she stared down at him, eyes full of love and concern, exposing her lovely breasts. Savage almost felt as if he should reach up and take one of her big dark nipples into his mouth.

"You must go one day?" she asked finally in a little voice.

He nodded, but added no explanation.

"It is the war?"

"Yes, the war," he answered as if that in itself was explanation enough. And it was. It was always the war. For years now, Savage thought, the war had been sufficient explanation – and excuse – for everything.

She nodded solemnly, as if she finally understood, and was not prepared to object to the simplistic justification he had given for his intentions and what had happened to her own tragic homeland. A long way off a clock chimed three. Otherwise all was silent – even the wind had died down. They could have been the last living people in the whole world.

Towards dawn, Elena came to him again. This time she was not the passionate virgin of the first time. This time she was a woman full of greed and sexuality, who knew what she wanted and was prepared to take it. Her hands scratched and tore at his skinny, but muscular body. She whispered and moaned in her native language. She kissed him time and time again, her cunning little pink tongue sliding in and out of his hard gaping mouth so that he was so aroused he had the devil of a time containing himself.

Over and over again, his thrust, his throbbing swollen loins against her. She responded feverishly, her lithe naked young body lathered in sweat. But when he tried to enter her she pushed him away almost angrily, as if she wanted to prolong this fervent, burning-hot sexual ritual for ever.

Finally, Elena could no longer resist and Savage thrust the tip of his aching penis into her. She squealed. She wriggled furiously. He couldn't hold back any more and grunting like an animal, he thrust himself deep into her. Elena's spine arched like the string of a taut bow. Next moment she was jerking herself back and forth with complete abandon, her teeth gritted, too, her eyes blank, savouring the cruel pillar of flesh, which seemed to be penetrating the innermost of her pleasure-racked body . . .

Two days later, with the old crone sobbing bitterly at the door, as if her very heart was broken, the lovers set out bravely into the dangerous unknown. Every man's hand was against them. But it didn't matter. They were in love and their love knew no fear, as long as they were together. When they were gone, the old crone dried her eyes on the end of her apron, crossed herself quickly and hobbled inside. With an air of finality, she slammed the door close behind her. They hadn't a chance, she knew that already.

Four

Furtively, lovers crept through the evening fog down a little country path. From the heights of the Elbe village of Geesthacht, it led to the river itself. Traffic on the Elbe had died down now. Further up the river, the mournful wail of a ship's foghorn and muted throb of an engine was heard. But most of the bargees, Savage reasoned, would already be in the waterside *Kneipen*, tossing back the local *lutt un lutt*, a dialect name for a small glass of schnapps followed by a small beer chaser.

They came to the towpath. Savage indicated the girl should stop. She did so immediately. Her reactions were more like a man's, he told himself. Elena knew they were in constant danger, but she didn't let it show. They crouched and stared at the dim outline of the railway bridge beyond the road, both of which spanned the Elbe. For a few minutes Savage thought they were deserted, unguarded. But then he detected the smell of a burning match. Someone had lit a cigarette on the road bridge, and it could only be a guard.

Savage nodded to Elena and she silently acknowledged him, indicating that she had noticed the sulphurous smell too.

He peered harder. There was no sign of a sentry on the railway bridge. Savage bit his bottom lip. Back in the camp they had given a great deal of study to the Germany road-and-rail system. The prisoners agreed that *all* bridges were guarded, so he would have to assume that the railway bridge would be guarded, too, but not as well as the road, where there was constant traffic. Besides the traffic that passed over it mainly went to Berlin, but there was a local line on the other side branching to the north and the ports of the Baltic – Lübeck, Travemünde, Wismar, etc., only thirty odd miles away. That was the line they were going to take.

He looked at the girl. Her face was shrouded, but he sensed that she was ready to go, to tackle everything, though she knew she faced a concentration camp or worse if they were captured. He'd suffer only a return to Wesertimke and a month in the cooler, at the most, on bread and water. For a moment, he thought he should tell her she'd done enough and should return to the old crone's farm while she was still safe. But then he realised she wouldn't obey him. Her love was overpowering. She wanted to be with him to the very end, whatever the outcome.

Swiftly he outlined his plan and, then, pressing her cold hand, whispered, "We'll do it, Elena."

"*Natürlich,*" she answered in German returning the pressure. "*Kein problem.*"

"*Kein problem,*" he agreed in the same language, for they had agreed to speak German now, however badly. It was less suspicious.

Five minutes later, they were cautiously edging their way down the towpath, feeling the damp cold of the fog as it rose from the great inland river and wreathed about their legs. All was silent now. If there were bargees up in the inns on the heights above, they were remarkably silent. Perhaps they were stuffing themselves with what in slang they called "fart soup", a potent mixture of peas and sausages. But silent as the little riverside village above them was, there was no denying that the sentry on the road bridge to their right was active enough. They could hear the stamp of his steel-shod boots on the tarmac, as he paced out his beat as stiffly as if he were personally guarding the Führer in Berlin.

Still, Savage told himself, they'd be able to skirt his red-and-white striped sentry box and the similarly coloured road pole, now hung with a dim-red lantern to warn approaching vehicles that they had to stop to be checked before they could continue their journey on the country road which led to Luneburg some thirty miles away.

Savage paused again.

Before them, some twenty yards away, lay the entrance to the side of the railway bridge. Marked by a huge metal sign a kind of low latticed door presumably used by plate-layers and other railwaymen to enter and check the bridge and brains. He indicated the sign. "*Da*," he said.

"*Ja*," she whispered back. That was the way they'd enter the bridge.

Crouched low, their gaze fixed almost hypnotically on the red glow of the unsuspecting sentry's cigarette, they crept gingerly towards the entrance of the railway bridge. Now there was no sound save the gentle movements of the dark water lapping against the bridge's support and the muffled tread of the sentry, alone with his thoughts. They reached the iron gate. With caution, Savage attempted to open it. It was stuck. He cursed under his breath. The damned thing was bolted. He prayed it wasn't padlocked as well. It wasn't. He breathed a sigh of relief. Then he set about drawing back the bolt. Elena tensed at his side, throwing glances at the red glimmer, as he drew back the rusty catch inch by inch.

It seemed to make a devil of a noise. Savage thought that Hitler could hear the the rusty squeak all the way off in Berlin. He felt a cold bead of sweat trickle down the small of his back. But still the sentry continued to walk his beat, stolidly.

"Nearly done," Savage whispered, hardly recognising his own voice. Elena nodded, not trusting herself to speak. Finally he'd done it and straightened, gasping, as if he had just run a race. For a moment he couldn't proceed any further. His right hand was shaking violently with the tension. Then she nudged him urgently. From the slope opposite, heading down from Geesthacht towards the river, there came the sound of a car negotiating the steep curve. It was someone connected with the sentry. Savage knew that instinctively. Perhaps it was the guard commander coming to inspect or change sentries.

Savage felt the adrenalin streaming through his veins. There was no time to lose. He tugged at the gate. It didn't move. The damned thing had rusted in place. He had no time to reason the whys and wherefores. The car was nearly round the bend. In a minute its blacked-out headlights would sweep their end of the railway bridge. He tugged hard. The gate flew open with a rusty squeak that sounded to him like a knell of doom.

Next moment the car swept round the corner. Its beam flashed upon them. The sentry challenged, "*Halt wer da*?" For a moment they were blinded, outlined a stark black, pinned down in the circle of light, clearly up to now good. The sentry must have thought so, for he cried, "*Halt . . . stehenbleiben oder ich schiesse . . .*" and, without waiting to see whether they would stop or not, he fired.

The sudden shot galvanised the two fugitives into action. With a grunt, Savage pushed the girl through the gate on to the sleepers and the line. "Run," he yelled as the sentry's bullet howled frighteningly off the iron stanchion near his head. Next moment, he had followed her through and was running all out and awkwardly towards the other end of the railway bridge.

The car started again. There was a screech of tyres. Shots followed. Cries of rage. Again, the searchlight beam of the car's headlights caught up with them, as other men in the car now joined in the wild firing. Desperately, the two of them zig-zagged the best they could between the sleepers. More than once a bullet cut the air just by them, as they raced for the cover of the far side, arms working like pistons, breath coming in harsh hectic gasps.

Next to him, the girl kept up. She needed no encouragement. If she were afraid, Savage thought, she didn't show it. She was a good trooper, ready for anything. But once again, he realised just how much was at stake for her. If she were caught now, there would only be one punishment – death.

Behind them, though they couldn't see it, the new arrivals were setting up a machine gun, with more accuracy and distance than that of the German rifle, to fire the length of the bridge.

But if they couldn't see what the enemy was up to, they were aware that if they didn't make the slight bend and the dark shadows beyond, they were going to die – *soon*.

Startlingly, frighteningly, the machine gun opened up. A high-pitched hysterical burst. White tracer zipped all about them. It sliced the leaves from the trees in a green rain. Slugs howled off the rails. Splinters flew everywhere. The air seemed filled with lethal, burning, flying, steel.

The girl stumbled. "Elena!" he yelled in absolute, overwhelming panic. He grabbed for her. Too late. Next instant she had pitched over the side of the embankment, disappearing into the darkness beyond and he was following her into the unknown in a shower of gravel and earth . . .

Müller looked up from the report and nodded, as if

confirming something to himself. Down below in the courtyard of the Prinz Albrecht Gestapo HQ, Berlin, they were shooting the latest two POWs who had been recaptured the night before. They were both naval officers, the kind that Müller needed for his plan, but they were useless to him now; they had been in the custody of the local military – where they had been recaptured – too long. Scores of soldiers and perhaps the same number of rubber-necked gawping civilians had seen them in that time. Even the Gestapo couldn't prevent that number of ordinary German citizens from relating what they had seen; so the POWs were now hopelessly compromised. They had to be eradicated.

He sniffed as the Gestapo officials below got on with their awkward task. It would have been easier if they had been able to tie them to a post and shoot them dead. But that was impossible. The Swiss cuckoo-clock bastards of the Red Cross, who would have to certify that the Tommies had been shot while trying to escape would want to see irregular wounds somewhere in their backs. Frontal ones, as inflicted by a firing squad, would have been out of the question; they would have given the game away. He dismissed the screams, shots and angry shouts coming from below and looked at the report once more.

It was clear, he told himself, that they were on the trail of another two escapees: Royal Navy men trying to cross the Elbe and heading north for the Baltic ports.

In their haste to get across the Lauenburg railway bridge, one of the escapees had left a haversack behind. It had been dyed a darkish colour, probably with the writing ink used in POW camps. The sack was definitely of English manufacture and bore on the inside flap a name, number and what Müller had been told by one of his aides, was a naval rank. An English naval officer all right. But no further clues had been picked up by the local garrison.

He sat back and rubbed his eyes with his massive paws – the fingers covered with dark animal-like black hairs – and thought. Down below one of the escaped Tommies was being chased around the yard by the fat, panting Gestapo officials. He had been hit. Still he hopped on fearfully, knowing what would happen if he fell down or stopped, the blood arcing from his shattered calf in a bright red stream, sparkling in the early morning sunshine.

Müller sighed. What bungling, hopeless amateurs these Gestapo men were; they didn't know the first thing about real police work. He was half inclined to stand up, fling open the window and yell, "Go for the back, man . . . the broadest part of the body," but in the end he didn't. Let them get on with it.

Müller's plan was simple: these Gestapo men would hand the escapers over to another branch of country police outside, who would know nothing of what had previously happened and who would carry out their part of the scheme. This group of Gestapo brutes would be responsible for the final part scene: the discovery and shooting of the escapers. Müller knew that they had to make it look real, that the marks on the corpses would convince the damned Red Cross that the Tommies were shot while trying to escape . . .

Müller stared a little while longer at the documents and the attached map of Mecklenburg, the area in which the two fugitives had last been sighted. He made his decision. He clicked on the switch of the intercom which connected him with his outer office. "Heinz," he called.

"*Standartenführer*?"

"These are going to be the two."

"Orders, *Standartenführer*?" Heinz, the born subordinate, who would probably die in a nice comfy bed of old age – Müller cynically reflected – thought it very efficient and military to answer in clipped hacked-off phrases.

"To be apprehended and arrested without any physical damage inflicted to their persons. Should any damage be done to either of them, I shall hold the officer in charge personally responsible. Clear?"

"*Klar, Standartenführer.*"

Müller clicked the switch off. The intercom went dead. For a few moments he brooded thus.

Down below they had trapped another POW. They had caught him in the small of the back. A dark red patch was spreading rapidly across his torn shirt. He wouldn't live long. Still, as all young men do, he had fought for life. But there was no chance – his hands now raised and clasped together in the classic pose of supplication, he quickly turned to face one of the officials who was going to shoot him. Lining up behind the first official were several more men, all ready, waiting to fire.

Müller told himself, watching the scene below but not really taking it in that once he had caught and briefed the two English escapees, he would be walking on thin ice, very thin ice indeed. But it was the only way he was going to pull it off. His heavy peasant face brightened. If it all worked out as he had planned, there'd be no turning back and his place and future in the other camp (he rarely used "Moscow") would be assured for ever. He would be the spy who had destroyed the German Fleet.

Down below, a heavy, fat Gestapo man standing behind the escaper – now bleeding but still on his knees, pleading for his life – paused. Silently, the heavy Gestapo raised his pistol. His face revealed nothing. He didn't even seem to take aim. He pressed the trigger. There was a stiffled scream of absolute agony. The boy pitched face forward, as the back of his head shattered like a lightly boiled egg struck by a heavy spoon. Hastily the killer cop stepped back to avoid the spurt of blood that might have spoiled the polish of his boots. Together, with the other Gestapo executors, he stared at the corpse. It was beginning to steam – they always did for a while – like the carcasses of the beasts that Müller remembered from the Munich slaughter houses of his youth.

Müller made a little sound. It might have been a sigh; it might not have been. He bent his shaven head over his papers once more. Down below the corpse started to stiffen . . .

Five

It was that old POW trick of getting into the centre of a town without asking questions of the "civvies", which was likely to be dangerous. All around Savage and the Polish girl in her ankle-length man's coat, workers streamed to the factories and shipyards. Most were on foot, but some were on bicycles, while others crowded at the tramstops, stamping their cold feet in the chill dawn air, waiting for the rickety ancient trams. All of them were as shabby as the two fugitives and all carried cheap briefcases, which didn't hold documents as they would have done in England, but flasks of cold tea and sandwiches for lunch.

Savage was waiting for the arrival of a tram that was particularly crowded indicating that it was heading for one of the central factories. Elena and Savage would follow it along the lines. To board and ride the tram would have been easier – and they were weary enough – but it wasn't a risk worth taking. In Nazi Germany, you needed damned identity documents for everything and they had none.

For the last two days, the two of them had been heading north-east using only country roads and avoiding villages wherever possible. They had food enough for yet another two days so that was no problem to eat. All the same, Savage had soon realised that by now a massive search to find them would have been launched. Ever since they had escaped at the railway bridge by the skin of their teeth, the Gestapo would have been on to them. More than once they had spotted police patrols and barricades on the main roads. Troops had been out, too, combing the countryside in long lines, beating grass and bushes, as fugitives – in the soldiers' minds – were nothing better than dangerous wild animals. Once they had nearly been discovered by a low-flying Storch reconnaissance plane, which had come in at tree-top height with its engine switched off momentarily. That had scared them and Elena, so tough and capable otherwise, had been forced to vomit with the shock. Thereafter she had not spoken for quite a while, until she had given him that brilliant, encouraging smile of hers and had whispered in German, "*Entschuldigung* – sorry . . ."

It was at that moment that Savage, so hard, so undemonstrative, was filled with an overwhelming sense of love. Now he knew he had done wrong to involve Elena in this unnecessary danger. All the same he knew, too, that nothing would harm her. He'd rather die than allow it.

Now they were approaching the centre of Wismar. Already he could smell that old familiar mix of gutted fish, sea, and rotting timber. They were close to the waterfront now; and now their problems would really begin. He gave Elena a little nudge and brought his forefinger to his lips, in warning. She responded immediately. She nudged him back and he knew everything would work out.

Steadily, they followed the tramlines, sticking to the ones which gleamed the most. For these were the lines which were most used.

Traffic was now getting even thicker. There were cars, mostly military, and horse-drawn carts, filled with produce from outside Wismar, going to the market. Savage spotted the *Hauptbahnhof*, which was adorned with the customary patriotic legend, "*Raeder rollen fur den Sieg*" – "wheels roll for victory". Savage sniffed. Not if he had his bloody way.

More and more sailors hove into view. There were those from the German Navy, no different to their matelot equivalents back in Pompey, Hull and Harwich: cocky young men, with cheeky eyes, looking at every piece of skirt, however old, as if they were there for the taking. Savage, however, was more interested in the merchant seamen, who filled the area around the main station. As they passed in their blue serge uniforms, he tried to pick up scraps of their conversation, his eyes lighting up when he heard they were speaking in Swedish. For it was a neutral Swedish ship that he was looking for this day.

Half an hour later they were in the dock area proper. It was the sort of shabby run-down area that Savage had seen in half a dozen continental ports on training cruises before the war. Here were the places that bored, thirsty, randy matelots sought out for a few hours of cheap pleasure among cheap people. Dingy bars and cafés reeking of stale beer and smoke, loud with raucous laughter and brassy music.

Here aged, raddled pros with dyed blonde hair and obscenely short skirts lounged about smoking in doorways with their bored seen-it-all-before gaze, offering their wares for a handful of coins. Barkers and pimps were there, too, trying to entice the wanderer to come inside their establishment for a quick thrill. At first their faces and mouths were full of promises but if their wares were turned down, the smiles and joviality would burn to pouts and slanging anger.

Next to Savage, Elena looked in wonder at the tawdry cheapness of it all and Savage told himself, though she had come from a great city she had probably never seen anything as seedy and sex-charged as this. No matter. These port hang-outs were dangerous too. The authorities might allow them to exist so that the sailors could get their "heavy water" off their chests. But they wanted to control them too. Such haunts of petty crime, VD and drunken fist fights had to be patrolled regularly and any potential outbursts of trouble stamped out right from the start.

Slowly, looking like two men – for at a distance, Elena, in her trousers and heavy coat, could be taken for a man – out for a casual day, the pair sauntered down the quayside beyond the harbour entrance. No one took much notice of them, even the twin naval sentries at the gate to the harbour, checking the passes of the stream of pale-faced, tired, undernourished dock workers, hurrying to their ships. It was just another grey day in the grey middle years of a long, long war.

Savage's feet were beginning to ache. As a sailor, he wasn't used to walking long distances, but he kept on, his face revealing nothing. At his side, Elena, a head shorter, did the same. In reality, their nerves were stretched to the limit, as their eyes searched for a suitable place to spend a few hours during which they would survey the harbour, looking for Swedish ships and ways to get on to them without being spotted by the ship's police and the odd bored naval sentry on patrol.

More than once they were about to turn into what they supposed would be a place – an inn – where they might carry out their task undisturbed when something had made them turn away. They knew when something spelled danger: above one inn door was a fading sign from pre-war days announcing, "*Jüden Unerwünscht*"; in the window of another was a large poster of Hitler with the initials of the Nazi Party scribbled on it, plus a number indicating that the pub was the meeting place or the local branch of the National Socialist Workers' Party.

Savage was a little surprised – he had always thought that the North German waterfront was strictly "red", anti-Nazi. Until Hitler's takeover of power in 1933, it had traditionally been the home of the socialist and communist parties. Still he gave no thought to the matter, but nudged Elena and the two of them hurried on without sparing either inn a second glance.

It was thus engaged that they were surprised by the sudden appearance of the fat *Schupo* at the corner opposite. There was no mistaking the local policeman with his black shako, ankle-length green coat and rifle slung over his shoulder. But what really caught their attention was the clipboard he held in his right hand – and Savage didn't need a crystal ball to guess that the information on it somehow referred to them. The fat cop was obviously on the look-out for the two fugitives.

They came to a sudden stop, as the policeman turned his gaze in their direction.

What were they to do? Savage realised, a little helplessly, that if they made a sudden move, the cop would sound the alarm, which would put an end to Wismar as a way out of the Reich. But could they just stroll on, knowing that the *Schupo* would probably stop them and ask for their papers, which were non-existent? Instinctively, Savage felt in his pocket. There rested his only weapon, a very primitive one at that: an old sock filled with sand. If the worse came to the worse, it could be used as a blackjack.

Fortunately, Savage was not going to have to use the crude club on the *Schupo*, for in that very same instant, Elena nudged him hurriedly and whispered, "Listen!" She cocked her head to one side to indicate that he should do the same.

He did so. For what seemed a long time, Savage didn't recognise that something strange was happening. But eventually he heard it: as early as it was, there was music coming from all sides . . . "*Das Oberkommando der Wehrmacht gibt bekannt . . . Es war im Monat Mai . . . Heute abend spricht der Führer . . .*" War communiqués, cheery songs, public announcements – they were pouring out on all sides from the pear-shaped "People's Receivers", which had, by law, to be kept on at all times so that the populace should know and appreciate what the 1,000-Year Reich was achieving for its loyal citizens.

But among all that noise, there was another tune that was definitely out of place.

For a moment, a puzzled Savage couldn't put his finger on it. But Elena soon enlightened him. Urgently, she whispered "*Die Internationale*", just as the cop started to advance towards them with the full majesty of the law.

"*Die Internationale*?" Savage echoed in bewilderment. Then he got it. "Of course," he exploded. "The communist . . ." He didn't finish. With the cop only a matter of yards away, the two of them moved into the "*Kneipe zum Hein Muck*" with apparent casualness and headed for the back of the smoke-filled room from which the anthem of the International Communist movement was coming. Casting a look over his shoulder, Savage caught a glimpse of the cop through the window. The *Schupo* hesitated in front of the dingy seamen's pub, realising it wouldn't be wise to venture into the place, and moved on, followed by the bold sound of international communism – and good will to all men . . .

"You're safe," a fat man with thick sensual red lips said, as the pair came face to face with him in the back room. "Or as safe as you'll ever be in this accursed country." He spat bitterly on to the sawdust floor and then took a great slug of beer from the lidded stein in front of him. His accent was strange, almost slurring. It was clear that it was not his natural accent. Was he frightened – aware that his voice might occasion a reaction in one of his listeners. Elena, wiser to these things than Savage, a native of a remote island cut off from the mores of continental Europe, had already given him one possible explanation for the man's accent. As the fat man had beckoned them into the back room, she had whispered, "*Zhid.*" A few seconds later Savage had understood the meaning of the Polish word: "Zhid" had to mean "Yid". The fat man was, of all things in Nazi Germany, a Jew!

If the fat man with the sensual mouth felt it strange to be a Jew in Nazi Germany, allowing the *Internationale* to be played in his waterfront pub, he didn't show it. He said in English (a pleasant surprise this time for Savage, who was straining himself by trying to converse in German all the while), "We must not fear them. We must show them our strength." He looked around the outer room, packed with Swedish sailors. Most of them drunk, even though it was so early the morning. "What could that policeman do against these men? Besides they are neutral. Germany wants no trouble with Sweden. Sweden is too important."

Surprised as he was by the strange turn of events, Savage nodded. He knew that supposedly neutral Sweden supplied Germany with most of its strategic goods.

"Ah well," the fat man continued, smirking at them, as if he were particularly pleased with himself, for some reason known only to himself, "We knew you and your kind would be coming this way. You English people from the camps always do."

For the first time Elena spoke and there was note of impatient contempt in her voice, Savage thought, as she said to the fat man in German, "Are you going to help us?"

"Yes," he replied in the same language, though this time he didn't smirk. Savage felt he had taken a dislike to Elena; why, though, he couldn't fathom." The Jewish man clapped his hands, and, as if by magic, the barman appeared bearing a tray. On it, he had two rather unclean bowls of steaming pea soup, each containing a fat greasy sausage. There were two hunks of bread as well as half a litre of foaming beer. "Eat first," he said inn English, grandly waving his pudgy hand with its bitten-down fingernails at the tray, "then talk."

Elena and Savage didn't need a second invitation. They hadn't eaten anything warm for two days now, ever since they had left the old crone's farm. The saliva of anticipation started to dribble down the side of Savage's chin and the fat man said, "*kinnwasser* . . ." then in English, "chin water, eh?" But Savage was too busy shovelling down the soup, in between great bites of the fresh bread, to comment.

Half an hour, later they were on their way. It was almost as if the Fat Man (he still hadn't given them his name) had known they were coming and had already planned everything. They were going to be smuggled aboard the Danish freighter *Kolding*. Savage had questioned him, but the Fat Man had answered easily, almost as if he had been prepared for the question, "The Nazis don't bother the Danes as much as they do the Swedes. After all Denmark is under German occupation. Who would want to escape from one part of Germany to another, as it were?" With an almost greasy smile on his blubbery face, he had answered his own question, with: "Of course, the thick heads of the local customs will only be interested in the ship's manifest to Denmark. They won't bother to check the *Kolding*'s next port—"

"Which is somewhere in Sweden," Savage had interrupted.

The Fat Man had smiled, as if he were pleased that others were as cunning as him.

Now, as they proceeded to the berth of the *Kolding*, helping to push the chandler's cart – piled high with provisions for the Danish ship – the Fat Man told them how they would go aboard with the rest of the loading crew and while the naval guards were being plied with Danish aquavit, they would be smuggled down swiftly to the anchor locker. Here they would remain while customs and immigration officials gave the ship the usual departure search, leaving that night on the tide.

The Fat Man assured them, "I have done it successfully before, I shall do it again." He had looked severely at the two of them, "Obey orders – *one hundred per cent.*"

They nodded their understanding and, at that juncture, Savage would have liked to have asked him a hundred questions, but he refrained. Somehow he didn't trust the Fat Man. Why was this man risking his neck to help them?

They continued pushing the heavy cart, one of many heading the same way to the berths and the waiting ships.

Six

If Lieutenant de Vere had been an emotional man, he would have blubbed. Still he was moved. After two patrols, which had been total washouts, he was now entering Harwich to the cheers of his comrades in the rest of the Twentieth Submarine Flotilla, who lined the decks of their lean deadly grey craft and waved their hats, while further off, the cruisers of the Light Squadron sounded their horns and sirens, too.

"Holy cow," de Vere called to his second-in-command, as the two of them stood proudly in the conning tower of the *Defiant*, with the crew in their best white jumpers lining the deck below, "you'd ruddy well think we'd sunk the ruddy *Bismarck* itself. What a carry on."

"What a carry on indeed, sir," his number one called back, as the gulls cawed and cried around the little craft, as if they, too, were joining in the welcome for the battered sub, its hide scratched a bright silver with near misses from the depth charges.

Only one member of those present on the deck that cold April morning was unhappy with the reception the submarine was receiving. It was the kidnapped shrimp fisherman, standing at the base of the conning tower under the watchful eye of an armed petty officer, muttering to himself in Frisian dialect about who was going to boil his shrimp now that he had been abducted by these "English naval gangsters".

An hour later, he was facing a whole panel of the

"English naval gangsters", who threw pointed questions at him without cease, speaking fluent German and, in one case, actually speaking with his own Frisian tongue. Outside in the office of the Flag Officer Harwich, de Vere was similarly having to submit to a barrage of questions, posed by an somewhat effete, yet broken-nosed Old Etonian, masquerading as a lieutenant-commander in Naval Intelligence. Fleming, an officer in the "Wavy Navy", had apparently come down from London specifically to take the prisoner back with him and find out the circumstances of his capture.

Fleming quizzed de Vere like some old salt straight off the quarterdeck of, a cruiser, say, who had been sailing the seven seas since Nelson's day, instead of being a temporary officer, who had probably learned all he would ever know about seamanship from weekends of "mucking about" in small boats in the Solent before the war, complete with Pimm's Cup and cucumber sandwiches.

As patiently as he could, de Vere answered the Old Etonian's questions, while the latter chain-smoked expensive hand-rolled cigarettes through a holder, looking rather like – de Vere couldn't help thinking – a not so camp Noel Coward. Ian Fleming, ex-journalist and future writer, currently a key member of Room 39 – the centre of Naval Intelligence in the Admiralty – was anything but a weed.

Fleming was out to make a career while in the Navy, enjoying every minute of the daily espionage games in which he was involved. It was a purely personal matter. Patriotism and the successful outcome of the war were not his first priorities. Fleming had more personal ambitions. Everything the war had forced upon him was to be stored up in his mind for future reference.

Finally Commander Fleming had had enough. He knew he had obtained all the information he was going to get from the young sub commander. But before he left for London with the prisoner and his escort, he chanced a final question. "Lieutenant de Vere," he said, "what do you think the Hun surface fleet will do now?"

De Vere was surprised. He didn't think Lieutenant-Commander Ian Fleming would think him capable of having an original idea in his head. Still he answered promptly enough, "There's only one thing the Jerries can do now, sir."

"And that is?" Ian Fleming narrowed his eyes to slits and let the blue cigarette smoke curl around them. It was one of his favourite poses. It made him appear very moody, mysterious and damnably attractive to the opposite sex.

"Come out."

"Why?"

"Because we seem to have driven them from the safest anchorage in the Baltic, well protected by flak, flyboys and the like. They wouldn't last long in any of the other Baltic ports once we've twigged where they're located."

"You mean bomb them out of the harbour?"

"Exactly, sir." De Vere was getting tired of being quizzed: Fleming picking his brains without letting on why.

Fleming savoured de Vere's answer for a few moments. "And then?" he asked finally.

De Vere shrugged his shoulders carelessly. "Search me, sir. You know the Hun? He has a mind of his own that works without any apparent logic." His voice picked up. "But of one thing you can be sure, sir."

"And what's that, Lieutenant?" Fleming snapped, not liking the young man's snotty tone one bit – didn't he realise he was talking to a superior officer?

"When he comes out, it'll be with a bloody big bang and if we don't watch out, he'll catch us with our knickers around our ankles."

The remark had triggered something off at the back of Fleming's mind, but he contended himself with wishing de Vere a "good afternoon" and going out into the courtyard where the staff car was waiting to take him to Harwich Station. His brain was racing furiously . . .

The first class compartment of the overnight train from Harwich to London was empty. Outside, the corridor was packed with troops, squatting on their kitbags and packs, laden with rifles, steel helmets, gas masks and the like – even the rack nets in the third class carriages would he occupied by the luckier ones, trying to get a "kip" – cursing the slowness of the wartime trains.

Fleming was totally unconcerned by the plight of the men who would do the fighting. After all, wasn't it what they were there for: to fight and die at the command of the brass hats from the War Office? But as he considered the problem of the missing German fleet, he did continue to eye the neat little Wren, who didn't look a day over eighteen, propped up on her kitbag, legs crossed, but all the same revealing a sizeable portion of delightful black-sheathed thigh. Idly, he told himself, she'd be worth a sin or two, although she was only a common rating.

Fleming's boss, Admiral Godfrey, Chief of Naval Intelligence, was not really cut out for this kind of work – he should have been on the quarterdeck of a cruiser, not presiding over Room 39. He was out of depth there among the smart young men of naval intelligence. He had come to rely on their advice and suggestions, especially those made by Fleming – and, as Fleming knew, Godfrey had the ear of no less a person than Winston Churchill, the Prime Minister, himself. Convince Godfrey of the scheme, which was beginning to unwind in his fertile mind like the coils of some deadly snake about to strike, and Churchill might well buy it. That would mean promotion, perhaps even the good "gong" that he coveted.

Fleming pursed his thin somewhat cruel lips, as he considered the plan, knowing that once Godfrey and Churchill had been sold the idea, their Lordships at the Admiralty would just have to do what they were bloody well told, whether they liked it or not.

Outside, the young Wren with the raven-black hair and innocent baby-blue eyes had given up trying to sleep in the crowded corridor. Instead she stared enviously into the empty compartment with its deep, red-plush cushions and seats The seats had even got frilly pre-war antimacassars on them. Now there was almost a look of longing in her eyes.

Fleming felt his lips suddenly go dry. He loved innocence in a woman. What fun it was to spoil it sexually – a game of wits, trying the virginal innocent to the limits and then beyond when she would do things that she had never even dreamed existed at the beginning of the relationship. Of all the sexual high jinks in which he had indulged himself since Eton, it had proved the most exciting.

Tentatively, Fleming, smiled at the young Wren. She blushed nicely and then after a moment smiled back a little hesitantly.

Thereafter followed a few moments of dumb play: nods, shakes of the head, a little warm waving, head shaken in refusal at the invitation to enter the compartment, a series of ever deeper blushes and then finally the nod of acceptance. A minute or two later, he was opening the sliding door so that she could drag her kitbag inside – it wouldn't have done for him, an officer, to help her – and then, "I say, I'll just pull down the blinds to the corridor . . . I think it would be safer . . . the guard, you know."

Numbly she nodded her agreement and sat down opposite him, her knees pressed so tightly together that he could see the whiteness of the bone through the delightfully sheer black stocking. Watson, he said to himself, remembering the Sherlock Holmes stories of his youth, the game's afoot . . .

It was.

Shortly before Peterborough, the long, slow troop train came to a sudden stop. The Germans were bombing the big city. They would have to remain in the countryside until the raid was over. Till then all lighting was to be extinguished and even the engine's boilers were to be dampened down in case the Dorniers droning overhead caught a glimpse of the stationary train. It was a situation that suited Fleming ideally: alone with the frightened young innocent in a darkened compartment – a bed on wheels, in fact. What could go wrong?

Nothing did.

The delight of it all, he breathed to himself, as he felt her shudder and stiffen when his hand rasped against the artificial silk of her black stockings. How her body tensed as those hot fingers penetrated even further! For a moment her right hand seemed as if it were about to push him away. But a hot kiss on her soft lips and she desisted . . .

It had almost been too easy. But he had forced himself to play according to the rules of the game, so that he extracted full enjoyment out of the actual deflowerment. How he loved that Victorian term with all its delightful degenerate connotations. "*I must . . . please don't stop me now . . . It won't hurt . . . I'll be careful, I swear to you . . .*"

An hour later when the train to London finally got the "all-clear" and could continue its snail-like pace to London, Fleming satiated now, with the girl snuggled warmly in his arms – he'd take her back to his flat for another session, once they reached the capital – he remembered Admiral Godfrey's words to him the week before when he had been looking into the case of the medium-spy, known as "Madame Clarrisa".

At the end of a confused meeting on the problem of the German high sea fleet, his chief had snorted in his usual quarterdeck fashion: "There must be a connection."

A slightly puzzled Fleming had retorted, "A connection between what, sir?" But Admiral Godfrey, his face a brick-red colour, perhaps due to anger, had not replied, leaving Fleming more confused than ever.

Now as Fleming prepared to move, his right hand still resting almost protectively on the Wren's throbbing loins, he saw the connection at last – and the way ahead.

The Hun would make a big ploy to cover the exit to the Baltic. Their planes would be in full force, fighting off nosey Coastal Command reconnaissance planes. They'd lay new and uncharted minefields to prevent RN subs and coastal craft from penetrating the Baltic to spy on their surface ships. In essence, the Hun would attempt to seal off the inland sea until the time came for their ships to make their major sally into the North Sea and against the British Home Fleet, if that's what they were after.

That time would come when the weather conditions were favourable to them – fog, low cloud, heavy rain and the like which would conceal their dash through the Baltic narrows into the open sea beyond. But there'd be a catch. The longer the German fleet's progress through the Baltic to that exit, the more likely the listening stations in Scotland and the British legation's secret operations in Sweden would pick up their radio traffic indicating movement westwards. So?

As the train slowed down and outside in the steamy fug of the corridor, the exhausted troops started to put on their heavy equipment, praying that the good ladies of the WVS would be waiting for them on the platform with mugs of hot char. Fleming had it in a nutshell. Bomb the hell out of every port along the Baltic, east of Wilhelmshaven, forcing the fleet ever deeper into the Baltic, perhaps as far as Danzig. Then when they did come out, it might well take them a day to reach the mouth of the inland sea, without any chance of returning to the shelter of one of the smaller ports – and in a day a damn lot of bloody nasty things could happen in wartime.

Fleming waited till the Wren had patted herself into shape, set her cap at a regulation navy angle and then helping her to put her heavy blue kitbag over her shoulder, he followed her down to the platform, admiring the pretty sway of her trim buttocks beneath the tight blue serge of her skirt. His staff car was waiting, as planned.

The rating behind the wheel looked at the two of them. Fleming's eyes narrowed threateningly. The rating saluted and held the door open. Fleming indicated that the Wren should sit in front next to the driver, while he took his seat in the rear – it wouldn't do for a lower rank to be seen sitting next to an officer when they arrived at the Admiralty. The Wren didn't mind, obviously. She was thrilled to be in a chauffeur-driven car for the first time in her young life. At her side, the driver, an old "three-stripper", told himself that the boss had been up her navy blue bloomers this night, he'd be bound.

But Fleming had already forgotten the girl. His mind was too full of the scheme he would soon be proposing to Admiral Godfrey at "White's".

Savage's Statement

"I shook my head – and the next moment bloody well wished I hadn't. It felt as if a red-hot metal skewer had been bored into the back of my bloody skull. I shook my head and everything swung into focus. I wish it hadn't. There was horror upon horror everywhere I looked.

"The RAF raid had caught the port defences completely by surprise. Just as we'd gone aboard with the supplies, the medium bombers – Wellingtons, I think they were – had come out of the sun, right across the water, mast-hopping almost, and had begun the raid. Brave bastards for Brylcreem boys, you had to admit that. One false move and they would have been in the drink themselves. Besides they had to be pretty nifty with their bomb-dropping. At that low height, if they'd timed it wrong, they could have blown themselves to hell and back.

"Now all was fire, fury and mass confusion. There were dead Danes and German civvies all over the show. Elena, thank God, hadn't been hit. I grabbed her – she was pretty dazed – and yelled, "Let's get the hell out of here before they come back." She protested: a woman next to her in the rubble needed help. But when she grabbed the woman's arm, the poor bitch toppled over. The back of her head was missing. Elena's face turned to horror – and we ran for it."

Listening to the stiff old man, I was amazed. There was a vital young man beneath that old-fashioned exterior propped up by the cushions of the Parker-Knoll.

"Somehow or other we got off the ship – there was no sign of the '*Zhid*' anywhere, but we weren't particularly concerned. Not only did we want to get away from the next flight of bombers, we also had to reckon with rescue parties. Once they came on the scene and started asking questions, who knows."

I nodded, but said nothing.

"God, it was like the end of the world, though. You can hardly imagine the horrors. I even felt sorry for the Huns. A woman ran up to us, for instance, completely naked, her hair on fire, screaming for help . . . another lay in the gutter, a dead baby clasped to her breast, still alive and writhing as the flames consumed her. I remember her whispering, '*Phosphor*'. The RAF had dropped incendiaries with the bloody awful stuff in it, you see. And then she shrieked 'Shoot me . . .' But nobody had a pistol – or the time. Everywhere everyone was trying to escape just like we were . . . Dante's *Inferno* and all that."

Again, I nodded and said nothing. Savage's story was horrific. But he wanted to tell me everything. I can no longer recall the precise words he used to describe all that he saw . . .

He and the girl had experienced the worse of a phosphorus attack. There were folks who had been hit by the deadly white pellets, which had imbedded themselves in people's skin and had continued to burn as long as they were exposed to air.

When the flames continued to rise and rise, these hapless people had run in circles like rabid dogs: men, women and kids running crazily, screaming hysterically, stumbling and falling, knowing that only water could save them from being burned alive.

Revolted, the two fugitives watched impotently as a woman, already blind, her face steadily being eaten away by the flickering white flame, fell into the shallow water off the quay and drowned, the water stiffling her terrible screaming in the end.

They stumbled on, eyes shielded against the searing flame, trying to find a way out of this hell-hole, blundering blindly through the burning streets, as the great fire storm thundered to its orgiastic climax, the houses on both sides shuddering like stage backdrops with, at regular intervals, whole buildings sliding down in an avalanche of bricks and stones.

"This is nothing to do with God," an old man quavered from a doorway as they fought their way out of the inferno. "It's the work of man . . ." He reached out one of his burned claws, like a charred twig, and tried to grab hold of Savage, pleading, "take me with you, friend . . . please take me . . ."

Savage recoiled with horror and, when that monstrous claw clutched his singed jacket, he lashed out with all his strength and sent the old man reeling back into the burning ruins.

On and on the two of them went – blindly. They didn't know where they were going. All they knew was that they had to escape . . . to escape from this crazy, doomed place. At his side, Elena cried, the tears streaming down her ashen face. Brutally, however, Savage dragged her with him, tears or not. She mustn't be allowed to break down now, he knew that implicitly. It would be fatal. She'd never start again. Who could under these conditions?

They passed a kindergarten. A collection of women and children lay in a neat line, fused together as they had stood, not a mark on them, their faces glowing a healthy red. The fire storm had choked the very air out of their lungs and killed them as they had waited to enter the place.

I remember Savage's face when he recounted the dreadful story.

"That nearly did for me, I can tell you," Savage said in a low voice, his mind obviously full of that terrible memory. "If it hadn't been for Elena," he hesitated momentarily, as if, even now, nearly sixty years later, the girl who vanished so long ago, could still tug at his heartstrings. "I don't think I would have been able to proceed any further. I'd have found a corner and just let it happen – death."

Looking at him now, even though the mark of death was already upon him, I didn't think Vice-Admiral Horatio Savage would ever have given in. It wasn't in the nature of the beast. But I didn't remark upon the fact.

Apparently, the lovers faced more horrors before it all finally ended: a team of horses, wild-eyed and panicked, their manes on fire, dragging a cart with a headless driver in the seat; naked babies from a shattered maternity home blown into skeletal trees, trapped in the blackened branches like monstrous human fruit; charred pygmies who had once been fully grown soldiers, their skin burst and oozing a purple juice like the syrup of overripe figs. Heat radiation sucking away the lives of trapped victims, their eyes bulging and glistening indicating that they were still alive . . . until the eyes themselves burst out of their skulls under that tremendous pressure and they were dead at last . . . *Horror upon horror* . . .

It was, however, when they came to the trapped Canadian that their attempt to escape came to an end and their lives were changed irrevocably. He was hanging from a large tree by his torn parachute, his right arm limp and useless, as if it were broken, looking down at the angry mob surrounding the place. They were shouting, waving their fists, with children throwing the cobbles they had turfed up from the pave. It didn't worry the Canadian in the blue of the RAF. He looked down, his face very pale as if he were in acute pain, and shouted back in defiance. "You kids, can't you even frigging pitch a rock right . . . Hey, one of you Krauts, don't look so dumb, get me down . . . My goddam arm is broken."

Shocked beyond all measure as they were, Savage could only admire the lone Canadian's bravery. His days were numbered. That was obvious. If the police didn't get here soon and save him, the mob might well lynch him. Savage knew it wouldn't be the first time that the victims of an RAF raid had taken their revenge on some unfortunate, downed crewman; it wouldn't be the last, either. German civilians, normally tolerant of POWs and the like, hated British terror fliers with a passion.

But there was another threat to the Canadian's life, which was approaching fast – the flaming inferno. Wafted by the wind from the sea, the flames were mounting higher and higher, jumping from street to street, rushing towards the Canadian suspended helplessly from the free. The trapped man was putting a brave face on it, but he knew that if the mob didn't pull him down and perhaps lynch him, the flames would get him. Perhaps that was why he called in broken German, no longer so defiant. "*Hilfe . . . ich bin verletzt . . .*" and then in English pitifully, "Come on . . . give a guy a break, folks, I can't make it by myself . . ." He looked round wildly at the sea of angry faces. "Shoot me if you like . . . but hell, I'm gonna fry up here in a minute. *Hilfe leute.*"

Savage looked at Elena. She was still terrified, but there were tears of pity in her beautiful eyes and he knew instinctively what she wanted him to do, whatever the cost to them personally. He cleared his throat and raised his blood-stained hand. "*Hor zu,*" he commenced.

Here and there, members of the lynch mob turned and gazed at him, wondering why this man, who was clearly a foreigner, was addressing them. But the rest continued their threats, raising their fists to the trapped Canadian, as he recoiled, trying to make his body smaller as the flames grew ever closer.

Savage raised his voice. "*Hor zu,*" he repeated. "Listen . . . Don't—" He stopped short. At the edge of the crowd, a fat policeman, minus leather helmet, his tunic singed and smoking, had pulled out his pistol, his fat paw trembling wildly. The Canadian had already seen him, and ceased his wriggling, his attempts to escape the encroaching flames. It was as if he knew he was going to die and was going to do so like a man. For one long instant the whole scene froze as if for eternity: Savage, the Canadian about to die, the flaming city, the hate-filled mob. It was a picture that the world's greatest artist could never have painted, even if such a painter had been present. It was something beyond the ken of even a genius: a scene that could never be reproduced. But, for Savage, it would be seared on to his mind's eye till the day he died.

And then a dying plane came winging its way in, both engines afire, the crew staring – petrified – through their perspex portholes. Even before they realised it was there, it smashed into the street and in an instant as the Vice-Admiral now croaked, "I knew it was the end. This time we were all going for a Burton."

He sighed. "When I look back now, it would have been better if we had done . . ." He sighed yet again. "I would have been spared a lot of heartache," and then he raised his voice and said, "nurse, bring the bowl. I think I'm going to be sick again." And he was.

BOOK THREE

Into Battle

One

Winston Churchill rose from the huge Victorian bathtub like a toothless, pink Buddha. The water dripped from his pudgy arm as the valet rushed across the tight bedroom at Chequers to offer him his false teeth on a silver platter.

The Prime Minister thrust them between his gums and grinned at the embarrassed delegation from the Admiralty, which had been ushered into his bathroom. Surprisingly, the Great Man himself had called his bodyguard, Inspector Thompson, to say, "Wheel 'em in, Inspector. They're sailors. They've seen plenty of naked rumps in their time, I'll be bound." A statement which had made Admiral Lord Pound gasp. Fleming, behind his chief, Admiral Godfrey, had grinned. It was a remark he'd note for the future. Indeed he'd make a note of the whole scene: the "King's First Minister", as Churchill liked to call himself in the fashion of the eighteenth century, receiving the brass hats of the Admiralty in bare buff. There was more to come.

Churchill stood up and nodded again to the valet. The valet snapped into action at once. As if by magic, he produced a large cigar, which Churchill momentarily savoured under his nose before lighting it, a maliciously cheeky look in his clever eyes, as if he were watching the admirals' reactions. Fleming chuckled to himself. The Great Man was toying with them and was enjoying himself immensely as he did so.

Standing there completely naked, his plump hairless body dripping with water, he waited till a footman appeared, beaing a tray with drinks and glasses. "Drinks, gentlemen?" he asked airily, as the footman waited for orders.

Admirals Pound and Frazier looked shocked. "But sir," Pound exclaimed, "it's still only ten in the morning. I don't feel—"

Churchill cut him short, "Never too early for a drink, Pound. Keeps a man healthy and flexible. There are too many sober-sided people about in this country, fighting the first war still. "He nodded to the footman. The latter poured him out a stiff peg of malt whisky, while the first one draped a fluffy white dressinggown around the Prime Minister's shoulders so that now instead of Buddha, he looked like an ancient polar bear which had seen much better days.

With Churchill in the lead, puffing at the big double Havana and carrying his large glass of whisky, they proceeded into the dressing-room, presided over by Churchill's sole bodyguard, the Scotland Yard inspector, and sat down the best they could on the spindly antique furniture.

Churchill took a careful sip of his whisky and Fleming noted that the Great Man did everything for effect. He wasn't really a hard-drinking, hard-smoking type. This show of anti-bourgeois behaviour was to put the admirals in their place; to make it clear to them that he didn't expect conventional wisdom and suggestions from them. He wanted dramatic, innovative policies and strategies. The young future writer, Fleming, realised that Churchill, ever since he had come to power in May of the previous year, had been battling against an entrenched establishment.

Now Churchill wasted no time. The show was over.

He wanted business – and results. "I've read your report, Fleming," he snapped. "You have done well by your chief. Well expressed and to the point. Good."

Fleming actually blushed. Admiral Godfrey looked pleased – and relieved. He didn't want to bear the brunt of Churchill's rage – the Great Man definitely had no respect for people; admirals could be fired at the snap of a finger and thumb.

"So, gentlemen, where do we stand?" Churchill answered his own question. "Here. The Hun wants to pull off some spectacular feat with his surface ships before the balloon goes up in Russia, when Hitler will have his hands full in that country." Churchill saw the looks on their faces and swiftly added, "Our special source of intelligence indicates that Mr Hitler will march east next month. So what can the Hun admirals do?"

"They'll attack one of our convoys and then make a run for it, back to the Baltic or north to Norway, perhaps south to their ports in occupied France – Lorient, Brest and the like," Pound finally got a word in. "They've done it before, after all."

Churchill looked at the slab-faced senior admiral almost pityingly. "It's a possibility, but a remote one. They might use one of our convoys as a *bait*. But would the Hun risk his great ships, such as the *Bismarck*, just to sink a few merchant men bringing corned beef from America to the suffering people of this land? I doubt it . . . I doubt it strongly, gentlemen."

Pound had been lectured long enough. In his no-nonsense manner – which in the past had made many a senior officer under his command quail – he snapped, "Pray, then, sir, tell us what the Hun intends."

Churchill ignored the heavy irony of the senior admiral's words. He knew that he had gotten a rise from Pound. So he smiled and answered, "Of course, I will, my dear

Pound. In the last bit of unpleasantness, the German Imperial High Sea Fleet was accused by its own people of sitting in its harbours on its iron-clad bum doing exactly nothing. Its reticence was supposedly based on false strategic assumptions. The result was the mutiny of the High Sea Fleet in 1918. Now, however, there is a new kind of strategic thinking aboard Mr Hitler's Navy."

Fleming wondered how Churchill could know all this, but he listened intently all the same. The Prime Minister's discourse was fascinating.

"That is, 'Don't let us be too careful this time'." Churchill shot a cocky sideways glance at his admirals, as if he were indirectly advising them not to fall into the same trap themselves. "The result?" Again Churchill answered his own rhetorical question. "The Huns are prepared for bold action – and, mark this, *losses*!" He paused to let his words sink in. "This time they'll go for our battleships, even if we do outnumber them, and risk all. In short, gentlemen, an attack by their great ships on our convoys will only be a ploy to lure our battleships to the scene for an all-out battle." He paused, and took a careful sip of his drink, a pensive expression on his face.

Now Fleming could see that the bantering, mocking attitude had vanished. The Great Man was serious. Fleming knew why. The British capital ships, with the exception of the *Prince of Wales*, which was still undergoing trials with scores of civvies still on board, were hopelessly outmoded in comparison with the Germans'. Even HMS *Hood*, Britain's largest and fastest ship, had been built in 1918. The *Bismarck*, on the other hand, had been laid down only a couple of years ago. If the Germans got loose, and attracted only part of the British Home Fleet, located far north at Scapa Flow, the enemy might well wipe the floor with the outdated, outgunned British ships. After all, back in 1939, it had taken five or six British cruisers to sink the modern German *Graf Spee*.

"So, gentlemen, what can we do?" Churchill was deadly serious now. The mocking look in his eyes had given way to one of determination and defiance, that same look which had seen Britain through Dunkirk and the Battle of Britain the year before. "We must be on the alert to mass our forces immediately once the *Bismarck* and her attendant ships make a break from the Baltic. As the Hun says, "*Klotzen* . . . er." He cursed under his breath. Obviously he had forgotten the rest of the German military term.

"*Nicht Kleckern*," a happy Fleming supplied the rest of the phrase.

Godfrey smiled at the cleverness of his aide. The two senior admirals frowned at such temerity from a junior member of the Wavy Navy.

"That's it," Churchill said. "Concentrate not dissipate. We must outnumber the *Bismarck*. We have to have that superiority in numbers, gentlemen, or there will be a tragedy that the Royal Navy will never live down . . ."

Sombrely, the naval party walked back down the gravel path to their waiting staff cars. They did so in silence, each man wrapped up in a cocoon of his own thoughts. The Great Man's words and his final warning had had their intended effect. Even Fleming felt subdued, his own private ambitions forgotten for a while as a result of what Churchill had said.

"There will be a tragedy that the Royal Navy will never live down." All the way back to London, Churchill's dramatic warning echoed through the caverns of Fleming's mind, and even the prospect of further perverting the willing little Wren that night could not divert his brain from Churchill's final statement, until Admiral Godfrey, sitting next to him at the back of the staff car, roused himself from his doze to say, "Old Winnie does go on a bit, Ian . . . But then I suppose all those frocks" – he meant politicians – "are like that, what?"

Dutifully Fleming agreed with his chief. But for once he knew this was not just the spoutings of a "frock". Churchill really meant it . . . A *tragedy* . . . But how?

Five hundred miles or so away that same morning, as the Wavy Navy party crept into a shabby wartorn London, with the barrage balloons tethered above Whitehall like lead-coloured elephants, Admiral Raeder and his staff were working out the details of *that* tragedy to come.

Now, time was of the essence. The Führer, ready to march on Russia, was breathing down Raeder's neck. He was to give the German people a victory and then, as far as the landlubber, Hitler – who was seasick even in harbour – was concerned, the German Surface Fleet had played its role in the West for good. But Raeder, as pedantic and thorough as ever, knew he had to cut corners now. There was no time to perfect things, even though he was risking his great ships, especially the pride of the *Kriegsmarine*, the *Bismarck.*

Despite the protest of his older staff officers, who thought like he did, he was sending his ships to battle without their full complements of fuel, ammunition, and even crew. "There is no time," was his standard retort, when one of his officers complained. "*Tempo . . . Tempo . . . Der Führer will es so. Klar*?" And, as always, there was no way that anyone could get round the Führer's edict.

Still, as Raeder looked out on the crowded docks below, from Danzig's Naval HQ, he felt a huge sense of pride – he was staring directly at the great ship, the *Bismarck.* Even as she was, only half prepared for battle, not even "worked up" properly – for they had had to cut its maritime trials short to meet the Führer's demands – she was an imposing, beautiful ship.

The *Bismarck* was the strongest battleship in the world. She displaced 50,000 tons, and forty per cent of that great weight was armour, best Krupp steel, of the kind that the Englishmen's older ships simply could not match. Yet despite this enormous weight of protective armour, she had a speed of twenty-nine knots and the British Navy only had one ship capable of catching her at that speed. It was the English battle cruiser, HMS *Hood*, which had a top speed of thirty-two knots.

Admittedly, the *Hood* had an impressive speed and could fire an awesome volume of shot and shell. But she had the fatal weakness of being a battle cruiser. Armour had been sacrificed for speed and Raeder, watching and brooding, knew exactly what her secret weakness was and what armour had been added to the Tommy ship since she had been launched back in 1918.

One week after Hitler and Raeder had finalised the operation the first piece of really bad news came in from France. It was conveyed by no less a person than Rear Admiral Karl Doenitz, head of the U-Boat Army. He had flown straight to Danzig from Brest where he had been inspecting U-boat wolf packs. Passing on this top secret information to the older admiral gave him the greatest of pleasure.

Without any ceremony, he was taken straight from the little airfield to the office where Raeder and a stern-faced Admiral Lutjens, commander of the *Bismarck*, were anxiously waiting for him. Doenitz commenced without preliminaries, his hard, lean, ruthless face concealing his delight at the bad news he had brought from occupied France.

"Both the *Gneisnau* and *Scharnhorst* will not be ready for sea in time, Herr Grossadmiral," he announced baldly.

"I have it from the Rear Admiral Enginsering, who is personally in charge of the French yards."

With a shaky hand Raeder felt for his old-fashioned starched wing-collar, as if it were suddenly unbearably tight. "Won't be—"

"Yes sir. The damage they suffered is too extensive for an emergency." Doenitz took his gaze from the stricken elderly admiral and looked at Lutjens. "You won't have the escort of the two battle cruisers now, of course."

Lutjens was of a different mould than the Grand Admiral. He snapped in his harsh north German accent, glaring at Doenitz, as if he would have liked to have strangled his scraggy neck there and then, "Of course." Then ignoring a triumphant Doenitz, he said to the stricken Raeder, "Sir, this means we must postpone or cancel the operation."

Raeder looked at him weakly. "Cancel . . . postpone?" he echoed.

"Yes sir. It stands to reason. All we've got in the way of an additional capital ship to support the *Bismarck* is the *Prinz Eugen* – and she's been damaged too. To make a success of this operation we need the strength and firepower of the two battle cruisers, *Scharnhorst* and *Gneisnau*. Now, according to Doenitz here," he didn't even deign to look at the U-boat commander, "we haven't got them. The op is now too risky. A decision will have to be made."

Raeder opened his mouth like a fish out of water. It seemed to take him an age to find his voice, while Doenitz watched, his contempt and delight barely concealed. Finally he managed to say. "We have to go ahead. You know why, Lutjens. If we postpone this operation for now and, even if the Führer were to approve of it, which I doubt, it will be summer before we can start again. Who knows then, if we will be putting to sea at all."

Lutjens opened his mouth, as if to protest again. Then he thought better of it; he knew there was no hope.

"There is no other choice, Lutjens," he heard Raeder say in a faint toneless voice, as if he were speaking to himself really and had already forgotten the presence of the other two admirals. "The *Bismarck* and the *Prinz Eugen* must put out alone . . . come what may."

The decision had been made.

Two

Savage groaned.

Slowly, tentatively he opened his right eye. He groaned even more. He wished he hadn't moved. It felt as if a red-hot poker was skewering its way into the bruised eye from the back of his bloody head. They really had worked him over the night before.

He would have liked to have drifted back into unconsciousness, but his sense of anger – and duty – would not allow him to do so. He had to work out what had happened to him since the air raid and what exactly his situation was now.

He forced both eyes open. The red mist drifted away and things started to come into focus. He was in a cell, blurred by his defective vision, but a prison cell without doubt. He attempted to sit up and realised the very next instant, his eyes were misleading him. His right foot was chained to the floor next to the cement slab which served as a bed. "Blast and damn," he cursed and closed his eyes momentarily. He visualised the scene after they had been pulled from the smoking rubble: he remembered those harsh words that rang with an air of finality, "*Geheime Staatspolizei – sie sind verhaftet . . . Kommen Sie mit.*" He realised was in a real mess.

Twice, the fat civilian from the Gestapo had beaten him up. It had been a routine beating. The Gestapo man, with the stump of a cheap unlit cigar clenched between his thick lips, had struck him time and time again with his brass knuckles and, when Savage had threatened to lose consciousness, he had dragged him to the cheap pail full of dirty water in the corner of the interrogation room and thrust his head into it until he had come up spluttering and choking for breath, but again ready for the next beating.

But at the end of it all, the torturer had been quite content with the information he could have easily got from Savage's POW camp records: name, rank and age. He had not even asked about Elena.

Now slumped there on the concrete slab, with the spring sunshine peering fitfully through the iron bars of the cell aperture, an alarming thought shot through Savage's aching head: *what had happened to the beautiful Polish girl, who had risked all in coming with him*?

But before he had time to set his poor addled brain to work on that mystery, a harsh shout came echoing down the long corridor outside. "*Achtung*!" But this was not the command Savage had heard often enough in Wesertimke POW camp. "*ACHT – TUNG*." It was the cry given only when some outstanding, feared personage was about to make his appearance.

Even in his weakened, battered state, Savage forced himself, with a rattle of chains, to sit upright on the stone bunk and run his dirty hand through his rumpled, blood-matted hair.

Just in time. There was an officious rattle of keys. His door swung open with a rusty squeak. His tormentor of the previous night hurried across the cell. Now his evil eyes showed nothing, but a sense of urgent duty and obedience, as if he dare not give any hint of his real personality – in case. Hastily he undid the chain and hissed in Savage's ear. "*Aufstehen, Mensch . . . aufstehen . . . los, dalli AUFSTEHEN*."

When Savage hesitated, the Gestapo man dragged him

to his feet and held him there, swaying badly until the blood returned to his legs and he could stand unaided. Just in the time. In that same moment, Savage heard the self-important stamp of boots in the corridor. The Gestapo man stamped to attention and his right arm shot out rigidly. "Heil Hitler," he barked at the top of his voice, as the small party swung into the cell, blundering against each other as they did so, as if they were not prepared to give way to one another because it was a matter of protocol and prestige.

Under other circumstances Savage might have laughed at these fat, arrogant Germans in their fancy uniforms, laden with braid and cheap tin decorations, each carrying a revolver in a holster at his belt, as if he half expected to be fighting for his life at the very next moment.

But there was nothing faintly comical about the little man standing in the midst, dwarfed by the heavy-set, over-fed Gestapo thugs. Even though he didn't know it at the time, Savage guessed this was the boss. Those cold dark eyes and shaven skull made that perfectly clear. Vaguely, the boss, if that was what he was, returned the salute and commanded not too loud, as if he expected people to strain if they wished to hear his words, "*Wegtreten! . . . Bitte.*

Immediately, the entourage turned as one and once more pushed and shoved each other in their attempt to leave through the narrow open door of the cell, while the little man waited, his heavy dark face revealing nothing. Finally he nodded to the man at the entrance, "*Scharführer.*"

The latter responded immediately. "*Sonderführer*!" he yelled, while Savage watched the various movements, only half understanding what was going on, but feeling as if he were watching the "Crazy Gang" at some Palladium knock-about farce, performing their crazy antics to illogical rules known only to themselves.

As the footsteps approached, the little man turned

back to Savage. "*Gestatten, Standartenführer Müller,*" he snapped, clicking his heels together noisely. "*Sie sprechen Deutsch*?"

Savage shrugged slightly. "*Ein wenig,*" he replied.

The little man named Müller rattled off a great burst of German, looking intently at the prisoner with those dark frightening eyes of his.

Savage looked up at him. "*Nix verstehen,*" he said helplessly, wondering why they had wheeled in such an obvious Gestapo bigshot to question him – just an ordinary "kriegie", who had had the misfortune to be caught red-handed. Then the thought flashed through his numb, befuddled brain with alarming speed, was it because of Elena? Did the fact that he was being aided by a Polish slave worker, a Slavic sub-human, warrant special attention? But before he had time to put his fears into hesitant German, Gestapo Müller (for it was he) shouted as if he were on some huge barrack square, "*Sonderführer*?"

Savage knew what a "*sonderführer*" was. They had had them in the camp: a kind of civilian with special skills, who dressed in a uniform like a soldier, but wasn't really part of the Army. This meant they had rights and privileges not accorded to someone who came under Army rules and regulations. But Savage had never seen a *sonderführer* like this.

It was the *zhid*, as Elena had called him. The fat communist Jew with the cunning dark eyes, who had played the *Internationale* so openly in the waterfront bar and had promised to help them escape to Sweden before the bombing. Now he was tucked carelessly into an ill-fitting brown uniform, with a swastika armband, and an oversized peaked cap gracing his head, an unholy grin on his broad face, as if he were enjoying the look of total, absolute surprise on the prisoner's face.

He bowed politely as he entered the cell and said,

"Good morning, Mr Savage. I hope you are feeling better." His look of happiness increased as he saw that the prisoner was now even more surprised by the fact that he knew his name.

But Gestapo Müller had no time for such pleasantries, especially when he didn't understand them. "Close the door, *Sonderführer*," he said sharply. "This damned place is full of big ears."

The *Sonderführer*'s smile vanished. He closed the door hastily and then listened intently, as the Gestapo boss fired a series of questions at Savage,

"All right," the fat Jew said finally, "this gentleman has a few questions to ask you. I shall translate. But I shall warn you now, this is what will happen if you speak one word of what is said here." He drew his right forefinger dramatically beneath his throat jowls, as if he were slitting a throat.

Savage was not impressed. Indeed his bewilderment had now been replaced by a burning anger. He snorted, "Where is the Polish girl . . . Eh, come on, out with it, or I'll tear you apart with my bare hands!"

The naked aggression in Savage's face must have scared the *Sonderführer*. For although Savage was tethered to the stone bed, he stepped back a pace or two, as if he feared for his life. Müller snapped, "*Los, mach' weiter, Arsch mit Ohren.*"

The "arse with ears" recovered quickly and answered, "The Polack woman will be all right, as long as you behave yourself, Savage. Now let's get on with it." He paused. Müller nodded. He took a deep breath like a diver about to jump from the high board. "How would you like to go to Sweden, *as a free man*?" he asked after a moment's deliberation. "From there your own people at the legation will ensure that you are sent straight home without being interned by the Swedes, as is usually the case." He paused and looked straight at an obviously puzzled Savage.

Savage was indeed puzzled. Everything was happening fast, even the *Sonderführer*'s English had improved dramatically since he had met him as a supposedly seedy Communist in the sailors' waterfront hang out. Dimly, Savage was aware that he had been caught up in some sort of mysterious plot in which he was just a mere cog in the wheel. But what was that plot and why had this – er – Gestapo Müller gone to such great lengths to entrap him, a humble escaped POW and junior officer in the Navy? What the hell was going on?

The *Sonderführer* seemed to be able to read the prisoner's mind for he added easily, "Rest assured that you will be doing nothing to harm your own country. On the contrary, you will be aiding it."

"Aiding it? But," he pointed to the shaven-headed chief of the Gestapo, standing there, arms folded impatiently, as if he couldn't get this business over with quickly enough. "But," he repeated . . . "Him?" He didn't seem able to clarify his thoughts any further.

"We're in this together, Savage. Now what is it to be? Are you with us? You scratch us and we'll scratch you, as I believe the English say." He smiled winningly. "What is it going to be?"

"The girl?"

"She'll remain here till the business is over. But you have our word on it, nothing will happen to her. Besides," the *Sonderführer*'s smile vanished as abruptly as it had come, "you have nothing to lose and everything to gain." He turned and hastily whispered something to Müller.

The latter nodded his shaven head urgently.

"If you don't agree, you die," the *Sonderführer* said. "You already know too much. So what are you going to do?"

Savage gave in. "As long as the girl is OK—" he didn't finish his sentence. The two of them, the fat Jew and the hard-faced Gestapo boss, were not listening, he realised. They were too eager to talk themselves. He waited . . .

Three

A high silver moon hung over the drifting wisps of night fog. It cast a spectral light on the grey sea of the channel. A wind was beginning to spring up. But as yet it was not strong enough to sweep away the vestiges of the fog. It looked as if the predictions of the weathermen would be right. Patchy, low-level fog would remain with them till mid-morning at least.

It was a forecast which made the officers on the bridge of the *Bismarck* happy. It made for difficult navigation. All the same the fog would give them the cover they needed as they slipped out of Danzig. By the time the high-level Tommy reconnaissance planes attempted to breach the port's defences and take photographs, they'd be gone and out into the Baltic.

Now, followed by the smaller, less powerful *Prinz Eugen*, the *Bismarck* ploughed steadily through the cold grey swell, the tugs falling behind into the gloom. The only sound that could be heard was deep, throbbing one – the notes of the great ship's powerful diesels and the steady pace of the many sentries. For Lutjens had ordered double look-outs and sentries for the great break out. One couldn't be too careful. Now they had a run of some twenty hours through the inland sea and that could be very dangerous, especially with the neutral Swedes – so important for the German war economy – sailing everywhere.

Lutjens, standing on the bridge, smoked silently and

reflectively. Well, he told himself, if any damned fat Swede got in the way and attempted to earn a few kroner by reporting the *Bismarck*'s presence in the Baltic, he was going to be in for an unpleasant surprise. He'd be at the bottom of the sea before he knew what had hit him.

Lutjens smiled wrily at the thought of some well-rounded Swedish skipper being confronted by the realities of this global, total war. That'd surprise the bastard, he concluded.

The Admiral dismissed the Swedes and, with his cigar cupped in the palm of his hand so that the red glow was not visible, he considered what it would be like. Action, as far as he was concerned, had been limited so far. Indeed the only time that a German surface ship had made a name for itself had been back in 1939 when Captain Hans Langsdorff's *Graf Spee* had captured the world's headlines.

Langsdorff had destroyed fifty thousand tons of British shipping in a month without the loss of a single German life. He had become a hero, decorated by radio by the Führer himself. That December von Langsdorff must have felt on top of the world, the Admiral told himself, as he pondered the fate of his predecessor. He would have believed that no ship in the South Atlantic could stop him and his beloved *Graf Spee*. Yet within a matter of days, his whole proud reputation had been shattered by a collection of inferior Tommy light cruisers. He had been trapped and, although he had volunteered to fight it out to the end, the Führer, not trusting von Langsdorff to do so, had ordered him to scuttle his proud ship. He had done so and thereafter had obviously felt there was no other way out but suicide. What a fate for such an able and brave officer!

Lutjens tapped the end of his cheap working-man's cigar and wondered what *his* fate would be if things went wrong. The Führer had no feeling for the sea and those who sailed it. As for Raeder, well, he was basically concerned with his own career and future; he would do nothing to help the *Bismarck* if she got into trouble.

"*Wie gekommen, so zerronnen*," Lutjens whispered to himself, as he stared at the spectral sea, as if he sought to find something there, and thought of those far-off days and the high hopes which had been shattered so brutally. He realised once again that there was nothing certain in this life, save death.

"Radar, sir,"

Lutjens turned, startled, shocked out of his reverie. He swung round. It was the assistant gunner controller, standing there like a frightened mid-shipman, "What is it, Guns?"

"Fishing vessels, right on our course."

"Ours?" he barked.

"No, sir. Swedes," The young assistant gunner controller answered with a note of trepidation in his voice, as if he expected an outburst on the Admiral's part.

It failed to come. For Lutjens had realised that this was the first of the imponderables that he was going to be face on this cruise to an unknown battle. An instant decision was called for. "How many?"

"Four, sir."

"Heaven, arse and cloudburst," the Admiral cursed. "All right," he made his decision, realising as he did so how calmly he could decide that in an hour or so a score or so of honest Swedish fishermen were going to die suddenly and savagely. "Liquidate them."

Hearing this harsh command, the gunnery officer paled a little underneath the weathered surface of his young face, but he recovered soon enough. Promptly, he touched a hand to his cap and snapped, "*Jawohl, Herr Admiral*!"

He turned and went, leaving Lutjens to stare at the sea,

alone with his thoughts once more. They weren't good ones. His decision had not pleased him, but it had to be done, he told himself. You couldn't fight a war without hard decisions.

For a moment the newsreel of the *Graf Spee* at Montevideo Harbour flashed before him: the bubbles of trapped air exploding on the surface, the mops and brushes floating foolishly on the surface, following a model of the ship that some rating had probably made in his spare time to take home to his mother as a souvenir of the *Graf Spee*, now mocking the great vessel which had been its subject; and a seaman's cap trailing its black ribbons behind it would this be the fate of *Bismarck*, too?

"Arse with ears," the Admiral cursed once again. "Great crap on the Christmas tree, what do you think this is, Lutjens, a seminary for well-born ladies of a sensitive nature! This is shitting war. Now get on with it, damn you, man!"

He shivered. He had burned away the rage with that crude outburst of seaman's language. Now he was the capable, cool commander once more. His fears had vanished too. On the contrary, he was filled with sudden energy and anticipation at the thought of wiping out the humiliation to the German Navy that it had suffered with the scuttling of the *Graf Spee*.

Lutjens pulled the collar of his naval greatcoat closer to his neck. It was growing colder. The fog had almost lifted now. The soft swell was bathed in a hard icy silver by the moon. It bathed the superstructure of the great vessel in its light too. It gave the *Bismarck* a shimmering, unearthly wraithlike appearance.

"A ghost ship, Admiral," the voices at the back of his cropped head whispered. "A ghost ship out for vengeance."

The voices didn't disturb the Admiral. He nodded as if

he approved of them, was used to them; as if they were part and parcel of his being. "Are you satisfied now?"

This time Lutjens didn't acknowledge those strange spectral voices. Instead he stood there a moment longer, feeling the immense power beneath his feet, listening to the rhythm of the mighty engines, drinking it all in avidly . . . absorbing the power and strength of *his* mighty ship. Before him the channel widened, as if it were inviting him to increase his speed, hurry to his date with destiny and what lay beyond . . .

The Junkers 88 night fighter had taken off ten minutes earlier from Jever Field in Schleswig-Holstein. Now, although it was still a little foggy, the pilot was managing very well with the aid of his radar and the light cast by the moon. He touched his throat-mike and called to the gunner mid-ships. "Keep your eyes peeled, Horst. Shouldn't be long now."

"Like a tin of peeled tomatoes," Horst replied cheekily.

Next to him, the co-pilot pressed his throat-mike and said to the pilot, "Skipper, do we really attack without warning?"

The pilot nodded, not taking his eyes off his panel of green-glowing instruments for an instant. "Yes – and there are to be no survivors, either." He gave a little shrug. "Total war and all that, you know, Kai."

"But if we're caught. They are after all neutrals—"

The pilot, the only party member in the Junkers crew took his eyes off the instruments for a moment, and pulling rank, snapped, "Listen Kai, I don't give a shit if they're Mongolians. We Germans will win this war, if we're hard enough, so there'll be no come-backs. One day soon, we'll be masters of Europe and that's that. I'll have no more of that kind of defeatist chat, understood, Kai."

"Understood, skipper," the co-pilot said a little miserably and, at the same instant, the mid-ships gunner sang out excitedly, "Got 'em in my glassy orbits, skipper. To port. In that break in the fog."

The pilot didn't hesitate. "Prepare for attack," he cried.

He tilted the nose down. The Junkers seemed to fall out of the silver sky. Suddenly there they were, a little cluster of boats, nets out, lanterns outlining their shapes in a stark black. It was a perfect target.

Eyes glued on the boats which were getting larger and larger by the instant, the pilot cried over the intercom, "Bomb aimer."

He didn't need to say more.

The bomb aimer, lying flat on his stomach over the glass and perspex observation, yelled back. "Bomb doors open . . . Taking over now, skipper."

"You're in charge," the pilot yelled back, eyes behind the flying goggles bulging with the pressure. Next to him the co-pilot felt that old mixture of fear and exhilaration, as the bomb aimer took over control of the Junkers, which was hurtling towards the sea as if intent on smashing itself there.

"Steady . . . steady now," the aimer yelled, "*yes*, hold that course, skipper, will you."

"Holding course!"

At nearly five hundred kilometres an hour, the Junkers headed straight for the boats. Next to him, thrust back against his seat by the tremendous centrifugal force, the co-pilot could have sworn he saw the startled white faces of the crew members staring up at this black angel of death, which had appeared so startlingly from nowhere.

"Now!" the bomb aimer yelled in a voice that the others could hardly recognise: it was thick and passionate, almost sexual. "*Bombs away*!"

"Holy shitting strawsack!" the co-pilot screamed, realising that the bomb aimer had released the bombs too soon; they were going to be the victims of their own weapon. "*BREAK . . . BREAK . . .*" Too late. Below, the first of the stick exploded, right on target.

A great gout of red flame shot upwards. The leading boats were blasted by an enormous blow torch, which seared their length and set their timbers afire in the very same moment that they disintegrated. But the Junkers was hit too. Suddenly, it rose high into the air at an incredible speed, as if punched by a gigantic fist.

Frantically, eyes bulging like those of demented man, the pilot wrestled to control the stricken night fighter. To no avail! The Junkers shimmied and slithered all over the night sky, while below yet another salvo exploded, drowning the screams of the bomb aimer, who had been ripped from pubis to throat by a razor-sharp fragment of bomb, his guts flowing from the scarlet wound like a steaming snake.

But no one had time for the dying man's shrill screams of absolute agony. Now the survivors were battling to save the plane before it was too late. Both the pilot and his co-pilot worked at the controls, trying to force the shattered nose upwards, while white hot glycol spurted from the portside engine and splattered all over the shattered cockpit canopy.

But they were out of luck. Mid-ship, the terrified air gunner baled out. They saw him, parachute half opened, as he sailed by them. He slammed directly into the starboard engine. The blades sliced his head off neatly. Complete with flying helmet, it flew apart from the headless torso gushing thick dark-red blood. It disappeared into the glowing darkness like a child's football, abandoned by some careless kid.

The co-pilot gave up. Not the pilot. "*Himmel, Arsch und*

Zugenaht," he cursed, his face hollowed out to a ruddy death's head by the light of the greedy little flames which were beginning to lick the length of the crippled plane's fuselage. With all his strength, muscles bulging through his thin coverall, he fought the controls. "Come on, you bastard . . . come on . . . stay up will you!" Next to him, the co-pilot buried his face in his hands and began to sob like some broken-hearted woman.

Fighting to the very last, though in his heart of hearts, the pilot knew it was hopeless, the shattered Junkers flew on. Behind, it left the sinking Swedish craft, as it skimmed the surface of the sea, virtually wave-hopping now, until finally disappearing altogether.

Four

Sven was already half drunk, though the sun had not yet peeped over the massed green ranks of the firs which almost ran down to the edge of the water. He had been there since before dawn. But, as yet, he had not had a single bite, and he was desperate. If he didn't catch enough fish to pay for his next ration of schnapps before the Swedish state liquor store closed promptly at noon, he would be sentenced to another long night without a drink. The thought tormented him. In the forest he could always trap enough game and soon the mushrooms would be reappearing, another part of his stable and free diet. But schnapps. That didn't grow wild and if he was caught manufacturing his own illegal alcohol from potatoes and currants, the cops would shove him behind bars for years; and then there'd be no booze at all. Christ Almighty, he had to catch some fish soon, or he wouldn't survive the rest of the day! He had long forgotten how to pray. As soon as he been freed from the stern dictates of the Lutheran church at the age of fourteen, he had forgotten his prayers immediately. Now, however, he folded his dirty calloused hands and, looking up at the morning sky, said, "Please God, let me catch some sea trout. They bring more money on the market. Please God . . ."

But on that May morning, God was perhaps looking the other way, for after another half-hour of fruitless casting and trawling, Sven took a tiny, careful sip of his rationed schnapps and gave up. He'd tried. It was now that, for once in his life, Sven Hansen struck lucky.

Wandering along the lonely remote beach in a half-drunken daze he spotted the severed head first. It didn't startle him – he was too far gone for that. Then he saw the body a little further on, with the heap of what he supposed for a while was scrap metal, but which later on the *Polis* identified as the cockpit of a German Junkers 88.

Sven's mind worked with the deliberate slowness of the chronic alcoholic. All the same, he was sober enough to realise that there might be something of value in the strange heap of still smoking metal that he could turn into schnapps. There was.

Two hours later Sven was roaring drunk on the proceeds of that surprising find and the local representative of the *Svenska Tageblatt* was urgently calling his Stockholm head office and a little later an unregistered telephone number not far away, crying excitedly over the poor line, "Here they've found a Junkers. A drunk. No, you can't talk to him. He's blindo. Found some Nazi Iron Crosses . . . flogged them for schnapps. But a Junkers all right . . . Might be connected to the missing fishing boats . . . I repeat, might be connected to the missing fishing boats . . ."

The news of the missing Swedish fishing boats in the Baltic and the remains of the crashed German night-fighters transmitted to the HQ of the British SIS in Stockholm, courtesy of the paid local reporter, struck home like a bombshell. The radio masts at the top of the embassy crackled. Teleprinters clattered furiously. Telephones and secure lines burned with the startling information, which all boiled down to that one overwhelming question: *is the Bismarck coming out . . .?*

Fleming had been aroused at his flat in the middle of the morning. The little naked Wren was still drunk from the champagne he had poured into her the night before and, as she had snuggled up to him cosily, he had tried to initiate her into the next stage of her "trip down the slippery slope", as he had called it to himself.

"Sometimes, Peggy," he had whispered, softly stroking her tousled hair, "a man is not always ready for – er – you know what."

She had nodded dreamily, not opening her eyes, indulging herself in her fantasy that the handsome young officer really loved her.

"Then only the most drastic measures will work so that a man can show his loved one that he really cares for her. But she will have to help, of course." He had pressed her plump young buttock gently.

"How?" she asked, still preoccupied with her silly girlish fantasies, with no idea of just how lecherous her companion was: a man who had seduced women ruthlessly and without remorse ever since he had been a schoolboy at Eton. Slowly, she opened one eye and looked up at him.

He had looked at her, as if he were burning with an unbearable love that would only end when death parted them. It was a look that he had practised many times in front of a mirror as a schoolboy. "Should I show you?" he asked and tenderly planted a gentle kiss on her smooth innocent forehead.

"Of course," she had responded, rising to the bait like an obedient trout, which she was, of course, he thought. "Anything for you, darling."

"Thank you, Peggy. You're a real sport. And remember, darling, I'd do the same for you any time."

"I know, Ian," she breathed, as he gently took hold of her head and brought it down to his chest.

She kissed it. Perhaps that, she thought, was what he expected her to do, the little romantic fool.

Emboldened, he forced her head a little further down his lean, pale-white body. He felt her stiffen. But it was only due to bewilderment. She was naturally wondering what she was supposed to do now. "Oh, how good you are to me, Peggy," he whispered with faked fervour. "Oh, you know how to please a man."

"Anything for you," she began in a muffled voice in the same moment that he pushed her down to his hairy throbbing loins and she gave what he could only categorise as a squeak.

"You all right?" he queried in an anxious, caring voice, which was becoming husky now with sexual tension. "Is this too much for you, dearest?" He felt himself sickened by the sound of his own voice, putting on this stupid bourgeois act for the girl's sake. But it had to be done. She had the makings of a good whore in her, he knew that now. Soon, with a bit more training and plenty of alcohol of course, he'd have her wild with frenzied excitement, ready to do just anything he wanted.

"Yes," she murmured uncertainly, her mouth almost touching the still dormant sexual organ, though he knew he wouldn't be able to control himself much longer: the intrinsic depravity of spoiling innocence was the best "Spanish fly" in the world. "But I don't . . ."

He bent and kissed the top of her head with fake tenderness. "Just . . . just take it in your mouth . . . Only for a moment," he added hastily. "As a sign that you love me."

"But isn't it . . . dirty?" she asked plaintively. "I mean—"

He kissed her again. "Just a single moment," he pleaded, feeling the movement, losing control over his loins. "For me, Peggy, darling."

She hesitated. Then he felt her fingers on him, guiding the erection in the direction of her tiny pink mouth, open already to expose the tongue, which he knew he could train to be as cunning as any Parisian whore's.

It was then that the telephone started to ring with startling suddenness and a moment later Admiral Godfrey was booming ever the air waves, as if he were still on the quarterdeck of the cruiser he had once commanded, "Get over here, tootsweet, Ian . . . The balloon's gone up at last . . ."

In Room 39, the headquarters of Admiral Godfrey's Naval Intelligence, the balloon had, indeed, gone up. Just as in Stockholm, all was hectic activity. Phones rang without cease. Messengers hurried back and forth, Dispatch riders, laden with leather message pouches and sometimes carrying .38 revolvers in gloved hands came and went, speeding off to various military bases with new orders and instructions. Elegant aides and naval staff officers, all bouncing lanyards and handkerchiefs doused in expensive eau-de-Cologne, came hurrying in, demanding new information for their chiefs – *bloody PDQ*."

And all the while, Godfrey's clever young men, including Ian Fleming, tried every angle possible to break through the German barrier of silence about the Baltic. For a while Fleming, with his talent at female seduction, was luckier than the others. Some time back, for an emergency such as this one, he had gotten drunk and had seduced one of the ugliest of the key secretaries at the neutral US embassy in London.

The woman, all buck-teeth, plaintive mid-Western accent and "long passion-freezers," as Fleming was wont to describe his conquest's underwear to his fellow officers, was madly in love with the aristocratic British officer. Twice she had betrayed key secrets relating to the ambassador, the Anglophobe, corrupt Joseph Kennedy, and had contributed in having him recalled to the States with his sons Jack and John. Now she was equally prepared to reveal what the US Berlin Embassy was sending back to London and Washington about the situation in the Baltic.

"Give me a drink, for God's sake," Fleming had gasped melodramatically to his laughing fellow officers after a "quickie" with her that midday in the back of a staff car. "The things I do for bloody England and the Empire." He had shuddered frighteningly. All the same he had brought back information which contributed greatly to the intelligence men's growing realisation that this was not another German feint, but the real thing.

"She said," Fleming whispered between sips of the single malt that Admiral Godfrey produced himself, while the others clustered around him, eagerly waiting for his findings, "that their Berlin Embassy press people have been put on alert for a key announcement from the *Tirpitzufer*." He meant the German Admiralty in Berlin. "They – the Yanks – have been warned to clear their lines to Washington. You know what that means? The Huns want President Roosevelt to be one of the first to know whatever they've got planned. If Roosevelt backs off and no longer supports Churchill, we've had it, chums." Fleming suddenly seemed to realise the gravity of the situation. For if anyone was intent in bringing the USA into the war on Britain's side, it was America's crippled president, Franklin Delano Roosevelt.

"So this is it, Ian?" Godfrey said.

Fleming lowered his glass. "I think so, sir. I don't think the Huns would go to these lengths without it being something big, really very big. The *Bismarck*, the *Prinz Eugen* are coming out of the Baltic at last and, as the Great Man said last week, it's not to stop a convoy filled to gunwhales with corned beef for the people of this country."

Godfrey nodded his understanding and looked at the huge chart of the North Atlantic and North Sea which graced one wall of Room 39. "The bulk of the Home Fleet is safe in Scapa Flow to the north there. We have various small task forces cruising off the coast to the south, west and one in the mid-Atlantic, bringing home a convoy. And there's one large one coming back from Murmansk in Russia. It's top secret but the Great Man has decided to help the Reds with some strategic goods before the shooting starts. Strange," he mused as an afterthought, "when Churchill has spent so much of his political life trying to eradicate communism. No matter. So, we've got the Home Fleet separated, but not too far apart and we have two convoys that the Hun might attack and destroy if he wants to achieve a quick propaganda victory without risking the *Bismarck* too much." He paused, as if he didn't know how to continue, which was in reality the truth. Godfrey was not a man for drawing long-term conclusions. He was more at home on the quarterdeck of a fighting ship than in the rarified atmosphere of Intelligence.

The others took up the challenge, trying to outguess the Germans, while the messages continued to pour in. But for the most part they were disappointing. The Baltic was shrouded in fog and, although by flying – illegally – ever southern Swedish air space, RAF reconnaissance planes had managed to penetrate the area of Danzig, intense flak had prevented them getting low enough to take serial photographs.

As Ian Fleming concluded around midday, as Peggy the Wren, temporarily attached to the Admiralty – thanks to Fleming's influence with Godfrey – brought in sandwiches and pink gin, "We're boxing in the dark, gentlemen. The Baltic is not going to reveal any of its secrets this day," he announced, taking a sip of his pink gin and knowingly winking to Peggy. She blushed and fled, revealing that delightful bottom of hers beneath her tight serge skirt and reminding Fleming that there were other perversions yet to come. The thought inspired him to add, "But let's not be despondent, gentlemen. We know the *Bismarck's* out – one." He ticked off the statement on one immaculately manufactured finger. "That she's after blood – two. And – three – she'll grab a quick victory somewhere or other before the Home Fleet can assemble and do a bunk for some close home base . . . probably in Norway or occupied France."

There was a mumble of agreement from the others, even from those who disliked or envied Fleming. But for once, he was wrong. Half an hour later, when they were on to their second pink gin, the usual grim-faced, armed RAF officer from Bletchley arrived, with his briefcase chained, as was customary, to his left wrist.

Hastily, they went through the complicated formalities and then, with the office door locked and the RAF flight lieutenant watching them suspiciously, hand poised on the holster of his revolver, Godfrey read out a message which was to be destroyed exactly sixty seconds after it had been seen. To a casual listener, it meant virtually nothing. But to them, it turned their world upside down.

It read: *"Lt Cdr Savage arrived Stockholm . . . Urgent Blood and Iron . . . Send Mossy to expedite. Hillgarth."*

The silence was almost gravelike as Godfrey handed the message wordlessly back to the RAF officer. He wasted no time. Holding it above the nearest ashtray, he zipped his cigarette lighter and burned it before their eyes. Then, saluting, he snapped, "I'll be on my way, gentlemen."

Without another word, he marched across the office,

unlocked the door and was gone, leaving them silent and unmoved like characters frozen into inactivity at the end of the third act of a fourth-rate melodrama . . .

Five

"E-boats, skipper," the look-out shouted, above the steady throb of the old destroyer's engines. "*Starboard . . .*"

The young captain of HMS *Bulldog* heard the bearing only vaguely, for he had already seen the two lean white shapes. They were racing straight for the little convoy, their scrubbed woodwork and pre-war polished brass gleaming in the fitful rays of the morning sun now breaking through the surface fog. "Bloody hell, that's torn it," he cried. Next moment he was bent over the voice tube, yelling orders down from the bridge.

The gunlayers were on target almost immediately. But the Germans reacted even quicker. The twin twenty cannon opened fire. At a tremendous rate they pumped a solid wall of glowing white tracer shells at the old destroyer and the first of the merchant men behind the escort. Almost immediately, the *Bulldog* started to take casualties, as the rigging came tumbling down and the wireless mast fell in a shower of electric blue sparks. A fire control party went down in the lower desk, a nest of flailing arms and legs. Screams and yells for help rose from all sides. Suddenly the lower deck was running red with blood.

But now the A and B turrets were responding. The bigger four and a half inches cracked. The ship, shuddered at the recoil. Spouts of angry white water hurtled upwards to left and right of the speeding crafts, their sharp prows knifing the water, throwing up combs of water. "Lower the range," the young skipper yelled desperately, as yet another vicious salvo of twenty millimetre automatic fire raked the destroyer: a thousand shells a minute running the length of the hull, ripping and gouging out the plates in sudden sparkling naked metal. *Bulldog* reeled dangerously.

But the skipper knew she was a tough old bugger. She could stand it. The E-boats, with their wooden hulls were a different kettle of fish. A lucky hit with one of the four and a half inch shells and that would be that. The Hun bugger wouldn't survive a minute.

Again, the two turrets fired. A burst of shells punched the leading E-boat. The German craft stopped. It was as if it had just run into an invisible stone wall. Next moment, steam and flames were escaping from its ruptured engine and she was sinking, with panic-stricken sailors throwing carley floats overboard or throwing themselves into the freezing water in which they wouldn't survive more than a few minutes.

Still the other E-boat kept up the attack. It swept round in a great angry curve, vanishing for a moment or two behind the sudden wall of flying water. For a moment the skipper of the *Bulldog* thought she was going to stop and pick up survivors of the other craft. That wasn't to be. A second later she came out of the fog of water, heading straight for the *Bulldog*, torpedo men, who had appeared out of nowhere, poised at her tilted bow.

The young skipper of the *Bulldog* didn't wait for the Germans to fire. Instead he yelled, "Port seven", in the same instant that the machine gunner in the open cage behind the bridge let loose with the round-barrelled, old-fashioned Lewis gun. Lead splattered off the leaping bow of the E-boat. One of the torpedo men flung up his arms dramatically, helplessly, a series of red buttonholes stitched abruptly across his chest, and disappeared over the side.

Instinctively, the other torpedo mate fired his deadly "tin fish", filled with two tons of high explosive. It slid into the water. An excited flurry of bubbles. Then it was speeding towards the *Bulldog*. But already the aged British destroyer was pulling away to port. Now the torpedo raced furiously towards its target, as if it had a mind of its own and was determined not to let the enemy escape. But that wasn't to be.

It hissed by the churning stern screws of the *Bulldog* by what seemed inches and hurried on. Behind the destroyer, its shattered mast almost touching the water as it swept round in that tight curve, the first of the little freighters, chugging along at the regulation convoy speed of eight knots, was not so nifty. Frantically its skipper tried to emulate the *Bulldog*'s manoeuvre. To no avail. The deadly torpedo struck its bow in mid-turn.

There was a blinding, electric flash of vivid violet flame. The freighter's bow seemed to leap out of the water. Next moment her back broke and she was sinking in two separate parts, the front end rearing up abruptly in a clifflike mess of shattered burning steel. A moment later and the second E-boat had broken off its attack and was surging away, audibly hitting each wave as it reached forty knots an hour, driving for the safety of the fog and Texel beyond . . .

That minor skirmish was the start of many that May day. German dive-bombers, the antiquated Stukas, easy meat for the British fighters, came over in swarms to fall out of the sky screaming, sirens going full out, to attack such coastal backwaters as Eastbourne, Southsea and the like. To what purpose no one seemed able to guess. At midday, off Withernsea in East Yorkshire, a run-down Victorian spa of no military value whatsoever, a German sub appeared and lobbed a few shells at the pier and what was left of the Victorian towers, where worthy middle-class citizens from Hull had once strolled and savoured the bracing sea air.

In London itself, the capital's air raid defences were repeatedly put on "red alert". Since the great German raid of 10 May, when 1,500 Londoners had died and double that number had been injured, the authorities had been expecting another attempt to put the capital out of action. Even the chamber of the House of Commons had been burned down to blackened walls and Churchill had wept. But the Germans, attacking everywhere, didn't chance heavy losses by attempting to bomb London once more. And it was this factor that caused the clever young men of Admiral Godfrey's Naval Intelligence section in Room 39 to continue to believe that these tremendously wide-spread German attacks were cover for the *Bismarck*'s foray into the open sea.

Still they were puzzled, and terribly worried. For if they came up with a definite statement on the *Bismarck*'s intentions, they knew this would influence their Lordships' deployment of the Home Fleet. As Admiral Godfrey, who had now taken to secreting a bottle of malt whisky in his office, to which he recoursed at regular intervals, remarked more than once, "Gentlemen, we'll only get one bite of the cherry – and God help England and the Home Fleet if we make a mistake. Please bear that in mind in your deliberations." And with that he would disappear into his own office for yet another sip of the whisky.

Thus it was, as more and more alarmist reports of German naval and air activity continued to pour in, the "clever young men", as Godfrey liked to call his intelligence staff, mostly civilians in uniform, waited with growing impatience for the arrival of the "Mossy" with its cargo from Stockholm.

Naturally they had looked up Savage in the Naval List and had soon found out that he had been captured the year before, imprisoned at Wesertimke and according to the "protecting power", in this case the Swiss Red Cross, escaped from the POW camp a couple of months ago. But how he had gotten to Sweden still remained a mystery.

That "urgent blood and iron", hadn't fooled them for very long either. "*Bismarck*, of course," Montague, ex-lawyer and now a member of the "clever young men", had exclaimed almost at once. "Remember that speech he made back in the 1860s."

"Actually, he said 'iron and blood'," Fleming had objected a little petulantly that he had not made the discovery.

"Oh don't be such a fart-carrier, Ian," Montague had snapped airily. "This is not a bloody seminar on German history, you know. So, our man – Savage – knows something about Bismarck, and it can only be about the Hun ship. Why else would Stockholm request one of our Mosquitoes to bring him back tootsweet? The Mossy is hardly off the secret list, after all."

When no one responded, the clever ex-lawyer looked around at the circle of glum and impatient faces and said, with forced cheerfulness, "Gentlemen, there is nothing we can do, but wait for the Mossy and Commander Savage. In the meantime, I suggest we collect our dear chief and convince him to invite us to a slap-up lunch at White's. For my part, I'm heartily sick of whale meat and boiled potatoes."

It was suggestion that was met by smiles on the part of the others, save Fleming, who would have dearly loved to have indulged himself in what he called a "nooney".

Thus those eager young men, mainstays of the Empire and upper-class system, ventured out into a bombed London, the shattered buildings peering through a fading fog of smoke turning the spring day into a weird November. They coughed in the acrid air as cinders wafted down like black snow. But the fact that the capital of the British Empire – "all that red on the map" – was in such a sad state didn't seem to worry them much. They laughed at the elderly bobby, who naturally saluted them, guarding a smoking ruin, now emptied of anything of value. They hooted at the sight of a taxi-cab, with the great billowing balloon of gas on its roof in lieu of petrol to propel it, and enquired whether it was going to take off for Berlin that night in retaliation . . . For basically, as clever as they were, they were careless people, born in the belief that things would always work out well for them and their kind. If their world was crumbling all around them, never to be restored, they didn't seem aware of it.

So they passed on their giddy, flippant way to the club, and five hundred or so miles away to the east, the *Bismarck* and its escort, the *Prinz Eugen*, sailed undetected through the Baltic narrows and then, gathering speed, headed for the safety of the Norwegian ports, from which they would sail to do battle with the "Tommies" at last.

The scene was set, the actors were in place, the drama could commence . . .

BOOK FOUR

Defeat into Victory

One

Dawn broke cold, grey, vicious.

A surprisingly cruel wind – for that time of the year – tore across the Denmark Strait. It ripped at the waves with its white fingers. It hurled the freezing cold spray over the look-outs, huddled in layer upon layer of clothing. It was no better on the bridge of the cruiser *Norfolk*. The wind buffeted the bridge party. It tore the words from their mouths. They were forced to speak only when necessary and when they did, the icy air stabbed their lungs like a razor-sharp blade.

Still the cruiser ploughed on. The bow cleaved the green heaving waves, never-ending, it seemed, in their determination to slow the *Norfolk* down, as she unwittingly sailed to her doom.

The men were on their toes, despite the conditions and the danger. All of them, down to the youngest "snotty" and rating knew the importance of their mission. The *Bismarck* and her escort the *Prinz Eugen* were out, heading for the "blue water". They had to find her and alert the leading ships of the Home Fleet before she managed to escape south. Breakfast, their only meal, had been cold greasy bacon, washed down with lukewarm milkless tea from flasks, though there had been a tot of rum. Now the captain had ordered the galley fires doused and the cooks on watch. Every available hand was needed on deck now. And the cooks, well-known throughout the senior service, as great moaners, obeyed without complaint.

On the bridge, the officers of the watch continued to scour the heaving grey horizon through their glasses, their eyes bloodshot with the strain. By now radar and radio were picking up enemy signals.

Back in Whitehall, the Admiralty could make little of them; as the captain of the *Norfolk* was informed in a terse signal, "*Colonel Bogey*." It was a strange form of communication from their Lordships, which puzzled the prim-and-proper young communications officer who brought the message to the skipper until the latter burst abruptly, and very surprisingly, into song, "Ballocks and the same to you . . . Where was the engine driver when the boiler burst . . . They found his bollocks . . ." Thereupon he grinned and informed the startled youngster, who had thought the skipper had gone mad with the strain, "It's all a cock-up, Perkins. Nobody knows nothing . . ."

In the end it wasn't the *Norfolk*, but her sister ship the *Suffolk*, which first spotted the enemy. Cruising at a leisurely eighteen knots, the *Suffolk* saw them in mid-channel. Instantly the radio operators bent over their desks, as up top they saw her in full detail: masts, funnels and huge guns, which spouted fire and smoke instantly.

The grey midday sky was torn apart by their elemental fury. One . . . two . . . three . . . four . . . Huge spouts of angry white water flailed upwards, and down below in the radio room, which shuddered like a live thing under the impact, the leading hand cried, "God in frigging heaven . . . it's the end of the frigging world . . ."

It wasn't. But to those who were there that May and who would live to tell their bloody and heroic tale, it almost seemed like that. The *Bismarck* had arrived. The battle had commenced . . .

"Here she comes now, chaps," the RAF Controller

announced over the tannoy system, which echoed metallically back and forth across Croydon Field. "Right on time. Watch your noddles, you down there on the runway, *please*."

Hastily the eager young officers of Naval Intelligence stepped back beyond the end of the flare-path.

One minute the Mosquito wasn't there, the next the beautiful wooden plane came hurtling down the runway at a tremendous speed, exhibiting why it could fly over the Reich totally unarmed; for the *Luftwaffe* hadn't a single fighter which could catch up with Britain's latest and most secret plane. Even Commander Fleming, the born cynic, was impressed. "By jove, sir," he exclaimed to Admiral Godfrey, "doesn't she set a cracking pace," and then they were submerged by the ear-splitting noise, as the RAF pilot throttled back and brought the twin-engined plane that had flown from Stockholm, with its all-important passenger, to a stop.

Now even before the little grey RAF utility truck could trundle out to the plane, the men of Naval Intelligence surged forward, eager to get a first look at the passenger hidden in the Mosquito's bomb-bay. Even Admiral Godfrey, despite his age, bulk and position, allowed himself to be taken with the mob of excited young officers.

A minute or two later, Savage was being helped out on to the tarmac, his legs still very shaky from the long tight trip, to face his eager interrogators. His features were gaunter than ever and there were two long lines etched deep about his mouth, indicating a man who had suffered a lot. But his eyes were his most striking features that May afternoon in Croydon.

They were naturally hard and aware, as they should be in a man who had suffered so much and had been near to death several times; but they were also puzzled, as if he couldn't understand these men, crowding around him, so eager, so well-fed, so content with life. It was as if Savage were asking, where have you lot been during the last years of the war . . . how have you suffered . . . where are your wounds?

But naturally the "clever young men" of Admiral Godfrey's Naval Intelligence section didn't know. Even if they had, it would not really have concerned them. They had nothing to be ashamed of. Let lesser mortals go out and die heroically. It was their job to help win the war and, when that was done, to carry on running the Empire, as they and their kind had always done. Undoubtedly they would die in bed of old age; it was their due and privilege.

Admiral Godfrey thrust out his hand, while the others waited eagerly to start questioning the puzzled young man with the emaciated, bitter face.

"Glad to see you aboard once more, Savage," the Admiral was saying as they started to move back to the waiting staff cars. "We can't wait to hear what you have to tell us about the escape, your encounter with this Gestapo chap M—"

"Müller, sir."

"Yes, Müller, and what he informed you about the *Bismarck*. How very odd indeed." He helped Savage through the open door of the big Humber blue-painted staff car, while on the approach road a motorbike headed towards the little convoy of waiting staff cars, going all-out. "I can't see why a person of that kind, the worse kind of Hun brute, should help us, Savage. Not for the life of me—"

"Do you think it was a plant, Savage?" Fleming cut in, sick of the Admiral's bumbling approach. "Some kind of Nazi ploy – a very clumsy one, if it is, in my humble opinion – to mislead us once we knew that the

Bismarck was on the high seas." Fleming leaned forward impatiently, as if willing the other man to speak up and solve the mystery.

Savage looked at Fleming, his face full of contempt as he got a whiff of the expensive eau-de-Cologne that this fellow lieutenant-commander used. "No, I don't think it is," he said slowly, his disdain for the other man all too obvious. "Why should he go to all that trouble to have me flown to Stockholm and have me delivered to the British Embassy. If that came out, surely he would have been in serious trouble with his own chief, Himmler?"

Fleming wasn't impressed by the argument. "Perhaps that chinless wonder of an ex-chicken farmer" – he meant Himmler – "might have been involved in the plot too."

"Ian," Godfrey cut his subordinate short. "Let Commander Savage tell his story first. Then we can make some decisions about it, eh?"

But Savage was not fated to tell his strange tale yet and when he did, it would really be too late. For, in that instant, as the petty officer had engaged gear and was about to set off for the journey back to central London, followed by the rest, the naval dispatch rider daringly swerved across the road, one hand held up in stern command, crying above the racket kicked up by his BSA, "STOP . . . PLEASE . . . STOP!"

"Silly bugger," the petty officer cried, "ain't even started yet. Want to frigging kill us all . . . and the Admiral on board as well?"

But no one was listening to the petty officer's enraged outburst, not even Admiral Godfrey. They were all staring entranced at the dispatch rider, who had appeared out of nowhere and had had the temerity to stop them in this high-handed un-regulations manner. Not that the DR was concerned. He was fumbling in the leather pouch he wore around his neck. What he wanted was a small sealed flimsy, which he handed to the petty officer with the command, "Give that to your senior officer, at once."

Under other circumstances, the petty officer might have given the rating on the bike what he would have called "a mouthful o' old buck". But not now, he was too surprised. He took the flimsy and, turning with difficulty, gave it to Admiral Godfrey, who, in his turn, passed it on to Fleming with the words, "If it's in clear, you read it, Ian. Left my spectacles in the office, dammit all."

Hurriedly, while Savage watched without any apparent curiosity, Fleming opened the message printed on oilskin paper. He glanced at it and announced, "It's in clear, sir . . . Shall I read it aloud . . . It's *very* important."

"Pray do so, Ian." He added then for the benefit of the driver, "Close the partition, petty officer."

"Sir," the driver answered dutifully.

Fleming waited. Behind, in the other cars, the young men of Naval Intelligence wound down the windows and craned out their necks, curious to know why they hadn't moved off now they had Savage out of the plane.

Ian Fleming whistled softly and then he looked up, "Admiral . . . gentlemen," he announced in a voice that he had once reserved for his odd appearances before the school in Eton Chapel, "the *Hood* is about to engage the *Bismarck* . . ."

Two

"It's the *Hood* all right, Admiral," the youngest officer on the bridge announced with the certainty of youth.

Admiral Lutjens remained undecided. He peered through the rolling low fog, while the rest of his middle-aged officers, who were too vain to wear glasses, did the same. Every now and again, he would catch a glimpse of the English squadron in the gleaming circles of his binoculars. "Are you sure, *Herr Oberleutnant*?" he asked finally.

"*Jawohl, Herr Admiral,*" the officer replied promptly, blushing furiously for some reason known only to himself. "It's the *Hood* all right. Can't mistake that silhouette, sir."

"Famous last words," Lutjens tried to grin, but failed miserably. But he thought the boy was right and there was no time to lose. What a great victory it would be, if he could knock out the pride of the English Navy at no cost to himself. He made up his mind. "Run up the battle flag – and permission-to-fire signal flag," he snapped. "We fight."

For a moment, the Admiral thought his middle-aged staff officers were going to open their mouths and cheer. After all, they had spent all their adult lives preparing for this moment; they were about to enter action at last. Instead they contented themselves with rapping out orders, making calculations and surveying the distance between themselves and the dark shapes on the tossing green horizon.

"*Fertig . . . fertig . . . fertig* . . . ready . . . ready . . . ready." From all sides the eager shouts came, signifying that the various divisions of the great battleship were ready for action.

Lutjens did the expected thing: the privilege of the fleet commander. "Stand by to open fire," he commanded. There was no sense of urgency or triumph in his voice at that moment. Instead he was doubtful, hesitant. Behind him one of the senior mates chortled happily, "Stand by for the waltz, girls." Lutjens frowned. How easy they were taking it.

He flashed a glance at the glowing of his complicated gold chronometer, given to him by the Führer himself. Very carefully he noted the time. It was Central European Time, zero five hundred hours and fifty-two minutes. "Eight minutes to six on a May morning in the year, 1941," he whispered to himself, knowing he would never forget that time as long as he lived. For perhaps it marked . . . He hesitated. Dare he say the words aloud? He did. "The end of the British Empire."

Next moment, all doubts forgotten, he yelled at the top of his voice, "*FEUER FREI*!"

"They're hoisting the open fire . . . open fire flags, sir," the young officer cried across to Rear Admiral Holland. Hastily the latter focused his binoculars. Below him the smoke from his own B-gun turret was drifting away. The *Hood* did not have the best of gun platforms, but Holland was not slowing down to give Guns, his gunnery officer, the kind of stability he needed for accurate shooting. That would have been too risky, especially as the *Bismarck* was within firing range.

Carefully he counted off three seconds until the Hood's first tremendous salvo detonated. They were firing at the *Bismarck*'s running mate, the *Prinz Eugen*; for it was Holland's guess that if the *Eugen* was seriously hurt, the

Bismarck, deprived of its escort, would make a run for it. At least, he hoped she would.

"Thar they blow," some rating yelled, carried away by the excitement of it all.

"They're on target," someone else cried, as the deckmen tensed for the result of the first strike.

Glued to his glasses, Holland watched as the first huge shell exploded to the starboard of the *Bismarck*. A miss. The knuckles of his hands holding the glasses whitened even more, the only sign of his frustration. The second strike was a miss, too. Again the shell fell between the two German ships, but closer. Holland could see how even the *Bismarck* trembled under the impact of the near miss. "Damn and blast," he cursed through gritted teeth. "Hit the bugger, will you!"

Next moment the third shell struck home. It hit the *Prinz Eugen*. A burst of intense black smoke rose, turning into a cloud several hundred feet high in an instant. In its centre a sudden cherry-red fire started to rage furiously. In its blinding ruddy glare, Holland, his eyes narrowed to slits, could see the *Eugen*'s radio masts come tumbling and slithering down to the deck in a series of angry blue and pink sparks. Almost instantly the German ship began to lose speed.

"We've hit the sod," Holland heard himself shouting, as if he were listening to someone else. "WE'VE HIT THE *EUGEN*!"

Now the Home Fleet, the greatest in the world, was beginning to close in on the insolent German intruders, who were making this cheeky attempt (so the British thought) to tackle the Royal Navy in its own backyard. The main Home Fleet had left its berth in Scapa Flow, sailed around the north of the British Isles in a westwards direction and was desperately sailing all out to cut off the enemy's escape route back to France, if that was the direction in which the *Bismarck* and *Prinz Eugen* would flee.

To the west of the Home Fleet, the two battleships HMS *Rodney* and *Ramilles* had taken up a back-up position in order to stop any attempt by the fugitive enemy to make a dash for the North Atlantic and the general direction of the American coast.

In the meantime, the *Hood* Force and the two cruisers, *Sheffield* and *Norfolk*, continued to engage the *Bismarck* and the *Prinz Eugen*, now waiting for the torpedo bombers from the aircraft carriers in the south to arrive and put the finishing touches to the destruction of these impudent Huns, who had dared to enter British waters like this.

The Bismarck's Last Voyage

Indeed the Admiralty started to feel complacent about the outcome of the running battle. The pressure started to ease. It was a foregone conclusion, wasn't it? The Huns could not escape; they were faced with too much British firepower.

At Naval Intelligence they were not so sure. By now Savage was beginning to open up, though as yet they couldn't quite believe his strange tale. Godfrey had told his officers privately during the several breaks they had been forced to make in their interrogation of the escaped officer (Savage, for all his tough appearance, was at the end of his tether, weakened by the year in captivity, his escape and the beatings afterwards): "In view of what the man's been through, we can expect him to be a little barmy. Who wouldn't under those circumstances, poor sod."

It was a sentiment with which the others agreed, save Fleming. He remained hard, cynical and sceptical. "Poor sod he might be, sir," he remarked acidly. "But if we're to accept even part of his downright crazy story – this business with the head of the Gestapo," he'd added with a snort of contempt, "Savage must have worked with the enemy, don't you think? Collaboration, if you like to call a spade a bloody shovel?"

The others had not risen to the bait. Indeed some of them, like Montague, had given Fleming looks of annoyance, which seemed to indicate that he should keep his damned prejudiced opinions to himself. But Fleming being Fleming had not even noticed. Invariably he was right and the others were wrong.

But as fantastic as Savage's story about his pact with Gestapo Müller was, the Admiralty were eager to know the details. If the Hun was really a secret communist working for the Bolsheviks, he would be in a position to deliver to them top secret German information. And it was a typical Russian ploy to involve a neutral third country in their devious plots. That country would think it was working in its own interests; in fact, it would be indirectly working for the Russians. So with a war impending between Soviet Russia and Nazi Germany, what better way to paralyse or seriously damage the German Navy before it could be used again in Russia, than to let the British do the job for the Russians. For the more far-sighted of their Lordships at the Admiralty, this could one logical explanation behind the strange agreement between Müller and the insignificant escaped British naval officer.

"You see, gentlemen," Savage had explained right at the start of his account, "Müller had me by the short and curlies, if you'll excuse my French. He was going to keep the woman – a Polish girl – who had helped me escape from the farm as security. As long as I promised to tell you and no one else about the *Bismarck*, so that he would not risk his own thick neck, she would be safe." Savage frowned uneasily at the memory of that meeting, "And if things went well, we could meet again after the war."

"Oh my God," Fleming had moaned softly in mock exasperation, "we'll have Vera Lynn on next warbling that sentimental twaddle of hers."

"Shut up, Ian," Godfrey had snapped, for once losing patience with his chief assistant. Typical sailor of the old school, a no-nonsense type – all the same he had commanded men for long enough to know when someone was speaking from the heart, and Savage was certainly doing that. "Let the man speak, will you."

Now Savage had finished speaking; his interrogation was over and, drained of energy as he was, he was hanging on strictly out of a sense of duty and the knowledge that if he made a balls-up of this business, it would be a totally defenceless Elena who would suffer.

Thus it was that when Fleming slowly began to think of the coming delights with the obedient and willing little Wren, Peggy, that Godfrey put down his afternoon tea and gobbled his last chocolate biscuit before anyone else had the temerity to take it. With an air of finality in his voice, he asked. "All right, Savage, we're going to get you back to your billet soon, so that you can get a good bath and as much shuteye as you need."

"Thank you, sir," Savage said with unaccustomed humility, for he had grasped that he was in the power of people who would use him as long as they needed him and then get rid of him swiftly and quietly. If he were ever going to see Elena again, and now that had become a priority in his life, he would have to play this clever game. He already knew far too much about what was going on on both sides of the pond. For the time he would play the game with his cards held tightly to his chest. So he controlled his anger, and added with seeming gratitude, "That's awfully kind of you, sir."

Godfrey beamed. He had obviously assessed his man correctly. "Let us assume that the *Bismarck* will soon have to make a run for it – the Admiralty tells me that she and her sister ship, the *Prinz Eugen* are under fire from our guns – where will she head for? Now this is vital. We can't waste time and ships searching all over the show for her, once she breaks and runs." He looked hard at the other man.

Savage was ready with his answer. "Müller, sir, told me that he knew that for certain, from two different sources. Grand Admiral Raeder's HQ in Berlin and even better from his own Gestapo officials in France, who seemingly know everything that's going on at service headquarters there." He paused and noted the power he had suddenly achieved. They were hanging on his every word, even that supercilious snob, Fleming.

"Go on," Godfrey prompted him.

But before Savage could continue, the door burst open and a red-faced admiral, his tunic wide open, his tie askew, eyes popping out of his head like these of a man demented, tormented beyond all reason, cried aghast, "the *Hood* . . . the Huns have sunk the *Hood* . . ."

Three

The *Prinz Eugen*'s second salvo came howling in like some great speeding express through a silent midnight station. The noise was tremendous, awe-inspiring terrifying. This time the second barrage didn't miss. The three huge shells slammed into the smoke-shrouded *Hood*. The main mast was hit. It came roaring down. Sparks and shattered metal flew everywhere. Shrapnel scythed lethally across the debris-littered main deck. Men and metal went down, ripped apart effortlessly. Everywhere there were dead and dying men, writhing and squirming in their death agonies in pools of dark-red, smoking blood.

The deck stowage caught light immediately. Within seconds the flames were crackling and blazing as high as the stacks. An instant later, the wind fanned the flames into a gigantic blowtorch of all-consuming fire. It swept the length of the huge deck, burning all in front. Ratings were turned into scorched, charred crouched pygmies in a flash. Boats went up like tinderwood. The grey wartime paint bubbled and sizzled like the symptons of some loathsome skin disease. In a flash all was horror and sudden violent death.

Still the great doomed ship came on in its final ride of death. It was as if nothing could stop her. Even in her death throes she was intent on closing with the enemy. After all, had this been the reason for her creation so long before?

It was just the target that the *Bismarck* needed. What

better kind of "blooding" for this totally new ship than the destruction of the pride of the Royal Navy – HMS *Hood*? Lutjens, on the bridge of the *Bismarck*, didn't hesitate. He made some swift mental calculations. He knew where and when to strike. There would be no excuse for the gunners this time, as there had been at that ill-fated *Battle of Jutland* in 1916. This time it was going to be a German triumph; it *had* to be!

Above Lutjens on the bridge, Fire Control made their calculations. Hastily they relayed them to an impatient, nervous Lutjens. He'd have the honour of issuing the decisive fire order. It was going to ensure his place in naval history, that of the commander who had sunk the *Hood*.

But it wasn't going to be all that easy. Even as he made his decision, the enemy shells raked the *Bismarck*. Great gouts of water shot up to starboard. Metal sang through the air. Lutjens yelped and grabbed a stanchion. He felt a stinging pain in his forehead. He reached up with a shaky hand. His cap had vanished. Something wet and warm was trickling down the side of his face. He had been hit. It was his own blood. The damned Tommies were not going to go down without a fight. Now it was to be a duel to the death.

He shook his head. Everything came back into focus once more. Holding up his hand to staunch the blood, he started to cry out his orders in a voice that he hardly recognised as his own; his voice was that shaky. But even as he determined to finish off the *Hood*, Admiral Lutjens knew that that would be the end of the attack. Thereafter, the Tommies would be after him like a pack of vengeful bloodhounds. They'd want revenge all right. He'd have to make a run for it and pray that he'd reach Brest before those English hounds of hell caught up with him

He made his decision. "Elevate A and B," he commanded.

Almost immediately the great steel turret hummed with electricity and began to swing round in the direction of the enemy. "Maximum height . . . plunging fire . . . two salvoes." Suddenly he felt, as if someone had opened an unseen tap in his body. All his energy seemed to flow out. He felt lethargic, as if he had just pounded the ribs of some hot whore in a mattress polka.

Then it happened.

The huge shells – one, two, three – plunged down at a tremendous speed. They sliced right through the *Hood*'s deck armour. They cut the steel plates like a hot knife through butter. Ammo commenced exploding. It was suddenly like Bonfire Night. Shells flew in every direction in a crazy pattern of multi-coloured light. The *Hood* started to tremble. It was an unbelievable sight: the enormous steel ship quivering frighteningly. The men on board trembled too.

On the bridge of the cruiser *Norfolk* they viewed the sudden transformation of the sky from grey to violet, to brilliant red and then to a smoke-distorted grey, once more with total bewilderment. What was going on a couple of sea miles away? What in God's name was happening to the *Hood*?

A moment later they found out. To their horror. Suddenly, the grey sky turned to livid, awe-inspiring burning fire. The *Hood* gave a violent shudder. Like a savage animal caught unexpectedly by a hunter's bullet and taken by surprise as its hindlegs start to weaken and give way.

A hellish boom. The *Hood* was shrouded by thick grey smoke. The cloud rose higher and higher. It commenced to lay a shroud over the dying vessel. Here and there, bursts of vivid cherry-red flames. That frightening, awesome trembling commenced once more. Plates sprung. Pieces of derricks clattered to the tilting deck or showered the water to both sides. Another mast came tumbling down. The ship's plane slithered slowly but inevitably along the deck. Slowly, almost comically, it went over the side and floated there for a few moments. Then the sea snatched it greedily and it disappeared. Now the *Hood* started to break apart.

Open-mouthed and gawping like village yokels, the men on the *Norfolk* watched the great ship go to her doom. Surely, their faces spoke, it couldn't be happening to the *Hood*? But it was.

She was racked by another terrible explosion. There was the wrenching, ear-splitting grinding of metal being ripped apart by force. Like some great grey whale surfacing for air, the whole of her bow rose higher and higher. Desperate tiny figures slithered its length, frantically fighting for a hold. In vain. They disappeared into the white frothy maelstrom below. A man dived from a shattered derrick. It was a beautiful performance like that given by some pre-war fleet champion before a crowd of admiring matelots. His dive failed. He missed his aim. Instead of the water, he hit the deck like a sack of wet cement – and burst open.

Now the watchers could hear the faint sad cries for help. "*Mercy . . . God help me . . . Don't leave me mates, I can't see . . . HELP . . . MOTHER . . .*" It was almost over now. Here and there the watchers shielded their eyes, turned away, heads bent, as if they could no longer stand the sight.

Abruptly, the bow plunged down again. Water shot up out of the centre of the fog of smoke. Higher . . . higher . . . hundreds of feet into the grey sky. More and more panic-stricken ratings flung themselves hopelessly into the freezing water. They knew they wouldn't survive more than a couple of minutes in that arctic sea. Perhaps they wanted to die quickly. Now the men of the *Hood* were beginning to die fast . . . by their score, the hundred . . . the thousand.

On the *Norfolk* hardened petty officers sighed. Those were their shipmates they'd gotten pissed with in Pompey, visited knocking shops with in Shanghai and Hong Kong, with whom they had paraded in half a score of glittering ceremonies all over the Empire "showing the flag". *Their oppos*! Now they were dying only a mile or so away and there wasn't one fucking thing they could fucking well do about it . . .

Lutjens pushed back his hair and wiped the sweat off his furrowed forehead. It was a ploy to dab his eyes at the same time; they were full of tears. It was the enemy dying, he knew that. But at the same time he was watching the end of a great ship and, like all sailors, that was something he hated to see. In the end all men, whatever their nationality and whether they were at war with one another or not, who went down to the sea felt the tragedy of a dying ship. This time Lutjens didn't give the order for the salvo which he knew would be the *Bismarck*'s last to fire at the dying *Hood*. He left that target task to "Guns".

Once more the *Bismarck*'s cannon boomed. A great swish. The howl of ton-heavy shells rushing across the sky. The terrible wind that swept the deck, as if the Devil himself wanted to wipe them all off the face of the earth into his evil clutches.

For what seemed an eternity, nothing happened. Had the *Bismarck*'s shells failed to explode? They hadn't. Next to him a hearty junior officer who had just come up from below to enjoy the spectacle, cried, "Holy straw sack . . . just cast your glassy orbs on that . . . *fer Chrissake*!"

A violent sheet of flame. It shot hundreds of feet high. A tremendous crash. Great white combers of water rushed towards the doomed ship. Startlingly forty-two thousand tons of steel started to disintegrate before their shocked gazes. The pride of the Royal Navy simply blew apart. One moment the *Hood* was there; the next she had gone, as if she had never even existed.

Metal showered the sea. The waves boiled in crazy fury. The oil slick caught light. Swiftly the tide of burning oil swept forward. It engulfed the men attempting to swim for it. Those on the carley floats didn't escape either. Their little craft were turned into instant death traps. Everywhere dying men pleaded with their God for mercy. But there was no mercy for the poor pathetic burning, drowning creatures. This day God was looking the other way.

Slowly, but surely the screams, the pleas, the curses against fate were submerged and muffled by the great cloud of thick black oil-tinged smoke which now arose until nothing more could be heard. On the *Norfolk*, the suddenly subdued matelots were glad. It gave them a moment's respite from the horror.

On the *Bismarck*, the men, too, were stunned. But not for long. Suddenly, the thought ran from man to man as if by some sort of naval bush telegraph: we've destroyed the pride of the English Navy! A wave of overwhelming ecstatic joy swept through the great German battleship. It went from division to division, deck to deck, mess to mess, right down to the sweating stokers in the bowels of the engine room. Suddenly discipline and strict military protocol were forgotten. Men embraced. Rank was forgotten. Officers shook hands, clapped petty officers on the shoulders, shouted joyously at humble ratings. They were like men seeing each other for the very first time, bringing some wondrous tiding.

The *Kriegsmarine*'s iron discipline, worse than that of the Royal Navy, based on the lash, relaxed for a few moments. Those who possessed illegal "flatmen", hip-pocket bottles of schnapps and *Korn* liquor broke them out and started toasting victory and this was the end of the terrible war. Others ran back and forth wildly. They punched the air, slapping shipmates across the back, "Good old shitting *Bismarck*," they cried exuberantly. "We knew she'd shitting well do it . . . That'll teach that drunken sod, Churchill. *Himmel, Arsch und Amerika*! . . . Now he can go and stick his Yankee cigar up his fat Tommy arse, eh!"

Men sang. Others, drunk on joy and schnapps, danced. Their comrades cheered. They made obscene gestures. There was wild talk of vaseline and bunks! They blew wet kisses. *Obermaat* Hansen, old, horny and totally depraved, gave one of his celebrated tuneful farts, modulated carefully to sound like "*Deutschland uber Alles.*" Drunks attempted to stand to attention to the sound of the national anthem coming from Hansen's well-endowed musical arse. They fell flat on their faces instead.

Up on deck in "officers' country" the celebrations were more subdued. But they celebrated all the same. "God in heaven," the junior officers chortled. "Think of the tin" – they meant decorations for valour – "the girls . . . girls with flowers. It'll be Christmas every day . . . roses all the way. Lads, we're going home to mother. Hurrah."

Suddenly and strangely, Lutjens no longer seemed able to enjoy his crew's joy. Abruptly he felt a sense of foreboding, as if he had been found guilty of a nameless crime and had to be punished. He knew not why.

An hour later, he signalled Raeder in Berlin, "Have sunk battle-cruiser *Hood*. Another battleship damaged and in retreat. Two heavy cruisers now shadowing. Fleet Commander." The message seemed to reflect his new mood. Lutjens had just announced a great victory, soon to be celebrated wildly throughout the Reich. But he suddenly took no joy in it.

Half an hour later he signalled Raeder once more. Now his sense of triumph had vanished completely. The signal was sombre. It read:

1. Engine Room 4 out of action.
2. Port stokehold leaking. But can be held. Bows leaking severely.
3. Cannot make more than eighteen knots.
4. Two enemy radio scanners noted.
5. Intend to run for St Nazaire. No loss of men.

Fleet Commander.

The wild intoxication of victory was past. Cold realism had taken over. Admiral Lutjens now had no illusions about what was to come. The Tommies had lost their *Hood*. They would make him pay for that. He had studied the English ever since he had been a teenage cadet. He knew as much about the Royal Navy as he did of his own *Kriegsmarine*. The English never gave up.

He had to make his escape now. There was no other alternative. Otherwise he was doomed. He ordered the retreat – and the escape.

Majestic, but a lot slower now, the great German ship sailed into the grey unknown. Behind her she left an empty sea. It tossed back and forth in its cold-green intensity. Far off the shadows moved too. But alone in that great watery waste there were three men – three men only – the sole survivors of the HMS *Hood* . . .

Four

Death came to the *Bismarck* on the morning of Tuesday, 27 May, 1941. From Friday onwards, the British Home Fleet, thirsty to avenge those who had destroyed the *Hood*, had been hunting the *Bismarck* frantically. After all, the prestige of the senior service was at stake. It was no use an official Admiralty spokesman announcing to a shocked and grieving British public: "And which of her great-hearted company would have been asked to be left behind on a day like this? God was very merciful to them. Their end was instantaneous and their fight an honest one in the greatest cause for which a sailorman ever put to sea." Even Churchill, the only wartime leader on any side who felt anything for the suffering of his people, wasn't satisfied. "They," he meant the dead *Hood* crewmen, "want revenge, not sentiment. Action this day. Get that *Bismarck* bastard!"

From all quarters the great ships converged on the *Bismarck*, as she twisted back and forth in intricate patterns and manoeuvres in an attempt to outwit her fiendish pursuers. For a while luck was on her side. The weather closed in and once, for as long as fifteen hours, the British ships lost contact. But with two aircraft carriers involved in the greatest chase of the war, she was found again. A coastal command flying boat spotted the *Bismarck* on the morning of 25 May. Thereafter the British never lost contact again.

By now Lutjens was a worried man. At first he felt he

could throw off the two old British cruisers shadowing him. With the weather and the poor quality radar with which the British ships were equipped, he felt he had a good chance of reaching the protection of the French coast before the fireworks really started. But the information, culled from tapped British radio signals, that he had been sighted from the air, changed the situation considerably.

Now things really started to go wrong. He ordered Captain Brinckmann of the *Prinz Eugen* to take up station in front of the *Bismarck* to minimise damage if the enemy came within gunnery range. But nerves right at the top were rattled. Brinckmann made a mess of the tactic. They almost collided and for a while Bismarck's steering mechanism jammed. Thereafter Lutjens retired to his day cabin and had three swift schnapps until his hands ceased trembling. Thereafter he washed his face and stared at himself in the washbasin mirror. The face of a dead man stared back at him. He looked away hastily.

By now the distance between the *Bismarck* and her pursuers, the two old British cruisers, had been reduced to 120 miles. The minutes to that final confrontation were ticking away rapidly.

Lutjens, glum, unable to raise a smile for his staff officers, which he knew was fatal – a commander must always radiate confidence – let *Prinz Eugen* go on on her own. Perhaps the British would follow her. They didn't. They continued their pursuit of the *Bismarck*. The Admiral started to despair.

Now the British, with the *Bismarck* only a hundred miles away and the aircraft carriers on station, began to apply the pressure. The British Commander, Admiral Tovey, ordered the ancient torpedo bombers from the aircraft carrier *Victorious* into action. The "stringbags", obsolete even before the war, were to slow the giant

German battleship down even more. Then the ships would finish her off with gunfire, once they came within range.

In patchy cloud the British came in to the attack. The gunners on the *Bismarck* spotted them immediately when they broke cloud cover. They threw up a tremendous wall of burning steel. The whole port and starboard sides of the German battleship erupted with fire. Still the pilots pressed on, wave-hopping, slowed down even more by the "tin fish" slung between the wheels of their fixed undercarriage. A plane was hit. It slammed down into the waves, turned turtle and lay there wallowing in the swell. No one got out.

The doomed squadron kept on. They seemed to be passing through a network of flame and smoke. Time and time the brave young pilots in their ancient planes disappeared into the smoking inferno. Yet they always emerged again. The lead plane got within striking distance. The pilot didn't hesitate. He fired his tin fish. The lightened Swordfish rose a good fifty feet into the air. Next moment the torpedo plopped to the waves and was up and running, heading straight for the *Bismarck*.

On the bridge Lutjens watched the wash as it sped towards the battleship, his hands clutching his binoculars turned into white-knuckled claws. He blinked. The torpedo had struck home. There was the great hollow boom of steel striking steel. The ship shuddered as the charge went off. Lutjens prayed fervently. His prayers were answered. The *Bismarck* steamed on, apparently untouched by the explosion at her bows.

As the surviving attack bombers turned to fly to their carrier before their fuel ran out, Lutjens forced himself to address the crew over the tannoy system. He boasted weakly that his ship had shot down twenty-seven British planes. It was a lie and even the stokers toiling in the bowels of the *Bismarck* knew it. They wiped their faces with their grease rags and whispered to each other, "The old man's lost his nerve. He's beginning to cream his skivvies."

Lutjens had. As soon as the announcement was over, he radioed Berlin to say that he was abandoning his attempt to lead his pursuers into a line of U-boats off St Nazaire, which was being hastily prepared by Doenitz. The latter raged and cursed to his young staff. "*Typisch*! What kind of piggery is this? The man ought to be in charge of a bimboat!"

Now a strange mood of apprehension and fatalism swept over the ship. They seemed to sense, even the dullest of the crew, that somehow their fate had been sealed. From being the terror of the sea, they had become a fugitive, hunted everywhere with every man's hand against them. Those who had charts kept looking at the French coast, trying to work out how long it would take the *Bismarck* to reach safety before the buck-teethed Tommies caught up with them.

Lutjens, not a religious man by any means, kept to his day cabin and prayed, and at the same viewed the weather, hoping fervently that God would make it break for the worse and give him one more chance to get away. More than often he thought of the fate of the *Hood*. Then he shuddered violently and had to get up and help himself to yet another stiff drink, his hand trembling violently, almost out of control. "In three devils' name," he moaned. "When will it all end? When?"

In Room 39, they felt the same. By now Godfrey's "clever young men" were hollow-eyed and shaky from too much black coffee, helped down by hidden sips of whisky and the Navy's favourite, pink gin. The Intelligence men simply couldn't relax. Even Fleming tried to take his mind off the great chase by thoughts of Peggy, the Wren, who wandered in and out at odd intervals, but he couldn't quite pull it off. He filled his mind with visions of her in various sexual poses. But they didn't work. Always, he came back to the "bloody *Bismarck*", as he was now calling the German ship.

Savage was the only man who did not seem outwardly affected by the furore, the constant excited comings and goings, the incessant jingle of the phones, the messengers. He sat in the corner near the polished coal scuttle – which Peggy brought in filled and burnished every morning, bending low so that Fleming had full advantage of her black-stockinged legs – wrapped up in a cocoon of his own thoughts. Now no one seemed particularly concerned with him; he had served his purpose and they were fully occupied with the details of the running battle between the *Bismarck* and the Home Fleet.

Savage had other things on his mind. All his life he had been a loner. Then Elena had come into his life. But for such a brief time. Now he was tormented by the feeling that he might have lost her for good and he'd have to return to that solitary existence, where his only love – his only life – was the Royal Navy. But what could he do about it? Was there some way that he could exert pressure on Gestapo Müller to ensure that whatever the outcome of the current battle, she'd survive?

Naturally Müller was now open to blackmail. His treachery could be revealed. But would the British authorities allow that? Looking at the clever faces all around him of men who knew how to use anybody and everybody to their own advantage, Savage felt not. Gestapo Müller's treachery would be used in due course for some more important matter than the life – or death – of a lone Polish girl. Suddenly Savage realised, as all sensitive people do some time or other in wartime, that he was not important. The "big picture", as the brass always calls the main issue, is what counts, not their petty lives with their petty worries and concerns. The brass pays lip service to the needs of the "little man", but it is that, merely lip service.

Savage dropped his head and Montague, glancing momentarily in his direction knew instinctively what was going through the ex-POW's mind. "Yes, chum," he said to himself, "one way or another, we're all bloody expendable . . ."

Admiral Lutjens had come to the same realisation, too. The Führer's signal, which he now held in a trembling hand, his eyes glazed with alcohol, though it could have been tears, made it clear that he was dispensable. It read, COME WHAT MAY, THE *BISMARCK* MUST ACHIEVE GLORY. UNDERSTOOD. LONG LIVE GERMANY! LONG LIVE OUR HOLY CAUSE!

The message had been read out to the crew – he could not bring himself to do it personally. There had been a few forced cheers. But not many. The men had understood Hitler's intention, just as he had. They were going to be sacrificed for the prestige of the National Socialist Reich. There would be no surrender. They would fight to the end and go down with their ship. Then Germany's honour would be satisfied. No one would give a damn about the hundreds of dead young men and their grieving relatives back home. They were merely cannon fodder, that's all.

Now captains of British ships in lost little ports, remote convoy duty, settling-down trials all over the North Atlantic slipped away unofficially from their assigned duties and tried to help in the search. These old forgotten skippers, who would never be promoted beyond their present command, smelt a fight. Signal after signal reached the C-in-C Admiral Tovey asking for permission to help find the *Bismarck*'s exact location and the Admiral felt he could do nothing to stop them.

The aircraft carriers closed in, too. It was against standard-operation-procedure for the lightly armed and armoured carriers to come within striking distance of a battleship. But now no one dare stop their skippers. It was said that everywhere stokers, trying to feed their engines to gain impossible speeds, were collapsing from heat stroke and exhaustion. Still the chase continued. For now everyone wanted to be in at the kill.

Now the end was near for the *Bismarck*. Yet her fate was still not finally sealed. The weather started to worsen. There was a rising north-westerly wind and an increasing swell. It was becoming ever more difficult for the "shadows", the great four-engined Sunderland flying-boats of Coastal Command, to keep on station. Tovey ordered his surface units to close up, whatever the risk, and not lose sight of the *Bismarck*. The result was that the HMS *Sheffield* soon received a blast from the *Bismarck*'s fifteen-inch guns. Like some tormented, cornered savage beast, the *Bismarck* was lashing out at anyone who came too close.

Still the destroyers went streaking in, a great white bone at their teeth. A profusion of torpedoes slid from their bows. Three hit. The *Bismarck* shuddered visibly and later the destroyer captains swore they heard her groan like some mortally wounded beast. An hour later the captain of the *Norfolk*: Signalled: "Enemy in sight twelve miles to the south of me . . . Tin hats on."

Minutes later *Rodney* followed with a similar report: "Enemy sighted." It was then that the C-in-C caught his first glimpse of the enemy. Veiled in the distant rainfall, a thick squat ghost of a ship, very broad in the beam was coming straight for him. Hastily he pulled on his "tin hat" and was drenched with rain water for his pains. Admiral Tovey didn't even notice. Already his ships were beginning to pound their target. The *Bismarck* commenced returning fire: thin orange streaks cutting the grey squally rain. "Battle bowlers on . . . on the bridge," Tovey ordered automatically, not taking his glasses off the enemy ship for one instant. "Here we go chaps. Nelson expects and all that . . ."

Five

The tension had been too much for Fleming. He needed relief from the constant nail-biting of the long chase which was now going into the third day. All that time he and the rest of Room 39 had existed on black coffee, pink gin and biscuits. By now his every nerve was tingling electrically; and ever since he had first discovered the pleasures of sex at Eton while he had been a member of POP, he knew there was one capital remedy against nervous tension – what he called, "a good rollicking bit of pokey-hokey!"

He had caught Peggy, the little Wren, as she bent down in the cellars to fill the burnished coal scuttle with the morrow's fuel. He had taken her completely by surprise. Naturally she had not screamed when he had crept up behind her and whipped up her skirts and then pressed himself against her, with "Now look, darling, what I've brought you." She let out a little whimper.

It was the whimper which had caught Savage's attention, as he had strode back and forth along the empty corridor above, lined with the oil painting of naval worthies in heavy wigs, striking the usual martial poses. Savage, as nervous and tense as Fleming – though for very different reasons – knew immediately what the whimper signified. Throwing his own concerns to the wind, he crept down the dark creaking old stairs that dated back to the eighteenth century to be confronted with the sight of Lieutenant-Commander Fleming, with his trousers around his ankles, prepared to enter the Wren, who was protesting but, all the same, had obligingly placed her hands on her knees to start the shock, as Fleming commanded, "Prepare to stand by for boarders . . . ha, ha."

For a moment Savage was dumbstruck. He hadn't needed a crystal ball to know what had been going on between the two of them. He had seen the looks that had passed between them every time she had entered Room 39. But he hadn't thought it right that an officer of Fleming's rank and experience should be fornicating, against King's Regulations, with a Wren, who was perhaps half his age and pretty vulnerable at that.

Even before he had decided what to do, he heard himself say sharply, "What's going on here, for God's sake? What's your ruddy game, Fleming, eh?"

The Wren jumped up. He could see the soft flesh of her plump buttocks shudder. She gasped just as Fleming's erection began to wither. A moment later the two of them were frantically grabbing at their under-clothing to cover up their nakedness.

For a long moment there was a heavy silence, broken only by the hectic breathing of the two lovers, caught by surprise. Then, with his flies done up in part, Fleming snapped in his best haughty manner: "Who the hell do you think you are, Savage – talking to me like that?" His thin face, with its broken nose, flushed a livid purple and automatically Savage clenched his right fist as if he were prepared to defend himself if Fleming came any closer. But he didn't. Instead he waited until the Wren had finished adjusting her skirt, not noticing that both her precious black stockings were badly laddered and beyond repair. Fleming nodded. Wordlessly, head bowed, face flushed with shame, she squeezed by Savage, as Fleming snorted, "What a damned middle-class prig you are, Savage. Besides what right have you to interfere in my affairs?" His eyes flashed. "Who knows just how pukka you are with your Gestapo Müller and supposed escape—"

"Shut up," Savage out in coldly, fully in control of himself. "Remember the position I've just found you in."

"One witness is no witness, may I remind you."

"No, with your reputation. Who do you think would believe you? You've blotted your copybook all too often. Just keep away from that Wren." Suddenly the thought of Elena flashed through Savage's mind. She'd been abused like the silly little Wren: an every man's beck-and-call, without any recourse to justice and protection. "Someone has to look after vulnerable girls like that."

"Join the frigging Salvation Army," Fleming was desperate to launch an attack – till he saw the look on Savage's emaciated face and changed his mind. Instead he contented himself with doing up the rest of his flies, saying softly, almost as if to himself as he did so, "You'll bloody well regret this, Savage, believe me." With that he was gone . . .

The end was near for the *Bismarck*. If the tension was still mounting in London, it had almost disappeared at the scene of action. The British, under the supervision of Admiral Tovey, knew they couldn't lose now. The odds against the dying *Bismarck* were overwhelming; it was only a matter of time before she went down now. In the *Bismarck* the mood was one of resignation. At the range she was being engaged, her Krupp armour was being holed like Swiss cheese. She was taking hit after hit.

By noon, a British salvo had ripped one of her turrets apart as if she were a tin can being opened by a particularly sharp tin-opener. That caused her to turn away and face what she might have thought were lesser and not so powerful enemies. But there was no escape. Shells continued to batter her from all sides. Everywhere there were great gleaming silver scars on her paintwork where they had slammed into her. Her deck was a shambles, with debris and wreckage everywhere, and angry little flames were beginning to erupt on all sides.

Desperately Lutjens ordered smoke. But the smoke screen had hardly commenced when, for some reason, it vanished once more leaving the dying ship naked to its enemies. Again shell after shell slammed mercilessly into the *Bismarck.* It was now almost as if the Tommies were using her as target practice, the broken Admiral told himself.

The crew's morale started to break at last. A stoker, his nerve gone, ran crazily through the explosions across the debris-strewn deck, heading for the bridge, shrieking, "You're mad . . . you're all mad . . . stop for—" The exploding shell caught him in mid-stride. His blood splattered on the buckled steel plates in great crimson gobs. He felt his bones breaking, urine and excreta streaming down his legs. For one second his contorted young face softened and a horrified Lutjens thought the rating was smiling up at him wearily. A moment later his severed head, encased in his steel helmet, rolled away and vanished into the scuppers.

Now the *Bismarck*, her rudders gone, was drifting aimlessly round and round, trailing thick black smoke behind her, the fire of her guns weakening by the instant, her life spluttering away in the ineffectual cannon fire of her shattered turrets. As the *Rodney* continued pounding her, great white columns of water rose nearly two hundred feet into the sky. Salvoes of that kind would have broken the back of the average destroyer and sunk her like a brick if she had steamed through one of them. Still, somehow, the *Bismarck* hung on. But not for long.

"Prepare the ship for sinking." The order now went out.

It was the last that anyone would receive from Admiral Lutjens. It seemed that he was no longer capable of making any constructive suggestions that might save the survivors. He was intent on going down with his ship. The men would have to look after themselves the best they could.

The engineer officers lit up the lower deck. Now there were brilliant lamps everywhere, illuminating the stark horror of the dying battleship: the shattered, crushed doors, the bulging split plates, the smoke gushing out everywhere, the dead lying abandoned. And men, hundreds of men, milling around stupidly. They had thrown away their combat gear and flash equipment. Now they were prepared for the ordeal in the arctic water that was to come, wearing inflated life-jackets and gas masks in preparation for the seawater hitting the electric motors and releasing their killing gases.

The *Bismarck* was sinking now. Lutjens had hidden himself. No one went to find him. They respected his wish to go down with his ship. Still there were those who felt he should have said something to the survivors. Instead Commander Gerhard Junack, the senior officer, present, barked, "Don't give up hope, comrades. Be careful when interrogated by the enemy. *Sieg Heil.*"

The response was listless. The great days had already been forgotten. The men knew they were facing death or years of imprisonment. The old world had vanished.

Junack gave up. In a weary voice, he ordered, "Abandon ship!"

It wasn't a moment too soon. By now the Tommies had shot out all the crippled giant's guns. They had left a smoking, lurching black ruin, which was clearly sinking. Tovey, feeling sickened at the sight, felt the ship was like a dog that had been run over. Someone had to put the dying beast down. He ordered his battleship to turn away. Next he had the cruiser *Dorsetshire* signalled. She was to sail in and finish the *Bismarck* off with her torpedoes. He was not going to risk his battleships in case the *Bismarck* had summoned up Doenitz's U-boats to torpedo them when they began to pick up survivors. But the head of the U-Boat Army had no such intention. His U-boats were spread across the French Atlantic coast waiting for the *Bismarck* to lead the Tommies into the trap. Now that the *Bismarck* wouldn't be coming, he didn't have the time to alter his dispositions. At least that's what he said later.

The survivors were hardly free of the ship when she keeled over to port. It was a frightening sight. Even those panicked sailors – splashing and slapping about in the freezing water as they tried to regain their breath – paused and stared momentarily, awed and strangely calm.

There was a frightening squeaking and groaning. The *Bismarck* was in its death throes. Later a handful of the survivors, men out of 2,400, swore they heard the screams, the pleas, the curses of the men who were still trapped at that moment, as they realised they were going to their doom.

A magazine exploded. Five hundred yards away the awed matelots of the *Dorsetshire* felt the shock, as if someone had just punched them in the guts. Majestically the *Bismarck* rose slowly into the air. Higher and higher. For what seemed an age that great steel tomb paused there. Then slowly, inexorably, she started to slide beneath the waves. They leapt up to receive her greedily, only to recoil hissing and spluttering furiously, as they felt the searing heat of her boilers.

On the bridge of the *Dorsetshire*, shocked and ashen-faced, the officers stiffened to attention without a command being given. They felt no sense of triumph at the end of this great ship, only one of loss. As one, they raised their right hands to the brims of their caps in salute

– the final tribute from the victors. Then with one last wild tumult of water, the *Bismarck* was gone.

The *Devonshire* steamed on to where the handful of survivors bobbed up and down in the oil slick. Not for long. A signal was coming through that U-boat periscopes had been sighted. Later it was reported that it was a false alarm, but that was later. So the cruiser steamed on, leaving the ocean silent and empty now, save for the mass of floating debris – and the one German on the rubber float, drifting aimlessly and sobbing, sobbing, sobbing, as if his very heart would break . . .

The Savage Conclusion

The smell of defeat was in the air that May afternoon, nearly sixty years ago now. Even the cool, fresh breeze coming in from the Baltic couldn't blow it away. The smell had settled on Wismar like a dreary grey dust. Now the port, which he had last seen four years before, lay in ruins, peopled by grey skeletons carrying their pathetic bits and pieces behind them in little wooden carts. Everywhere, there were demobilised veterans of the defeated *Wehrmacht* in their shabby grey uniforms, begging for cigarettes at street corners or fighting bitterly for the wet butts the foreigners had tossed into the gutter. All was grey, save for the ruddy, healthy British soldiers – rifles over their shoulders – who strode down the bomb-shattered streets purposefully like creatures from another world.

Captain Savage tapped his driver on the shoulder and ordered, "See if that road there, Jones, leads to the harbour." His voice was stiff and awkward, for he was still recovering from the throat wound he had received in the Channel in the winter.

Jones said, "The Admiral's arriving by train from Hamburg at fourteen hundred hours. We don't want to miss him, sir."

Savage forced a smile for the rating's sake. "Any admiral who arrives by train, Jones, *ought* to be missed. Don't worry. I'll get you to the station in time. Just want to make a little sentimental journey."

Jones wondered what kind of sentimental journey the boss wanted to make in this arsehole of a place, but he didn't comment on the matter. Officers were a funny lot at the best of times and everybody knew Savage's explosive temper. So he kept his mouth shut and concentrated on weaving in and out of the line of shabby, grey whores offering their services to the Tommies.

Now Savage started to recognise the odd place in which he had found himself after his escape from Wesertimke in what now seemed another age. But now, in place of the leather-helmeted Hun cops directing traffic were the hatchet-faced British MPs, the Redcaps. Standing there in the swirling grey dust, they urged the Army trucks to move on between the bombed harbour docks, daubed with the slogans of the defeated Nazi Empire, "*Better Dead than Red*", "*Never Again 1918*". And over and over again that defiant "*Victory or Siberia*".

Grimly Savage nodded to himself. These days "Siberia" was just up the road where the lines of the Red Army commenced. That's why the Admiral was coming in. Their Lordships wanted to have a look-see at the former German Navy's resources, just in case the Russians got too uppity and decided on trouble. Churchill himself had ordered the check to be carried out. If there was ever going to be another war, Winnie had decided the Huns would be on our side.

Savage sighed. It was a crazy world, he told himself.

The jeep slowed down to avoid the scores of potholes, caused by the Brylcreem boys. There were beached wrecks everywhere, flying the white flag of surrender, with bored matelots in steel helmets guarding the German ships. Savage knew he should shout at them and order them to get their "fingers out". But he wasn't really interested in naval discipline this afternoon. He had come here in the hope that he might still find her, though after four weeks in a defeated Germany and four years after they had parted, he hadn't much hope of doing so.

"Naturally, Harding," he explained, as he sat bolt upright in his wheelchair, surrounded by his medicines and "bloody pisspots", as he called the nursing home's plastic bedpans, looking weaker now than the first time I had gone to hear his story, "I'd tried the usual agencies of the time, UNRRA, Military Government, the Swiss Red Cross . . . but nobody really seemed much interested in the poor Poles." He had flashed me one of those bitter looks of his, but I thought most of the fire had gone. Vice-Admiral Horatio Savage, I told myself, was beginning to fade.

The jeep turned the corner. Before Savage lay the naval harbour, filled from end to end with wrecks, some deep in the water so that only their funnels and masts were visible. Others had been tossed over on their sides like children's toys by the blast of the RAF bombs. One or two were beached in the shallows, as if they were stranded metallic whales.

Then he saw her. Her deck was pocked with bomb shrapnel marks like the symptoms of some hideous, loathsome skin disease and she was listing to the water around her, blue and greasy with oil. "Get closer, Jones," Savage ordered, noting an odd tingling, electric feeling in his hands and a sudden shortness of breath. He was getting excited, too bloody soon, he told himself, as the rating manoeuvred his way the best he could towards the wreck.

"It was the *Kolding* all right, Harding, you know the old Danish tub, which was going to smuggle us to Sweden." Savage paused, as if he was thinking how different his life might have been if the *Kolding* hadn't been hit.

Perhaps, he wouldn't have been here, a lonely dying old man, surrounded by medicines and "bloody pisspots", if he and Elena had have made it.

I looked at the old man. His face revealed little but there was a wet sheen to his faded eyes. I felt embarrassed for him. I looked away, out of the window.

Outside a hearse had drawn up. Two men in black suits were leaning against the big old Bells smoking discreetly, with their cigarettes cupped in their hands. Another of Mrs Hakewell-Smythe's "clients" had gone the way of all flesh.

Savage saw me looking out of the window and said in that old bitter fashion of his, "the harlot" – he presumably meant the owner of the "Hollies" – "always says, the finger had writ and passed on." He snorted impatiently. "The sooner it does me, the better. Then I'm out of here."

"Don't say that, sir," I tried to appease him. "You have years left, and besides, I want to get your whole story down. You can't snuff it on me – *yet*."

He obviously liked that, for he forgot about the funeral outside and said, "It was the *Kolding* to which the traitor had taken us from the *Hein Muck* pub, which had gone in the bombing, too, I found out later, Harding. So once again, I had come to a dead end – or so I thought." He paused as if he were trying to recall the full details of that May day so long ago, before he attempted to relate them to me. "It was then that I met the Hun."

I thought it better not to interrupt and ask which "Hun".

"He looked like an ex-officer, naval type, I suppose. Obviously down on his luck, poor bugger. Ankle-length overcoat devoid of badges of rank, concealing a missing leg. Instead he had a peg-leg and crutches. As you know, Harding, I don't go much on the Hun, but I felt sorry for this chap. Looked like a gentleman."

* * *

On any occasion I would have laughed at the description. Who talks like that these days? Who's a gentleman for that matter? I'm not, for sure. But I let him carry on, feeling we were progressing now. For, although I was not particularly interested in the Polish girl – she was obviously long dead in 1945 – I *was* keen to learn more about Gestapo Müller, Eichmann's boss. I'd checked with the German authority concerned with finding missing war criminals in Ludwigsburg and, of course, the Simon Wiesenthal Center in LA. There Gestapo Müller, if he were still alive, was still number one on their list of most wanted war criminals.

"Yes?" Savage had demanded coldly – after all it was forbidden to talk to Germans except in the line of duty. "What is it?"

The German's pale, half-starved face flushed a little, but he was no longer in a position to be proud as he had once been as the second-in-command of the *Prinz Eugen*. "I saw you looking at the wreck of the *Kolding*," he said in very good English. "I was here in 1941, waiting for my ship when she was sunk."

That got Savage. He reached in his pocket and brought a round tin of Capstan out. Offering it to the flushed German, he said, "Take a handful for yourself." The officer hesitated and Savage urged, "Go on. I've still got plenty from last month's NAAFI ration."

Whether or not the German knew what Savage meant by NAAFI ration was not clear, but he couldn't resist the temptation of the cigarettes, the only valid currency in Germany that year. He took a handful, trying not to be greedy and bowing his thanks as he did so. "I can pay," he began.

Savage cut him short. "Don't think about it, please."

Jones's eyes widened at that "please". The old man hated

the Jerries like poison; now he was saying "please" to one of them. Wonders would never cease.

"That's how I came to meet *Herr Kapitanleutnant* Jensen. He had his leg cut off by a bloke he called the "Pox Doctor" during the *Bismarck* business. Not a bad bloke for a Hun. Indeed we corresponded for a couple of years before he snuffed it." Savage sniffed at the memory for some reason known only to himself.

Outside Mrs Hakewill-Smythe was saying, "Please don't take the body past the front door, gentlemen. I don't want my clients to know that people die here . . . And oh, by the way, if you have a replacement for her, there's a hundred in it for you as long as she or he only lasts a couple of months."

I didn't comment. Instead to keep the momentum going, I said hastily, "And it was this Jensen who led you to Gestapo Müller?"

"In a way, Harding. I thought if I could find him, he'd give me a clue – even if I had to beat it out of him personally – to what had happened to Elena."

"And he did?"

"Yes, in a way," Suddenly there was a note of resignation in the old sailor's voice, as if he were realising for the first time that he was coming to the end of his story and that he had known all along that it was going to be an unhappy one.

Somehow or other, and it had involved a lot of wire-pulling, even a few threats, Savage and his new naval assistant on German Naval Matters, Unit 30 (a unit that would never be found in the Royal Navy's Order-of-Battle) arrived in the British sector of occupied Berlin.

Berlin was worse than Wismar: a sea of ruins, occupied now by the soldiers of four victorious allied armies, with their officials trying to restore some sort of order to a capital that had been under the Red Army's siege for nearly a month. All the same, Jensen, now in British battledress with a self-designed flash on the sleeve proclaiming he was a petty officer in German Naval Matters, Unit 30, was very resourceful. Plentifully supplied with packets of NAAFI fags for bribes, he greased the wheels everywhere, making Savage's task much easier.

"You know, Jensen was more like one of us, Harding. Not a bit like the typical Hun," he confessed, as we sat there, listening to the sound of the departing hearse and the normal cackle of the demented old ladies below. "If I hadn't have known he was a Hun, I would have taken him for one of my own staff. What?"

"What," I agreed and left it at that.

Over the month or so that Savage managed to wangle in Berlin, Jensen did his best to follow Gestapo Müller's trail through Berlin in the last days of the war: from his post in Hitler's bunker, the couple of days he had spent in Eichmann's hide-out in a cellar-shelter beneath the Kurfurstenstrasse until his apparent final disappearance, once the allied secret services had commenced asking about the man who knew more about German counter-espionage – especially against the Russians – in World War Two than any other.

For a while, the trail had gone dead, and Savage had gone into a black mood. Then Jensen had struck lucky. He had hobbled into the lobby of the senior officers' mess, which Savage was using as his HQ, announced by the club steward and, when the latter had been out of earshot, he whispered excitedly. "They've found him, sir."

Savage's black mood had vanished in an instant. "Gestapo Müller? Where, man, don't waste time. Let me get my hands on the bastard . . . I'll get the truth out . . ." The words had trailed away when he had recognised the look on the crippled German officer's face and he had said in a subdued tone, "All right, Jensen, tell me."

Jensen, who by now knew the reason for this British officer's long search, said softly, "In a grave in the old Jewish Cemetery in *Berlin-Mitte*. Apparently one of the grave units, employed by the Russians, buried his corpse there last week." His voice faltered, "Sorry, sir, I couldn't bring you something—"

Savage wasn't listening. He signalled to the nearest steward, "Double whisky for two."

The white-jacketed waiter looked as if he were about protest that Jensen was a German, but Savage didn't give him a chance. "You heard me," he snapped. "Look sharp now!"

The waiter looked sharp . . .

"It was one of the worst days of my life," Savage said softly, his gaze far away as he recalled the scene at the makeshift grave in the old Jewish cemetery, where ironically enough they had apparently buried that arch anti-semite Gestapo Müller. "It is not something I care to recall, Harding, but it's seared on to my mind indelibly."

I said nothing. I waited instead, realising yet again how much he felt.

"Jensen had found some poor old Hun pathologist down on his luck. He was making a living, so Jensen said, as an 'angel maker'." He saw I didn't understand and added quickly, "Abortionist, getting rid of unwanted babies. But Jensen had offered him two tins of Woodbines to have a dekko at the body to make sure that it was Gestapo Müller's. Naturally I was praying it might give us some clue to the whereabouts of Elena. A long shot, I know, but that was what I was hoping, while the grave-diggers toiled away by the light of Jensen's lantern. And I was right. It didn't disappoint us. It gave us *more* than a clue sadly."

The sad-faced doctor sighed like a man who was sorely troubled. He looked up from the mess of clothing, uniform and human parts spread across the freshly disturbed soil, while the grave-diggers watched patiently, leaning on their shovels and sipping the "Bass Best Pale Ale", again supplied courtesy of the NAAFI.

All was silent now in Central Berlin. The curfew was in place and all of them, save Savage and Jones risked being arrested for breaking it if the Russians caught them. But that didn't seem to bother them, German and British – they were too interested to hear the broken-down pathologist, who was now wiping his dirty hands on his patched *Wehrmacht* trousers before he commenced his statement, which Jensen would translate.

Savage puffed at his cigarette, the end glowing in the early autumn darkness. It had been a long search. As eager as he was to hear what the "sawbones" had to say, he could wait a few minutes more now.

The doctor cleared his throat. It was an unpleasant sound and, to Savage, it didn't seem healthy; perhaps the German doctor needed to see a doctor himself. Finally he started to explain his findings and Jensen attempted to do his best, his face worried in the yellow light of the lantern, as he tried to translate the difficult forensic medical terms. "There is some – er – putrefaction and the maggots have obscured the details of the wounds, which look a couple of months old. If I had a – er – lysol bath to kill the maggots, I could tell you more. "He shrugged his painfully thin shoulders. "But I haven't. However, it is clear that all three of them died violently."

"*Three*?" Savage exclaimed sharply.

"Yes," the pathologist, whom Jensen called the "Pox Doctor", looked surprised. "I said three," he added in

English, while Savage looked at him in the wavering light of the lantern, open-mouthed with surprise like some half-witted village yokel. He nodded to Jensen and the latter brought the lantern closer, as the doctor drew back the tarpaulin from the exhumed grave. "You see – a very shallow burial," he went on, as Jensen translated. "The bodies disintegrated more as we scooped them out. But they are definitely the parts of three bodies."

"Gestapo Müller – in three parts," Savage said, totally bewildered as he stared at the bloody remains, alive with maggots.

The pathologist smiled cynically and said something quickly to Jensen. The latter hesitated. "A lot of people like Müller have wanted to disappear these last few months – like taking a dive in a U-boat, we call it. He left some identification papers in the grave and that was that. Perhaps he's in South America already, for all I know."

"And they are all people in their mid-twenties," the pathologist added in German, as if he had understood Jensen's explanation. "A quarter of a century younger than Müller, who is – was – forty-five. As old as the century." He laughed hoarsely.

In the silence, Jensen held the lantern closer so that Savage could get a better look at the three corpses, or what was left of them. "All are headless, sir, you see," he said softly, as if he realised what this discovery meant to his new master. "You can see he was making it harder to identify them and cover up his tracks. He probably bribed the graves commission man to 'find' him here like this."

Savage nodded his understanding.

"I did find something, however," the pathologist broke the heavy silence.

Savage looked up, but he wasn't interested now.

Another trail to Elena had ended nowhere. "On the woman," he added in English.

Jensen looked sharply at his old shipmate. "The woman?" he queried in English for Savage's benefit. He could see just how low the Tommy was.

"Yes, this one is a woman," the "Pox Doctor" replied in the same language and then in German. "Her abdomen has not been subjected to the blowflies which lay the maggot eggs. So it is relatively intact." He bent down to the middle piece of "flesh" (that was the only way that a horrified, repelled Jensen could think of the three corpses) and with his bare hand he wiped away the soil caused by the grave-diggers. "You see the vagina. Still intact. The legs are slightly spread, as you can observe, and I'm guessing but I think she had had sexual intercourse before she died so violently."

The "Pox Doctor" wiped his hands once again and reached into the pocket of his shabby tunic. "This is interesting. It's in Polish. But you know me and foreign tongues—"

Savage cut in. "Let me see that," he ordered harshly.

Obediently the "Pox Doctor" dropped the dusty amulet into Savage's outstretched palm, as Jensen brought the flickering lantern closer. Hastily Savage blew off the remaining dirt and held it to the yellow light. The others waited tensely, wondering why the Tommy seemed to become so tense about a piece of enamel, cheap at that, with a Polack inscription on it.

Time passed leadenly. Still they waited. The Englishman seemed transfixed, staring at the object, suspended from a silver-plated chain, also cheap, as if he were hypnotised by it.

Jensen cleared his throat finally and asked, "Is it important, Captain Savage?"

But Savage couldn't answer. His mind and memory

were a million miles away. That night in the old crone's barn when he had first made love to her, she had told him about the amulet which she had worn around her neck and the picture it had contained. It had been given to her by her mother before the Germans had taken her from Warsaw. The portrait, cheap and crude, had been that of the Black Virgin of Cracow. Her mother had ordered her to keep it on her body, always; it would bring her luck and keep her out of harm's way.

That night, lying naked for the first time and feasting his eyes on Elena's young nubile body, he had spotted it resting between her breasts, where she had hidden it before the brutal German searches. "It brings luck," she had whispered lovingly.

Then he had bent down and kissed the nipple of each beautiful breast, replying in whispers, too, in case the old crone heard, "From now on, Elena, I bring you luck. *Verstanden*?"

"*Verstanden*," she had agreed and then they had made intense, passionate love.

Now she was a headless corpse. Savage swallowed hard and the tears welled up, hot and blinding, in his eyes.

Jensen saw them. Gently he took Savage's arm. "I think it is better we go. It is long past curfew. We want no trouble, Captain Savage, do we?"

Numbly, Savage nodded. Jensen took his hand, holding his lantern high so that the Englishman could see his way out of the shattered old Jewish cemetery. Obediently, like a chastened, hurt child, the one-time "Hun eater" allowed himself to be led. A few moments later they had disappeared into the silent night, broken only by the grunts of the grave-diggers, as they returned the soil over the body of Elena and her comrades in death . . . It was all over.

Author's Note

At that last meeting, I promised Vice-Admiral Savage that I would look into the matter of Gestapo Müller's grave more thoroughly when I went to Germany. I did. The officials of the section of the Bavarian State Ministry concerned were, as usual, very helpful, exceedingly so. One wonders how a similar British department would have reacted if I had to come to them, enquiring about a supposedly long-dead British war criminal.

They knew about the first grave in the old Jewish cemetery and about the second one, also in Berlin, which bears the legend, "To our dear papa . . . from his children." It has also been excavated *twice*. Naturally it does not contain the remains of our "dear Papa". So where is Gestapo Müller?

According to the Bavarian officials, Gestapo Müller – the head of that dreaded organisation which was feared throughout Europe for years in the 1930s and 1940s – was forgotten for years after the preliminary enquiries about his fate in the immediate post-war years. Then in the late sixties, two Mossad agents were arrested trying to break into his "widow's" flat in Munich while she was in hospital. Thereafter the rumours started once more.

Gestapo Müller was spotted alive in many places, from Albania to the Argentina. Once more he became Germany's most wanted war criminal; and even today though he would be a hundred years old, he still heads the Bavarian Agency's list of wanted men. But where did he go? One of the officials, who shall remain nameless, took me aside after I had surveyed the relevant documents and like two old "queens" sizing each up in the lavatories, he told me – "unofficially" of course – what the Bavarians thought.

"It was the CIA of course. They had spread the rumour that he had gone over to the Russians in '45. In reality he had worked for them against the 'Ivans' and then they had smuggled him out through Switzerland to the States and Langley. Here he was promoted to the rank of general, worked for them as Europe's top expert on Russian spy networks before he retired with a new family, American, somewhere in the wilds of West Virginia."

I accepted all this without blinking an eyelid. (Obviously my informant in the Bavarian WC had never been to the "wilds of West Virginia." I nodded in agreement, as he concluded with, "Typical *Ami*, you know, Herr Harding. A very devious people, the Americans. I wouldn't trust them as far as I could throw them, *nicht wahr*."

Nicht wahr, indeed!

I was going to call Savage immediately when I got back with my news. But it was too late. Instead there was a letter waiting for me which would have made the call and a journey to the "Hollies" unnecessary.

It wasn't much of a letter. For the envelope contained a poor, blurred photograph. It was obviously an amateurish effort. Later I discovered it had been taken by no less than Mrs Hakewill-Smythe.

Even Mrs Hakewill-Smythe's cheap snap could not conceal the tawdriness of the "naval" funeral, as she called it: a squad of boys from the local Sea Scouts, a Marine bugler and a portly old boy from the Royal Naval Association, heavy with polished medals, but looking either drunk or confused (perhaps both) in the standard brass-buttoned blazer and beret.

"We did him proud," Mrs Hakewill-Smythe gushed in her accompanying note. "It was a real naval send-off for a brave navy man. There must have been at least half a dozen of my clients from the home present at the ceremony and the *Gazette* did him proud, a whole half column. They would have sent a photographer, but there'd been an accident on the by-pass and naturally the paper needed him out there that morning . . ."

I put down the note and thought to myself, what can one do? Grin and bear it? I suppose Savage would have said in his wartime slang that he still affected all those years later, "Roll on death and let's have a go at the angels." Who bloody well knows?

So he had died: Vice-Admiral Horatio Savage, DSC, MC, a sailor who had fought at Dunkirk, escaped from Wesertimke, been wounded at Walcheren . . . and endured it all stoically to live into our own Brave New World.

Today, a year after the Admiral's death, all I can do is quote that last line from Fitzgerald's *Great Gatsby*. It seems apt enough. "So we beat on, boats against the current, borne back ceaselessly into the past . . ."